Dorothy Lyle
In
Avarice

Book 1 of:
The Miracles and Millions Saga

A Series of Novels
By Ella Carmichael

Print Edition
Copyright © 2017
Ella Carmichael
All rights reserved

This eBook is copyright material and must not be copied, reproduced, transferred, distributed, leased, licensed or publicly performed or used in any way except as specifically permitted in writing by the author, as allowed under the terms and conditions under which it was purchased or as strictly permitted by applicable copyright law. Any unauthorised distribution or use of this text may be a direct infringement of the author's rights and those responsible may be liable in law accordingly. This book is a work of fiction and, except in the case of historical fact any resemblance to actual persons, living or dead is purely coincidental.

Nobody can go back and start a new beginning, but anyone can start today and make a new ending.
~Maria Robinson~

ALTERNATIVE TITLE

*Dorothy Lyle
Forgoes Love forever
And in the Midst of her Grey Life
Discovers she is
Rich Beyond the
Dreams of
Avarice*

PROLOGUE

Joshua O'Keefe awoke with a start and groped for the switch of his lamp. As he flicked it on, the person sleeping in the foldaway bed under the window emitted a deep moan of resentment. 'For feck sake, man,' Deco protested. 'We've got an early start tomorrow. Is it necessary to keep me awake half the bleedin' night?'

Without answering, Josh turned off the lamp, rolled out of bed and left the room on silent feet. He spotted a strip of light under his sister's door and tapped on it gently. When he heard her voice calling to him, he pushed it open and peered inside. To his relief, he saw she was propped up in bed, wide awake and working away on her laptop.

'I had the weirdest dream,' he told her sheepishly. 'I'm a bit freaked out.'

'Well you needn't think you're sleeping in here,' Diane half-smiled at him, her green eyes vivid in her oval face. 'Drink a glass of water and you'll be grand. It's no wonder you feel strange after all the shit you and Deco imbibed over Christmas. The best thing you can do is treat your liver to a week off. What was it about? The dream I mean.'

'I dreamed you and I were toddlers,' her brother rubbed at brown eyes that itched. 'The four of us were spending Christmas together. It was just you, me, Mum and Dad. It was like something from one of those annoying Christmas movies.'

'Sounds cosy,' his twin replied, her voice heavy with irony. 'Did you happen to notice any divorce papers tucked under the tree?'

'No,' he frowned. 'I opened this massive box with a red bow on the top, and there was a puppy inside. I can't remember what happened next, but when I woke up my heart was racing like the Formula 1. Do you think it means something?'

His twin perused Josh's face for a moment, noting the way the fair hair flopped into the big brown eyes, and the hooknose that was too large for his boyish face. She did her best to sound patient when she replied, 'With a bit of luck, it means Mum is planning to buy us an extra special belated Christmas present. Maybe when she got back to work, there was a year-end bonus waiting for her.'

'So you think the dream might be about gifts?' her brother asked hopefully. 'You don't think it has anything to do with marriage or puppies?'

'Christmas is well and truly over, Joshie,' Diane told him gently. 'If miracles exist in this world, and I'm not for one minute suggesting they do, you can bet your ass ours won't involve our parents reconciling after fifteen years apart. Why don't you try to get some sleep? You promised to help me shop for Mum's present tomorrow. It isn't every day a woman turns forty. The least we can do is make a bit of an effort.'

The young man sighed heavily and rubbed his hand through his already tousled hair. 'Sorry to be such a wuss,' he mumbled. 'Night, sis.'

He withdrew from the room and made sure the door was closed tightly behind him. In bare feet and wearing only grey boxer shorts, he wandered into the kitchen of their rented apartment. To his profound relief, he discovered an untapped bottle of ice-cold water in the fridge, and helped himself to a tall glass.

Still feeling shaken from an emotion he could not quite identify, he stood at the window and stared down into the courtyard of the apartment block. A couple of late night revellers weaved their way across it, alternatively clutching each other for support and then shouting raucously.

Josh sipped the water and his thoughts turned to his mother. He hoped she was all right and his odd dream was not some sort of weird portent. Diane was a very level headed girl, and if she believed it had something to do with gifts, he was undoubtedly worrying unnecessarily.

1

'Your daughter is in my power and will be executed unless you do exactly as I say. Wire twenty million dollars to the following account by noon tomorrow, and your little girl will be released unharmed. If you ignore my instructions, or contact the authorities, you will never see her again.'

Dorothy paused outside the window of her neighbour's cottage. It was only open a fraction, but because it was the perfect height for her ear, she had no trouble hearing what was going on inside. Due to his superb reading voice, which was totally at odds with his everyday country bumpkin drawl, Horace was occasionally contracted by a small media company to act as a narrator for their audio books.

Like the majority of his paid employment, the compensation received for his labours was modest at best, although he seemed to enjoy the work, and never refused a gig if he was lucky enough to be offered one. Dorothy was hesitant to interrupt him when he was practicing for an upcoming job, but felt compelled to do so. Not least, because she was clutching a casserole dish that contained the remains of a beef stew, and was determined to offload the unwieldy burden before she caught her train.

She tapped on the front door and waited impatiently for the owner of the cottage to make an appearance. The mahogany entrance had been lovingly restored by Horace when he purchased the house some eight years earlier, and painted a lively shade of royal blue.

As Dorothy stood shivering in the bitter January air, she remarked to herself for perhaps the thousandth time that she and the single slab of ancient tree stood exactly the same height. The rare visitors Horace received always commented on the fact that the entrance was scarcely large enough to accommodate a garden gnome.

The pavement on which Dorothy stood shivering ran past the front garden of her own semi-detached house, then dipped as it crossed the entrance to the laneway leading down to the long-abandoned property known as Bluebell Wood, and kept going until it reached Horace's abode, a mere ten yards away. Unlike the majority of other houses in the area, his cottage was set so close to the concrete runway, it actually looked as if it was resting upon its marl grey surface.

Given this proximity to the road, together with its diminutive size, Dorothy was amazed the cottage had not been snatched up and demolished by an eager developer, keen to acquire the substantial garden and lay the foundations for an apartment block.

Indeed, when word had first leaked out that Old Hen Cottage, as it had been known for many years, was sold at last, the neighbourhood waited with baited and disapproving breath for a planning notice for just such an apartment building to appear. Dorothy and her neighbours were ready, willing, and able enough to begin the lengthy process of defeating the application by sheer strength of numbers, to say nothing of old-fashioned determination.

Dorothy Lyle was by nature a peaceful woman, but in this instance, it was *her* view and property value in jeopardy, and likely to suffer the greatest loss as a result of such construction. She professed herself battle-ready, and mentally girded her loins with a garment which bore a strong resemblance to Frodo's magical chainmail in *The*

Lord of the Rings. Having donned the attire, she was all set to march in the vanguard of warriors who would defend Bluebell View and its inhabitants from the evils of a sky rise.

Almost disappointingly, it had all come to naught. It soon transpired that Horace Johnson, formerly of the county of Somerset in the United Kingdom, had purchased the property because of its one hundred and twenty-foot-long garden, and would sooner have razed his beloved cottage to the ground than consider letting any developer within a league of it.

When it dawned upon the other residents that their new neighbour was essentially a harmless hippie type, whose only ambition was to renovate the interior of the dwelling, and replace the ancient outbuildings with new ones of identical size which would accommodate his myriad hobbies, they heaved a collective sigh of relief and returned to the normal business of their daily lives.

Dorothy put away her imaginary chainmail and, despite some initial qualms over the latest addition to the neighbourhood, soon reached the conclusion that God had smiled upon her when he sent Horace Johnson to her neck of the woods.

Fast forward eight years or thereabouts. The unlikely pair had not only become firm friends, they had also come to rely upon each other in a multitude of minor ways. This was the main reason Dorothy found herself outside Horace's door on a cold January morning, clutching a dish of food.

Over the years, she had gotten into the habit of bringing him any leftovers she might have which she would not need herself. In all the time she had known him, Horace had never once refused an offer of food from her; hence she kept right on bringing it. The offerings had increased in volume since the previous September.

Her nineteen-year-old twins, Diane and Josh, had moved out of the family home four months earlier so they could be closer to their college on the North Side of Dublin. After almost two decades of cooking for a family, Dorothy found it virtually impossible to prepare food for only one person, and Horace had inevitably been the beneficiary of the extra portions.

She raised her arm to knock again, but before her gloved hand made contact, the door swung inwards and Horace was revealed in the opening. The reason for the door's shortness of stature was due to a minor architectural feature that became clear when it stood ajar. Horace and Dorothy's eyes were level but, unlike his neighbour, this was not because the man in question stood five feet tall in his bare feet.

Rather, it was due to the eight-inch drop immediately inside the front door. Some called it dangerous, some called it quirky, some called it downright annoying. Dorothy had given up calling it anything many years earlier. Whenever she crossed the threshold of Old Hen, she took care to negotiate the drop with sufficient care and, so far at least, had suffered no ill effects from the unexpected downwards plunge.

When Horace spotted the casserole dish, he smiled one of his rare smiles. It was not easy to detect through the bushy black beard, although Dorothy knew it was there by the way his eyes lit up. In the morning light, they looked more green than brown, and were flecked with grey.

He had allowed his hair to grow during the winter months, which meant it was now shoulder length and looked as if it had not been washed for quite some time. She had been inside the cottage many times over the course of the years, and was well aware the first thing Horace did before he officially took up residence was to completely refurbish the bathroom and install a cutting-edge shower.

Ergo, she seriously doubted the hair was actually dirty. It merely tended to look that way whenever he allowed it to grow. Horace seemed to relish the black looks he often received from passersby whenever he took his dog for a walk, looking like nothing less than a tramp.

'It's not like you to cook a big meal on a Thursday night,' he drawled in his Somerset brogue.

'It was imperative I remain very calm last night,' Dorothy replied earnestly. 'I felt the best way to do that was to spend the evening in the kitchen. The result was I made a tonne of food. I froze some of it, but I thought you might like this casserole for your lunch.'

Under the hair, Horace's expression grew concerned, and his brow furrowed. 'Is everything all right with you?' he enquired gently. 'Why did you need to stay calm? Are the twins well? Is it your parents? Perhaps you should come in and have a cup of tea and tell me about it.'

She carefully extended her arms and offered him the dish. 'I can't stop because I have a train to catch,' she told him firmly. 'I'll explain it to you another time. Nothing is wrong; it's just I have something on my mind. Quite a number of somethings, if you must know.'

'Your eyes are shining,' he sounded almost accusing, as he accepted the dish of food. 'Have you met somebody? If you have a new boyfriend, why don't you just say so? Is it a man from work?'

She snorted through her cute little upturned nose. 'Don't be ridiculous,' she said definitively. 'I have big news, but you'll have to bear with me for the time being. All will be revealed soon enough. Now I really must dash. Enjoy the grub. See you later, Hairy Bear.'

With that, she turned on her heel and headed for the train station. Horace stood in the doorway and watched her until she was out of sight. Amanda Flynn emerged from the house on the opposite side of the road and noticed his abstraction.

She was wearing her full length, brown winter coat and accessories, and was all set to walk the five hundred yards to the doctors' surgery where she was employed as the receptionist. It was her job to open up each morning, and she was already running two minutes behind schedule. Being of an enquiring disposition, she could not resist pausing to see what was up with Horace.

He was looking even more bear-like than usual in his russet coloured cable sweater and a pair of patched, corduroy trousers of indeterminate hue. Amanda spotted the dish in his hands and surmised that their mutual friend had deposited it with him on the way to the station. 'Everything okay, Horace?' she called curiously.

He reluctantly withdrew his eyes from the tiny speck that had become Dorothy in the distance, and transferred them to Amanda instead. 'Have you noticed anything odd about Dorothy this week?' he asked, raising his voice so she could hear him above the din of the morning commuters.

Amanda shrugged. 'She's been mad busy at work, and wouldn't even go to the cinema with me the other night, even though I begged her. She says she's intending to work long hours for the next two weeks so the payroll department is on top of everything by the end of the month. Personally, I think she's mad. The staff at that place haven't had a pay rise since the downturn started back in 2008, and I know for a fact she's already overworked. If it was me, I certainly wouldn't be putting in any extra hours. The more you give, the more they expect. They'll be wanting blood next!'

On that cheerful note, Amanda waved gaily, then began to walk in the opposite direction to Dorothy. Horace remained standing in the doorway and watched her leave. He had the strangest feeling something monumental had happened to his neighbour. Something which would not necessarily bring her the happiness she so richly deserved. He frowned.

The sound of Trotsky's bark from the interior recalled his master to his duties. With a final glance around the neighbourhood, Horace stepped back and firmly closed the heavy door on the traffic and elements. He was still frowning.

2

'If you fail to follow my instructions to the letter, your daughter will die,' said the vaguely robotic voice. Startled out of her abstraction, Dorothy jumped slightly in her seat.

'Sorry,' the young girl sitting next to her grimaced apologetically. 'I haven't quite got the knack of my new iPad. I didn't even know there were audio books on it. My boyfriend must have loaded them on there to surprise me.'

Dorothy smiled understandingly, then returned to pretending to read the slim paperback novel she had tucked into her serviceable black handbag, prior to leaving the house. Since boarding the urban train that serviced the coastal area around Dublin, appropriately named the DART, she had not read one word of the book.

She was using it merely as a cover in case somebody attempted to strike up a conversation with her. Even at 8.15 on a freezing January morning, you never knew what commuter might be feeling chatty; hence it was best not to take any chances.

To further perpetuate the fallacy, she turned a page and gazed sightlessly at the printed words. Of all the things she should be planning on this most life changing of mornings, she found herself unable to stop thinking about Horace Johnson of all people.

It was not that she did not value the man as both friend and neighbour. It was just that it was highly inconvenient of him to be invading her thoughts this way, and on such a day. She sighed heavily and then quickly turned another page so anyone overhearing her would naturally assume the novel's plot was both intense and dramatic. Horace was the reason the twins were living on the far side of the city.

There! She had said it. The Hairy Bear who lived next door and spent his days teaching guitar and whittling pieces of wood into animal shapes, was the reason her children were now sharing an apartment in Santry, instead of residing safely at home with their mother where they belonged.

It all began when fifteen-year-old Josh expressed the desire to learn acoustic guitar. Dorothy had the idea of approaching Horace, who readily agreed to provide lessons in exchange for a modest fee and the occasional meal. Josh had taken to the instrument like the proverbial duck, and his best friend, Deco, soon joined him.

Back in 2006, Derek Moynihan's mother and stepfather ran an independent mortgage brokering business, and were riding high on the wave of financial success generated by the so-called Celtic Tiger.

They professed themselves willing to pay for any number of music lessons for their only son, and suggested an academy of music as an appropriate institute of learning. Deco laughed in their befuddled faces and told them Hairy Horace was good enough for him, and could he please have a few quid and a box of groceries to pay the man?

Josh and Deco were soon strumming along happily together, and occasionally setting music to some of the lyrics Horace was known to jot down during his more reflective moments. The experiment was a success, and the Lyle family grew even closer to their hirsute neighbour. Dorothy was especially grateful to him for providing a much-needed male role model for her son, who only saw his father five or six times a year at best.

A year later, when sixteen-year-old Diane asked her mother if she would be willing to pay for Horace to provide chess lessons, Dorothy did not hesitate. Far from worrying about what might develop in the little house next door, she was delighted to see her daughter taking an interest in the game and even joining the society at school.

The fact that Diane had signed up because she fancied the captain of the chess club in no way fazed her mother. Regardless of her motivation, the important thing was the girl was embracing something other than fake tan and social media.

Under Horace's tutelage, Diane grew so proficient over the year that followed, she soon had to take steps to ensure she only occasionally beat the boy of her dreams at the game. Diane's aspirations to become a chess master became the joke of the family. Dorothy smiled to hear Josh and Deco challenging her diminutive girl child to a game, followed by them sulkily admitting defeat an hour later.

During Diane's final year at school, she admitted to her mother how much she was struggling with English. 'They expect us to read like a million novels and plays and poems, Mum, and it's all so boring. What am I going to do? I'll never get into college if I fail English,' she whined during the first term.

Dorothy did not for a minute believe Diane would fail the subject, although it was true she needed to achieve a high grade if she was to get accepted on her course of first choice, studying economics and modern languages at

Dublin City University. She decided to take the necessary steps to ensure her daughter's ambitions were fulfilled.

Horace did not like to discuss his past, except to say he had been raised the only child of strict Presbyterian parents in a village called Burrowbridge. He attended the local grammar school until he was eighteen, and then went to work in the family's golf hotel, where he was training to take over as manager from his father.

When he was only twenty-one, his parents died tragically in a motor accident, and left him what he described as a tidy sum. He put the hotel and family home on the market, and waited impatiently for the funds they generated to materialise. As soon as the moola was safely in his hands, he moved himself, his dog, and his few meagre possessions to Shankill in the Republic of Ireland, where he purchased Old Hen Cottage for its location and substantial garden.

There was no mystery about him, he assured Dorothy on many occasions. Somerset, and Burrowbridge in particular, held few happy memories for him. He had been desperate for a fresh start in a place where no relations were likely to come crawling out of the woodwork, and lucky enough to have the means at his disposal to buy a dwelling place that suited his needs.

Dorothy would have believed his story if not for the fact that he knew so much. He might try to hide it, but she was certain Horace was a highly-educated man. In all likelihood, his parents *had* run a hotel, and they may even have wanted their only child to join them in the business, yet Dorothy was certain her neighbour had attended university after grammar school, and had not been an apprentice manager at all.

She often speculated as to whether or not he had been a teacher back in the UK, or at least a trainee teacher who had gotten into trouble with a student. Horace had a certain wide-eyed simplicity about him which would inevitably attract a predatory, teenage female, and as he was without guile, he naturally had few weapons at his disposal to repel such attacks.

Dorothy wished he would confide in her, but after acknowledging that if *she* had lost her career over an indiscretion with a teenager, she would be loath to admit it, wisely let it go and refrained from pressing him for details pertaining to his past. Her suspicions about his real profession were further solidified when she spoke to him regarding Diane's plight.

Horace readily agreed to assist the girl with her English studies, and assured Dorothy he would have her daughter exam-ready well before the June deadline. He seemed enthusiastic about the project, and Dorothy hoped his pupil did not let either him or herself down.

Horace was as good as his word. Between January and May of 2010, he transformed Diane O'Keefe from a B minus to an A plus student of English. He also insisted they work on her French, German and Italian together so she would be well prepared for university life. 'The economics will be tough enough without you having to worry about French verbs,' he told her earnestly.

Diane chuckled at this and, her green eyes twinkling, professed herself surprised to discover her chess tutor had a working knowledge of so many languages, considering his background.

Nonplussed, Horace blinked at her from behind the glasses he occasionally wore for reading whenever his eyes felt strained.

'My old headmaster was a real language nut,' he said slowly. 'He believed there was a strong possibility my classmates and I might end up migrating to the European mainland to find employment. Ergo, he encouraged us to learn as much of the local lingo as possible. He even ran a special language club for those of us who were quick learners. My parents supported me in my endeavours because I was able to converse with the overseas hotel guests, and we used to get fantastic reviews because of it. I also know a couple of words of Spanish, if you'd like to learn how to order a botifarra.'

Diane had known Horace since she was eleven years old, and was not fooled by this story for one instant. Nonetheless, being a kind hearted girl, she decided to let him off the hook, and obligingly began to discuss the job market.

'Not much has changed since you left school,' she told him blithely. 'My only hope of getting a decent job is to have modern languages, and even then I'll be lucky if I get to stay in Ireland. It's some comfort to know things aren't much better back in good old Burrowbridge.'

When the story was relayed to Dorothy over the dinner table, she decided that Horace had probably been a trainee English and modern languages teacher at an exclusive girls' school when scandal struck. Her heart went out to him. He had lost everything over one error in judgement, and now found himself scraping by in a country that was rapidly becoming the scrapheap of Europe.

His capital had been eaten up over the years by the cost of living in Ireland, and even though he did not exist on the breadline, he was by no means comfortably situated. She was pleased her salary allowed her to recompense him for tutoring Diane, especially as her daughter was flourishing under his guidance. Horace himself seemed happier and more relaxed than he had for a long time.

Dorothy never saw it coming.

Not in her wildest dreams did she ever imagine that her beautiful daughter, who resembled a pixie princess with her blonde hair and vivid green eyes, would fall hopelessly in love with a man ten years her senior. A man who looked as if he should be living in a cave on the side of a mountain, and who had more than once been mistaken for a homeless person.

She had no premonition of the axe that was about to fall, until a white-faced Horace came to see her the day after his twenty-ninth birthday. A day that fell precisely three weeks before the exams were due to begin. He knew Diane was not around because she and her best friend, Emily, had gone swimming for an hour to give themselves a well-deserved break from their studies.

When Dorothy opened the front door that Saturday morning, she was surprised to find Horace standing on her doorstep looking pale, shaken and clammy. Convinced he had contracted summer flu, she invited him inside and insisted on making him a hot whiskey.

Clutching the beverage in his muscular, grubby hands, the young man confessed that Diane had offered herself to him the previous evening as a birthday gift. He was badly shaken because he had been awake all night rehearsing what to say to her.

In a trembling voice, he assured Dorothy that he had never encouraged the girl to think of him in that way, and had certainly never laid a finger on her. He begged her to help him extricate himself from a situation which was likely to bring nothing but pain to a fragile, eighteen year-old.

A stunned Dorothy made her neighbour finish the drink. Then she told him in her best motherly tone that he was not to concern himself any further, because she was going to deal with the situation and nip it in the bud. She sent him home with orders to go back to bed for a nap.

She had ample time to mull the situation over in the hours before Diane returned home. She was inclined to believe her precocious daughter was playing a game with the burly, hairy neighbour. Diane had been dating the captain of the chess club for many months, and seemed blissfully happy with him.

When Di arrived back, she was alone, Emily having headed home to hit the books yet again. Dorothy told her they needed to have a serious chat. She sat the girl down, and gently requested an explanation for her strange behaviour.

In preparation for the answer, she already had a speech prepared about the cruelty of playing with other people's emotions. Dorothy was left both shocked and appalled by her daughter's response. Diane perked up when her mother began to talk about Horace. She immediately confessed all, and professed her undying devotion to the man.

'But what about Matthew?' Dorothy reeled in shock. 'I thought you were mad about him.'

'Matthew?' Diane regarded her mother in disbelief. 'Why would I be interested in a boy when I have a real man next door? I've been using him as a decoy because I don't want folks to know about me and Horace until it's all settled between us. People are so weird about age differences and boring shit like that. Horace was very coy when I spoke to him about it yesterday, but that's because he's a little old-fashioned, and thinks he doesn't deserve me or some such nonsense. He'll come around once he realises nobody minds about us being together.'

In a panic, Dorothy summoned her best friend, Simone, who fortunately was working in the area, and frantically explained the situation to her. The friends converged on Diane and set about the task of persuading the girl that Horace did not love her, did not desire her as a woman, and had no intention of marrying her and moving her into Old Hen Cottage as his bride.

It took them two hours, but the message finally got through. Dorothy had no choice but to witness the heart literally breaking inside her adored child's chest, and fight back her own tears of rage and pain.

For two days, Diane withdrew completely from the world and remained locked inside a self-constructed container of despair and loneliness. She refused any sustenance except water, and only left her room to use the bathroom. Most of the time, she lay on her bed staring at the ceiling.

When she was not doing that, she was sitting in a chair by her window, staring down into the garden of Old Hen with deadened eyes. When Emily came to visit, Diane barely acknowledged her presence. Emily was almost as broken hearted about the situation as her friend. She admitted to Dorothy that Diane had confided in her about her feelings for Horace, and assured her they were reciprocated.

'I don't know what she sees in him, Dorothy,' Emily sobbed at the kitchen table over a cup of coffee. 'I know he's not a bad fella or anything, but he's not exactly a catch compared to Matthew, is he? I don't know what to say to her to make her feel better. I know you're right, though, there's no way he's in love with her.'

A stunned and equally baffled Joshua was the one who hypothesised a possible solution. When he tentatively suggested it to his mother, she was horrified at the notion.

However, after another day spent witnessing the pain her daughter was enduring, she could bear it no longer. She marched into the girl's room and informed Diane that if she got out of bed and returned to her studies, and sat her exams as she had been planning to do for the past eleven years, she would never have to lay eyes on Horace Johnson again, if that was what she wished.

A two-bedroom apartment would be rented for the twins near their university of choice. The money to pay for it would come from the college fund their father had created for them a decade earlier. It might make things financially tricky if either wanted to do a masters' degree after graduation, but the family would cross that bridge if they ever got to it. If Diane wished, her days in Shankill, living next door to Horace, were numbered. But only if she hit the books and got her life back on track.

Diane continued to lie on her bed, staring at the ceiling and processing this development for a full seventy-seven minutes. Dorothy knew this because Josh sat on the floor outside his sister's bedroom door and timed her. When she had finished thinking it over, Diane got out of bed, took a shower and brushed her teeth vigorously.

She put on one of her favourite dresses, went down to the kitchen and ate a large salad for lunch. She told Dorothy and Josh she was intending to spend the rest of the day studying at her desk, and did not want to be disturbed unless they were making a cup of coffee. Then she asked her mother if there was any chance she and her brother could get away for a holiday as soon as the last exam was finished.

Dorothy almost cried with relief. Since January, she had been putting money aside each month for a holiday for herself. She had been in the process of planning it with her neighbour and anticipated travelling companion, Amanda, when disaster struck in the form of unrequited love.

She mentally consigned her own plans to the dustbin, and eagerly told the twins how much money she had saved. Without hesitation, she told them she had intended it to be a surprise and suggested they go online and see how far they could make the budget stretch. If they asked nicely, maybe their grandparents might be persuaded to top up the funds for their eldest grandchildren who so richly deserved a treat.

The ploy worked. Dorothy's parents, Pat and Joey Lyle, willingly pledged a couple of hundred euro as an early birthday present for the twins, and the Spanish holiday was booked.

3

Diane returned to her studies and also continued her relationship with Matthew as if nothing had happened. If she did not actually sail through her exams, she attained the points she needed for the course which was her first choice.

While the twins were on holiday, Dorothy and Amanda, who had experienced a cocktail of emotions ranging from disappointment to incredulity over the change of plans and the reasons behind them, viewed ten different apartments. By the time the travelling pair returned to Ireland, their mother had identified three student-friendly complexes she considered suitable for her offspring.

Diane professed herself ready and willing to shake the dust of Shankill from her feet forever, and said she would like to leave as quickly as possible. Dorothy begged her to reconsider and at least remain in the family home until the end of August. She assured Diane that Horace had hardly been seen since the beginning of June. It appeared the young man was avoiding Diane just as much as she was avoiding him.

Diane was not convinced, but Amanda assured the girl her mother was speaking the truth. On the first day of the Leaving Certificate exams, Horace had been spotted leaving Old Hen with Trotsky by his side, his guitar slung over one shoulder, and a large backpack strapped to his person. He had not returned until he knew for certain the twins had left for the airport.

Nobody knew for sure where he had spent the intervening weeks, although they suspected he had slept rough up in the mountains for the duration of the exams. Since his return, he was only ever seen outside the walls of the cottage between the hours of ten and eleven in the evening. The local fuel station stayed open late, and this was where he had started to buy his milk and other essentials, under cover of darkness.

Amanda informed Dorothy that, in addition to groceries, Horace had taken to purchasing a minimum of three bottles of whiskey, or other spirits, every week. This pertinent fact was not mentioned to Diane. Amanda and Dorothy assured her there was no need to rush off as if she had done something wrong, and urged her to spend time searching for the perfect apartment.

Diane reluctantly agreed to the scheme, and spent the month of August with Josh, Deco and Emily, locating a home they all deemed suitable, and making the necessary arrangements for the big move. The choice was soon made, the college fund plundered for the deposit and first month's rent, and the bags packed.

Josh and Deco spent three days driving Dorothy's blue Focus to and from Santry, piled high with boxes of possessions; while at the other end, Diane and Emily unpacked it all and made the place look homely. By the end of August, without Diane ever again coming face to face with Horace, the twins left the home they had shared with their mother since they were seven years old, and at only thirty-nine years of age, Dorothy was left with an empty nest and a heavy heart.

Still on the DART, she turned a page and glanced out of the window. Only three more stops to Tara Street. She really needed to put these sad thoughts behind her and focus on everything she had to achieve today. The situation with Horace was all in the past now, hence there was no sense in dwelling upon it.

Diane had remained with Matthew, the chess lover, for a further three months and then, much to his shock, ended the relationship. She had grasped hold of the silken threads attached to the shattered pieces of her life and pulled them back together again.

Life went on for Diane O'Keefe without the presence of Horace Johnson, and Dorothy thanked God for it. Of course, that did not stop her worrying what the effects of such hurt and despair would be on her daughter in the long-term. Her sisters, Orla and Gemma, and her friend, Simone, who had seen with their own eyes the devastation Horace's rejection had wrought, did their best to reassure her.

'We all had our hearts broken when we were teenagers, Dottie,' Simone said reasonably. 'It didn't stop us moving on and getting married to other people. It's all part of the growing up process. Diane will be fine in a few months. I wouldn't mind betting that this time next year she won't even remember who the hairy fella next door *is*, never mind have any feelings left for him.'

'Simone's right, Dottie,' Gemma said impatiently. 'You fret way too much over those kids of yours. Just because you're a lone parent, doesn't mean you have to worry enough for two people. Stop fussing over the girl and give her a bit of space, and she'll be over the big, hairy fecker before you can say, here comes a young Adonis-type to woo my beautiful, intelligent, witty daughter.'

On the face of it, Gemma and Simone had been proven correct. Dorothy reminded herself of this as the train pulled in at her destination. Determined to push all thoughts of lost love aside for the rest of the day, she alighted and headed for the exit along with dozens of other commuters. It was not raining, which meant she made good time to Lower Abbey Street.

She did not immediately enter her destination. Instead, she walked past the building a couple of times, and also stared into a couple of shop windows. She had the advantage of being small and virtually invisible, and for once was grateful for her lack of stature and general air of insignificance. In her long, black coat, sensible heels and old handbag, she would have blended in anywhere.

She noticed the headline of a newspaper an elderly man was holding. There had been a knife attack in New York City earlier in the week, resulting in four deaths and a litany of other injuries. News of the horror had been slow to reach Ireland, and the details were only emerging now.

The elderly man saw she was reading the back of his paper and smiled at her politely. 'Knife crime is so personal,' he told her in a surprisingly musical voice which was definitely not Irish in its origin. 'The young man must have been full of hate.'

Dorothy blinked away a sudden tear and hurried off before she disgraced herself. There was a middle-aged man with an expensive looking camera slung around his neck hanging around a large building. She stopped to exchange a few words with him, telling him she had a job interview scheduled in five minutes and was feeling nervous.

The man was bored and did not mind passing the time of day with her. He could not fail to notice the woman's enormous brown eyes as they seemed to examine him. For a second, he felt as if he was being probed by an alien life form, and shivered inside his grey raincoat.

He shook off the inexplicably weird sensation and lifted his camera as if to protect himself from an unseen force. The woman spotted the gesture and smiled impishly. Then she bade him goodbye and strolled into the building without a backward glance. Dorothy approached the main reception desk and greeted the young woman who was seated behind it.

'Good morning,' said the woman politely, 'may I help you?'

'I'm expected,' Dorothy replied with a smile. 'My name is Dorothy Lyle, and I'm here to collect my winnings.'

4

'I have a gun pointed at your daughter. In precisely one minute, she will be dead, and there is not a damn thing you can do about it.' Dorothy looked around for the source of the voice.

This was the third time today she had been privileged to overhear somebody else's audio book, and was beginning to wonder if it was a sign of some sort. She was standing on a sun terrace on the twelfth floor of the Falcon apartment building, which meant the reader could only be in a limited number of locations.

It seemed likely the voice emanated from the roof garden above her, although it was difficult to judge, given that the wind had picked up. Whoever was up there definitely had the volume on their new Christmas iPad turned up too loudly, that much was for certain. Why didn't he or she just put their headphones in?

On cue, a woman spoke, sounding exasperated: 'Where the hell are my headphones? The rest of the residents don't want to listen to my new audio book, even if it is fresh from the iTunes stores. God be with the days when I used to go to the library every week and try to find eight books I had never read before.'

Dorothy smiled to herself. God be with the days before technology indeed. She was tempted to call out to the reader on the rooftop and ask her for the name of the novel. It sounded good, even if some poor girl was being held at gunpoint so her parents could be either fleeced for cash or tortured at an emotional level.

She decided against interrupting the stranger and possibly even scaring her, and instead returned to her previous occupation, which involved gazing out over Dublin city and admiring the views. A robin landed on the steel railing only metres from where she was standing and chirped at her winningly. Dorothy smiled at the bird and heaved a great sigh of contentment. With the intensity of an eighteen year-old girl who believes herself to be madly in love, the Space Ache flared in her chest.

Stop that nonsense this second. Don't spoil this moment for me, she silently urged. Not for the first time, she speculated as to whether or not it could hear her, and not for the first time questioned her own rationality in posing such a question. Was it not bad enough she suffered from a mysterious ache in her chest which no doctor had been able to diagnose in more than six years, without attributing some form of conscious thought to it? Was it possible she had been reading too many Dean Koontz novels?

Dorothy took a few deep breaths. Then she sent a positive message of love and support to her heart chakra. The pain rapidly subsided, and she returned to appreciating the panorama stretching in front of her. She loved the views from this apartment. She squinted slightly and was positive she could see as far north as County Kildare, and as far south as County Wexford.

With a jolt, it dawned upon her she had lost all track of time and hastily checked her watch. She supposed that, generally speaking, a woman who could afford to spend a cool million on one apartment would not be obliged to rush back to the office for a two o'clock deadline.

Alas, life was not always that simple. Even though it was Friday, she did not intend to leave work until six at the earliest. Her in-tray was currently home to eight inches of paperwork, and she aimed to have every last millimetre of it resolved and cleared before another week had passed.

She did not intend to give Premier Payroll and Accounting Solutions any excuse to contact her after she left. If this entailed working late every night between now and her final day at the office, it was a sacrifice she was prepared to make. She could almost feel her wings unfurling. Her new life was beginning, and Dorothy was determined not to allow anything or anybody to stand in her way.

Walking inside once more, she allowed her eyes to rove around the duplex. It had been decorated in a minimalistic style, and was essentially a blank canvas. Most of the rooms had hardwood flooring or tiles, with walls painted either matt white or other pastel shades.

The blinds were wooden and screamed quality. The furniture was large, modern, and clearly expensive. Tucked away in a corner, six sturdy, brown storage boxes were stacked in a tower, and she was willing to bet these contained the CDs and other personal possession.

There was some sort of cutting edge DVD rack fixed to the wall which was empty. Somebody had taken the trouble to pack the personal stuff away but had not bothered to remove the boxes. They had clearly lost heart. Even though the apartment was spacious and airy, it was also cold and a little austere, giving Dorothy pause for thought.

For a moment, she questioned her own choices and actions. Should she even be here? There was no doubt the apartment was amazing from the point of view of space and location. It even had stairs for pity's sake! The property itself was not the issue.

She was positive she would soon have it more homely and welcoming when she added her own possessions. When all was said and done, what she really wanted was a house on the coast. It did not have to be the size of a castle, as long as it had four bedrooms, a cute little pool, and a pleasant view.

All week, Dorothy had worked away at her desk. All week, she had done her level best to maintain her usual demeanour as she helped the payroll staff deal with the tough queries. All week, she had liaised with the HR department with regard to holiday entitlements and sick pay. All week, she had striven not to go up to the rooftop of the Premier building and holler her news to the city at the top of her lungs. All week, in a quiet corner of her brain, she had begun to build a picture of the type of house in which she would like to live.

After much deliberation, she concluded the obvious and best solution would be to build her own home. If she chose that route, she would be able to customise it in the early stages. It would make far more sense than purchasing a readymade property and then remodelling it. That said, until she located a suitable site for such an establishment, she could not even begin to think about the build process.

Was there any possibility Simone would come home and design a house for her? After all, what was the point of your best friend being an architect if you could not call upon her to help you plan your dream home? Sadly, such an event was unlikely to occur. Dorothy's BFF, the aforementioned Simone Redmond, was all loved-up on the Australian continent, and would soon be involved in an exciting business venture with her new partner.

Even if she *did* return to Ireland, it would be unreasonable to expect her to design a house when she had no clue as to where it would eventually be located. Although there were plenty of plots available, the good ones were in short supply. Their owners were holding them back because the market had plummeted after the property bubble burst. Anybody attempting to sell a piece of Irish soil in 2011 would be lucky to achieve half of what they would have done a mere five years earlier.

In the meantime, Dorothy needed a new place to live. *If Diane O'Keefe doesn't want to visit Shankill, then perhaps Charlotte Quay would suit her better.* Maybe, just maybe, this apartment would make a good stopgap. The Falcon residence would certainly befit her status as arguably Ireland's luckiest woman. She could not class herself as Ireland's richest woman. A well-known executive, who, according to the *Sunday Times Rich List*, was worth in the region of eight billion, had the honour of holding that title.

Dorothy sniggered quietly. She had never moved in the same circles as anybody worth eight billion, or even eight million for that matter, and did not anticipate doing so any time soon. Her musings on millions were interrupted by the arrival of a tall, slim man in his late thirties. 'Have you seen enough, or would you like to go around again?' he enquired of her in his subdued way.

When Saul Newman first opened the door to Dorothy, he had been something of a revelation. His face was long and thin, and his eyes were blue under a pair of slightly bushy grey eyebrows. He was attractive in a pale and tired way, and was certainly wearing an expensive suit, even if it did hang on his slim frame as if he had recently shed a few pounds.

She tried and failed to remember the last time she had encountered such a sad man. He had an enormous black cloud comprised of sorrow and grief, hanging over him like a giant bird of prey. Even his subdued voice at the end of the phone had not prepared her for Saul in the flesh.

When Dorothy was a teenager, she often envied her peers who had talents that far outreached her own. She was not naturally artistic like Simone. She was not a mathematical whiz like her friend, Vivian. Nor could she play the violin like her pal, Naomi. While boys considered her attractive, she was not a natural flirt like her other friends, Amy and Bel, and often missed opportunities in that department. This was partly due to a sheer lack of know-how, as well as a tendency to be too honest in her dealings with the opposite sex.

What Dorothy *did* have, and what she assumed everybody else had as well - that was, until she reached the tender age of nineteen and discovered her error - was the ability to read people. The ability to see, quite clearly, into the heart of another, and to read their hopes and intentions. Dorothy Lyle had the uncanny ability to take a sneaky peek at another person's soul.

Nowadays, you could hardly turn on the television without stumbling across somebody claiming to be able to chat to the deceased, but back in the seventies and eighties, folks did not talk much about psychic ability. She would not have known what they meant, even if they had.

Dorothy had no reason to believe she was different. If she sometimes knew what was going to happen before it happened...well, that was feminine intuition. Nobody, not even her dad, who was the ultimate cynic, doubted the existence of that. Of course, the only time it did *not* work was when she really needed it to. When she had an important decision to make, or when it was vital she understand another person. Over the years, she also noticed it was difficult to read, with any degree of accuracy, those who were closest to her. Yet she could gauge a complete stranger within seconds.

'Saul,' she approached him carefully, the same way she might have done a very nervous puppy. 'Do you think we might sit down and talk for a few minutes? If you can spare the time?'

After a momentary hesitation, he gestured towards one of the long sofas facing the enormous plasma screen. Following his lead, Dorothy sat down, and he perched next to her, clearly ill at ease. 'Is this your apartment?' she asked, sensing the conversation was likely to be the emotional equivalent of wading through treacle, but nonetheless determined to persevere.

'No. I'm trying to sell it on behalf of my half-sister. Anna Sadler is her name.'

'Why is she selling?' Dorothy probed gently, in the hope of lulling him in to telling her the story. Something was going on. There was some sort of problem. She could almost feel it swirling in the air around her. She was determined to find the underlying cause, and still had sixty-five minutes to spare. There were always plenty of taxis cruising around Grand Canal. If she hailed one, she was positive she would make it back to the office in the nick of time.

'Anna was married to Phil Doheny,' Saul replied morosely. 'Have you heard of him?'

'The drummer with the Steel Tulips? Didn't he pass away last year? I seem to recall Dublin was overrun with crying musicians for a week. It was bizarre, yet incredibly sad all at the same time. That was for Phil, wasn't it?'

'That's right. He died nine months ago.' Saul wiped a hand across his face. 'It's actually quite ironic. He would have thoroughly enjoyed his own funeral. He was always a party animal. That's how he met Anna. She was putting herself through college by working for a catering company, and one night they got a gig handling one of Phil's parties.

'Anna was working away in the kitchen, trying to make some finger food look more appetising. She was wearing a black dress and a white apron and thinking about her thesis. Suddenly she looked up and saw Phil standing in the doorway watching her. He couldn't take his eyes off her. Phil always used to say it was love at first sight for him, and he never looked at an apron in the same way again. They were married a year later.'

He paused but Dorothy remained silent, hoping for more. He soon began to talk again. 'Ten years ago, they moved to the UK for Phil's career and he did really well, but Anna always missed Dublin and talked about coming back someday. Phil felt London was his spiritual home and he would rather have stayed there, but Anna started to put pressure on him after the first baby came along.

'Then, two years ago, Phil's grandparents and aunts died within six months of each other, leaving him the sole heir. Between the four of them, they owned two adjacent plots of land where the family had lived for over ninety years. They'd had offers for the houses during the property boom, but were at an age where they wouldn't leave their homes for any amount of money.

'When Anna discovered Phil had inherited land in Ireland, she insisted they take a look. Long story short, after much persuasion, Phil agreed to move home and build Anna her dream home. They asked me to design it.' Here Saul paused. 'I'm an architect,' he said, by way of explanation.

'Yes,' Dorothy replied gravely, wondering what was coming next. 'Go on, Saul. What happened?'

'They had plenty of dosh. Phil made a pile from his recordings in the early years, and the Steel Tulips had a major tour in 2008 that netted him five million pounds. They moved home with their little boy, Aidan, who was four at the time, and purchased this apartment for two million.

'Anna was over the moon. Phil was chipper enough once he realised he could pop over to London any time he felt like it. He soon realised Dublin isn't such a bad place to live. Especially if you happen to be something of a rock legend.' Saul paused and a shadow crossed his face.

'And then?' Dorothy prodded gently.

'It took a long time to complete the designs and get them agreed by the planning department, but there wasn't any mad rush because they had this place. They said they would rather wait an extra year and get it right, because the new house would be their forever home.

'Last February, we eventually got the green light and started clearing the site. We began by demolishing the houses and outbuildings belonging to the older generation. The site is on three and a half acres and has full coastal views. There's no doubt it was a fantastic inheritance for the guys.'

Now that Saul had begun to speak, he seemed to be loosening up and finding it easier. Dorothy made a concerted effort not to breathe too loudly, in case it dawned on him that he was sharing his family history with a complete stranger.

'Nine months ago, we had cleared as much as possible and were good to go,' the architect continued. 'The contractors and diggers arrived on site and so did I. We had a fantastic first day. Anna and Phil asked the local priest to come around and bless the land. We even opened a few bottles of champagne and toasted the project.

'Anna had just announced that she was four months pregnant, and was buzzing with the news. Everybody was in great form. The lads were delighted to get the work. Most of them had been scraping by for months, if not years. Lots of them had been on the scratcher for ages…eh…the dole, I mean. I was delighted to get going after the months of delay. I was the project manager, you see.'

'I see,' she murmured, although Saul did not seem to notice and kept talking. 'Anna, Phil and Aidan were plain, old-fashioned excited. They stayed for ages to watch the men at work, and then eventually headed off. Anna asked Phil to drop her off in Malahide so she could visit some of her old friends. After that, Phil was supposed to take Aidan home.' Saul paused in his recital and looked in to Dorothy's face. 'Do you remember that huge pileup last spring on the M50 motorway? The one around the Westlink toll bridge involving about twenty vehicles?'

'Yes,' she whispered.

'Phil dropped Anna in Malahide, and then headed home via the motorway. We're not sure why, because he always drove through the city centre if possible. He hated the M50. He used to say Irish motorists had no clue how to use the lanes correctly. You would think he was English to hear him talk, instead of born and reared in Stoneybatter.

'We think he was taking Aidan out for dinner, but we'll never know now. Some arsehole tailgating a flatbed lorry caused the pileup when the truck had to unexpectedly brake. Phil rear-ended another vehicle and spun out of control. His sports car ended up under an eighteen-wheeler. He was almost decapitated, and Aidan was virtually broken in two with the force of the impact. Even in his booster seat, he didn't stand a chance. His little body was crushed to pieces.'

Saul put his head in his hands, but remained soundless. Dorothy merely sat there, a helpless witness to the silent heartbreak.

'When Anna heard the news, she collapsed,' Saul lifted his head and spoke again. 'She was rushed to hospital, but it was too late. She lost the baby. She was in such a state of shock, for a while we wondered if she would die as well so she wouldn't have to face the truth. That baby would have given her something to live for, but now she has nothing.

'She blames herself, of course. She was the one who wanted to leave London, and she was the one who wanted the swanky house. She's absolutely convinced if she had been in the car that day, they would both still be alive. But she wanted to tell her friends about the new baby and the house.' Saul stopped speaking and stared at Dorothy.

'That's why the apartment is up for sale. Anna never wants to lay eyes on it again.'

He suddenly sat up straight, as if they had just enjoyed a perfectly normal conversation about blinds and rugs, and looked at her expectantly.

'Saul,' Dorothy spoke the words slowly. 'Where is the site on the coast? Is it for sale as well?'

He frowned, clearly not expecting that particular question. 'Anna intends to put it on the market in due course,' he replied. 'We made the decision to sell this place first before focusing on the site. It's virtually impossible to shift a plot of land these days unless you have a cash buyer, and they're in short supply as you know.'

'I understand that,' she said patiently. 'But where is it? Is it in Dalkey or Killiney?'

'Of course not,' Saul frowned again. 'Phil inherited the family land in Howth.'

'Howth?'

'That's right. In Dublin 13. On the North Side of the city. The little peninsula bit.'

'I haven't just disembarked off a plane from Moscow,' Dorothy replied snippily. 'I know where Howth is. I also know it rhymes with both. It's just I was expecting you to say Greystones or Killiney, or somewhere like that. I never really saw myself living that far north of the river. I used to take the kids there sometimes when they were younger. It's a small place.'

The architect shrugged. 'You never have to travel far in Howth to find what you want. You're only fifteen minutes away from everything.'

'I think it would be worth me taking a look at that plot of land. Assuming you're prepared to show me,' she spoke the words quickly, and then held her breath.

'Do you mean to say you're not interested in this apartment?' His voice was bitter, as if to say 'I knew it. A timewaster!'

'I'm prepared to offer you one million for this duplex, although I'd like to see the site as well.' She patted his arm reassuringly. 'I intend to build my own house and I'm looking for a suitable area. I must admit, I had sort of been thinking of Greystones. I think it's beautiful there. What's your opinion? It's on track to get a new marina as well. At least that's what I've heard.'

Saul looked bemused. 'But, Dorothy,' he protested, 'you'll have the stamp duty and legal fees on top of the one million smackers for this gaff. To say nothing of the moving costs and annual management charges. Anna is going to want a chunk of moola for the site, which, by the way, will be virtually impossible to get a mortgage on in the current economic climate. Unless of course, you happen to be having a torrid affair with a high-ranking banker? Are you?'

'No,' she replied shortly.

'In that case, are you yourself a high-flying banker?' he persisted.

'I am not a banker,' she replied coolly.

'In which case, do you have those kinds of funds at your disposal?' he asked somewhat tersely, clearly suspecting he was being led down the garden path by this rather tired looking and slightly odd little woman.

'I do indeed have the funds at my disposal,' she replied. Reaching into her handbag, she withdrew a piece of paper. 'Take a look at that photocopy,' she said, and offered it to him. Saul accepted the piece of paper and examined it for a full minute.

Then he lifted his head and stared at her. Then he scrutinised the paper again, before rather absentmindedly folding it in two and placing it on his knee. After a ten second wait, he re-opened it and studied it once more. After a further minute, he handed it back to her, a flabbergasted expression in his blue eyes. 'So, you're…' he trailed off.

'Correct. I'm last Friday's mystery winner,' she confirmed for him. 'The one that, so far, the press have been unable to track down.'

'But, Dorothy…' he spluttered.

'Yes?'

'That means…' he trailed off again.

Dorothy saw she had her work cut out with this one. She hoped she would not ultimately rue the day she met Saul Newman. She tried an encouraging smile and said, 'Let me make it a little easier for you. Last Friday night, I won the Euromillions lottery jackpot.

'It also happened to be my fortieth birthday; ergo I was already experiencing a degree of emotional turmoil, as I'm sure you can appreciate. First thing this morning, I went over to the lottery offices and, as you can see from that copy, they gave me a cheque. Can you believe they couldn't pay me by electronic funds transfer in this day and age? After a visit to the Irish Citizens' Bank and depositing the aforementioned cheque, and opening one of those high interest accounts, I came over here so I could meet you. I love this apartment and would like to buy it.

'That said, my heart is set on a detached house with coastal views and a nice little swimming pool, which I intend to build for myself. If anyone had raised the issue this morning, I would have said it could take months if not years to find the right location for that house. Then you tell me you might have a piece of land for sale which just happens to be on the coast, and I would dearly love to see it.

'It's really not that complicated. I hadn't anticipated getting involved in any property deals on the first day, but sometimes the universe throws opportunities our way, and it's up to us to catch them and not mess around.' She stopped talking and watched him expectantly.

'May I see the copy of the cheque again?' he asked quietly.

With a resigned air, she reached into her bag and, withdrawing it once more, handed it over. He perused it carefully, and then raised his eyes to hers. Sad blue ones met calm and kind, monkey-brown ones.

'Dorothy,' Saul spoke slowly and carefully. 'You just won more than one hundred and thirty-eight million euro, and broke the record for the largest Irish win ever.'

'That's right,' she agreed cheerfully. 'I have to be back in the office for two, so perhaps you could call me later to make the arrangements for a viewing out in Dublin 13. That's the little peninsula bit.'

5
One week earlier

Much like an unsuspecting target with a sniper zeroing in on her head, Dorothy was blissfully unaware of what was about to befall her. If she *had* known, she might have felt considerably more enthusiasm for the chore in which she was engaged.

However, somewhat unusually for her, she had not the smallest inkling of what lay ahead. As a direct result of this lack of prescience, she threw her groceries into the basket in a rather desultory fashion, and speculated on the possibility that she might be genetically predisposed to hate shopping.

Perhaps it was the period of time she had wasted on Victor-The-Moron that was the root of the problem. Sad to say, that phase of her life had turned her off many things. Romance, spaghetti bolognaise, skirts and ice cold water, to name but a few.

She firmly pushed all thoughts of her hideous ex-boyfriend aside. There was no need to devote perfectly good energy reflecting on those dark days. For a full year, she had been Victor-Free, and was currently entrenched in the Post-Victor phase of her life. Instead of burning calories pondering life with the sad loser, she focused her attention on choosing a bottle of wine which was palatable without being ridiculously expensive.

She glanced at her watch. It was the timepiece her parents had bestowed upon her on the occasion of her thirtieth birthday, and was beginning to show its age. She hardly noticed the scratches on the band any more, she only cared that the watch still functioned. The hands showed 8.06 p.m. A mere six minutes earlier, she had disembarked from the DART at Shankill station.

Even though it was a bitterly cold January evening, and she should be hurrying home to the warmth of her house, she took the decision to pop into her local express supermarket with a view to picking up a couple of essentials. Dorothy was of the opinion that she would not make it through what remained of her fortieth birthday without what a health professional would undoubtedly refer to as a crutch. In layman's terms, the aforementioned prop translated into a minimum of one bottle of wine.

In due course, she made her selection from the relevant shelves and, taking no chances, threw two bottles on top of the small loaf of multigrain bread already in her basket. She chose a pasta based convenience meal at random, and it joined the other groceries.

She had no intention of cooking this evening, yet urgently required sustenance since she had partaken of very little except birthday cake all day. She made her way to the front of the shop and took her card from her wallet.

The employee at the register did her best to look interested in yet another customer. She was a nervy looking young woman of about twenty, who had bitten her nails down to the quick. Despite her own troubles, Dorothy felt a measure of sympathy for the girl. She was stuck behind a cash register on a Friday evening, when she should have been out having fun.

As she carefully lifted her precious bag of alcohol and junk food off the counter, she smiled at the cashier and wished her a good evening. The girl looked startled and stood a little straighter, as if it had suddenly dawned upon her that she might not be invisible after all.

As Dorothy left the shop and started towards home, a gust of wind almost swept her off her feet. Both hands were full of bags, which meant she was unable to pull her black, woollen coat any tighter against her body.

After pausing to catch her breath and swear a bit for good measure, she continued on her way. A bus trundled past, and she moved further away from the road in case it splashed her coat and flat shoes with muddy water.

She had left her favourite three-inch pumps in her desk drawer, all ready for her feet to enter them once more when she returned to work after the weekend. For today was Friday and, even though it had the misfortune to be her fortieth birthday, at least she did not have to contemplate the office until Monday morning.

She slowed her footsteps as she passed Horace's door, tempted to knock and ask him if he wanted to come over and share the wine. At the end of the day, misery loves company. *To hell with it!* She quickened her pace and moved on. She was more in the mood for Amanda's company tonight, but her friend's house was cloaked in darkness. This was hardly surprising, as she had a healthy social life, and was rarely home before midnight on a Friday.

When Dorothy reached home, the light from the street lamps illuminated her Focus sitting safely in the driveway. Even in the half-light she could see the small front garden looked tidier than it had that morning. She wondered if Horace had wandered over while she was at work and raked up some stray leaves and debris. It was the sort of thing he *would* do.

She sighed as she inserted the key into the lock of her three-bedroom semi and pushed open the door. Horace was well aware she was struggling to forgive him for essentially driving Diane away, and was always trying to make it up to her in small ways.

I know it wasn't his fault. These things happen in life, and there's no rhyme or reason to it. I just miss them both so much. There are times when I feel as if I lost as much as Diane did when he rejected her. At least she has her whole life ahead of her, while I'm looking forward to precisely nothing.

Taking care not to drop any of her bags or tread on the post strewn on the doormat, she flicked on the hall light while simultaneously pushing open the door to the sitting room. She was greeted by a blessed wave of heat. The central heating had been on for a number of hours, albeit on a lower setting than usual. In an attempt to be both eco-friendly and economical, she had taken to reducing the thermostat by at least one degree.

Using the light from the hall to guide her, Dorothy walked to the far side of the room and pushed open the door to the kitchen. Using her elbow, she flicked on the light and saw that everything was exactly as she had left it. The room was small, clean and dated, but at least it was hers and she was home safely and was grateful for that.

With a sigh of relief, she set her bags down on the one countertop that was a decent size and appliance free. Working quickly, she unpacked the shopping and, after locating the best corkscrew at the back of the drawer, opened one of the bottles of wine so it would have a chance to breathe. Returning to the living room, she switched on the two floor lamps, drew the curtains, and ignited the gas fire. After all, it was her birthday so why shouldn't she splurge?

Only then, did she remove her coat and hang it on its special hook in the hall. The door to the bathroom was located beside the hook. Instead of picking up the post, she went in and turned the control on the shower to hot, determined one way or another, to get some heat into her cold and aching limbs.

She removed her clothes and threw her underwear and shirt into the hamper. She folded her grey trouser suit as neatly as possible and placed it out of harm's way. She hoped to get another year out of it, and it was her intention to drop it off at the cleaners the next day, on the way to visit her parents.

For Dorothy had lied to just about everybody who cared about her with regard to her plans for her fortieth. She told her colleagues she was meeting friends for dinner, and consequently would only be able to join them for a couple of post-work drinks. She told her mother and sisters she was going out for dinner with friends, but would join them for celebrations on Saturday. She told her friends she was going out with the girls from work.

She had not bothered to tell her dad anything. He had not remembered any birthday since his own back in 1953, and only recalled that day because, in the mistaken belief that he would be taken more seriously by his parents, had been looking forward to reaching double digits for some time.

The lie regarding the dinner plans seemed to have successfully assuaged her mother's suspicions. Nonetheless, Dorothy resolved not to accidentally answer her phone unless she was standing next to running water.

At least that way, she could pretend to be in a restaurant, having yet another copious goblet of wine poured for her by a smug waiter.

Her mother had very sharp hearing when it suited her. There was always the possibility she might correctly surmise that her second child was hiding out in solitude, intending to get quietly drunk because she was incapable of facing the outside world or her own limitations as a human being.

Still, Dorothy concluded, when dealing with an Irish Mammy it was best to err on the side of caution. She called her mother from the pub and did her best to sound excited and breathless, as if she might be in the middle of a major flirtatious episode.

Pat Lyle was delighted to receive a call from the birthday girl, and thrilled to hear the clamour of revelry in the background. She was over the moon to discover the proposed dinner companions were mostly singletons who would not feel obliged to rush home to loving spouses and children two minutes after dessert was finished. She wished her middle daughter many happy returns, and said she was looking forward to seeing her the next day. Not just for a proper chat, but also for a celebratory meal with the whole family.

Dorothy felt a stab of guilt pierce her conscience as she disconnected. She was getting so good at lying she may as well write a book and see if she could make some money at it!

Pulling a shower cap over her shoulder-length, brown hair, she shot a glance at her own reflection in the floor-to-ceiling mirror before stepping under the hot water. It was a very swift glance, for she was not happy with the appearance of that woman, and had not been for some time.

There was no denying that in the days prior to meeting Victor, she had looked younger and healthier, and been twenty pounds lighter. At first, the natural progression of a relationship in its infancy had caused her to gain weight, as the new couple spent many a happy evening enjoying romantic meals and drinks together. However, as the months wore on, she had grown to rely more and more on wine to get her through the evenings. Not for nothing was alcohol known as liquid fat.

Earlier in the week, she had paid a visit to her local gym because they were running a new year special offer. The fitness instructor, who looked about twelve years-old, had forlornly informed her that she was three stone overweight. In addition to that sobering fact, her face, despite its excess fat keeping it relatively line-free, had a grey tinge, not unlike the rest of her life.

In her younger days, Dorothy had always been regarded as a pretty girl. In addition to an oval face with a delicate chin, a cute little upturned nose and good cheekbones, she had a pair of large brown eyes that tended to have a faraway expression. Alas, time and tide, and most recently, Victor Hines, had all taken their toll.

While she did not possess a face that would make small children scream and run away, she could no longer be classed as pretty. These days, the best descriptions she could hope for were 'average' or 'not too bad for her age'.

Standing with closed eyes under the single jet of water, she rubbed the general area of her heart, as it sometimes helped to ease the discomfort she had nicknamed the

Space Ache. There were days when she scarcely noticed it, but today was not one of them.

Perhaps not surprisingly, the mysterious pain had been niggling at her all day, and now began to throb in earnest. 'Please make it stop,' she said aloud, trying not to snivel. 'I can't handle the Space Ache tonight of all nights.' The throbbing stopped as suddenly as it had begun.

'Thank you,' she sighed gratefully. She began to wash her body with peach scented shower gel, and grimaced as she felt the way her jelly belly jiggled. Come Monday, she would think about the gym membership, but right now there was no point in dragging herself even lower with thoughts of excess body weight.

It was not all bad news. If she were to be unexpectedly kidnapped by insurgents while vacationing in a resort close to the equator and held captive for a month, she would undoubtedly possess the fat reserves which would enable her to survive far better than her skinny fellow prisoners. Besides, fat was nature's way of keeping the body warm, and in her opinion this was always a good thing.

Dorothy hated the cold. For that reason, images of homeless people lying shivering in doorways upset and annoyed her more than anything else, because seeing them made her acutely aware of her own vulnerability. She pictured herself living without heat or comfort in a bleak and unforgiving world and grew very angry.

She often contemplated getting involved with one of the homeless charities as a volunteer but, quite frankly, did not believe they would want her. She did not view herself as a stupid or lazy person, but accepted she lacked the spark of creative energy which some folks possessed in abundance. She was certain that, in the fullness of time, the charity would lose patience with her and suggest she spend more time with her family.

Finished with her ablutions and wrapped in a jumbo-sized towel which had started its life as a deep lilac shade, but subsequently morphed into a washed-out grey over the intervening years, Dorothy slipped her feet into a pair of equally ancient slippers and wearily climbed the stairs to the first floor.

Inside the relative security of her bedroom, she switched on the lamp and pushed the button on the radio next to her bed. The room was a respectable thirteen feet-square, and large enough to accommodate her double bed, lockers and large wardrobe cum chest of drawers combination unit.

She rummaged in the top drawer of the chest until she found a pair of old and comfortable knickers. They were an unattractive shade of grey, but she concluded that since she was the only person who was going to be looking at them, it hardly mattered. *Must have a clear out of those drawers one of these days. New year and all that positive shite.* She dried her lower extremities briskly then pulled on the underwear.

The base of her divan bed housed two extra drawers. She rummaged about in one of these until she found an old pair of navy jog pants with an elasticated waist, and a couple of long-sleeved cotton tops. She pulled the pants on over the greying knickers, and then set about drying off her top half.

Instead of putting on a bra, she pulled a plain white top with a support panel over her head and shoved her arms through the pencil straps. Then she scrambled into the T-shirts as quickly as she could before the cold got a chance to set in. As she shoved her arm through the final sleeve, a memory briefly flared of Victor's obsessive need to dry every square millimetre of his flesh two or three times before he considered himself sufficiently arid.

With a sense of shock, she realised it had been many months since she last remembered this habit. It was definitely a good sign she had forgotten at least one of Victor's annoying traits. A voice on the radio began to sing about how much they needed the mighty dollar.

'That sounds a bit like me,' she mused, as she listened to the words. 'And I certainly agree all that glitters ain't gold.'

At school, the choirmaster told Dorothy she was a mezzo. It meant her voice was completely unsuited to the song about the dollar, which was being sung by a deep-voiced male. She could not have cared less, and belted out the lyrics as she dragged on a pair of slightly newer, furrier, and warmer slippers, slapped on a dollop of anti-aging moisturiser, and tied her hair back in a ponytail. She had not had it cut for some time. A trip to the salon was an expensive luxury in recessionary Ireland, and she wanted the twins to have new phones for Christmas.

She gazed at the photograph of her two babies which was perched on the room's single shelf. She perused their beloved faces and willed herself not to cry. She would see them tomorrow for the big birthday celebrations along with the rest of the family.

Diane was still very reluctant to visit Shankill, and often suggested meeting her mother on neutral territory. On the weekends she *did* venture home for a visit, she tended not to leave the house if she could help it, and if they were going out in the car, was always the last to jump in before it pulled away. Even Josh was beginning to lose patience with her antics, and it was left to Dorothy to plead with him for forbearance.

'Give her more time,' she begged. 'It hasn't even been six months since it all blew up. In another six months, she might be utterly indifferent to Horace, and not care if she falls over him raking up leaves out the front. It's very fresh right now, and she still feels humiliated by the whole episode.'

'She was crazy about him, Mum, and the worst part of the whole sorry mess is she was totally convinced he was in love with her as well and wanted to marry her,' Josh looked appalled at the very notion. 'I like the fella a lot, but he's not exactly what you might call a catch, is he? What the hell was she thinking?'

'She got all confused with her emotions and saw something that wasn't there,' his mother told him soothingly. 'Horace was as shocked as any of us when he learned the truth. We need to give her more time and be patient, Joshie. Maybe one day, they'll find they can be friends again.'

Josh's expression said it all. 'I can't see those two ever being civil to each other again, Ma, never mind being friends. Emily says Di won't even mention his name. It's as if he's dead to her. She doesn't want me and Deco to have anything to do with him either. She says she'll consider us traitors if we do. We've known the fella since we were kids, Ma. We can't just cross the road when we see him coming.'

His mother sighed. 'You know what they say about love and hate being two sides of the same coin, sweetheart. What you're witnessing here is a representation of that. If you and Deco want to occasionally visit Horace, that's fine. Just make sure your sister doesn't get wind of it. Be tactful for her sake, if nothing else.'

After a little more persuasion, Josh agreed to be discreet about his on-going friendship with Horace, not to harass his already-fragile twin, and allow her time to adjust to her change in circumstances.

6

Dorothy paused in the act of straightening the duvet and instead picked up her pillow and began to knead it between her hands. She regarded the piece of furniture with its wooden headboard and lilac cover.

The spare locker on which no man had dumped his phone or coins for over a year only enhanced the sense of splendid isolation. It had been many months since a man had rested his head on the plump pillows situated on the right-hand side, complained bitterly about the heat of the room, or moaned because she had changed the fabric softener just as he had gotten used to the aroma of the old one. It was a lonely looking divan and no mistake.

It went without saying that she had never expected to find herself travelling solo at this time of her life. Two years ago, she had felt it safe to assume she would be married by the time she turned forty, and would form part of what she liked to call the Couples Club. A club where very few members seemed to worry unduly about the quality of their relationship, just as long as they were part of one.

Alas, instead of putting her energies into planning a wedding, she expended them on devising a scheme to evict Victor from her house before he realised he was being dumped. After many weeks of sleepless nights and serious chats which led precisely nowhere, she had surprised herself by successfully seeing off the sad loser in the run-up to Christmas 2009, without one drop of blood being spilled or one tear shed.

It was a victory. More than that, it was a triumph. After waving off the man who had been the means by which she had wasted months of her life in an ironic manner that sailed right over the fuckwit's head, she returned to a life of sleeping alone. Regretful another relationship had bitten the dust, but grateful the snoring, shite talking, moronic monster was no longer around to torment her.

Dorothy shrugged as she ceased to pummel the pillow and turned off the radio. Being alone was better than wasting away within the confines of a toxic relationship any day of the week. It was just such a shame it had all worked out so badly and left her, emotionally speaking, out in the cold.

The sense of isolation she had been experiencing since September was reminiscent of those days she had endured while trapped in a deeply unhappy marriage to the twins' dad, Declan. The situation had been further exacerbated by the absence of her oldest friends.

The previous August, Simone had taken off to Australia with only a couple of weeks' notice, while Amy had been living in France for what felt like forever. Bel was never far away, but had a hectic social life, a devoted husband, and two teenage boys to run around after.

If not for Amanda across the road and Horace next door, Dorothy knew she would not have survived the past couple of months half as well as she had. She felt a twinge of guilt at this, well aware she had not appreciated Horace's efforts to support her in a way he deserved. She resolved to, once and for all, put the past behind her and get their friendship back on track. Just not this weekend, and certainly not this evening. Right now, all she wanted to do was sit in her chair and get quietly drunk.

She plodded downstairs in her slippers and finally paused to collect the heap of mail from the doormat. When she entered the sitting room, she found it toasty warm from a combination of fire and radiator. That was when she spotted it.

She had been in such a rush to dive into the shower earlier, she had not noticed the parcel perched on the corner of the sofa. She never used the piece of furniture unless she had guests, preferring her own comfortable recliner. She knew who it was from and did not spend time examining it.

It was too big to balance on the arm of her chair so she put it on the floor and leaned it against the side of the recliner. In that way, it would be within easy reach when she eventually sat down. Then she went back to the kitchen, threw the pile of post onto the worktop and spent a few minutes clearing out the other bags she had brought home.

She carried her birthday cards back to the sitting room and arranged them artistically on the mantelpiece. Then she stood back to admire her display. There was no hiding a birthday in a payroll department, no matter how much you might be inclined to do so. A date of birth was one of the core pieces of information that ensured the smooth running of any such department. Attempting to hide the anniversary of your birth would be the equivalent of working at Starbucks and hoping your co-workers would conveniently fail to notice your addiction to skinny lattes.

In addition to the cards, the girls from Premier had surprised her with a cake and balloons. They were a riotous, joyful bunch all morning, until she wondered if it would be less exhausting and painful to simply hurl herself out of the office window. After all, they were situated on the seventh floor, high indeed by Dublin city standards. Alas, health and safety guidelines restricted the opening of any aperture by more than three centimetres.

While not exactly ready to appear on her own show (possibly entitled *Way too Fat for 40,* or *You are Fat, go sit in the corner looking contrite*), Dorothy was very curvy, and unlikely to squeeze through the teeny weenie gap of availability. As an alternative to ending up in a bloodied crumpled heap on the pavement below Premier, not unlike a scene from a CSI based drama, she resolved to go with the flow and try not to scream.

So what if the girls were young and excitable. It was not their fault her life (such as it was) was well and truly over, with about as much chance of a future as a Snickers in the hands of a chocoholic.

When the alarm clock began to emit its shrill wail on Friday morning, she had seriously contemplated the idea of calling in sick. In many ways, she *was* sick. In her heart, she was sick at the idea of the Big 4-0, as it was known. What was so big about it, anyway? In her opinion, the fortieth birthday should be banned in the same way floor thirteen was often banned in buildings.

Those were her thoughts as she hit the snooze button and considered the impending shower with a sense of dread. The arctic weather had returned with a vengeance, and the cold was seeping its way, not only into the bedroom, but also into her heart and soul.

Having lain with the duvet pulled up to her chin for ten minutes reviewing her options, Dorothy concluded there was no point in putting off the inevitable and got up.

Rather, she moaned resentfully, and then dragged her 40-year-old ass out of bed.

After showering, she dressed in one of her better work suits and a fairly new white blouse that did a good job of disguising her belly flab. In honour of the day, she chose a neat pair of stud sapphire earrings which had been a Christmas present, and applied more makeup, perfume and lipstick than usual.

Satisfied she had made herself as presentable as possible, she set about getting the same 40-year-old ass to the office. At least it was Friday. As she made her way to the DART station, she sincerely thanked God, the universe, and any beings who might be watching over her that today, of all days, was Friday.

It was the quality of her life that was the killer, she admitted to herself as she spent the afternoon pretending to work, but in reality wallowing in self-pity. Or, more accurately, the lack of quality. The listless drifting had taken a firm hold and become the norm. If her life had a colour, it would undoubtedly be grey, the hue of wet cement. She often wondered how she would react if something truly good should unexpectedly happen to her, but seriously doubted she would have the energy to either appreciate or enjoy it.

As she composed an email to the HR department, she considered all the possibilities before her. She came from a long-lived family, that much was certain. Look at Aunt Eileen, who had recently received a letter and cheque from the president, congratulating her upon becoming the latest Irish centenarian.

It was extremely likely Dorothy had another forty years ahead of her, which meant today was merely the midway point. Perhaps the time had come to call a halt to the pity party. Perhaps the time had come to draw a line in the sand and start facing up to things.

She would go back to that gym and focus on losing the rogue three stone and become strong and fit again, just as she had been for most of her life. She would take better care of herself, and drastically reduce her consumption of alcohol. She would spend more money on clothes, shoes and cosmetics. She would have her hair done six times a year and hang the expense.

Instead of succumbing to the loneliness, she would embrace the solitude of the house. Instead of viewing the twins' absence as a bad thing, she would look upon it as a positive change. Perhaps she would turn one of their old bedrooms into a fitness area, and the other into a sacred space where she could lay out her crystals and candles and start to meditate again.

She had gotten out of the habit during the time Victor had lived in her house. He was the sort of man who had not hesitated to make disparaging comments regarding other people's habits and beliefs, despite being fatally flawed and downright stupid himself. Perhaps she would even travel a little if she could save enough dosh.

Seated at her desk, Dorothy shuffled some paperwork and tried to look busy, although all the while her mind was in a whirl of conjecture. What about the dreaded subject of romance? She had reached an age where it was almost impossible to meet an appropriate mate. Unless one should happen to wander into the payroll department and miraculously take a shine to her, it was unlikely she would bump into a suitable male by traditional means.

Should she perhaps consider a spot of online dating since it was all the rage? She pulled a face and hoped none of her colleagues would notice. Some years earlier, Amanda, her well-meaning friend and neighbour, had signed Dorothy up to an internet dating website.

For a while, she had gone along with it. Partly so as not to hurt her friend's feelings, and partly (she supposed) because, deep down, we all retain a small iota of hope that we will find that special somebody and all will be well with our own small world. Looking back now, she wondered what she had been thinking in allowing herself to get involved in such a scheme. Maybe she was just fussy. When a woman reached a certain age, she did tend to become extremely picky. Maybe she was just unlucky. There was no doubt not even the most liberal of her friends or family would describe her as blessed in matters of the heart.

On the other hand, perhaps it was simply because every man she met online had turned out to be a sex mad fitness freak, on the hunt for a woman who would worship, adore, and take care of him. Then there was the age thing. Every man over the age of 35 was looking for, and considered himself entitled to, a woman aged between 18 and 25.

This was a common theme running through the profiles. The men who had entered a minimum age of 30 as a requirement in a partner had turned out to be lying. They did not want to be perceived as the type of men who would pursue 18-year-old girls. This was precisely the kind of men they were, yet they were choosing to lie about it. Naturally enough, this flagrant lack of honesty made them seem even worse than the ones who were blatantly seeking 18-year-old girls.

After six soul destroying, heart wrenching, eye opening and quite frankly, stomach-churning months, Dorothy gave up on the online dating and went back to raunchy paperback novels and the electric blanket for entertainment and warmth. 'Hope is an odd and dangerous concept, and makes so called grown-ups act in some truly bizarre ways,' she told herself.

Removing a number of documents from her in-tray, she pretended to peruse the top one, although in reality was not seeing the words. She was thinking further on the subject of romance. What would 2011 hold for Dorothy Lyle? What would she choose for herself?

She made her decision while clearing a few sweet wrappers out of her desk drawer and throwing them into the wastebasket. She discovered a decrepit chocolate bar, which met the same fate. *That part of my life is over now. I can manage the next forty years alone. To hell with them all.*

Certainly, she liked the *idea* of a boyfriend. Every single woman liked the *idea* of a companion for those cold winter nights. She fully appreciated the seasonal and social advantages to having a partner. She hated attending weddings and other family events alone. She enjoyed having an escort as much as the next woman did. Just not every day.

Her problem was not that she disliked men, or did not appreciate their good qualities. Dorothy's problem was that she could not be fecking bothered to either tolerate or make room in her life for one.

What kind of woman tied herself to a human being who considered the zenith of the human condition to be (in no particular order) a cold beer, a plate of food, an oversized TV, and a girl in a bikini? Not her. Not Dorothy Lyle. Not anymore. That ship had long since sailed.

The notion that she would ever again hitch her wagon to that of some testosterone-ridden, attention-craving, grumpy, overly tall, sports-mad, controlling, mother-obsessed, bossy, opinionated, unkempt, beer-swilling, boob-fixated, constantly hungry, frequently horny, male of the species, was frankly laughable.

The decision was made. From now on, she was out of the dating game. Done with men. Single forever. She waited for the sense of despair and dread which must surely follow such a drastic decision, but it never came.

She wondered if perhaps this was a sign from her guardian angel that she was on the right path and was, in fact, meant to be solo. Perhaps the universe had a plan for her which did not allow for a relationship. It was an interesting thought.

It would explain a lot, she ruminated, as she tackled some shredding. One of the team would have happily done it for her since she was the head of the department, but performing the simple chore gave her a few private minutes to think.

Returning to her desk, she checked nobody was loitering before logging into her private email account. Sure enough, she had a message from Bel wishing her a happy birthday. She and Gerald were having a fabulous time in Italy, and had taken at least one hundred photographs. They were looking forward to celebrating with her upon their return, and had found her a fabulous gift. Sadly, there was no mail from either Amy or Simone, which meant she would have to check again later.

Dorothy logged out and spent the next couple of hours in a meeting with Rita, her assistant. Rita was looking forward to the team enjoying a few birthday drinks after work, and had already warned her husband and children that she would not be home to make dinner for them.

Dorothy had been dreading the enforced jollity and socialising all morning, but that was before she made her plans for the remainder of the year. She suddenly felt more positive, and had not minded spending a few hours in the pub with the girls.

Nonetheless, she never lost sight of the fact that, before her new life could begin, she would first have to survive her birthday weekend. There was no point in pretending she could do this without the aid of some legal-yet-addictive substance. Like wine or chocolate, or possibly both.

A forty-nine-minute commute away from Premier Payroll and Accounting Solutions, Dorothy strolled into the kitchen and poured herself a large glass of red wine with one hand, while powering up the oven with the other in a professional manner which suggested she had performed the same ritual countless times before.

A replacement oven was long overdue, yet she hoped to get another year out of this model. Now she lived alone, all of her appliances were under considerably less pressure. *What's the point in splashing out on a fancy new oven just for one person?*

When she had pierced the cellophane lid of the packet as per the instructions and placed it on the middle shelf, she set about examining the small collection of birthday presents she had received so far. The girls from her department had tried hard to find gifts well-suited to their boss. Louise had presented her with a little book called *Angel Numbers*.

Liz had given her a spiral bound notebook depicting a frolic of gyrating fairies on the cover. Finola had chosen a miniature crystal guardian angel, the type she would be able to hang from her rear-view mirror. They had tried hard to get a buzz going, and she had been touched by their kindness. After all, it was not her team's fault her life had been so grey and meaningless of late.

Feeling guilty for being such a party pooper, Dorothy suggested they take turns flicking through the little angel book to see what number they landed upon. It was not the correct way to use it, but none of the payroll team had time to go searching for signs from their angels hinting at what numbers they should be investigating.

When Dorothy's turn came, she slowly allowed the pages to flow through her fingers. When she felt a tingle in her lower spine, she stopped and opened the little book. She had landed on 111. This very quickly caught everyone's imagination.

Whenever you see the sequence 111, it is a sign of a golden opportunity. It means a doorway has opened up in which your intentions and goals will manifest extremely quickly. The angels have taught me to focus my thoughts and intentions whenever I see this number. It's not unlike making a wish when a cake with candles is presented to you.

The team had grown quite excited when she read the paragraph aloud. Handing over her new notebook, the girls insisted she make a manifestation list. Over birthday cake, and with plenty of assistance from her colleagues, Dorothy covered no fewer than three pages with a wish list. This included, amongst other things, a celebrity-slim body, a Hollywood smile, and a house with a pool.

7

Still in her kitchen with the oven humming away contentedly next to her, Dorothy sorted the normal post from the junk mail which, despite the recession, had not reduced one whit in volume.

Once she had crammed the unsolicited correspondence into the overflowing recycle bin, she checked the letter from the bank was nothing more than a machine generated piece of sales crap, and nothing urgent. Satisfied she had done her duty by Friday's post, she picked up her glass of red and left the room.

She returned to the living room and settled herself comfortably in her recliner. Then she carefully deposited her glass of wine on the small coffee table she kept next to the chair for exactly such a purpose. She determinedly exhaled as much of the air from her lungs as she was able, and felt her shoulders relax a fraction. She followed this with a large gulp of the wine.

Delicious. Good choice, Dottie girl. Many happy returns of the day. Twisting slightly, she eyed the parcel still resting against the chair. She could put off the evil moment no longer. The time had come to open the birthday present Horace had left.

The mystery gift-giver could only have been him. Apart from the twins, who had called earlier to say they were sending her positive birthday thoughts from a city centre watering hole, he was the only other person who held a key to her house. Because Horace did not have a traditional job, and was seldom away from Old Hen, he was the obvious choice to be a key holder, and was also entrusted with Amanda's.

Dorothy surmised he must have dropped by earlier with his little surprise. That was very likely when he had noticed the garden was full of detritus, blown there by the January winds, and had taken the time to tidy it up.

A more normal man might have sent her a text to wish her a happy birthday, and perhaps even mentioned he had left a little something for her. But not Horace Johnson. He did not possess a phone of any style or digital persuasion.

Horace was inclined to be eccentric, and shunned modern technology on principle. He despised phones in particular, and tended to view them as tools of the devil.

His attitude would have been amusing if not for the fact it was incredibly annoying. There had been many occasions over the years when she had urgently needed to speak to him while stuck at work, and been unable to make contact.

Four years earlier, she had even offered to buy him a phone. An offer which he firmly but politely refused, saying they were teeming with radiation and liable to cause brain tumours.

Taking care not to accidentally brush against her glass and cause it to topple over, Dorothy leaned her torso to the side until the fingers of her right hand grazed the brown packaging of the parcel. She got a firm grip on it and gently eased it upwards and over the arm of the leather chair. Using both hands, she hoisted it into the air a couple of times to gauge its weight.

It was a frame of some sort, of that she was certain. *Maybe he's gone and framed one of those soppy poems he sometimes writes. I do so enjoy a love poem. Not.*

The paper was brown and thick, and resembled the stuff one often saw shop assistants using in old movies.

Horace had even tied it up with twine, for all the world as if he was living in post-war Europe when goods were still in short supply.

Dorothy shook her head over this, as she gently pulled at the approximation of a bow and the string came undone. She was about to roll it around her finger with a view to saving it, but in a fit of birthday frivolity flung it onto the mahogany coloured carpet instead. She would tidy it up tomorrow when she was past all the birthday nonsense.

She did not intend to leave the warmth of her bed until noon at the earliest, and had very little planned for the afternoon except a couple of essential household chores. She would have to start getting ready to go out at six, because she was due to catch the seven o'clock DART to Blackrock. The entire family were planning to congregate at one of their favourite restaurants for the purpose of celebrating Dorothy's birthday.

She already knew what she was going to wear. She had purchased a dark blue dress with a sprinkling of sequins around the neck for her Premier Christmas outing, and intended to give it another airing on Saturday. Who knew when she might next get a chance to wear it and, even on sale it had cost the best part of one hundred euro.

Even taking into account staying in bed until noon, and beginning the beautification process relatively early, there would be ample time to pick up pieces of string or any other debris which might be lying around the house. Let Saturday take care of itself. Tonight she was forty, and determined to bear the ordeal with fortitude, rigour and vino.

Dorothy took a deep breath and ripped off the brown parcel paper. Her mouth dropped open ever so slightly. The picture was twelve inches high and roughly nine inches across. The frame was made of rosewood. She knew this because it was Horace's wood of choice for carving, and she had been privileged to see some of his finished pieces over the years.

Many had been sold off to keep the wolf from the door, although he had retained a magnificent headboard which he attached to his own large bed, together with a rocking chair which Dorothy doubted could have been improved upon by a master craftsman.

Rosewood was expensive and not easy to come by, and she guessed the picture frame had been carved from off-cuts of the chair which he had carefully salvaged and preserved. There were no visible seams in the corners of the frame. It was as if the four sides had effectively been melted into each other, which she knew was impossible.

She pulled the wooden gift closer to her nose and sniffed it experimentally. Linseed oil. Another favourite of her neighbour's. Dorothy firmly grasped the frame in both hands and held it away from her body so she could better admire it. There was a beautiful sheen to the wood thanks to the oil he had applied, but that was only the beginning.

Horace had carved three magnificent dragonflies at the base of the frame, using the relief method. Consequently, the 3D, winged creatures looked as if they might take off at any moment and fly out of the wood. *How long did that take him for feck sake!*

He had not stopped there. The picture inside brought a tear to her eye, although she did not dare to remove one hand from the precious object to wipe it away, in case it fell to the floor and broke. It would never do to destroy something so wondrous. Another tear quickly followed the first one as she gazed rapturously upon the faces of her children.

Using only charcoal, Horace had caught their very essence. Josh's hair flopped into his eyes over a pair of large, dopey eyes which were identical to his mother's. The hooknose he had inherited from his father was too large for such a slim and youthful face. The young man in the picture wore a typical Joshua O'Keefe expression - determination mixed with humour.

Next to him, his sister's eyes glistened with mischief. Her cheekbones and chin were all her mother's, although her eyes were very like her father's, bright, sharp and questioning. It was impossible to tell from the portrait that they were an unusual emerald green shade which often left her open to accusations of using coloured contact lenses.

Diane's long blonde hair hung around her oval shaped face and her cute little upturned nose was totally at odds with her twin's beak. She was half-smiling as if she had a secret.

She did have a secret you great, hairy, dopey eejit. She was madly in love with you. Even on the day you sketched this picture, she was probably sitting there posing for you and imagining a life of wedded bliss with you and your dog in your funny little cottage. With you taking commissions for pieces of furniture and giving guitar lessons to earn a crust, while she...what exactly was she planning to do? Wait around until your ship came in?

Dorothy very carefully pushed the base of her chair in a downwards motion until she was sitting fully upright. Still clutching the picture, she eased herself out of the recliner and approached the mantelpiece.

Using her elbow, she flicked her birthday cards onto the floor and replaced them with the gift from Horace. She centred it on the mantle and leaned it carefully against the wall, making sure it was steady. She was tempted to leave the cards lying on the floor as well, but decades of habit kicked in.

She picked them up and rearranged them on either side of the gift, being careful not to obscure any of the picture as she did so. Satisfied that everything looked as well as possible for the moment, she also retrieved the discarded piece of string. She would return it to Horace tomorrow, together with the brown paper, in case he might want to reuse them.

She would drop by on the way to the station to thank him, and bring some sort of food offering and the bottle of brandy she had won in the Premier Christmas draw. She rarely drank spirits, and knew he would appreciate the bottle far more than she would. Having reached that decision, she relaxed and returned to her chair.

It took a few seconds to locate the remote because in all the excitement of opening the parcel she had let it fall to the ground beneath her recliner. Once she had retrieved the gadget and brushed the dust off its grey surface, *must do a spot of vacuuming tomorrow before I go out*, she turned on the television.

As she did, Dorothy wished for the 111th time she owned one of those flat-screen models that did not require four strong men to carry it. Out of habit, she watched what was left of the nine o'clock news and caught the recap of the headlines. She wondered why she bothered, as these days the news was seldom good. In the Middle East, somebody called the Conger had assassinated a British executive who had long been suspected of selling arms to the wrong side.

Dorothy was intrigued by the name Conger, and spent a few minutes speculating about the type of person who killed others for money. She wondered how Interpol knew it was this Conger person who was responsible for the murder. Were they merely guessing, or did he or she leave a calling card? She found it difficult to picture a deadly, female assassin, but as they were frequently depicted in the movies, there was no reason to question their existence. Perhaps the Conger was a girl who suffered from debilitating PMS?

There had been another major earthquake which had wiped out hundreds of homes, and killed tens of thousands of her fellow earthlings. This news made her frown, creating a deep furrow in her brow. The world seemed to be falling apart. No wonder so many folks believed it would end in 2012. Dorothy shook her head at the folly of the human race and their crazy notions. As if the world would suddenly cease to exist simply because of a date in a human calendar.

In domestic news, unemployment was on the rise, as was the rate of inflation. The country's leading economists predicted that house repossessions would exceed ten thousand within two years.

Dorothy sincerely hoped this exaggerated number was nothing more than scaremongering, designed by news producers to boost audience ratings. Where were all of these dispossessed families to go if the mortgage providers had them evicted? Were they to set up camps on the side of the road, as had happened in California a few years ago?

The oven timer beeped and she heaved herself up out of the chair and went to serve up her dinner. She put her plate on a tray with a knife, fork and paper napkin and took it back to the sitting room. She was usually quite disciplined about eating at the table, but there was no way she was dining in splendid isolation at the kitchen table tonight.

As she worked her way through the meal, she watched a few minutes of a sit-com, but was not really seeing it. Instead, she was running through the different scenarios which might result from mass repossessions by the banks and other lenders.

Then, reminding herself it was her birthday, and she was trying to stay positive, she snapped out of it. She went to rinse her empty plate and left it in the drying rack, then collected her laptop from its usual spot on the kitchen table, keen to see if the two pals who lived abroad had emailed her.

Sure enough, she had messages from both women, wishing her many happy returns of the day, and commiserating with her on turning forty. The tone of Amy's email was rather low. After Dorothy had read the message through twice, she decided it was no wonder. Her latest romance appeared to be in trouble and she was not doing a good job of hiding it.

In the attached photograph, Dorothy could see her friend had lost weight. Amy's short frame was not as pear-shaped as it had been when she had taken off to France many months earlier, clutching the proceeds of her much anticipated house sale, and with Donal Mulligan by her side.

At least she still had some sparkle in her eyes and looked like a woman on a mission, with her brown hair pulled back in a ponytail reminiscent of her teenage style. Dorothy smiled at the memories of her school days with Bel, Amy, Naomi, Simone and Viv. Hitting reply, she began to type.

~~~

From: Dottie8888@chatulike.ie
To: ANorris@talkalot.com
Date: January 7th, 2011
SUBJECT: POOR ME. 40 TODAY. BOO HOO.
Hi, Amy chick!
Thanks for remembering. I won't pretend it's easy, because it ain't, although all things considered, the day has been good. I even decided to join the local gym and get fit again, but not until next week. Sorry to hear things are not going too well between you and Donal. Is it the strain of all the building work?

I well remember when my friend, Maura, and her partner built their own house. They almost ended up separating as a result of it all. They got there in the end and are still happily together, so don't go throwing in the towel or anything drastic like that. I really hope the situation improves, and you and Donal work it out.

Earlier today I swore off men for the rest of my life. I thought I might get a bad feeling afterwards, but I didn't. On the contrary, I felt very well. Do you think it's possible God wants me to remain single? That doesn't mean you should do the same. I know you love Donal and vice versa. I wish I had some money so I could send you a chunk for your barn.

I had better go because I still have to reply to Si and I am a little tipsy. I really should go to bed, but Marty Lovegood is starting soon. Si never liked him that much, but I think he is very cute and would make an excellent boyfriend. You could take him anywhere and he would never be at a loss for words. I hope the sun is shining in La France. Talk soon. Love Dot xxx

8

When the *Late Night Show* started at ten minutes past ten, she was still coherent. The gas fire had heated the room to her preferred temperature. To Dorothy, this meant nicely warm, although in the past, guests had described it as stiflingly hot. Hence it very much depended on whose opinion you sought on the subject.

She topped up her glass and relaxed into her recliner, marvelling at how well Marty was looking in a particularly stylish, navy pinstriped suit, silver grey shirt and deep purple tie. His face was long and his hair just grey enough at the temples to lend him a distinguished air. She had Googled him and discovered he was thirty-nine, only a year younger than she was.

Dorothy was looking forward to the show but to her profound disappointment, the first interview was with an apparently well-known sports personality. Well known to everybody except Dorothy.

'Who is he?' she muttered in vexation, as the tall man walked on. 'Do they not understand it's my fortieth, and my barest minimum requirement is Harrison Ford decked out in Armani? Ideally singing happy birthday to me.'

The interview seemed to last forever. By all accounts, the nation could not get enough of Tyrone O'Sullivan. It transpired the young man was a tennis player, and would potentially be the Great Irish Hope for Wimbledon 2011. After twenty minutes, Tyrone thankfully finished his poetic waxings on the subject of tennis and left to rapturous applause.

The next guests were a couple in their thirties who had recently won a million smackers on the Monday night lottery. After collecting their winnings and thinking things over, they had taken the decision to move to Greece and live on the beach.

In Dorothy's vaguely sodden state, it sounded very similar to the final scene of *The Shawshank Redemption*. The one where Morgan Freeman strolls down the beach, laced shoes slung over the shoulder, all set to embrace a sun-drenched Tim Robbins, who is, of course, busy repairing a boat, or partaking in some other nautical activity.

It was quite an interesting interview, especially in comparison to Tyrone and his - my fastest ever serve was recorded at two hundred and fifty-nine kilometres per hour, but who's keeping score, arf arf - ramblings, although Dorothy still found the couple somewhat annoying.

They appeared to be possessed of the bizarre notion that taking their million and running away from their loved ones would solve all their problems. Even Dorothy Lyle, a woman with minimum hope for the future, knew that running away was seldom the answer. Having tried it once, she had reached the conclusion that, while in the short-term it was a perfectly viable option, as a long-term solution it had a low success rate.

I got lucky. The whole thing could so easily have backfired on me. Thanks be to God we acquire wisdom with age. Most of us anyway.

The couple left the set and rather than pausing the show, Dorothy used the ensuing break to dash to the toilet and replenish her wine. She made it back to her chair within the designated three minutes, and was just in time to see the next guest taking her place in front of Marty, and hear her being introduced as the latest artistic sensation.

The girl went by the name of Gráinne Byrne and had recently won an award for her sculpture entitled *Death of a Tiger*. The young woman chatted to Marty with great confidence, as if she had been born to sit under studio lights, being interviewed on live television.

Dorothy envied her poise and confidence, to say nothing of her talent. She experienced a momentary sadness when she acknowledged she would never achieve even a fraction of what the 19-year-old had during her few short years.

Having acquitted herself with honour and only been patronised by Marty once or twice, Gráinne left the studio, grinning like the teen she was. Marty signed off and Dorothy waved to him and blew him a kiss as the credits rolled and he was played off by the resident band.

She didn't bother to channel surf and instead let the commercials play in the background as she took up her laptop once more and re-read Simone's mail. She sighed heavily. She really missed her best friend. Nonetheless, judging by recent correspondence, it was clear Simone was very happy. Given that her married years had been tempestuous, and her subsequent divorce both acrimonious and protracted, the situation certainly merited gratitude. Dorothy shook off the sudden anxiety that swept over her, firmly clicked on the reply button and began.

~~~

From: Dottie8888@chatulike.ie
To:SRedmond@chatchat.com
Date: January 7th, 2011

SUBJECT: THE BIG 4-0

G'day Si!

Thanks for the mail. I won't pretend it's easy turning 40, because it's horrible. So far, I am getting through the day well enough, and trying to stay positive. The Space Ache was bad earlier, although it's better this evening. I went for a few drinks after work and now I am hiding out at home and have just finished watching Marty Lovegood, your not so favourite TV presenter.

Bel and Gerald are at a wedding in Italy, the lucky feckers. What do Australians make of the word feckers? Do they understand it's not abusive? Have you had to stop saying it in case you give offence? It means Bel is not here to save me from myself, although I will see her in a week's time.

You will be pleased to hear I have decided to join a gym next week, once I am over the whole birthday trauma. I have also sworn off men for the rest of my life, but more on that another time. As you have started a new romance, I don't want to whine about the opposite sex and put a downer on things.

Amy is still in France with Donal, refurbishing the barn and the holiday lets. She says they are having a few problems. It can't be easy working on a big project like that, because it always ends up costing more than you first anticipate. I am sure that is what is putting a strain on the relationship.

Well, it's bound to be either money or sex isn't it? During the time they have been together, she has never complained about Donal in the bedroom department. Although (don't tell a soul I said this) he can be a bit of a fascist at times. Perhaps he is all nag and no shag? Ha ha ha ha. Seriously, I should have my own show.

Work is okay. Same shit different day as I heard one of the girls describing it. There have been rumours circulating about more lay-offs and wage cuts. You might recall the trauma I endured (and you by association) two years ago when we had a round of redundancies. That purge left Rita and me the old ladies of the department.

Premier kept on the four youngest members of the team because they were earning the least money, meaning things have been more pressurised since then, because naturally the girls are not experienced and need plenty of guidance. There are days when Rita and I feel like throwing in the towel, but we are both stuck because there are no jobs out there. At least there are, but only a handful, and the competition is fierce. Better the devil you know and all that.

I think it's unlikely the company will lay anybody else off, but if the rumours are true about the cuts in pay then I will find it hard to manage. Even the 60K I earn (which is not a bad salary these days) is stretched to the limit with the cost of living here.

I am also trying to pay down a little extra on the mortgage each month as a basic precaution. It's a habit I got into when I got my promotion, and I am loath to stop doing it. I am luckier than most people, in that I bought my house before the property bubble began to engorge in front of our very eyes, but it's still a large mortgage for one person.

Ergo, I'm afraid I can't see myself being able to visit you in New South Wales for a while yet. We were very disappointed you didn't get home for Christmas, but maybe you'll get back this year. Are you really living in a place called Boomerang Beach?

I know I should have said it before now, Si, but I hope you know how happy I am that you have met somebody. Who says that there isn't life after thirty-nine?? Isn't it pure fab Des finally came to his senses and your divorce was granted before you left? One less thing to worry about.

Charlie sounds fantastic (of course) and I look forward to seeing a few pics of him. Hopefully, we will all meet up before we get much older. The idea for the bar and surf school sounds wonderful, but I know what you mean about difficulties in raising finance. Are the banks down there lending money?

You wouldn't stand a chance of borrowing a red cent if you still lived here because all funding has dried up. The average person is paying for the errors made by others. There is no justice in the world. I only hope things are better where you are.

I was watching a lottery winning couple on the TV earlier. I can assure you if I should be lucky enough to win a decent sum, I would not be forgetting you and your bar. Even ten thousand would be great, never mind a million. Maybe I should think about playing the lottery more frequently.

I tried setting up an online account once, but I got so frustrated I soon gave up. Why would a seemingly reputable organisation tell you they will hold your numbers for fifteen minutes so you can create your account? Only to inform you at the end of the fifteen minutes - after they have taken your date of birth, mother's maiden name and card details - that your application cannot be completed until you post them a signed photocopy of your passport!

I don't object to the principle of sending it to them. I just can't understand why they don't ask for it at step one instead of step eight. When I complained, and asked why they took all the sensitive information first, before asking for the passport, they told me it was their policy to eliminate under-age gambling. In other words, they didn't answer the question.

That's the lottery's idea of customer service. What a pack of self-satisfied, condescending morons. I may complain to the

Department of Justice about them when I'm feeling more energetic.

There's a big Euromillions draw tonight. It has been rolling over for more than six weeks, which means the jackpot is enormous. The smaller prizes aren't too shabby either. Even if you only matched five numbers plus one star, you could still potentially win a million.

You won't have it in Oz, but we're all pretty excited up here in the northern hemisphere, even if the odds of winning are something like one in a billion. Kathleen from the office offered to get me a ticket when she was buying her own, and in honour of the day I reluctantly handed over the six euro.

Do you remember that little statue of Ganesh you gave me a few years ago? I keep it on my desk at work. I rubbed his head and asked him to plough a path ahead of me, removing all obstacles to abundance and any fear that I might have of moving forward with my life.

I had better go. I still have to register my meter reading before the electricity company sends me a highly inflated bill. Take care of yourself and say hi to Charlie. Please stay in touch. Don't forget the pics of your surfing hunk. Love ya. Hugs. Dot xxx

~~~

Dorothy grabbed her handbag and located the scrap of paper on which she had recorded her meter reading. With a flourish, she keyed it in and pressed the submit button. In a self-congratulatory moment, she decided to clear her bag of all the old superfluous receipts she had been hoarding.

As she did not own a real fire, she contented herself with simply ripping up the rubbish and creating a neat pile. As she worked, she flicked over to the Sky Arts channel where somebody was playing a jazz piece.

With a jolt of horror, she remembered she had omitted a piano from her wish list, and heaved herself out of her recliner so she could grab her new notebook. She took the opportunity to top up her wine glass at the same time, and then made herself comfortable in the chair again, gently replacing her drink as she did so.

In her smallest writing, she added piano to the list in between 'Liposuction' and 'Spend more time in nature'. As the notebook was open, she decided she may as well include more detail and refine it. At the bottom of the page, she wrote, 'Banish the grey. An End to Fear. Embrace Life. Go Dorothy Go!'

She managed a self-deprecating smile as she read it back. She would burn the pages soon enough, but for tonight it was helping to keep her sane. After all, a woman had a right to dream, hadn't she? Then she turned her eyes heavenwards, or at least upwards, for who knew where heaven was situated?

'Sorry I forgot about the piano, Lord,' she said aloud. 'But if you could see your way clearly to sending me one, I would be most grateful. Of course, I've never had a lesson in my life. My parents told us we had to choose between learning to play a musical instrument and Irish dancing lessons. Orla was desperate for the dancing and Mum didn't want her going alone, ergo I've never had a lesson! Hence, Lord, I'll need a tutor as well, if you wouldn't mind. I'm pretty sure Horace only teaches guitar. Thanks and Amen.'

The till receipt which had been handed to her at the shop earlier in the evening was among the discards.

Dorothy scanned it, and marvelled at how much money she had spent in less than twelve minutes. Fortunately, she had not lost, mangled, or ripped to shreds her lottery ticket. It had become entangled in her receipts, as all lottery tickets inevitably do unless you put them into your wallet without delay. Having located it, she decided she may as well check it before shutting down her computer.

She opened a new tab on internet explorer and typed in the website address of the lottery. Once the site was fully loaded, she clicked on the box labelled Prizes and Results, and then the box marked Euromillions.

She located the winning numbers and scribbled them at the top of her list, noting there were more Irish winners than usual. *That sort of cash injection will be handy for the crumbling economy. I wonder if the millionaire couple shared their win with anybody, or will all that lovely lolly be spent in Greece. God knows the Greeks could sure use a capital injection right now.*

She closed the laptop but could not be bothered getting up to put it away again. Instead, she carefully placed it on the carpet and gently pushed it with the tips of her fingers so it slipped under the recliner. Then Dorothy calmly compared the winning numbers she had scribbled at the top of her wish list with the ticket Kathleen had purchased on her behalf from the kiosk at Pearse Street railway station earlier that day.

And so it was that, on January 7th, 2011, on a cold Friday evening which also happened to be her fortieth birthday, fortune smiled upon Dorothy Lyle. By the time she rested her head on the pillow that night, she was one of the richest women in the land, and very likely one of the drunkest.

By anybody's standards, she had acquired an enormous amount of cash. However, these riches were not accrued by dint of hard work, talent or skill, but merely by a combination of luck and chance, and possibly the power of 111. The manifestation number.

9

Dorothy left Saul Newman at the Falcon apartment with his mouth hanging open and, faithful to her cunning plan, took a taxi back to work. She clocked in with one minute to spare, then dashed to her office on the seventh floor and stashed her handbag in an empty drawer.

Her colleagues were working away happily enough in the main open-plan office, with absolutely no inkling that a multimillionaire was sitting scarcely ten feet away from them. She made sure nobody was hovering nearby, and then brought up her favourite property website. She could not resist one more glance at her new pad.

Saul was fairly certain his sister would accept the offer, but had promised to phone later with an update. Dorothy asked him not to call before eight, as she wanted to be safely home before they spoke again.

She explained to the architect how nobody in her office was aware of her changed circumstances. A flabbergasted Saul agreed to make contact shortly after eight and, in something of a daze, escorted her to the front door of the apartment building.

She wondered what her friends' reaction would be to the Falcon purchase, and regretted that none of them were around to share the moment. At least she had the comfort of knowing she would be seeing Bel and Viv on Monday evening. She had sent both friends a text, asking them to meet her as a matter of urgency because she had BIG news to share.

She also invited her sisters, Orla and Gemma, saying she had something important to discuss with them. The twins had not been told of the arrangement because

Dorothy wanted to speak to them away from the rest of the horde when she was good and ready to do so.

The get-together was arranged for seven o'clock at her parents' home. Joey and Pat had not been at all put out at the idea of their house being used as a point of rendezvous. On the contrary, they were looking forward to seeing her and the girls, and had offered to lay on a few refreshments.

They said they were itching to hear her news, but if it was regarding a new boyfriend, would she please bring the fella along so they could meet him. Their daughter informed them her news had nothing whatsoever to do with a relationship, but assured them they would be very happy by approximately eight o'clock on Monday evening.

Pat Lyle was disappointed and puzzled to learn the big news did not involve a man in her daughter's life. If Dottie had not embarked on a new relationship, she demanded of her husband, what could she possibly have to tell them that was so important? She resigned herself to a couple more days of conjecture, while her husband resigned himself to a house without peace.

Having made the necessary arrangements for the big news-breaking evening, Dorothy was left with the weekend to decide how much of a gift to give each person. She knew from listening to Oprah (the font of all wisdom regarding such matters), the best way to handle these situations was for the giver to determine the amount in advance, then stick to the decision come hell or high water.

In other words, the newly rich person should decide how much largesse they were inclined to dispense. This would negate the need for the non-winners to have to ask for a specific sum or, worse still, to be left hanging, not knowing if they were in line for a cash hand-out, or perhaps a car or holiday.

Never having found herself in a situation even remotely similar to this one, Dorothy was torn. If she gave too little, she would in all likelihood be deemed miserly. If she gave too much, she might regret it later. Worse than either of those two scenarios, she might inadvertently create an expectation that there was more to come.

She needed to decide on a sum which would be generous enough to make her friends and family feel they had received a reasonable share of her win, yet at the same time send a clear message it was the one and only gift.

Staring blindly at a photograph of the contemporary kitchen units in the Falcon apartment, she admitted to herself that, regardless of the expectations of others, she was unwilling to become the source of infinite hand-outs. She really needed to get it right first time. *God sent me the money so I can do some good. Should I even bother trying to explain that to everybody else, or just give them a chunk of moola and hope for the best?*

Well aware she was overanalysing, she resolved to put the matter out of her head until that evening. Then she closed the website and put her head down, determined to clear the top ten most urgent items from her in-tray before clocking off.

~~~

From: Dottie8888@chatulike.ie
To:SRedmond@chatchat.com; ANorris@talkalot.com
Date: January 14th, 2011
SUBJECT: CRAZY BIG NEWS FOR A FRIDAY.

Hi Simone, Hi Amy,

I have big news so I hope you are both sitting down. This time last week, on my birthday, I won the lottery. Please email your full bank details so I can send you some money. I know it sounds crazy and, believe me, it is.

I am still in shock and keep expecting to wake up and discover it was all a dream. I spent most of last weekend in a daze, but fortunately I had a hangover and nobody thought much of my strange behaviour. Even though I saw the whole gang on Saturday for my birthday dinner, I didn't dare utter a word to the family. I couldn't call the lottery company until Monday, and I didn't want to get everybody's hopes up in case it all turned out to be a massive mistake.

I am home now. I had a hectic day and am glad to be safely tucked away in my little house. I went to the lottery offices this morning. Can you believe they couldn't pay me electronically? I had to take a cheque! That meant I had to go all the way over to the Irish Citizens' Bank on O'Connell Street and lodge it. I made them give me a few photocopies before I handed it over.

I had a lovely little chat with my new best mate, Ken, who is the branch manager. He almost wet himself when I told him my story, the poor wee tyke. He opened a 90-day account, which means I will be gaining some interest on the dosh while I decide what to do next.

I only put 90% of the money in there, and lodged the balance into my current account so I can spend it. He is also going to arrange for me to have a new credit card, a type that doesn't have a limit. Did you know you could get those?

It has taken me a full week to collect the winnings because the money had to come from Bruges or Berlin, or somewhere like that. The lottery company doesn't keep large amounts of cash in Dublin. Well they do, but only enough to cover the Irish draws, not the Euromillions. I have this image of a convoy of armoured trucks full of gold bullion, driving in a convoy up the quays, but I know that's just silly. Ha ha.

I took the DART in as usual and got off at Tara Street, and from there it was only a short walk. The folks at the lottery were very pleasant and congratulatory; hence I forbore to mention their condescending email regarding the opening of online accounts. Nor did I mention I was considering making a complaint against them to the Department of Justice. I didn't feel the timing was quite right.

There was only one journalist hanging around, and I managed to escape his notice by being sneaky. When I got inside, I had to wait for a few minutes because the staff weren't quite ready for me so early on a Friday morning. They insisted on opening a bottle of champagne but I only indulged in a sip or two. I had a busy day ahead of me and you know how it makes me giddy.

They offered me advice, as you would expect. I assured them one of my first tasks would be to hire a financial guru, and they must have believed me because they didn't try to force the issue. Perhaps they could see I'm past the age of being foolish (if such an age exists).

It's a pity you weren't able to go with me because you would have enjoyed it. I miss you! It's bad enough that Bel only got home from Italy this evening. She would have had a ball today because this sort of thing is right up her alley. I'm sure Viv would have come with me if I had asked, but I knew she had an important meeting with her accountant, and there was no way I was going to suggest she cancel it and drive all the way up from Wexford to hold my hand.

There has been lottery fever here all week because the press have been unable to discover the winner's identity. It was extremely fortuitous that Kathleen bought the ticket at a railway station. It makes the winner impossible to trace, ergo it's driving the press nuts. Anybody even caught glancing through the window of a BMW dealership has been viewed with suspicion by friend and neighbour alike.

So far, my cover has not been blown, but that's because I haven't told a living soul. You guys are the first to know. Naturally enough, I chose the no-publicity option. I could tell the folks at the lottery were a little disappointed at my decision. They seem to think it will only be a matter of days before the news leaks out anyway, although I'm not so sure.

After all, who's going to tell the media I'm the winner? My friends? My family? I don't think so, do you? It's true you do have to be on your guard. There are still stories appearing in the papers about the last Irishwoman who won a large amount on the Euromillions, and that was six years ago. Not that I expect to be seeing my name in the papers any time soon, if ever.

Once I am a little more organised, I'll scan the photocopy of the cheque and email it to you. Whatever you do, don't say a word until everybody knows because it will spoil the surprise. I can't wait to see their faces.

I resigned last Monday, not long after I made the call (the signal was surprisingly strong from the broom cupboard) and confirmed I had the winning ticket. I composed a letter during the lunch break and at four o'clock I was able to grab fifteen minutes with the finance director. I told him I was leaving the company due to life-changing events.

I got the impression he thinks I'm sick and is terrified to enquire too deeply, which suits me. It wasn't a big lie. After all, you can't get much more life changing than a lottery win. My final day will be the last Friday in January. I think I can just about hold out until then and hand over to Rita.

In some ways, the company are glad to be losing me because they need to cut back on the salary bill, but at the same time I had to push for early release because it's a busy time of year. I only persuaded them to give me this morning off because I told them I had some important legal matters to sort out, and now they are convinced I am making my will. I must actually do something about that, now I mention it. I haven't looked at it since the twins were small.

I am attaching a link to my new apartment which is on Charlotte Quay near Grand Canal in Dublin 4. I was celebrating my resignation by surfing the web and stumbled across it. I couldn't resist making an enquiry, even though I knew it was a little premature.

According to the boffins, I should be taking my time and devising a plan for the future, not looking at one of the most expensive pads in Dublin. The general wisdom states you're not supposed to make any substantial purchases for at least six months. Ah, well. Life's short. Might be dead next week.

A man with a sad voice called to tell me more about the apartment and before I knew it, the appointment was made. I'd be sad too if I was trying to sell a duplex (yes, it's two apartments on separate floors joined together by stairs) in recessionary Ireland. Anyway, he has sold it now, so hopefully he will be feeling a little better soon. I will be back next week with the update. Don't forget those bank details. Love Dot xxx

~~~

Dorothy glanced at her watch. It was not yet nine o'clock. Saul had called at five past eight to break the news that Anna was only too pleased to accept the offer. She expressed her delight with the outcome and gave him her solicitor's details. When he tentatively suggested they go ahead and make the appointment to view the site in Howth, she agreed with enthusiasm.

She sensed relief emanating down the line, and guessed he was hoping she had not lost interest in the piece of land now she was on track to buy the apartment. She explained she was still working fulltime, and had to listen to a five-minute lecture from him about putting herself first and getting on with her new life.

Once Saul had gotten this off his chest and made a few noises about financial advisers, he offered to meet her in Howth on Sunday. She had noticed earlier in the day that he was wearing a wedding band, and said she did not want to disrupt his weekend by dragging him away from his family.

He assured her his family would be more than understanding about the situation, and pressed her to agree a time and place. Knowing she would be hard pressed to fit in a viewing while still working, her protestations were only half hearted, and the arrangement was swiftly made. When Saul rang off he sounded almost relaxed, and she was glad for his sake that things were picking up.

Pleased she had brought Amy and Simone up to speed, Dorothy turned off the gas fire and wrapped her blue scarf around her neck. As there was a strong possibility she would be delayed next door, she had already taken the precaution of setting the *Late Night Show* to record.

It was time to tell Horace her news. She had the rest of the weekend to do it, but as she was on something of a roll, wanted to get it out of the way tonight. No doubt she would be up until all hours anyway, since there was very little chance she would get any sleep, and was even contemplating asking Amanda if she had any Xanax or alternative sleep-inducing medication secreted in her medicine cabinet for emergencies.

After a momentary hesitation, Dorothy went into the kitchen and opened the fridge. The previous Saturday, the family had bestowed birthday presents aplenty upon her. These included a bottle of champagne and a litre of Bacardi. Her hand hovered over the champagne.

Horace had never struck her as the kind of man who enjoyed a glass of vintage Krug. If they were going to have a celebratory drink, they may as well do it properly. She pulled out the bottle of chilled Bacardi, together with a sealed carton of cranberry juice.

She glanced at her handbag, but as it was already full to bursting, pulled a carrier bag from her stash and dropped the carton into it. Then she gingerly tucked the bottle on top, hoping the juice would protect it. She left the bag on the worktop and went to pull an old black fleece on over her grey sweatshirt and scarf.

Satisfied she was wearing sufficient layers, she lugged the bag of booze and her handbag as far as the front door, flicking off all lights as she travelled. She left the one in the hall alone. Having double-checked she had her keys, she stepped outside and gave the door a tug. She inserted the key and turned the deadbolt, well aware Horace would ask if she had locked up properly, and scold her about security if she admitted she had only pulled the door after her.

Shivering in the cold night air, Dorothy shoved her keys into the outside pocket of her bag and walked past her car and through the front gate. In addition to the old fleece and sweatshirt, she was wearing a pair of faded jeans and scuffed black leather boots. The outfit enabled her to take as long a stride as her short legs would allow.

In daylight, walking the ten yards to her neighbour's house never bothered her, but after dark was a different matter. She always felt vulnerable when traversing the pavement at the top of the lane leading down to Bluebell Wood.

As far as anyone knew, the house had been abandoned by its owners sometime in the late sixties. It had been a substantial residence in its heyday, and home to a growing family who had abandoned it virtually overnight and never returned to claim it.

To the horror of local residents, the property had become a squat and drug den during the seventies and eighties. Eventually, the local council bowed to pressure and boarded it up. They even traced the legal owner and offered to buy it from him with a view to converting it into social housing units.

The man in question refused to sell, or even engage in discussions with the council. Worse still, he paid the fines they levied upon him over the years, and continued to absent himself from both Shankill and his responsibilities.

The house was surrounded by two acres of wooded gardens and grounds, which continued to be used by local children as a sort of adventure playground. Sensing a lawsuit waiting to happen, the council took steps to have the entire boundary fenced off and warning signs erected. Even the druggies gave up trying to gain admittance after that, and sought out easier accommodations.

As far as Dorothy knew, only Horace and Trotsky made use of the old place these days. His own garden backed on to the grounds of Bluebell Wood, a piece of serendipity Horace did not hesitate to use to his advantage. One of the first things he did after taking up residence in Old Hen was remove some of the bricks in the back wall of the cottage and replace them with heavy, timber doors that opened centrally.

When both doors were pushed outwards, they met the chain link fence surrounding the neighbouring property. Horace set about cutting himself a man-sized hole in the fence, thereby providing an access point for himself and his wheelbarrow. In this way, Bluebell Wood essentially became part of Horace's garden.

His comings and goings between his cottage and the big house never disturbed anybody. On the contrary, he could often be relied upon to top up a needy neighbour's stock of firewood from the stashes he kept in the wood.

Having acquired a petrol chainsaw during his first year in Shankill, Horace made it his business to cut up any fallen trees or branches, and make good use of the unwanted timber. He had piles of logs of varying ages dotted throughout the wood, and only kept a month's supply in his own fuel store. Unhindered by either the authorities or the neighbours, Horace and his pet continued to take advantage of the gardens without disturbing anybody.

Over the years, he had carefully uprooted a number of plants from the grounds and replanted them in his own much-beloved shrubbery. His garden was the envy of the neighbourhood, yet none resented him for it because of the sheer amount of man hours he had dedicated to it over the years.

Most of the neighbourhood were well aware that Hairy Horace had the run of Bluebell Wood, but could not have cared less. They accepted he was essentially harmless, and could be counted upon to raise the alarm if there was a resurgence of antisocial behaviour. Not because he was inherently law abiding, but because he would not tolerate any vandalism in an area which he considered to be of such natural beauty.

10

Despite her anxiety concerning the dark laneway, Dorothy reached her destination without incident. After transferring the plastic carrier to the hand already holding her bag, she tapped gently.

The door opened almost immediately and Horace loomed in the opening. 'I was hoping you'd drop by,' he said without preamble. 'For the first time in a decade, I regretted not owning a phone. I was actually on the verge of popping over to see you. Are you sure you and the twins are all right?'

Dorothy blinked at him in the light escaping from the cottage. 'What are you wearing?' she asked in amusement.

He lowered his chin and peered down at his torso, then raised his head again and stared hard at her. 'It's my Christmas gansey,' his tone implied it should be obvious.

'A gansey?' Dorothy's lips twitched in amusement. 'You know you're an Englishman, right, and not from Tipperary? Who gave you the...eh...gansey?'

'Mrs Wilson from up the road. I've been keeping her borders tidy and mending holes in her fences.'

'Do you like it?' Dorothy dubiously eyed the garment. The sweater was knitted in bright red yarn. Spread across the front was the head of a white and brown reindeer, complete with scarlet pom pom for a nose. The sweater was an unusually tight fit on a man whose wardrobe consisted of loose clothing garnered from charity shops and jumble sales, and strained across his chest and shoulders.

She knew he had a hard body from all the firewood he chopped, to say nothing of the miles he walked every week, but it had been many months since she had seen him in anything other than a baggy top and had the opportunity to admire his muscle tone.

Horace was eyeing her in return and seemed baffled by her sudden interest in his wardrobe. 'Of course I like it,' he replied patiently. 'It's pure wool and very comfortable. I've asked Mrs Wilson to knit me a larger size for next Christmas.'

'Gosh,' Dorothy replied breathlessly. 'You mean there's more where this one came from?'

'Please come in out of the cold and stop behaving so strangely.' The laidback country drawl that made Horace sound remarkably like a character from Tess of the D'Urbervilles was suddenly gone, and his voice changed to one which was considerably more reminiscent of an old-school BBC newsreader.

When challenged about this schizophrenic aspect of his nature, he always claimed he could turn the voice on and off at will because he was able to perfectly mimic his former headmaster. Dorothy was not certain about the veracity of this claim, and wondered if he had studied drama in his youth.

He had shown up in Shankill when he was in his early twenties which meant, in theory at least, he had not been afforded many opportunities to do much during the short span of his old life.

Nonetheless, she reasoned, there was no sure-fire way of knowing what sort of hand he had been dealt. Perhaps Horace's parents had been members of the local amateur dramatic society, and family evenings had been spent mimicking their friends and neighbours and putting on shows. Anything was possible.

'Dorothy, please come indoors this minute, and stop dawdling on the doorstep like an unwelcome Jehovah's Witness,' the young man sounded almost hostile now.

Sensing he was genuinely annoyed, she pulled herself together and carefully manoeuvred her body down the drop to the kitchen. She tended to think of it as the kitchen, although in reality Horace's house was nothing more than one very large room.

The first thing his builders had done when they started working on Old Hen was to knock down the ramshackle extension housing the bathroom, and replace it with a well-insulated bricks and mortar alternative.

They kitted out the new room with fixtures and fittings considered first-rate at the time. When that job was finished, they set about mending the ancient roof and making it waterproof once more. During this process, it became necessary to rip out the boards forming part of the makeshift attic and, due in the main to the resulting mess, the stud walls separating the four individual rooms were also demolished to make the job easier.

The roof was restored to its former glory and, at the request of the new owner, the workers left the freshly fitted and blessedly rot-free rafters exposed so they could be admired by all.

The rotten windows were the next thing to find their way into the skip, and these were soon replaced with modern, draught-proof, double-glazed alternatives. The flagstones needed a little TLC, although it was agreed by all involved in the project that the slabs of stone had withstood the test of time admirably, as had the chimney.

The delighted architect discovered this relic from a bygone age was the sole means of support for the cottage.

Horace was equally pleased with the news, and decreed the cottage should remain open-plan, in its natural state. Instead of the four tiny rooms the previous owners had occupied for seventy years, Old Hen morphed into one large space, with a central chimney and fireplace which essentially acted as a support beam. An added bonus of this layout was the fire could be seen from both sides of the room, while also providing a natural partition.

Still clutching her bag, Dorothy remained standing in what she thought of as the kitchen side. To her right were the sink and fridge, together with a number of fitted pine units under an oiled teak worktop. On her left was a large, scrubbed pine table surrounded by six chairs. Behind that stood an oversized oak dresser awash with Horace's clutter. His guitar was lying on the table, as if he had been sitting there strumming it and impatiently waiting for her to show up and explain herself. Next to it was a large teapot covered in a purple knitted tea cosy.

'New tea cosy?' she muttered, wondering if she was going to be shouted at for her trouble.

'Mrs Magee isn't up to knitting jumpers, but she's highly skilled at the tea cosies,' he sounded calmer now that she was actually indoors, and had slipped back into his usual and considerably less intimidating drawl. 'I told her she should try to sell a few of them because they're top notch, but she said she's too old for that malarkey.'

'Do you take care of her garden as well?'

'Occasionally. When her son is too busy to help out. He has one of those office jobs.' Horace uttered the word office in a way which suggested Mrs Magee's son was in league with a platoon of demonic beings. Dorothy fought hard to resist the urge to giggle for fear of irritating him again and calling forth the BBC newsreader.

The fire was blazing away merrily and there was a definite aroma of apple emanating from the logs. It was the only source of heat in the cottage and by rights she should be feeling the chill.

Standing there in her fleece, she suddenly felt overwhelmed by the heat and went to set her bags down on the table so she could take it off. Horace obligingly took it from her and hung it on a wrought iron black hook next to his own battered raincoat on the rear of the front door.

Above the line of hooks was a small plaque made of rosewood which had been attached to the door with almost invisible screws. Carved into the wood were the words: Mellita, domi adsum. Dorothy knew they translated as: Honey, I'm home, and her lips twitched as she read them. Horace was often vastly entertaining, even when he did not intend to be.

She cast her eye over the work surfaces. They were clear of debris and slightly damp as if he had washed up and scrubbed everything vigorously. She knew by the lingering smell he had eaten fish pie for his supper. It was a speciality of Amanda's, and Dorothy was willing to bet her friend had deposited a portion with Hairy Horace during her lunch break from the surgery.

The two windows looking out over the road and the side window above the sink all had their curtains drawn to keep out the winter night. The fabric with its pattern of red and green apples had come from the attic of her own house, when she unearthed seven metres of it during a major clear out some four years earlier.

Not wanting to throw it away, she had, with some trepidation, offered it to her neighbour. He had professed himself delighted with the find and the next time Dorothy visited Old Hen, she discovered it had been used to make curtains for all the windows, both front and back. Horace freely admitted a friendly neighbour had cut and hemmed the fabric for him in return for his services with a paint roller in her spare bedroom.

He had strung the finished product onto lengths of plastic coated wire, and there the curtains had remained ever since. Dorothy wondered if they had ever been washed during the course of the previous four years, and strongly resisted the urge to sniff them.

'Dorothy,' Horace enquired gently, 'are you drunk? Shall I make you a cup of valerian root tea? I have a jar of it out in my storeroom.'

She tore her eyes away from the apples and eyed him in fascination. 'What's valerian root when it's at home?'

'It's a natural sedative and perfectly safe,' he replied impatiently. 'I harvested it myself, which means you can rest assured no pesticides were used on it. If you're suffering from your nerves, it might be just the thing to settle them. Shall I fetch the jar?'

'Much as I would love to hear about the process of harvesting valerian root,' Dorothy smirked, as she reached into the carrier bag. 'I'd like to table that suggestion for now. How about you forget about making hippie brews and help me celebrate the biggest news of my life?' She extracted the Bacardi and waved it at him. Then she set it down on the kitchen table and went back for the juice.

Horace looked none too impressed by these antics. 'Sweet Jesus in heaven above!' he exclaimed. 'Please tell me you haven't gone and taken up again with that Victor fuckhead!'

'Not quite,' she grinned at him. 'As I told you this morning, my news has nothing to do with romance. I won the lottery.'

Horace put his hand to his chest and in so doing covered the reindeer's pom pom nose with a large, hairy paw. His nails were long for a man, and there was a thick layer of grime under them. It would have looked disgusting on most men; although on him it seemed normal.

'That can't be right,' he said firmly. 'Mrs Wilson says nobody has won the jackpot for weeks. She's very excited because tomorrow night's big prize is five million euro. She says if she wins, she's going to give one million to each of her four children and keep the rest for herself. She wants me to help her choose a cutting-edge lawnmower when she's a millionaire. She bought six lines today, even though I warned her against wasting her money because it's a mug's game.'

Dorothy was staring at him in wonder. 'Are you and Mrs Wilson lovers?' she enquired curiously.

In response, Horace opened and closed his mouth a number of times. 'She's almost eighty years of age,' he sounded vexed. 'What sort of sick fuck do you take me for?'

Dorothy giggled at the aggrieved expression on his face. 'Just checking,' she replied gaily. 'I hope you like cranberry juice. See if you can find two clean glasses and a few ice cubes, there's a good lad.'

She thought he might continue to argue, but instead he went to the kitchen corner and obediently rummaged in one of the two, eye-level cupboards. He emerged with two tall glasses with Smirnoff logos that looked as if they might have been filched from a public house.

He peered inside the vessels and, as a precaution, rinsed them under the mixer tap. Dorothy carried the bottle of Bacardi over to the worktop and poured a generous helping into each glass.

'Vodka would be better,' Horace grumbled, 'but I seem to recall you can't tolerate it.'

'Correct,' she smiled at him brightly. 'Any ice?'

His fridge was the type with a miniscule freezer compartment at the top, and from this he gingerly extracted a green, compartmentalised tray full of frozen water. Each piece of ice was in the shape of a Christmas tree, and looked as if it had been there for some time.

'I don't suppose they go off,' he said, as he carefully pressed a couple of the trees into each drink and returned the tray to the fridge. The ice in the glasses made a comforting hissing sound as it mingled with the spirits.

Dorothy poured a modest measure of the juice on top of the transparent liquor and passed the carton to Horace so he could put it in the fridge. She picked up both glasses, handed one to her neighbour and raised her own to chin height. 'You should drink a toast to me, Horace Johnson of Burrowbridge,' she said lightly. 'It isn't every day a man like you gets to partake of alcohol with the fortieth richest woman in the land.'

'What do you mean by a man like me?' he sounded suspicious.

'I mean a man who doesn't mind being seen in public wearing a jumper like that. Gansey, I should say.'

'I told you before, it's pure wool. Why are you behaving so strangely?'

Indoors, his eyes were more brown than green, and she took the opportunity to examine him while she was up close. Since her visit earlier in the day, he had made an effort to brush his hair and tied it back with an elastic band. He looked younger when it was pulled back like that. It was easy to see his high forehead was unlined, and the only wrinkles he had were a couple around his eyes from squinting at the sun. There was no grey in either his hair or beard and, given how much time he spent outdoors, his skin was in good condition and not especially weathered.

He had a neat, snub nose, and his black eyebrows lay flat against his forehead and were a perfect oval shape. It was the beard that made him look like a man in his fifties, she decided. Even when he trimmed it during the summer months, he never fully shaved it off, and she could not recollect ever having seen his naked face. 'What do you look like under that horrible beard?' she asked thoughtfully, her fingers itching to smooth his hair.

'The spitting image of some long-dead relation,' he replied drily.

Dorothy lifted her left hand and gently touched his right cheek. 'You don't smile as much as you used to,' she commented gently.

'It's been a long winter and it's still only January,' he growled softly. 'Come back in June and you'll find me as jolly as a sand boy.'

She dropped her hand. 'I won't be here in June. Why don't we sit down and I'll tell you all about my crazy week?'

After casting her a look full of reproach, Horace led the way to the other side of the fireplace. Dorothy preferred this area of the cottage. Not only was it well away from the street, it was more spacious than the kitchen side and had been decorated in a more homely way.

Tucked away in the corner, not far from the rear windows, was Horace's large bed with the attached headboard he had made himself. On the opposite side of the room was the desk where he kept the tools he used for his small carvings, as well as his charcoals and pastels. As usual, the desk was awash with a collection of wood shavings, pictures, and poems which were works in progress. Dorothy resisted the urge to have a good poke around to see what he was working on.

One never knew with Horace. It might be a carving of a bird, or it might be a sonnet to the beauty of a plum, or it might be a sketch of a stray dog. He was a man whose talent was only equalled by his lack of order and direction.

Horace did not believe in keeping to a strict timetable, and was occasionally heard to say if it was routine he wanted, he would have remained in the UK and continued to work in the family business. As her host busied himself rearranging the little side tables he utilised whenever he had company, Dorothy examined the mantelpiece.

There was a silver-framed photograph of her neighbour and his parents taken when he was about five years of age. Given the dress code of the eighties had been nothing if not flamboyant, neither his father nor mother looked as if they had been slaves to fashion, and were dressed very conservatively in a dark suit and simple blue dress respectively. The boy Horace was grinning widely at the camera, and bore no resemblance to the Hairy Bear who was busy rearranging the furniture.

There were a number of other framed photos on the mantle, including a sepia one of his grandparents decked out in the traditional garb of farmers, although the one that caught Dorothy's eye was an unframed sketch balanced between a photograph of Old Hen in a somewhat derelict condition, and a large dog who had passed away many years earlier, and whose name escaped her. She stared at the sketch in consternation.

'Horace?'

'Yes?'

'Why is Sharon Dooley from across the road posing naked for you?'

'Never mind that,' he said impatiently. 'Take a seat please, Dorothy, you're making me nervous with all this fidgeting.'

11

Dorothy obediently went to sit in her usual chair in front of the fire, only to discover it was not her usual chair. Gone was the rather dilapidated armchair which had resided in the same spot for as far back as she could remember. It had been replaced by a gleaming rosewood rocking chair.

This was almost identical to the one Horace had made for himself, except in one significant feature. It was compact. He had added a padded cushion in a fetching shade of cerise, which looked as if it had been purchased from a shop as opposed to a jumble sale. There were some words carved into the back of the piece, although she was unable to understand them as they were in Latin.

Dorothy examined the item of furniture for a few seconds longer, and then moved to sit in it. She carefully lowered herself onto the padded seat and set her glass of Bacardi down on the small table Horace placed at her right side.

She relaxed back into the chair and gave a little exploratory nudge with her feet. It began to rock backwards and forwards in a smooth, lulling motion. The back was high enough to reach the top of her head, and he had carved a shallow crater into it which provided her skull with a comfortable resting point.

The dimensions were a perfect fit on her short frame, and her head came to rest in the spot as if the chair had been made for her. There was no doubt in Dorothy's mind the piece had been designed with the smaller person in mind. She wondered if Amanda has seen it yet and what she had made of it.

'Beautiful chair,' she kept her voice light. 'How long did it take you to make?'

'Six months in all,' he replied quietly. 'I didn't have much time to work on it last year, but the Christmas period was very quiet, which meant I was able to catch up with lots of little jobs.'

'Sorry I didn't see much of you over Christmas. I hung out with the family a lot of the time. I take it you spent it with Mrs Wilson.'

'I popped up for an hour and had my dinner there, but I left soon after and had my pudding back here. Two of her sons and their wives were visiting, and I wasn't about to disrupt her family with my presence for any longer than necessary. Trotsky and I had a lovely relaxing afternoon listening to music.'

Here, he gestured towards the back of the room where an old record player he had unearthed at a car boot sale took pride of place on its own shelf. Next to it was perched his collection of classical music, all on vinyl.

Dorothy knew the conversation was veering towards dangerous territory, and was not in the mood to discuss or debate the great Maestros of the world. She took a large swig of her drink and surveyed him gravely.

'Horace, are you having an affair with Sharon Dooley? A woman of thirty-eight, who, I might remind you, has a husband and three children.'

By now, he had thrown another log on the fire and made himself comfortable in his own rocker. 'I wouldn't exactly call it an affair,' he replied mildly. 'Her husband is away a great deal, and she gets lonely. It's a convenient arrangement for us both, although that's as far as it goes. He's talking about moving the family closer to the city centre, hence there's a strong possibility she might not even be living in Shankill much longer.'

'Perhaps Sharon's husband sees more than you realise, and wants to take his wife as far away from Hairy Horace as he can get,' Dorothy suggested sarcastically.

He shrugged in response and said, 'I seriously doubt he's that observant. I think he's fed up with the commute, and has his eye on a swanky school for the eldest. Either way, it doesn't really concern me. I'm not trying to take Sharon away from him or anything weird like that.'

'But you don't object to making hot passionate love to her whenever the opportunity presents itself,' Dorothy replied crossly.

He shrugged again. 'She doesn't object to the beard and she's a very nice woman. Trotsky likes her as well.'

Upon hearing his name spoken, a large black canine with a shaggy coat made a rumbling noise from his bed in the corner near the window. At almost ten years of age, he was long past his youth, and the Giant Schnauzer that was Trotsky Johnson took considerably longer to stand up and walk across the room than the exuberant puppy she had first met back in 2003.

He bumped his head against Dorothy's arm to say hello, then went to his master for an affectionate hug. Clearly feeling he had fulfilled his duties as host, Trotsky returned to his bed and curled up again.

'He's a good age for his breed,' Dorothy remarked.

Pain flashed in Horace's eyes, although he said nothing.

Oh shit. Does Trotsky not have long to live? Have I gone and put my foot in it?

'If you pass me my bag, I'll tell you about the lottery,' she smiled, hoping to distract him.

Horace set his glass down on his own little table and, after jumping up out of the chair, strode off around the side of the fireplace to fetch the bag. When he returned with it, he set it down on the table he had placed between the chairs. This was the largest of the three, and was often referred to as the pizza table, because it was the ideal size to accommodate an extra-large one in its box.

Dorothy rummaged in the bag until she found the photocopy of the winning cheque. With a sudden fluttering in her chest, she passed the piece of paper to him with some trepidation.

'I won the Euromillions,' she uttered the words succinctly.

Experiencing a surge of relief that she had crossed an imaginary line and could not take the sentence back, she picked up her glass and relaxed back into the new chair, nursing her drink. If Saul's reaction was anything to go by, Horace would need a few minutes to compose himself.

She was correct. It took him a full five minutes to process what was on the piece of paper, and Dorothy spent that time gently rocking and reviewing the minimalist décor at Falcon. She was in the middle of mentally redecorating her bedroom with soft furnishings when he interrupted her.

'You weren't joking,' he sounded stupefied. 'You very likely *are* the fortieth richest woman in the land.'

'Told ya,' she grinned at him.

'So when you said you won't be living here in June, you actually meant it?' he sounded worried now.

'I bought an apartment.' She delved into the side pocket of her bag until she located her phone. 'I took a few pics of it today, just enough to give you an idea of what it's like. I was hoping you and I could take a trip to see it together.'

She held out the phone so he could see the screen, and Horace stared at a photograph of the small drawing room at Falcon. She moved on to the next picture which was of the stairs leading from the corner of the drawing room down to the entertainment area one floor below. His mouth dropped open.

'It's quite substantial,' she smiled at him. 'I got it for a million euro, and when you consider what it would have cost during the height of the property boom, I think I did quite well. I'm going to use all the existing furniture for now, because I'll be busy enough getting used to my new life without worrying about choosing new stuff. It's a tad bare and cold at the moment, so I'll need lots of soft furnishings to jazz it up.'

He stared hard at her and she saw from the expression in his eyes that her revelations had rocked him to the core. 'You're leaving Shankill?' he asked hoarsely.

'Hopefully by the end of February,' she deliberately kept her voice even so as not to add to the drama. 'I'm looking forward to setting up home in my swanky apartment, although I'm the first to admit it *is* rather large for one person. Perhaps I'll make my mother happy and get a boyfriend.'

She chucked to herself as she imagined how thrilled Pat would be if this event actually came to pass, although her neighbour did not join in. He stood up and held out his hand for her almost-empty glass. 'I'll get us a top-up,' he croaked.

She gladly handed over her tumbler and he walked off on unsteady legs. As her phone was already in her hand, Dorothy eased herself out of the rocker and, as discreetly and quickly as possible, took a picture of the Latin sentence carved into the wood on the back.

Her phone was two years old and did not have internet access, which meant she was unable to run a search. Besides, Horace would be back at any second, and she did not want to be caught prying. As an alternative, she texted the image to Josh with a message: *Please translate and text back to me. Do NOT mention to anyone else. Love Mum x*

She returned the phone to her bag and moved the whole thing to her lap, leaving the surface of the pizza table clear. Once again, she shoved her hand inside and this time emerged with a thick envelope. It had not been easy to fit it in earlier, and she had been forced to sacrifice a hairbrush and can of deodorant to her desk drawer in order to accommodate it.

Still, it had been worth it. There were thirty items in the envelope. She extracted them one by one and stacked them in three separate towers. Horace returned with the drinks and placed hers on her individual table. He reclaimed his own seat and took a large swig of his drink. 'What's that?' he asked woodenly, with a vague gesture at the towers on the pizza table.

She smiled at him brightly and said, 'It's thirty thousand euro. For you.'

In response, he placed his drink on his own table and buried his face in his hands. 'I don't believe this,' he muttered. 'You tell me you're leaving Shankill, and now you're giving me money.'

'I know it's all been something of a shock,' she replied soothingly. 'But in a few days' time you'll be used to the idea, I promise. This isn't very much money in comparison to the amount I won. I know the capital you had with you when you came to Ireland is all gone, and I want you to be able to do something nice for yourself for a change, and not have to be scrimping all the time and taking any odd job you can get your hands on.'

'Abite nummi, ego vos mergam, ne mergar a vobis,' came his voice from the cave of his hands.

Dorothy exhaled heavily and took a large swig of her drink to steady her nerves. When Horace started speaking Latin, it invariably indicated he was emotionally invested in the current situation and, alas, not always in a good way. 'I'm going to assume what you just said means something along the lines of: Get thee behind me evil money,' she said with a hint of sarcasm.

'Close enough,' he muttered, and raised his head to stare at her accusingly.

'I know you don't trust banks,' she said coaxingly, 'which is why I brought cash. It also means you won't be done for gift tax. I thought you might like to go on holiday and soak up a spot of culture. Do you have a favourite country, or city?'

Horace eyed the stacks of thousands with deep unease. 'I went to Vienna when I was a teenager and I've always wanted to go back,' he said quietly. 'A trip like that wouldn't cost thirty thousand euro, Dorothy. That's far too much.'

'I'm planning to give Amanda ten times that amount,' she replied impatiently. 'I won almost one hundred and forty million smackers, and I'm offering you a paltry thirty thousand so you can buy a few treats. Most people would feel insulted to be given so little.'

Horace moaned loudly, then leaned his head against the back of his chair and began to rock back and forth in a frantic motion. 'I don't believe this,' he said plaintively. 'You're leaving Shankill next month.'

'I'm not moving to Mars for feck sake,' she said crossly. 'I'll only be on Charlotte's Quay. You can take the DART to Lansdowne Road anytime you fancy a visit. I'll even set aside a bedroom for you and Trotsky if you like. There are five of them.'

He stopped rocking and turned his head so that he could see her better. 'Trotsky and I come to stay with you in a swanky flat?' he said in disbelief. 'Does that sound like us?'

'Well, no, it doesn't,' she admitted. 'But I'm going to miss you, Horace, and I hope you won't desert me just because I no longer live ten yards away.'

'I'll stay in touch,' he growled, 'but don't expect me to come and visit you. I hate apartments. I feel claustrophobic when I know I can't walk outside and feel the earth under my feet.'

Dorothy drank some more Bacardi and cranberry and told herself not to give up just yet. 'Are you not pleased for me?' she hoped she did not sound as pathetic as she felt. She had not expected him to be overjoyed about her change in circumstances, because he genuinely believed in living the simple life and had a horror of excess, yet at the same time she had not anticipated this level of antipathy either. What the hell was wrong with the man?

Sensing he had upset her, Horace sat up straighter and did his level best to regain control over his emotions. 'Of course I'm pleased for you,' he said firmly. 'I just wasn't expecting any of this, and it's come as something of a shock. I hope you'll be very happy in your new home.'

'Thank you,' she replied timidly, knowing full well he did not mean a word of it. Determined to push her advantage, she gestured at the piles of cash. 'You could bury most of it in the garden,' she suggested softly. 'You could spend five thousand on a holiday and a few things for the house. You'll need a digital camera if you're going to Vienna. I hear it's very picturesque. I expect Mrs Wilson will dog sit Trotsky, if you promise to bring her back a nice gift.'

Horace busied himself rearranging the piles of thousands. He stacked five of them on top of each other, and then made three piles of the remaining bundles. 'That's not a bad idea,' he said, making a gargantuan effort to sound grateful. 'Thank you for your generosity, Dorothy.'

'You're welcome,' she replied, and went back to her drink, grateful he had stopped being so belligerent, even if he was making a poor job of hiding his true feelings on the subject.

She thought about standing up and taking her leave, but was reluctant to part from him while he was in such a strange mood. She offered him the envelope, and he packed the cash into it in a manner which suggested he had done it before. Then he walked over to the bed and tucked the bulky packet under his pillows.

Dorothy took the opportunity to admire the colours on the throw that was spread out on top of the duvet. She knew the Americans would have referred to the item as a comforter, an adjective totally suited to it.

A magnificent silver and white swan had been lovingly quilted onto a background of indigo and pearlescent mauve. The creature was framed by a copse of willow trees, and towering proud and tall over these was a single species she knew was a sweet chestnut. A dog was lying in the shade of the tree with his head resting on his front paws. Dorothy's favourite part of the quilt was the top right hand corner where a mass of golden stars and crescent moon had been carefully sewn onto a large patch of indigo. The person who made the quilt had loved its owner dearly, of that she was certain.

When Horace first arrived in Shankill, he had been on foot and travelling light. When he moved into the house a few months later, he brought his quilt with him. Except for the ten weeks of warm weather they usually enjoyed between July and September, it had been on the giant bed ever since.

Every summer, he arranged for one of his neighbours to wash and line dry it when the weather was good, but not so hot there was a risk of bleaching the vivid colours. At first, the neighbours had been a little surprised by this unmanly behaviour, but that was before Horace disclosed the source of the comforter.

It transpired his mother had made it for him as part of his eighteenth birthday present, and it was one of the few items he still possessed which reminded him of her. After hearing this, the neighbourhood women fell over themselves offering to wash the quilt every year and, as a result of their ministrations, it had been well maintained and was still as vibrant as the day Dorothy and Amanda helped Horace unpack it, and discovered that one of the most beautiful objects they had ever seen had been used to wrap a collection of poetry and prose books, many of them written in the dead language of Latin.

With the cash safely tucked away, Horace returned to his chair and polished off his drink. Dorothy gladly accepted another one, and forced herself to make normal conversation for the next forty minutes.

She wished he had a television so they could sit together and do something normal on a Friday night, but one of the joys of visiting Horace was accepting the acute absence of all technology. She was often amazed he did not eschew electric lights in favour of candles, or the record player in favour of a windup gramophone.

She was tempted to suggest he use some of the cash to buy a television and satellite dish, but decided she was better off quitting while she was ahead, and while he was at least projecting the appearance of a man resigned to the changes afoot. She began to yawn at the end of the third drink and he offered to walk her home. She gladly accepted, and while she pulled on her fleece, he went to put a leash on Trotsky.

Horace pulled his old brown raincoat on over his reindeer sweater and pocketed his front door key. They set off together in the cold night air, with Trotsky eagerly sniffing for any cats that might have the temerity to cross his path. When they reached her house, Dorothy quickly unlocked the door and pushed it open so she could see his face in the light from the hall. Horace looked sad, although for the life of her she did not fully understand why.

'There's no need to leave Shankill,' he said gently. 'I could help you look for a bigger house around here. Maybe you could even build your own. There's a decent plot for sale not half a mile from here with a fabulous view of the sea.'

She patted him comfortingly on the shoulder. 'I know you mean well,' she smiled sadly, 'but I have my own reasons for wanting a fresh start away from here. I hope you understand.'

It was on the tip of her tongue to add the words, it's nothing personal, but in good conscience she could not utter them. If not for his presence in Shankill, she might be sorely tempted to go and check out the available site. If it was the one she was thinking of, it would make an ideal location for her new house, and she would still be a stone's throw away from her friends, to say nothing of the seashore.

It was a moot point. Horace was entrenched in the Shankill community, and Dorothy was not prepared to pass up the opportunity that had been presented to her to see more of her daughter. Living half a mile away from the man who had shattered her vulnerable young heart was not distance enough for Diane O'Keefe, not by a long chalk.

Horace seemed to pick up on some of Dorothy's thoughts, and in the light that streamed from the hallway, his face darkened. His jaw clenched and his eyes glinted with an emotion she was unable to identify.

'Goodnight, Dorothy,' he said gruffly. 'Thanks for everything.'

She watched him walk away with Trotsky bounding on ahead, delighted at such an unexpected treat. Instead of heading home, Horace turned left and strode up the road at an alarming rate, desperate it seemed to be well away from her orbit.

Dorothy closed the door and locked it securely from the inside. She was tired and looking forward to bed. She hung up her fleece and scarf and then went upstairs to turn on the electric blanket, grateful she no longer had to worry about the ever-soaring energy bills. As she made her way back downstairs, she heard her phone beeping inside her bag. She carried it into the sitting room and switched on one of the lamps so she could see who was texting her.

Josh had sent two messages. The first read: *Deco and I will pop around for dinner tomorrow, if that's okay. Di not coming. Says she's too busy with projects.*

Dorothy quickly typed a reply before she forgot, telling her son that he and his friend were both welcome, and she would roast a chicken to mark the occasion. She was grateful he had not suggested a Sunday visit, since she would have had to make her excuses.

She had no way of knowing how long her trip to Howth was likely to take, and did not want to rush such an important decision. She opened the second message and perused it. She read it twice more to make sure. Then she slowly sat down in her recliner and allowed her body to relax.

She closed her eyes and considered all possible implications of the words Horace had carved into the back of the new rocker. The second message from Josh read:

Domus et placens uxor = A home and a pleasing wife. Something you want to tell me, Mother?

Ten minutes later, Dorothy hauled herself out of the recliner and got ready for bed. Despite an exhausting week, it took her a long time to fall asleep.

12

When Dorothy awoke on Sunday morning, she was pleased she had not allowed Josh and Deco to coax her into having more than two glasses of wine the night before. Saying they were going clubbing, they had left the house at nine o'clock, and she had not attempted to detain them.

Neither had she pressurised them into making a return visit. Neither of the young men had seemed in any way suspicious about this blatant lack of motherly fussing, and sauntered in the direction of the station without a care in the world. She waved them off with a sense of relief.

It had been incredibly tempting to blurt out the entire story over the roast chicken dinner, and she had to forcibly remind herself that she had a plan for the twins which could not be rejected on a whim.

She went to bed shortly after ten, and expected to feel buoyant and energetic on Sunday morning, but in truth felt drained. Going the extra mile at work, together with keeping her colleagues in the dark, had been tough, and she could not resist a twinge of guilt at the way she was excluding them.

On top of all that, she had experienced the adrenalin rush of collecting her cheque, swiftly followed by offering for the apartment, and then the showdown with Horace. Last but by no means least, she had sat at the dinner table with her only son, and not uttered one word on the subject of his mother being a newly created multimillionaire.

Despite her good intentions, such behaviour was the very worst kind of deception. Was it any wonder she was shattered? She was certainly not in the mood for driving any great distance, especially to the far side of the city, and felt a rush of gratitude for the convenience of the DART.

She made a decent breakfast of eggs and wholemeal toast, which she consumed with a large mug of strong coffee. The sustenance provided a much-needed energy boost, and as she dried her hair and slapped on her makeup, she felt ready to face the day and conquer all obstacles.

As the wind was bound to be fierce in Howth, she made sure to wear a pair of thick tights under her trousers, and a thermal top under her shirt and jumper. *Gansey, sweater, jumper. Ain't linguistics fun?*

There was no rain forecast so she did not bother with an umbrella, although she took the precaution of wrapping her warmest scarf around her neck and making sure she had the cosy gloves Amanda had given her for Christmas. After a visit to the bathroom, she was ready to leave, and cast a final glance at her reflection in the mirror. The face staring back at her looked drab and exhausted. It truly was ironic. *Money doesn't solve all problems, Dottie. At least not overnight.*

She gathered up her usual black bag, which was considerably lighter after offloading thirty thousand smackers, and double locked the front door behind her. She took a quick mental inventory of her belongings before setting off for the station. It was the perfect alternative to driving, especially as it would give her a better idea of what normal life was like in the Howth area.

She slowed her pace as she walked by Old Hen, although all was quiet and the windows were shut tightly against the weather. She continued to walk, but had only travelled another ten steps when she heard Horace calling her name. He was in his usual oversized drab attire, and had Trotsky by his side on the leash. 'If you're off to the station, I'll accompany you,' he said quietly.

They strolled in companionable silence for a minute until he was ready to speak. 'I'm happy for you, Dorothy,' he said gruffly. 'Please ignore my little outburst last night. If there's anything I can do to assist with the move, you only have to say the word. And thank you again for the money. I buried most of it at first light. Trotsky was delighted. He loves the digging game. We discovered a most interesting bone.'

Dorothy smiled up at him as she walked. 'It's been a shock to us both,' she told him warmly. 'I'm meeting the family in Rathmichael tomorrow evening for the sole purpose of breaking the news. I don't have to tell you what madness will then ensue.'

He chuckled. 'I hope your mother doesn't lose the plot entirely. Will you be staying overnight with your parents? Would you like me to keep an eye on the house?'

'No thanks. I intend to drive home so I can get up at my usual time for work on Tuesday.'

He frowned. 'But why are you still working? Have you not resigned?'

'Of course I've resigned, silly, but I don't leave until the end of the month, and I intend to honour my commitment to the company right up to the last minute. I don't want any phone calls in February asking me to go back in to sort out some mess or another. It's only two weeks of my life.'

He chuckled again. 'You're a gas woman,' he said, the expression sounding very odd in his British accent.

Horace left Dorothy at the station, and she enjoyed a blessedly uneventful journey to Howth. She had not brought a book, or even an MP3 player, and entertained herself by admiring the views of the coastline and considering what new clothes she should buy. Nothing too elaborate or expensive for now, that was for sure.

When the train pulled in at the station, she glanced at her watch and saw she had thirty minutes to kill before Saul was due to collect her. That suited her very well, as she badly wanted to check out the area. When she emerged from the station, she noticed that many of her fellow travellers were heading towards the West Pier, and decided to follow them.

She soon realised the majority of the ramblers were out to avail themselves of the fresh produce the restaurants and delicatessens had to offer. It was all too touristy for her taste. She loved it, of course. Who would not enjoy visiting such a town? Even on a cold January day, there was a warm and friendly buzz about it. Nonetheless, did she really want to live in such a small place, on the North Side of the city, miles away from her friends and family?

She felt sure her parents would be far from impressed when they discovered what she was contemplating. When Horace asked her where she was headed, she had given him a vague response, not wanting him to know about Howth when he was only just coming to terms with the idea of Falcon.

Even though he would enjoy the area, she knew he would be unimpressed by the notion of her living so far away. Dorothy sighed heavily as she examined a collection of lobsters in a shop window. She had only been in the area for twenty minutes, and was already regretting her decision to view Anna Sadler's plot of land.

After a while, she grew bored of the shops and strolled back along the pier. On impulse, she decided to walk along the slipway by the harbour, which was home to the yacht club as well as the lifesaving hut. Most of the yachts and other boats were covered in tarpaulins, although she admired the few that were visible through the wire fence. She could not imagine ever being the proud possessor of a luxury vessel, yet it was early days. After all, never was a long time, and who knew what the future might hold?

There was no doubt as to the function of the majority of boats in the harbour, because they reeked of fish. Dorothy shivered when she imagined being out in the Irish Sea in winter, and could not help but feel a degree of sympathy for the men who worked the trawlers. It was then she saw it, and initially assumed her eyes were playing tricks. A dark, furry creature bobbed about in the waters, close to the boats.

'It can't be,' she said to herself.

'Look, love, a seal,' a man who was standing nearby called to his wife.

It *was* a seal. Without warning, the Space Ache flared in Dorothy's chest, and a tingle began at her lower back and ran up her spine. She shivered inside her old woollen coat, and rubbed hard at the area around her heart. The seal turned its head and stared at her, and she experienced a floating sensation as if she was swimming alongside the creature.

Dorothy looked at the seal and the seal looked back at her. For a second or two, she caught a glimpse of a man dressed from head to toe in black. His face was covered by a mask, and one of his large hands gripped a long gun in a manner which suggested he was entirely comfortable with the weapon. The image was gone as quickly as it arrived. She stood motionless, staring out at Howth harbour asking herself what the hell was going on.

'The clairs are getting stronger,' she whispered, then quickly glanced around to make sure the strolling couple had not overheard her. They would doubtless think her a mad woman when they heard her talking to herself about a mysterious woman called Claire, who was possibly a professional bodybuilder.

However, the gift of claircognizance was not a woman, and together with clairvoyance, clairaudience and clairsentience, was only one of her abilities. *Why is it more powerful now? Is it because of the money? I always assumed that as I grew older, the clairs would grow weaker. But since my birthday, they're stronger than ever. It must be because my life is changing so rapidly and suddenly.*

Doing her level best to snap out of it and push all thoughts of her abilities aside, to be pondered later in the privacy of her own home, Dorothy turned away and began to walk back towards the station.

Grateful she had worn the extra layers, she patiently waited near the DART building and indulged in a spot of people watching to pass the time. After a few minutes, Saul pulled up in his rather old, battered, and frankly dirty, four-wheel drive. Given that many architects had lost their livelihoods since the economy had plummeted into a downward spiral of misery and austerity, Dorothy was not surprised to discover his car was past its best.

'How are you enjoying Howth so far?' he enquired politely, as soon as she was buckled into the seat next to him. He was more chipper today, she noted, presumably because he had a firm offer on the apartment, and finally some good news for Anna.

'To be perfectly honest with you, Saul, I find it all a little touristy. I used to bring my twins here when they were younger, and I always felt sorry for the natives living on this side of the peninsula. They seem to have a perpetual line of day-trippers passing their doors. Plus, I've always thought of Howth as mainly hills, four-wheel drives, and big houses with even bigger gates. I don't think I've ever seen so many properties with entry phone systems and CCTV cameras. I'm not sure it's me.'

Saul nodded in apparent agreement. 'It's true this side is the busiest because it's closest to the shops and the main road to the city. I agree with you about the hills as well. If you were a Howth resident, you'd very likely purchase a four-wheel drive pretty quickly. As for security, you can have as much or as little as you like. That's a personal choice. My recommendation would be to install extensive security in the initial stages. It's much easier to do it that way, than it is to retro-fit it later.'

'I suppose that would be sensible,' Dorothy nodded thoughtfully. 'Is that what Phil and Anna were intending to do?'

'Absolutely. They planned to install state-of-the-art wiring into the house as it was being constructed so they wouldn't have to worry about it for many years. Once you have the wiring in place, you can run everything off it, not only security. You can set up a home network that will allow you to access all of your systems from every room. It all starts with good wiring, and don't let anybody tell you any differently. There's no point in having a fifty-thousand-euro sound system, if the basic cabling is cheap and doesn't function. You'd have to arrange a meeting with the electricians and installers in the planning stages about the technical specs. Assuming things got that far, of course. We don't want to get ahead of ourselves.'

His laugh sounded rather forced, although she refrained from comment. *I'm not one hundred percent certain I understood what he just said. A home network?*

They reached the end of the town centre and Saul was forced to take a right as he had run out of road. The street became a hill, and Dorothy sighed quietly so he would not hear her. At least the range of shops and restaurants was good, and it would be fantastic to have all the fresh fish on the doorstep. If she lived here, she would in all likelihood be able to arrange for a regular delivery.

'The site I'm showing you today is not one that your average day tripper would be able to access,' Saul told her, as he navigated the latest hill. 'Unless, of course, they happen to be travelling on one of the ferries to Dublin or Dún Laoghaire, and decide to leap off and attempt the swim to your house. So if it's the idea of tourists passing your front door that worrying you, then fear not.'

He actually smiled, which cheered her up no end. She was sure she was wasting his time and, despite his assurances to the contrary, felt guilty for dragging him out of the house on a Sunday.

After driving a further two kilometres, Saul hung a left, followed by another right, and drove along a gently winding road. A selection of houses on both sides came into view, and Dorothy examined them critically. For the most part, the properties were substantial in size and well finished. Naturally, they had big gates. After all, this was Howth.

The thought flashed across her mind that some of them looked almost prison-like. Then she reminded herself the gates were nothing more than security features, hence there was no need to be melodramatic. One house was currently under construction and when Saul slowed the car, she assumed this was their destination. To her surprise, he pulled away again almost immediately, merely having slowed to allow the bus to pass.

'It's handy it's on a bus route,' she commented. 'In case I get bored driving my Hummer.'

He immediately perked up and looked interested. 'Did you order a Hummer?'

'Eh no, Saul, I did *not* order a Hummer,' she sniffed in disgust. 'Those things are like tanks. I saw one on the M50 the other day and it was a pink limo of all things! I haven't even thought about cars yet. I've been way too busy getting used to being rich. A Hummer indeed!'

The car slowed again and he gestured to his left. 'Just so you know, that's a private road over there. It leads down to the lighthouse and a couple of residences. It's unlikely you would find yourself under arrest if you accidentally wandered down there, although it's certainly not encouraged. Don't confuse that entrance with your own, that's all I'm saying.'

'It's not *my* entrance,' she replied irritably, 'and the only thing confusing me is you. Where exactly are we?'

'We're on the Baily and this is Thormanby Road. The site is around the corner.'

Sure enough, seconds later, they stopped outside a pair of wrought iron gates securely fastened by a chain and giant padlock. Seemingly out of nowhere, Saul produced a key. Jumping out of the car, he removed the lock and pushed the gates wide open before hopping back in.

'At the moment, it's difficult for two vehicles to comfortably pass, although it could be widened if you wished,' he told her, as he nosed the car through the entrance.

One thing Dorothy could not fail to notice was that all of the houses on the easternmost side of the road had sloping driveways. This track, for that was how it could be best described, was no exception. For the first thirty yards, it sloped downwards at a steep angle. Then it levelled out, and the car continued to descend at a more gradual rate.

It was impossible to look either left or right as the lane was enclosed by a dilapidated hedge to the right and a crumbling wall to the left. She was still trying to get her bearings when the architect said, 'Here we are.'

With that, he turned right and pulled onto a patch of concrete large enough to comfortably accommodate twenty vehicles. There were no buildings in sight and Dorothy recalled what he had told her about clearing the plot in readiness for the new foundations. When she glanced back up the hill, she could see houses situated far higher up the Baily, with vast numbers of trees and shrubs dividing them from their neighbours.

She noticed something looking suspiciously like an orchard. When she enquired, Saul confirmed it belonged to the Doheny clan, and formed the western periphery of the property. The site was substantial, and the orchard only stretched the length of half the boundary line. Next to it was what appeared to be a vast acreage of long grass and briars. The architect saw the mess had caught her attention.

'Phil told me that forty years ago, the family used to grow a lot of their own produce on that patch of land. They even grew their own spuds. Back in the eighties, their health began to deteriorate, so they stopped working it and let nature reclaim it. Phil was thinking he might clear it one day and turn it into a paddock. He thought it would be nice for his kids to have ponies.'

His breath caught in his throat as if he was fighting back the tears, but Dorothy remained silent and allowed him time to gather his thoughts. Saul made a gargantuan effort to pull himself together, and began to point out the other boundaries to the parcel of land. Even with him doing this, she could not quite get a feel for the size of the plot, although that was not the architect's doing. The Irish Sea was solely responsible for this deplorable lack of focus.

They were standing literally yards away from the coastline, and Dublin Bay stretched out before them, with nothing to impede the view. A ferry was approaching at that very moment, and she saw what Saul meant about the tourists. There were only two ways to access the house. Either down the narrow winding lane or across the water. *You would have to be a mermaid to attempt it.*

She could clearly see the Baily lighthouse on its own little protruding part of the peninsula. It looked close enough to touch, and even in the winter bleakness it shone like a white star in an indigo sky. She also had unrestricted views of both the Wicklow and Dublin mountains.

The towns of Dalkey and Killiney appeared so close, Dorothy smiled at the irony of it all. Saul caught her attention once more by touching her arm and pointing. 'See that little bit of rock jutting out over there? That's called Lion's Head. Your borderline is right next to it. You also have a piece of shoreline that's big enough to launch a boat. Would you like to see it?'

Feeling rather overwhelmed, she nodded silently, and side by side, they set off walking. Saul guided her on a makeshift pathway which was less stony and more level than the rest of the ground. Absorbing her surroundings, Dorothy could not comprehend how Phil Doheny's family had managed to live for so many years on such an uneven parcel of land. They must have been goat people!

She was tempted to ask Saul what sort of design he had come up with for such an irregular, hilly surface, but decided to defer her question indefinitely. She did not wish to create the false impression she was genuinely interested in Phil and Anna's house design.

After all, what suited one person would not necessarily suit another. She would be as well to start the design process from scratch so everything would be to her own taste. Now she had the apartment, it would not matter how long it took. Assuming she purchased this site, which was by no means a given.

13

After a couple more minutes of scrambling, Dorothy and Saul arrived at the side of the cliff that separated the land from the sea, and came to a halt close to the edge. They stood and stared down at the choppy water. The drop was not especially high, although a fall onto the rocks below would very likely result in serious injury.

There was no doubt any residents of the property would have to exercise caution, especially if there were pets or children around. Dorothy spotted the dilapidated remains of a low-level barbed wire fence running along the cliff top, and shuddered at the idea of such a monstrosity. She pictured an elegant little railing in its place, and smiled to herself.

She made an effort to pull her thoughts back to Saul since he was gesturing at the landscape and pointing out features. When she had seen enough, the architect suggested they turn north, and she duly obliged. The pair walked for a few minutes until he indicated the small shoreline belonging to the site.

It was not exactly a beach, at least not the kind you would see while on holiday, being somewhat stony and drab in appearance. It was separated from Lion's Head by a tatty fence turned green and grey from age.

Dorothy assumed this unsightly mess was the boundary line. If it was replaced with a decent barrier, it would certainly deter unwelcome guests because they would have to jump into the water and somehow scramble onto her beach in order to access her land. *It's not your land, Dottie; please try not to lose the run of yourself.*

The beach itself was easily accessed by a set of stone steps, and there was an accompanying concrete slope for launching boats. Looking at it objectively, she admitted that for anybody with an interest in water sports or angling, it would be fantastic. She was not sure if it would be legal to launch a jet ski from there, as the local council were strict about such matters, but you could certainly keep a small boat. She wondered what her dad would make of it. Horace would enjoy it, of that she was certain. Assuming she could entice him away from Shankill long enough to admire the Howth vista.

'Wow,' was all she felt able to enunciate, even though she knew the architect was looking for more.

'Well, you said you wanted coastal views,' Saul was grateful even for that one syllable, and jumped in encouragingly. 'You can't get much more coastal than this unless you move to the South of France. You would be very private here, and there are plenty of golf clubs and other amenities in the area. The neighbours keep themselves to themselves, although I'm sure they're fine once you get to know them.

'Phil met a few of the locals, and he said they were a friendly bunch once they got chatting. You'd need a gardener and a handyman, of course, since you're…eh…a single lady. You wouldn't be able to manage a place this size alone. On top of all that, it would be a good investment for the future. When the property market eventually recovers in another decade or thereabouts, you'd be sitting on a prime piece of real estate, and that's no exaggeration. In the meantime, you could kick back and enjoy the views. After you built a house to live in, of course.'

For the second time in an hour, the tingling sensation started around Dorothy's lower back, and she pulled her coat tighter against her body. She did not want the architect to see how shaken she was. 'I need to think about this for a few minutes. Let's walk back to the car,' she replied, hoping he would not notice the way her voice quivered.

With Saul occasionally assisting her over the more treacherous terrain, the duo strolled companionably back up to the parking area. Upon reaching the dirty vehicle, Dorothy turned around and stared out to sea.

'I could wake up to that every morning,' she whispered. 'Every single day for the rest of my life, I could open my eyes to that view.'

Saul pretended not to hear, and obligingly edged away in order to give her space. Dorothy was experiencing inner conflict the like of which she had not known for many years. Not for a moment had she considered the possibility of her new acquaintance showing her something so out-of-the-way and unusual.

In her naivety, she had been expecting a site close to the town centre, perhaps with a view of Claremont beach. Yet here she was, standing on over three acres of rubble, tree stumps, brambles, nettles and hills, and the clairs were in full throttle, urging her to buy it. There was no doubt in her mind the tingles meant precisely that. Dare she ignore them?

Dorothy shoved her hands deep into the pockets of her coat and walked away from Saul so he would not be able to see her face or hear her voice. She fixed her eyes on the southern coastline stretching out before her. 'Come on then,' she said somewhat crankily. 'If you genuinely want me to buy this slice of a hill, miles away from my family and friends, then show me a definite sign. Otherwise no deal.'

Almost before the words had left her mouth, the terrain wavered in front of her eyes. and the debris-strewn patch of land with its sprinkling of trees and briars disappeared. It was replaced by an image of a basketball court on which two men were playing.

The taller of the two appeared to be bald, while the smaller man had a full head of black curls. Even though she was unable to make out the words, Dorothy could sense them shouting at each other as they played.

As she watched, the smaller man dodged around the bigger one with the agility of a kitten and, grabbing the ball, tucked it under one arm. He leaped into the air and caught the basketball hoop with one hand, while dropping the ball into the net with the other.

Clearly deeming this feat of athleticism to be insufficient, he remained hanging from the hoop, swinging like an Orangutan and hollering victoriously at his large companion. The taller man approached the hoop and turned around so his back was to the swinging man. The curly haired Orangutan dropped from his hanging position and landed on the bigger man's back. Both men roared with laughter, apparently finding these antics hilarious.

Almost immediately, the image wavered and the men disappeared, to be replaced by the views of Dublin Bay. Dorothy rubbed at her chest abstractedly. She was shocked to find herself missing the two men, and wondered who they were.

She moved a little further away from Saul, in case he was tempted to interrupt her thought processes. *Well, you asked for a sign, and that was precisely what you got.* How was she to explain this when asked why she had chosen to buy the rugged, uneven plot of land, miles away from everyone she knew?

She could clearly picture the look of revulsion on her dad's face, if she told him that not only had a seal in the harbour eyeballed her and seemed to be sending her a message, she had also seen a vision of two men playing basketball. She sighed heavily. That was the trouble with the clairs. You could not go around telling folks about them. Not if you wanted to live a normal life that was. She had made that decision many years earlier.

At nineteen years of age, Dorothy had been travelling in a car with her five closest friends, when she had seen a vision of the vehicle ploughing into a cow, resulting in the deaths of Bel and Viv, and the rest of the group being hospitalised for weeks. She had begged the driver to slow down, and approach the upcoming level crossing at a snail's pace.

Notwithstanding the fact that the railway line in question had been out of use for many years, an irate Simone had given in to her friend's demands. As she rounded the corner in her clapped out Toyota, they were amazed to see a member of the bovine community standing stock still in the middle of the old train tracks, regarding the vehicle with absolute apathy.

Simone had pulled the car over and they all demanded of Dorothy how she had known. When it dawned on her that out of the six girls in the car, she was the only one who had sensed anything out of the ordinary, she took the instantaneous decision to lie. Instead of explaining the vision, Dorothy simply told them she had experienced a Very Bad Feeling, and they had accepted the lie, grateful to be alive. That day set the pattern for the rest of her life.

In the years that followed the Cow Incident (as it became known), she and Simone had occasionally discussed it in a small way, although she had never once shared with her best friend the full extent of her ability. As far as Simone, or indeed any of her other friends knew, she sometimes got Bad Feelings or Good Feelings about things, and often had an uncanny ability to spot if a person was lying, or if there was trouble brewing.

They could handle this much because they had known her forever and took it very much in their stride. But that was the extent of it. Dorothy did not object to this state of affairs. After all, if any of her friends wanted to spend time with a psychic, they could always go and have a crystal ball reading or something of that nature. There was no need for them to be subjected to her crazy thoughts, visions and ideas. She did not doubt they would soon grow bored of her rattling on about them, if she insisted on trying to mainstream them into their lives.

That approach had been all well and good in her old life, but now everything was changing. While her abilities might not exactly be growing, they were certainly making their presence strongly felt. If she did not start to share some of what she was sensing, seeing and feeling, she ran the distinct risk of driving herself crazy.

No sense in worrying about it now. Perhaps I'll know when the time is right to share something. Maybe I should be more trusting. Perhaps being more open about that side of things is all part of my new life. Yikes. Not a scary concept at all.

She slowly returned to the car where Saul was waiting patiently with his hands shoved deep into the pockets of his corduroy trousers. 'I'm definitely interested,' she told him. 'That said, I would like to negotiate separately for the land and house design. The concept you came up with for Phil and Anna may not suit me, although I'd love to see it out of interest. It might even give me a few ideas for my own house. That is, if you don't mind.'

'That's no problem,' he replied gravely. 'We can start the ball rolling on the site, and we can have another meeting about the house designs in a few weeks. Or even in a couple of months, whatever suits you. There's no rush now you have the apartment.'

'Excellent. Thank you, Saul,' she smiled at him gratefully.

They scrambled into the car, glad to be out of the sharp wind, and he drove her back to the station. After giving him her opening offer, Dorothy returned home to Shankill in the same way she had come.

She did not encounter Horace between the station and her house, for which she was grateful. She did not want to lie to him anymore that day. She would wait until the land was hers and she had a design for a suitable house before breaking the news of this fresh purchase.

Even though she was resigned to it, she could not help wishing there was no work the next day. There was no getting away from the fact she had commitments to fulfil before her new life could begin properly.

While Dorothy thought about the many things she planned to do in the coming months, Saul Newman went to visit his sister in her sad and lonely apartment in Donabate. He gently broke the news about the latest offer from the strange little Euromillions winner.

Not quite believing she was so easily able to dispose of the piece of land that had been the start of all her troubles and the ruination of her life, Anna Sadler agreed to sell the site on the Baily to Dorothy Lyle for the knockdown price of €390,000.

When Saul called on Sunday evening and reported the good news to Dorothy, she was pleased. At the same time, she asked herself if she was somehow profiting from Anna's misfortune. She sensed that, once again, the architect was relieved to have the matter resolved so speedily for his sister's sake. After thinking it over, she came to the conclusion it would be better not to dwell upon Anna's troubles, but instead to be grateful for what she had been lucky enough to acquire.

14

Dorothy experienced a moment of empathy with a basted turkey, but wisely resolved against dwelling on the widespread slaughter of innocent avian. Instead, she stretched her legs out on the plinth, closed her eyes, and made a concerted effort to relax her shoulders.

She should be luxuriating in the sensation of having cocoa butter applied to her exhausted body instead of brooding about farmyards and feathers. Zara, the therapist, lifted Dorothy's arm in order to more ably apply the butter, and she could not help but notice the instrument the girl was using bore a startling similarity to a pastry brush.

She forcibly dragged her thoughts away from baked goods. She was feeling pretty peckish after her morning's exercise, and was only supposed to be contemplating the salad awaiting her at lunchtime. *Who would have believed being so rich could be so exhausting?*

Incredibly enough, the five weeks which had passed since her birthday had been the busiest of her life. For a woman who had given birth to twins at twenty years of age, this was saying something. Before winning the money, she had been emotionally drained.

It was a sad irony that unexpectedly finding herself one of the wealthiest women in the land had almost tipped her over the edge into nervous exhaustion. It was wishful thinking to believe an injection of cash, no matter how significant, could undo in less than a month, the damage that years of unhealthy eating, self-blame and, dare she say it, alcohol abuse, had perpetuated on her mind, body and spirit.

Three days earlier, she had left the offices of Premier for the final time. Now the nine to five lifestyle was a thing of the past, she was certain her quality of life would drastically improve. Rarely had a woman been more grateful to exit a building than Dorothy that day.

She almost skipped through the revolving door shortly after four o'clock, clutching her little statue of Ganesh, two bags of parting gifts, and a selection of other personal effects. She had by no means been unhappy at the company, and was grateful to them for giving her a job in the first instance. However, like any other relationship, when it was over it was over, and no amount of hanging around and hoping for the best was going to change things.

Despite the occasional twinge of guilt, she had resisted the urge to divulge her secret to the staff. When the time was right, she fully intended to give her ex-colleagues a suitable gift from her winnings, although this would have to wait for a more appropriate moment.

She acknowledged how likely it was they would judge her harshly when the truth became known, although it was a chance she was prepared to take. This delay was not because she intended hiding her winnings forever. She had no aspirations to buy an estate in darkest Donegal or deepest Roscommon, and spend the remainder of her days cowering behind its high walls.

She fully intended to go out into the world and enjoy her money to the best of her ability. That said, Dorothy was a cautious woman who was well aware there was a time for everything. Telling over one hundred employees of a company, while you yourself were still working alongside them, that you had won more than one hundred and thirty-eight million euro, was simply asking for trouble. She hoped she was not so foolish as to go actively seeking that level of madness while her plans were still in their infancy.

Zara finished spreading the butter, then wrapped her client in a garment which forcibly reminded her of one of her mother's tablecloths. The head massage began. Dorothy sighed with pleasure and hoped she would not fall asleep and miss any of the action since that would be a felonious crime indeed.

Zara dug her fingers into Dorothy's scalp, which was as tight as a warlord's grip on a UN aid drop, and proceeded to gently manipulate it within an inch of its life. Dorothy wondered if the girl could be tempted away from Champneys Health Spa, with the promise of a considerable pay rise, in order to facilitate the massage process every day back in Dublin. As the treatment continued, she mentally pressed the rewind button inside her head, and relived her movements since the day she collected her cheque.

For the most part, things had gone pretty much according to plan. When Anna Sadler accepted her offer of a cool million for the duplex, she readily agreed to include all furniture and fittings as part of the deal. The other woman sent a message by Saul to say she was relieved at the latter part of the proposal, and for Dorothy not to feel she was taking advantage in any way.

Both siblings had been dreading the inevitable disposal of five couches of varying lengths and design, three recliners in different finishes, two enormous TVs, the contents of a gym, one extra-large oak desk, a dining room set and two queen size beds, just for starters. While

Dorothy looked forward to the day when she would refit the apartment to her own taste, she was more than happy to avail of the existing contents for now, as it would mean the barest minimum of shopping, prior to taking possession.

Potentially, her move would be completed in one day. She would literally have to make up her new bed and transfer the utilities to her own name. After that, she could consider herself the newest resident of Falcon Apartments. It was a deeply satisfying thought. In fact, the cleaners would be in beforehand and would probably make up the bed for her if she asked. *Oh, I don't mind undertaking that one small task for myself.*

Zara was taken aback to hear a chuckle emanate from the small woman lying on her plinth who, heretofore, had been extremely quiet. When the girl enquired if all was well, Dorothy hastened to reassure her that she had merely been daydreaming about her new apartment.

Being of a lively disposition, Zara immediately launched into a description of the new house she and her boyfriend were in the process of buying. Used to the girls who had worked for her over the years, Dorothy left half of her brain on autopilot. While Zara happily expressed her views on the subject of gas versus electric, and laminate versus carpet, she allowed the fully functioning half of her brain to continue its review of recent events.

Overall, the meeting with her family and two of her closest friends had gone well. Upon hearing the news, her mother had briefly fainted and had to be revived with scotch. Initially, her sisters had been sceptical, and inclined to believe Dorothy was playing a prank. As one, they lifted their hands and impatiently pushed brown locks of hair back off the oval faces they had inherited from their mother. Two pairs of piercing blue eyes, a genetic gift from their father, glared at her accusing.

Dorothy had spent a sleepless Sunday night, rehearsing what she was going to say to them, to say nothing of determining the amount of the cheques she was planning to write during her Monday lunch break when the office would be as quiet as the grave.

She was in no mood for her sisters and their attitude. She promptly told them that, regardless of what the psychologists might say, there was no real benefit to having been born the middle child, because you were always stuck between the firstborn-who-is-never-wrong, and the youngest-who-must-be-cosseted-at-all-costs.

She advised them to get over themselves and stop being so suspicious, before handing them a photocopy of the winning cheque as evidence. After that, they came around quickly enough and apologised for their scepticism, although not before Gemma stated it was a myth that being the eldest was a licence to be infallible, while Orla insisted it was not her fault she had been born last, and demanded to know why everybody always picked on her.

Her dad and Bel both reacted in a similar manner. They each sat stunned, gawking at Dorothy without uttering a syllable. Bel's little elfin face settled into an expression of disbelief coupled with rapture, while her blue eyes grew almost misty with joy. Joey's careworn countenance had grown an alarming shade of red.

He had thrown himself into his favourite armchair and remained incommunicado for a full two minutes. Joey and Bel had always been good friends, and neither of them had ever been shy about expressing their opinions upon any given subject, hence it was amusing to watch them reduced to absolute silence. Even if that blessed relief did not last very long.

Upon hearing the news, Vivian began to twist her long blonde hair in agitation, and her brown eyes had grown huge in her face as she grinned like a maniac. Ten minutes later she was still grinning, but had begun to pace the floors in her high heels, all the while wringing her hands in a manner better suited to a Dickensian character.

Dorothy had had the presence of mind to bring along four bottles of champagne, which Gemma and Orla fell upon in their haste to open. She was careful to only take a sip during the toasts because she had work the following day. She did not intend to stay over in her parents' house, because she wanted to sleep in her own bed.

The only person who understood why she had not simply walked out of her job was her mother. Pat was a great believer in loyalty to the employer as well as seeing things through. Bel, on the other hand, did not understand one iota. She was inclined to view Dorothy's attitude to working three weeks' notice as a minor brain defect, possibly brought on by stress-related abundance.

As Bel had not had to work since the day she discovered she was expecting her first baby, her attitude did not particularly surprise Dorothy. She was, however, a little disappointed to learn that Joey, Viv, and her sisters were inclined to agree. They made no secret of the fact they considered her a wee bit deranged because she was still at the office.

They could not seem to grasp that she had been with the company for over a decade, and merely wanted to leave in as professional and civilised a manner as possible. Ideally without all the fuss and gossip a sudden and impromptu departure would naturally trigger.

Finally, irritated and frustrated, Dorothy gave up trying to justify herself. In the hope of effectively shutting them up on the subject, she handed them their cheques.

Ironically, it was her parents who had caused her the most anxiety. After all, they had been married for the better part of forty-five years. To each other. Would they be offended if she gave them the same as the girls, but split between them? Would they think her mean if she gave too little? Would they think her a show-off if she gave too much? Would they care as long as they got something? After all, they were her parents. How likely was it they would sit in judgement upon her?

Joey's pharmacy business had always ensured the Lyle family had never gone without. Since inheriting the family home back in the nineties, Pat and Joey had moved into their autumn years even more comfortably situated than when they had a growing family to support. Nonetheless, they still maintained the same attitude towards money as they had in the early years of their marriage. This was, save first and spend second, and only then if you had the means at your disposal.

They did not believe in greed, materialism, credit, or overspending. How would they feel when their daughter presented each of them with a cheque for one million euro? After much internal struggle, Dorothy decided to give her sisters and friends two million each and the same to her parents, but split between them. Just in case they had widely differing ideas on how to spend the loot.

She had conducted some research into the tax implications of giving away large sums. In line with many European countries, all Irish winnings were tax-free. That said, once any of the moola was gifted to a third party, it became taxable income. There were a few minor tax breaks for close family, but even taking this into account, they would all have to be careful they were not inadvertently stung for an unexpected, to say nothing of astronomical, tax bill.

'I had to send Amy and Simone's by international transfer. I wish they were here. I miss them so much,' Dorothy told the group sadly, as she extracted what she needed from her handbag. She handed each of them an envelope containing two cheques. The first was for two million euro, and the second was made out for an amount she estimated as adequate to cover the tax charge.

As she passed the envelopes, she explained how they could lodge the tax cheque into a high-interest account until the time came to pay it over to the revenue. As they were already safely in the 2011 tax year, they would (theoretically at least) have more than twenty months interest accrued by the time a tax return would be required.

'I decided to give you it all now, instead of dishing it out in dribs and drabs over the next year or so,' she chose her words carefully, and crossed her fingers inside her own head. 'I know it might not make the best sense from a tax point of view, but I felt it would be cleaner that way. To give it all at once, I mean.' Hoping she had made her point without hurting anybody's feelings, she stopped speaking and allowed them to process.

For thirty seconds, not a word was spoken as they examined the contents of the cream coloured envelopes. All of a sudden, the room erupted in squeals of excitement, and Dorothy was almost crushed in the stampede, as bodies flung themselves at her, all determined it seemed, to break every rib in her torso while hugging her to express their gratitude. *That went well.*

Even though she stayed until close to ten, happily discussing the disposal of their newfound wealth and polishing off the champagne, the words 'show-off' or 'miser' never once entered into the conversation.

Gemma, Orla and Bel ended up quite tipsy, and Gerald had to be summoned to chauffeur the trio home. When he discovered the reason for the impromptu celebration, he became almost incoherent from excitement and gratitude.

After he hugged Dorothy to within an inch of her life, he said if he had known what was afoot, he would not have griped at his wife for dragging him away from the TV on a cold January night. Viv happily accepted Pat's offer of a bed for the night, stating that notwithstanding the fact she was drunk, she would have been too excited to drive home to Wexford even if sober.

Back in Champneys, Zara moved in a southerly direction and commenced the foot massage. Dorothy had to stop herself moaning aloud with sheer pleasure, and quickly returned to her life review.

The fortnight, up to and including her final day at the office had been hectic, and she had lost five pounds without even trying. This was mainly due to drastically reducing her wine intake and cutting out unhealthy food. This had not proved much of a challenge because she found she was too excited to bother with anything that might be bad for her. Now she had the resources, she fully intended to put them to work, and her first mission was to make herself over.

That was the main reason she was currently lying on a plinth, somewhere far north of London. It had been Bel's idea to sign up for the twelve-day transformation programme. Dorothy had initially been reluctant. This was not only because it would mean leaving Ireland for so long, but also because she did not enjoy flying.

When she consulted her solicitor, Robert McCaul, and Saul Newman, her new architect acquaintance, they assured her that a mere twelve days away would be neither here nor there in the great scheme of things. Rather than trying to dissuade her, both men encouraged her to take a break.

Dorothy did not know if this was because she was getting on their nerves, or simply because they felt she needed some time out, or possibly even a little of both. Coming to the conclusion their motives were immaterial, she went ahead and made the booking.

~~~

From: Dottie8888@chatulike.ie
To:SRedmond@chatchat.com; ANorris@talkalot.com
Date: January 20th, 2011
SUBJECT: IT'S ALL NEW!
Hi Si, Hi Amy,
Sorry to send a joint mail but I have so much to tell. Yes, in answer to both of you, I still get the strange pain in my chest that started all those years ago. I am always aware of it lurking in the background, although I can go for weeks at a time without it causing real pain. Of course, there are times when it

sort of flares up like arthritis and can be extremely uncomfortable.

The pain doesn't last very long, usually only ten or twenty minutes. Sometimes it sort of hums as if it's happy, although that's rare. Perhaps hum is a bad word. It sort of vibrates at a very low frequency. That hasn't happened for a long time. It has been strong for the past few weeks and I have been acutely aware of it, but that may be from all the excitement.

I am hoping it will ease off now my life is changing for the better, but who knows what will happen? I suppose I really should see an uber-expensive specialist now I'm so wealthy, but the Harley Street doctor I saw a few years ago was considered one of the best in the world, and he couldn't find one damn thing wrong with me. I think more tests would only be throwing good money after bad, to say nothing of the added stress of being poked and prodded by medics.

I am expecting the purchase of both apartment and site to go through fairly quickly. No mortgages are required, and neither property was ever owned by the local authority, which is a huge benefit. There do not appear to be any right-of-way issues with the site, which should speed things up.

The annual charges on the apartment are astronomical, although I am not quibbling over them as it will only slow things down. I am starting to get excited about moving. I have decided to stick with my usual solicitor, Robert McCaul, for the time being. I asked him to look at my current will, which he did. He says that, under its terms, the twins are well protected in the event of my death, because they will inherit the money on deposit.

However, I am under orders to have it completely rewritten because, as my circumstances change, it will not be adequate. He has offered to start the process next month, once things calm down. Unfortunately, I think I may have upset Bel a teeny bit. She is somewhat miffed because I will not be giving Gerald my legal business, especially as he is now a senior partner in Morgan, Morgan & Kinsella. I am very fond of Gerald. After all, I've known him since I was seventeen years of age, for feck sake.

Nonetheless, despite having known me since I was a teenager, he has never once in all of those years, offered me any advice, free or otherwise, or indicated in any way that he would welcome my business. Not even during those nerve-wracking days when I was purchasing the house.

I don't feel particularly guilty about it, but at the same time I don't want Bel to be upset with me either. I really need her now because this is such a crazy time for me. I told her I don't want to mix business with pleasure, which is true in many ways.

She suggested we go on a break to a place called Champneys in the UK, and I agreed. I hate flying, as you know, not because we are up in the air (which I like), but because of the security, the cramped conditions, and the way the passengers are herded as if they are livestock. Do those idiots at the airport really believe we are all carrying bombs inside bottles of shampoo? Honestly, talk about keeping morons with clipboards in employment.

I mentioned the flying thing to Bel, and she suggested we charter a private jet because her friend Trish has done it a few times. At least her husband's firm has done it in the past for the senior management outings. I don't mean to be bitchy, but I have met Trish a few times, and she is one of those women who like to take personal credit for everything.

If her husband worked as a janitor in the Treasury Department, you can bet Trish would be telling everybody he was second only to the minister himself, and essentially running the country's finances.

I went ahead and booked the jet, and it will be an adventure for us. Bel is looking forward to the treatments. I have signed up for something called a 12-day transformation package. It runs from Sunday to Friday.

This means we will be back home in time for what Bel likes to call Valentine's Weekend, and what I like to think of as The Shittiest Time of the year. Back soon with more news. Glad you got the money safely. You don't have to keep thanking me. That's what friends are for. Love Dot xx

15

In all the years spent living what was already beginning to feel like another woman's life, Dorothy had never spent more than the occasional day at a health spa. She was unsure how to approach her 12-day stay at Champneys, and resorted to the web for inspiration.

After an hour of intense research, she concluded the best way to begin the process was to invest in new luggage. Ideally, the type that would last for many years, and would not have to be regularly replaced because it fell apart or went out of style.

It was Bel who suggested they take a trip to the Louis Vuitton department in the Brown Thomas store on Grafton Street, and see if anything caught Dorothy's eye. Even though it was Sunday, a day Bel usually reserved for family time, she thoroughly enjoyed the shopping expedition.

She agreed wholeheartedly with her friend's selection of three different sized cases from the monogram canvas range. Even though the patent finishes were exceptionally stylish and appealing, the choice of size was very limited. At least with the more traditional signature Vuitton look, Dorothy would be able to add additional pieces as she identified her needs.

Bel, however, soon lost her smile when she discovered the record-breaking Euromillions winner did not intend to shop for her clothes at BT. When her pal casually mentioned she planned to replenish her wardrobe from high street shops, Bel was aghast.

Dorothy had already donated or dumped more than half her existing wardrobe. She had kept hold of her two best work suits for the final week, although these items were also destined for the clothes bank. With the exception of a handful of bits and pieces which she thought her sisters might like, it was her intention to get rid of every single scrap of clothing she currently possessed, and start afresh.

She had booked ten personal training sessions at the spa, and hoped to lose a minimum of one stone and drop two dress sizes by Easter. Dorothy did not see the sense in spending thousands on designer gear she would inevitably end up giving away two months down the line.

Bel disagreed. In fact, she came dangerously close to exploding when she heard this rationale. She argued that, with more than one hundred and thirty million in the bank, her friend should not have to make any purchases from the same shops the unemployed and students frequented.

To placate her, Dorothy agreed to purchase a selection of items from the store of her choice, providing it was not ridiculously expensive designer wear. Bel calmed down and agreed it might be a little early to go mad with couture. They compromised by visiting the House of Fraser in Dundrum.

Dorothy had the presence of mind to top up her credit card while her bank manager was arranging the new one. Two hours after crossing the threshold of the Dundrum Shopping Centre, she was patting herself on the back for such foresight. When she left the women's clothing department, she was in possession of no fewer than three Seafolly one-piece swimsuits, intended for use in the Champney's pool. She was also the proud owner of one Orla Kiely evening dress, two pairs of Ralph Lauren wide-legged trousers, a vast array of Dickens & Jones tops, as well as a MaxMara long-line cardigan, to name but a few.

At the till, the sales assistant rang it all up then called out a figure that made Dorothy blink rapidly and glance worriedly at Bel. In response, her pal grinned happily and suggested she make use of her credit card. Dorothy pulled herself together long enough to take her wallet out of her bag and, with hands that trembled, handed the card to the smiling girl behind the desk. The women gathered up the purchases and, with Bel still chuckling in amusement, made their way to the shoe department.

Dorothy immediately felt more comfortable because she did not object to spending money on footwear. She had always been a size four, and did not anticipate the situation changing any time soon. Nonetheless, she tried to choose items she knew would also appeal to her sisters in case she wanted to pass them on at a later date.

Orla and Gemma took the same shoe size as she did and were of similar height, although Dorothy was the petite child of the family, standing exactly five feet tall in her bare feet. Unfortunately for her self-esteem, she was also the heaviest by a good thirty-pound margin.

Of all the items she purchased that day, only one, a beautiful Jaeger silk tunic top, was a size fourteen. The others were all size sixteen, and one pair of trousers was even an eighteen. It was very lowering, but she cheered herself with the thought of the much-anticipated twelve days at the health farm, under the watchful eye of a personal trainer.

An hour later, the ladies left the shoe department, having acquired a selection of Dune and Yves Saint Laurent pumps, as well as Radley and Carvela boots in different shades and styles. Bel insisted Dorothy purchase a pair of Michael Cors mesh shoe boots, which she agreed to, even though she was not certain they were her style.

Bel was not forgotten during the orgy of retail. Dorothy treated her to a magnificent Anoushka G silk chiffon maxi dress, as well as a pair of Carvela evening shoes. As they were on the verge of leaving, the women remembered they had overlooked the lingerie section, to say nothing of sleepwear and a new coat for Dorothy.

Leaving the multitude of purchases with an obliging sales assistant, they made a mad dash back to the outerwear corner. Dorothy chose a Tommy Hilfiger cashmere overcoat for herself, even though it was far from being the most exciting one on display. She was not yet ready to experiment with extreme style statements, and resisted her friend's attempts to coerce her into buying a Biba leopard print, knee-length number.

She did capitulate to Bel's wishes on some items, the main one being a Jacques Vert evening jacket to wear at Champneys. Dorothy would have preferred a new fleece in case it was cold in the UK, but was not particularly surprised when Bel firmly vetoed this garment and returned it to the rack with a derisory sneer.

In the sleepwear section, Dorothy grabbed a selection of comfortable-looking pyjamas, as well as a pair of moccasin slippers. Then she stood back and allowed Bel to choose a range of lingerie and nightdresses for her. She suspected the majority would never see the light of day, but by now was past caring.

She felt certain if she did not escape from the shop very shortly and procure a cup of tea, she would likely self-combust. It did not take Bel long to make the selection, and a bone-weary Dorothy was soon standing in front of yet another cash desk, handing her plastic to a smiling assistant.

After collecting the multitude of bags, the women put their heads down and returned to the multi-story car park as quickly as possible, determined not to be sidetracked by anything on display in the windows of the other stores. They crammed what bags they could into the substantial boot of Bel's BMW next to the Vuitton, and threw the remainder on the back seat.

It was already dark outside as Bel carefully manoeuvred the overflowing vehicle up the ramp and out on to the main road. When she paused at the first red light, she laughingly commented that the contents were worth almost as much as the car itself. When Dorothy asked if she was intending to treat herself to a new vehicle any time soon, Bel replied that she had promised her husband she wouldn't make any substantial purchases for at least six months.

'Gerald says we mustn't allow the money to go to our heads,' she told her friend earnestly. 'If we squander it on cars and suchlike, they won't be anything left for investments or serious purchases. I'm sure I'll buy a new car in due course, just not yet. It's not as if I have any issues with this one. I've loved this Beamer since the day Gerald surprised me with it for my birthday.'

As Bel negotiated her way through the Dundrum traffic and pointed the car south, Dorothy privately admired her friend's common sense approach to her newfound wealth, and wished she could absorb some of it by a process of osmosis. She privately resolved to take a break from retail for a while, and felt grateful there was only a small shopping mall at Champneys which mainly sold sportswear and orthopaedic shoes.

Bel successfully delivered Dorothy and her multitude of goodies home to her little house but refused the offer of coffee, saying she really needed to get home and get a few things done. Dorothy felt guilty at having monopolised her entire Sunday, but Bel waved this off as immaterial, stating she had enjoyed the orgy of retail enormously, and did not begrudge a minute of the time spent.

Dorothy waved her pal off, then heaved a sigh of relief as she carried the last of the bags indoors, firmly closed the front door and turned the deadbolt against the evening air.

It had just gone six o'clock and fortunately none of the neighbours gave any indication they noticed how much merchandise she had brought home. It was a cold winter's night, and nobody was paying much attention to anything except his or her television screens. There was smoke billowing from the chimney of Old Hen but no sign of its owner hovering outside either his own house or hers.

As a precaution, and much to Bel's amusement, Dorothy had thrown an old sheet over the enormous Brown Thomas bags containing the Louis Vuitton, before removing them from the car.

She noticed the lights were on in Amanda's house, and felt guilty for not yet having shared the big news with her neighbour. She had not hesitated to share her tidings with Horace, but admitted she did not have the energy to deal with Amanda right now.

She fully intended to tell her friend about her good fortune and give her a gift, but not until she returned from Champneys. She urgently needed a break and a chance to get her head around everything that had happened in recent weeks. She was sure Amanda would forgive her for the delay once she saw the size of her cheque.

After showering and changing into something comfortable, Dorothy sat down to drink her tea and review her selection of goodies. The fancy luggage looked very odd in her small sitting room. After a while, she got sick of staring at it, and put it upstairs in Josh's old bedroom.

She laid out all her purchases on Diane's bed, ready to be packed for the trip. Even though she knew that, technically, she was disgustingly rich, she was sobered by the amount of money she had spent. A small part of her hoped her parents would not find out she had burned through the best part of five thousand euro in less than three hours at Dundrum. And that was after she had handed over what amounted to a deposit on a small apartment for the luggage.

She smiled when she pictured the appalled expressions on Pat and Joey's faces but only briefly. Recognising she was exhausted and overwhelmed by her change in circumstances, she took herself off to bed, grateful she only had one more week to endure at the office.

The extra hours she had put in during her notice period paid dividends. The final five days, while busy, were not anywhere near as hectic as they might have been. When Dorothy sat down with Rita during her final morning at Premier, there were only a handful of relatively minor items still outstanding.

Rita assured her she would be well able to manage. Then she offered to help with the final bit of desk cleaning and general sort out. When she asked if everything was all right with her boss, and whether she should be worried for her, Dorothy assured her second in command that things were very much all right, although she would not be able to provide more details for a while yet.

When Rita tentatively enquired if she had met a wealthy man and was all set to marry again, Dorothy gave her a secret smile. Rita immediately relaxed, and her eyes sparkled with the anticipation of spreading such a juicy nugget of gossip.

At one o'clock, the finance director took the payroll team out for a long lunch. He presented Dorothy with a card and generous voucher for Brown Thomas. He also made a very nice speech, in which he thanked her for all her years of service to the company.

When the group returned to Premier at three o'clock, they were all a little tipsy. Dorothy spent the final hour chatting to anybody who dropped in to say goodbye, and making sure she had not forgotten anything. She was not sad at the thoughts of leaving, although she felt a tinge of regret at having to leave behind so many colleagues without being able to share the truth with them. She resolved to get them together when the time was right, and give them a gift they would not forget in a hurry.

After a final round of hugs and tears, she eventually escaped and made it home to Shankill by five. At exactly forty years and four weeks old, Dorothy collapsed into her recliner once more. This time, it was only for as long as it took to demolish a cup of tea and send a couple of texts. After a twenty-minute breather, she forced herself to get up again. She spent the remainder of that Friday evening and a chunk of Saturday in preparation for her trip.

On January 30th, a limousine taxi delivered her and Bel to the service centre designated for those passengers choosing to fly by private jet from Dublin airport. Fortunately, Eamonn, the driver, knew where he was going, because Dorothy had no clue, and she was certain that Bel, for all her big talk, would not have known either. She was pleased she had agreed to Bel's suggestion and chosen this method of transportation.

Eamonn was helpful and knowledgeable, and there was ample space in the car for the luggage. After they exited the limo, Dorothy discreetly pressed a substantial tip into his hand and said a little prayer he would not be offended. Eamonn ran his hand through his grey hair and his blue eyes smiled kindly at her from his lined and frankly, dad-like face. Then he passed over his business card and assured her she could call upon his services at any time. He did not seem offended by the tip.

'I'm surprised you didn't book a stretch limo, Bel,' Dorothy teased, as they walked into the service centre.

'Don't be silly, Dottie, this isn't a hen party,' was the vaguely acidic reply.

The private jet had been a real revelation. The security checks were minimal. Dorothy had naively assumed she would have to go through the usual rigmarole of taking off her shoes and having her lipstick scrutinised.

I don't think these men and women quite appreciate how potentially lethal a bottle of shampoo can be. They look rather relaxed. I wonder if I should mention I have a nail file in my bag.

The luggage restrictions were also a real revelation and a source of genuine delight. What it boiled down to was that, as long as the crew could fit the bags on the plane without endangering the passengers or contravening aviation law, you could bring as much as you liked!

The crew took their tail number, welcomed them on board and performed the necessary introductions. Captain Merryville was a tall man with a mop of silvery grey hair and a smile capable of melting rock. Dorothy saw the way Bel scrutinised his posterior as he walked away, and pretended to be shocked.

'You know I've always had a thing for men in uniform,' the other woman smirked unrepentantly. 'He's some hunk, isn't he? I wonder if he's married.'

'*You're* married,' Dorothy raised a condemnatory eyebrow.

'I'm not thinking of *me*, Dottie,' Bel replied impatiently. 'You're the one who's been single forever. Have you ever considered dating a pilot? What do you think of the uniform? Pretty hot, eh?'

There was no time for further discussion regarding the charms of Captain Merryville as just then another member of the crew arrived to ensure their handbags were stowed away safely. After the usual demonstration of the safety features, Dorothy gratefully accepted a cup of green tea from the attendant then stretched out in the luxurious surroundings. She was amazed at the sheer size of her seat, which more closely resembled an armchair. She sipped her tea and wished her sisters were there to share the experience.

16

Under the guiding hands of Captain Merryville, the small jet touched down on the asphalt at Luton with scarcely a bump. Dorothy was out cold and Bel had to shake her awake.

Neither woman could recall her ever being truly relaxed mid-flight before, and giggled at the discovery that it took travelling by private jet to finally lull her to sleep. The crew sprang into action and unloaded the women and their luggage in record time.

The captain came to bid them goodbye, and Bel spent a minute batting her eyelids at him as she tried to extract details pertaining to his personal life. Feeling utterly mortified that a woman she had known since the age of five would stoop to such measures, Dorothy gritted her teeth and told herself to offer up the torment as penance for all her bad behaviour as a child.

Thankfully, Bel could only dawdle for so long and they were soon exiting the airport in search of their car. Bel seemed blissful unaware her behaviour had been in any way embarrassing, and chatted gaily all the way to their destination.

By two o'clock, they had been safely delivered by yet another limousine driver (who originally hailed from Cork) to the front door of Champneys, all ready for check-in. Dorothy had reserved two suites on the ground floor, as close to the pool as she could get.

She considered it fortunate there was availability at all, because they had left it very close to their departure date before booking. It had crossed her mind that Bel might be offended at being allocated her own suite, as it would be more usual for them to share a room.

Far from complaining, Bel was thrilled, and behaved as if she had been expecting nothing less. After this, Dorothy wisely refrained from even mentioning the arrangements. They each had a king-sized bed, which she hoped would make it easier to sleep.

Dorothy's main motivation for booking separate rooms was because she wanted to be able to come and go to the gym and pool at all hours without disturbing her friend. She intended to make good use of the facilities and did not need Bel, who was as thin as a length of rope, constantly pleading with her to relax.

Dorothy booked an hour of Reiki for herself, as well as a session of Shiroabhyanga. She had never tried it before, but it claimed to be the ultimate Ayurvedic treatment, which meant she was more than willing to give it a go. In a moment of daring, she added on a colon hydrotherapy treatment as well as an anti-cellulite sculpt.

As luck would have it, Champneys kept a standalone computer for guests' use in the older part of the building, close to the log fire. She tried hard to resist the lure of both computer and fire as much as possible as she was there to focus on her fitness, yet found herself unable to resist emailing Simone with her latest news.

~~~

From: Dottie8888@chatulike.ie
To:SRedmond@chatchat.com
Date: February 8th, 2011
SUBJECT: WINE AND CRAZY DREAMS
Hi Simone,

Champneys is wonderful and I highly recommend private jets, which is something I never thought to hear myself say in this lifetime or any other. I have an appointment with the personal trainer every day, and she has given me plenty of diet and exercise information to take home.

I bought every lotion and potion the therapists recommended. I must be the best customer they've had for years. I love being able to buy what I want, whenever I want. Talk about a novelty!

I am soooo glad I let Bel talk me into buying all of those clothes in Dundrum, because dinner here is smart casual. We actually have to remove the white robes and slippers and get dressed! As usual, Bel was right and is now feeling pretty smug. I told her to book anything she wants (it's all my treat, of course), which means we don't see much of each other between meals. She is having her treatments or relaxing with a book, while I am off being tortured by some incredibly fit sadist or having my entire body wrapped in foil.

When we first arrived, dinner times were a bit of a chore. Bel cannot seem to accept the fact I have to reduce my calorific intake if I am to lose weight. Especially the booze. I have to cut down on the wine if I'm to shed this three stone. She's taking it rather personally, as if I'm trying to spoil her fun. She keeps ordering wine, and I have to find new and interesting ways to dispose of it.

It would be quite funny if it wasn't so annoying. Some of the serving staff copped on to what was happening after the first few nights, and they have happily become co-conspirators in the subterfuge. They keep swooping in with a glass showing only residue, and substituting it with such sleight of hand, I'm beginning to wonder if perhaps they are all circus trained. I'm getting very good at slipping ten-pound notes into their hands.

It's a successful system and one to remember. It helps that Bel has such a small bladder and is always nipping to the loo.

I don't think Bel is hugely impressed with Champneys, although she can't say much about it because she was the one who suggested we stay here. I don't think the surroundings are as sumptuous as she was expecting, and we are certainly not tripping over celebs around every corner.

The fitness trainers are quite strict with those of us who are on the transformation programme, which is also irritating her because she feels we should be letting our hair down a little. She wants to take off tomorrow and spend the day in London, but I don't want to mess up my fitness schedule. After all, that's the main reason I am here. We can go to London any time we fancy, but if I fall at the first hurdle of my weight loss programme, I may as well give up now and stay fat.

The only other little annoyance (if it could be called that) is the strange dream I have had for the past two nights. It's very weird and I really need to tell somebody about it, so here goes.

I'm lying on a sun lounger reading a magazine. The lounger is sort of floating in the air above a swimming pool (well it is a dream) and it's all chrome and leather and looks totally impractical to have anywhere near a puddle of water, never mind a pool. My dream self must have a very daring interior designer.

I'm looking at a photograph of myself in the magazine. There's a man standing next to me in the picture and I'm pretty sure he's wearing a tuxedo, although I can't see his face.

The pool is wide, possibly thirty or even forty feet across. It's lined with aqua green tiles that make it look like the bottom of the ocean. Incredibly, inset within these tiles are what seem to be thousands of blue and silvery grey mosaics laid out in the pattern of a blue whale. The whale is life-sized because the pool is so long, easily sixty feet.

There are dozens and dozens of little lights in the water, making it sparkle. The lights are not only in the pool, they're also in the ceiling and they resemble starlight. The entire effect is absolutely stunning.

At one end, there are two diving boards, and in between them is some sort of tower. Or maybe it's scaffolding. I'm not sure. When I look up, I can see there's a sort of gallery running around the perimeter of the pool house, and behind this are enormous glass doors letting in lots of light.

So I'm lying there on my floating chair looking at the pic of myself as if it's all perfectly normal, when I suddenly notice a tall figure at the far end near the boards. It's definitely male. My spine gets all tingly. He sort of runs up the stairs to the scaffolding in a very show-offish manner. Then he hesitates for a few moments as if he's assessing the situation. He glances in my direction as if he's assessing me as well.

My heart goes pitter patter. He raises his arms over his head then executes a perfect dive and hits the water with knife-edged precision and disappears. After what seems like just a few seconds, he resurfaces at the shallow end, obviously having swum underwater the entire length of the pool.

He starts to swim up and down at incredible speed, his long arms and legs propelling him through the water for lap after lap without seeming to falter or tire in any way. When he eventually pauses, he swims over to the poolside. He reaches up and grabs my lounger and pulls it down so it's resting on the water instead of floating above it. (So not weird or anything). Then he casually flicks water at me. 'Don't be lazy, Boss,' he says in a deep voice. 'C'mon in, the water's warm. I won't let ya drown.'

My poor heart skips a few beats. Get this, Si! Not only does he have an American accent, he sounds just like Sam Elliot, the actor. I promise you, Simone, I haven't seen the man in anything for months; ergo I have no clue as to why my dream man has his voice! I stare at him, but no matter how hard I try, I cannot bring his face into focus. I say to him, "Is the water really warm, or is this one of your usual scams, tough guy?"

And he replies, "That's an affirmative, Boss. Sahara daytime temperature, just the way ya like it."

You are not going to believe what happens next! I sit up and I suddenly find myself standing at the foot of the tallest diving board, which must be three metres high. I start to climb the ladder. I know I have no business doing this because I've never dived in my life and I'm not likely to start now, at my age. I reach the top and I'm standing on the board. I look down and I realise how deep the pool is.

The only reason I can see the bottom at all is due to the lights. I feel as if I'm standing at the edge of an abyss. I can see the whale even more clearly from this height, and it's sort of breaching out of the water. Then I realise it looks that way because the pool slopes quite steeply. I look at the man who is waiting for me in the shallow end and he sort of gives me a little wave as if to say, "Go ahead and dive".

Next thing you know, I've taken a deep breath, bounced and launched myself off the board. Just before I hit the water, I wake up in a state of supreme relief! I have a tight feeling in my chest, although it's not like the Space Ache, and I have the tingling in my lower back.

For the past two nights, I have had the exact same dream and quite frankly, it's getting a little disturbing. I am positive I am not resting properly, and I was exhausted during the walk I do every morning with all the other fatties. What if I have it again tonight? Any thoughts? Hi to C. Dot x

PS: I was talking to your mum last week. She is in good form but missing you. There is no way she and your dad would be able to manage the long flight to Oz. They are well aware of this and are not planning to do anything crazy so don't worry about them. I told her I had offered to send you a ticket, but she understands you are very busy right now.

~~~

The following morning when she awoke, Dorothy elevated both arms towards her bedroom ceiling and shouted. 'Okay! Okay! I get it! You want me to build a crazy pool that looks like something from a James Cameron movie so a dolphin man can swim in it! As soon as I get home, I'll speak to Saul! Thanks, by the way, and Amen!'

~~~

From: Dottie8888@chatulike.ie
To:SRedmond@chatchat.com
Date: February 9th, 2011
SUBJECT: YIPPEE!
Hi Si,
I got your text. I agree they are frustrating, not enough characters. Charlie was quite right. As soon as I said aloud I would speak to Saul about the pool, the dream stopped. We are due to have a meeting as soon as I get home because he wants to show me the house he designed for Phil and Anna. I feel fantastic now, as if a great weight has been lifted from me. The Space Ache has eased off as well.

Thanks for your advice and thanks for not calling me a nutcase. I wasn't sure about telling you at first, but now I am glad I did. What sort of skin does Charlie have? They have a full range of products for men here so I will get both of you some of the lovely potions and courier you a nice parcel of goodies. It's not as if I have to worry about baggage restrictions on the flight home. Yes, I am sure I have lost more weight. Proper mail soon. Hi to C. Dot xxx

~~~

When the personal trainer weighed and measured Dorothy on her final day, she was pleased to discover that, not only had she lost another eight pounds, she had also lost an inch from around her waist and thighs.

She felt and looked more toned and revitalised. Determined to keep up the good work back home, she carefully packed all of the leaflets, brochures and menus she had collected into her largest Louis.

Feeling very much like a new woman, she happily paid the astronomical bill the two pals had run up. After thanking the staff for their help, she left Champneys with a smile on her face, looking forward to the new life that awaited her.

As she watched the motorway flashing by on the return journey to the airport, she pondered the next things on her to-do list. She had to explain her change of fortunes to Amanda, of course, although the two most important people in her life had to be told first.

The entire family had been under strict instructions not to utter a word to Josh and Diane until their mother had a proper chat with them. It had caused much controversy, and her parents had been quite shocked and annoyed by her attitude. Dorothy stood firm and insisted she knew what was best for her own children. Telling them her big news promised to be fun.

17

Against the express wishes and advice of her parents, twenty-year-old Dorothy Lyle married twenty-two-year-old Declan O'Keefe because she was expecting his baby, and because she truly believed they were in love with each other.

She pointedly ignored the voice in her head that urged her not to proceed with the wedding, but instead to fake an illness, or find some other way of postponing the nuptials until she was older and wiser.

Sadly, Dorothy was young and foolish, and like many before her, was convinced she had found The One. Consequently, she steadfastly blanked the tingling sensation in her lower back which warned her all was not well, and her anticipated marriage was an error of magnificent proportions.

Pat and Joey assured their daughter that since they were not living in the dark ages, there was no need to rush into wedlock just because she was pregnant. Despite their best efforts to make her see sense, Dorothy went ahead with the marriage, neither understanding nor acknowledging the concerns of those who loved her best.

For the first, but sadly not the last time in her life, she fell for a man who was only capable of self-adulation, a love against which she could never hope to compete.

For the first two years, she battled to make things work. It wasn't until the occasion of their second wedding anniversary she finally accepted what the inner voice had been trying to tell her from the beginning.

Not only was Declan lacking as a human being and a miserable failure as a husband, the only love he was capable of experiencing was saved purely for himself. Alas, by the second anniversary the die had been well and truly cast, and it was too late for Dorothy to undo the terrible error she had made.

Long before reaching the age of forty, she had given up all her illusions regarding the Catholic Church, and only entered one when it became necessary to do so. In her opinion, she was more than capable of finding her way to the creator without the assistance of the old men in the Vatican.

Nonetheless, back when she was twenty, she had not yet come to the realisation that she was not the sort of woman who required an antiquated institution to show her the way to God. Therefore, as per the custom of the day, the parish priest presided over the nuptials in the church near her childhood home.

Afterwards, the wedding party moved on to the local hotel. As they were standing on the front lawn, with the photographer bossing them around, Dorothy glanced over at her husband, her young heart overflowing with love. She soon wished she had not bothered. Declan did not appear to be even remotely happy at finding himself a newly married man.

Worse than that, he seemed positively detached from his surroundings, as if the entire proceedings were beneath his notice. With a sinking heart, Dorothy noticed he also emitted a distinctly contemptuous vibe. It was as if nothing about the day, particularly the bride, meant anything to him. At her own wedding, of all possible times, Dorothy got one of her Very Bad Feelings, and during the months and years that followed she was destined to get many more.

When the twins came along four months later, they were a welcome addition. Even though having two babies to care for when she was barely out of her teens was extremely hard work, she did at least feel that somebody loved her. Declan's absence of affection was inexorably making itself known to her, because by then he was making less and less of an effort to hide his lack of regard for her.

They lived in a small apartment in West Dublin, where Declan was employed in his father's auto parts shop. Dorothy began to dread the sound of his footsteps at the end of the working day, as it was the prelude to yet another evening spent listening to his snide comments about how wonderful his life had been prior to meeting her, and how all he ever had to worry about was where his next pint of beer was coming from.

These remarks were always coupled with the contemptuous glances at which he excelled. No matter how many years passed, Dorothy never forgot how his eyes used to glint with malice over his hooknose, as he derived pleasure from the hurt he was inflicting upon his young spouse.

The family celebrated the twins' first Christmas in Ireland, then shortly after their first anniversary, packed up and moved to London. Declan's brother, Liam, had been living there for the past two years and running his own building firm. After a major family discussion, the O'Keefes decided that Declan should join his brother in what was bidding fair to be a successful enterprise. They even went so far as to put up the capital which would enable him to buy a share of the venture and implement new plans to take it forward.

Even though it meant leaving her friends and family behind, when Dorothy was apprised of the scheme, she raised no objections. She lived in hope that the change of scenery might somehow jumpstart the marriage. Besides, she now had two babies to care and provide for, so what was she supposed to do? Tell her parents her marriage was a disaster after barely a year?

She was the one who had insisted on marrying Declan. It behoved her to accept her responsibilities and give the relationship a fair crack of the whip. After all, they were both young. Perhaps in a new town, away from the old haunts, they would finally gel as a couple and possibly even fall in love like other folks did.

It did not take Declan long to make his mark in the building trade and, for a while at least, he seemed happier. Dorothy began to hope her wish had been granted, and they were about to embark on a new phase of their lives where their relationship would be a more normal one. This hope seemed to be confirmed scarcely three months after the move, when Declan announced his intention of purchasing a family home for them.

Almost before Dorothy knew what was happening, she was installed in a beautiful three-bedroom house in an upcoming area of Highbury. In a manner that was kind for him, Declan told her to buy what she needed for the house. He spent long hours at the company with Liam, a dedication that paid dividends.

Financially speaking, things progressed more smoothly than Dorothy would ever have dreamed possible, and she unexpectedly found herself married to a man with prospects.

Unfortunately, the same could not be said of the relationship. The initial euphoria of being a man of property soon wore off, and whatever resolutions Declan had made concerning his behaviour were soon forgotten. His father, Billy, had always been able to curb his son's excesses in the past, but without that constant steadying influence, Declan soon began to treat the move to another country as a get out of jail free card, and essentially began to live the life of a single man. He remained under the family roof, and to the outside world at least, gave the impression he was a good husband and father.

However, behind closed doors he either ignored Dorothy and treated her as if she was part of the furniture, or alternatively barked orders at her as if she was an indentured servant. As the months wore on, his behaviour deteriorated, and the ache of loneliness she felt for her friends and family back home became almost physical.

Only the twins kept her going. Joshua and Diane were healthy, happy babies, who freely gave of their affections to their young mother. In later years, she often wondered what the outcome would have been if the children had not given her something to live for during those early years with Declan.

Hoping a change of lifestyle would do her good and keen to make new friends, Dorothy decided to attend an evening class, and set about finding the most suitable one. The one that appealed the most was expensive, giving her pause for thought.

During the fifteen months of their marriage, Declan had not exactly kept her short of money. Nevertheless, he was a controlling man who took considerable pleasure from the fact that his wife often had to approach him and request funds for her and their children. Well aware he would never willingly give her the hundreds of pounds necessary to pay the fees, Dorothy was forced to embezzle money from her husband whenever the opportunity presented itself.

Each evening when he got home from work, Declan would dump his dirty clothes on the floor and leave them for her to pick up. Each evening, she carefully went through his pockets and removed any paraphernalia which might upset the delicate mechanism of the much-cherished washing machine.

Every night for three months, she stole one pound from her husband's pockets. She kept the stash secreted in a tampon box with a false bottom which was just enough of a disguise to fool a casual observer. When she eventually broached the subject with Declan, he raised neither interest nor objection to the scheme, as long as he was not expected to participate or support her in any way.

He was firmly entrenched in the business and had little thought to spare for his wife's activities. Dorothy heaved a sigh of relief and headed down to the college to complete the necessary application forms.

She began to study accounts and payroll in the September after the twins turned one. With the addition of sixty pounds from her children's allowance, she was able to afford the registration fee as well as the books and equipment she would need.

When it dawned upon Declan that the course was not free of charge, Dorothy told him her parents had sent her the money and suggested she learn how to type and do bookkeeping, in case she wanted to work part-time when the twins started school.

He could hardly question the veracity of her statement, and since he did not like Joey Lyle, whom he regarded as being far too honest and outspoken, made no attempt to contact the Lyles, and therefore asked no more about it.

The neighbours tended to be standoffish at the best of times. They regarded the young Irish couple as upstarts who should not have been in a position to buy a house in such a property hot spot when couples twice their age were struggling to do so.

One of them, a woman called Josie, gradually began to thaw, and suggested that Dorothy might like to use her youngest sister, Brenda, as a regular babysitter. Dorothy was delighted at the visible signs of thaw as well as the notion of a regular babysitter, and was quick to approach the young woman.

Every Wednesday evening for thirty-eight weeks, Dorothy paid Brenda to look after the twins, and took a bus to the college. She made friends with a fellow student called Rudy, who always gave her a lift home so she would not have to catch the bus after dark. In return for his kindness, she made a point of helping him with the course work because his next promotion depended on him getting good grades.

She soon picked up the essentials of payroll, as well as manual and computerised accounts. It came easier to her than it did to some of the other students, including Rudy, for which she was profoundly grateful. She had barely managed to scrape the money together for the books and fees, and did not have a Plan B if the experiment had turned out a failure.

Her petty pilfering continued throughout the year. Every week she had to pay Brenda the going rate because Declan baulked at the notion of being left alone with the children, and always took off to the pub on college nights. Dorothy was grateful for this absence.

Truth be told, she preferred the arrangement. The twins were very fond of Brenda and as the months wore on, it suited her to know they were in safe hands while she was at college. It was a stressful time for Dorothy, but in the end it was worth it. During the June the twins turned two, she heard she had passed her exams with distinction and received her certification.

By the time she completed the course, Dorothy had been aware of Declan's affairs for some time, and had officially ceased to care about them. Their sex life had been a one-sided transaction while it lasted, and had as good as disappeared as soon as they said, 'I do.'

She was not especially bothered about the other women. In many ways, she felt they were doing her a service, and almost pitied them. It had been a long time since she had found Declan's touch anything other than repulsive, and wondered how any woman could willingly share his bed. She was forced to share it in order to maintain the status quo, but always went to bed before him and feigned sleep whenever he entered the room.

There were a number of occasions when he sought intimacy with her, mainly because he knew she did not want it, although his attentions ceased abruptly when he experienced an unexpected bout of erectile dysfunction. He informed his wife that she was to blame for this lack of performance, and accused her of trying to destroy his manhood in addition to making a mockery of his life.

Dorothy crossed her fingers and prayed she would always be the cause of a flaccid member in the man she was rapidly coming to despise.

No, it was not his frequent absences from the family home, or even the knowledge he was having sex with other women that upset her. It was his active dislike of her that hurt the most, and the way he derived a degree of pleasure from her pain which was almost sexual.

Too late, she recognised how incredibly naïve she had been. Blinded by youthful infatuation, she had failed to realise he had gone through with the marriage under a misguided sense of obligation due to her pregnancy, and regretted it almost instantly.

His parents were an old-fashioned couple with traditional values, and Dorothy suspected they had pressurised their son into doing the right thing by her. Well, the O'Keefes had not done her any favours. With all of her heart, she wished she had listened to her own parents' counsel, and stayed at home with her babies and taken her chances as a single mother.

With the arrogance of youth, she assumed she knew best and, as a direct result of her own folly, now found herself in a strange country with two toddlers relying upon her and hardly a bean of her own money. Completely dependent on a man who did not love her. Worse than that, dependent on a man who disliked her intensely, and blamed her for trapping him.

He did not even have enough respect or basic human compassion to attempt to hide his disdain, not just for her but also for their life together. He still made regular references to his 'glory days' before he had the misfortune to meet her. Those were dark times indeed and unknown to Dorothy, they were set to get a helluva lot darker as the months progressed.

Having accidentally discovered things were done differently in the UK, she put the twins' names down for a local nursery soon after they moved into the new house. There was a large one in Highbury with an excellent reputation. This was subsidised by the council, and as a result had a long waiting list.

Shortly after receiving her qualifications, the children were offered a morning placement. Dorothy raised the subject with Declan, who flatly stated he had zero intention of paying for his children to be looked after by strangers so his wife could laze around the house even more than she already did.

Having already anticipated this response, Dorothy agreed he was very likely right to veto the idea. 'I read somewhere it's not considered unhealthy for little boys to be interested in dolls,' she said, as she put his dinner in front of him. 'I'm sure Josh will be fine once he's older. It's hardly surprising he's taking such an interest in Diane's toys when she's the only other child he ever really sees.'

By the end of the meal, Declan had agreed to the twins attending nursery on a morning only basis, then stormed out of the house in a fit of temper.

The next day, Dorothy accepted the places, then went to the library where she spent three mornings typing up her CV and searching for a part-time job. A local hotel that could not afford a fulltime or experienced bookkeeper offered her a trial period. The salary was not exactly generous, but since Declan had agreed to pay the nursery fees, she was able to put almost all of it by in the secret bank account she had opened for herself.

The hotel chef occasionally offered her food parcels to supplement her income. Dorothy did not know if he had any ulterior motive in slipping her those parcels and did not care. If she had to sleep with him, or indeed any of the other staff in order to keep her job and maintain the status quo, she would gladly have done so. It was not as if her husband would care or notice, and truth be told, she would have been grateful for any hint of human kindness or gentle touch.

Neither the chef, nor anyone else for that matter, ever propositioned her. It was only as she grew older that she realised they must have had some inkling of the truth of her situation and pitied her. She often said a prayer of thanks for the employees of that hotel who had taken a chance on a young girl. For it was the job with its pitiful wage packet which ultimately enabled her to break free.

The idea for the driving lessons popped into her head one day when she was passing the test centre and felt the familiar tingle in her lower back indicating the clairs were trying to attract her attention.

Before she could talk herself out of it, she walked into the local driving school and booked her first lesson. It took four months to learn to drive on the Highbury streets. Partly because she could only afford to take one lesson per week, and partly because she was always rushing to collect the children from nursery. Even though she passed her test on the first attempt, she had no memory of it afterwards, and privately considered it a miracle.

18

By the time the twins turned three, Dorothy had purchased a used car spacious enough to comfortably hold her and the children, as well as two car seats and a pushchair.

To her everlasting shame and regret, one of the early casualties of a less than perfect life with Declan was her relationship with Josie. After a humdinger of an argument pertaining to Dorothy's horrendous taste in men, the other woman dropped her like a hot potato, and also advised Brenda to have nothing more to do with the family.

Rudy's career blossomed, but sadly for Dorothy, the new job he loved so much took him to the other end of the country. She began to wonder if she was cursed in the arena of relationships until fate intervened once more.

After assisting an elderly neighbour to his front door after he stumbled on the road, the pair struck up a friendship of sorts. Karl had lived in the same house for the past sixty years, and was not impressed when he realised the residents he regarded as blow-ins were snubbing Dorothy.

Having been around for eighty years, he was also something of an expert on men like Declan. He offered the use of his driveway to his new acquaintance so she would have a secure place to keep her car, thereby providing few chances for her husband to discover the existence of the vehicle.

The other neighbours unwittingly covered for her, their dislike of Declan ensuring they went out of their way to avoid him. Indeed, most of them would rather have stuck needles in their eyes than get involved in a conversation with the Irish buffoon from number 13, Rowntree Avenue.

The general animosity towards her husband worked in Dorothy's favour. Declan never discovered his wife had a part-time job or had learned to drive, passed her test, or bought the vehicle. On the days she worked at the hotel, she was home every day by two o'clock, and except for those evenings when Declan was 'out with the lads', his dinner was on the table every night on the dot of six.

He neither knew nor cared what she did as long as his home was kept clean, his children looked after, and his wife did not get under his feet or ask anything of him. Dorothy doubted he ever spared a thought for her or wondered how she spent her time. If asked, he probably would have said she sat around all day watching television and drinking coffee.

During the final year of the marriage, he chanced to come home early and discovered an empty house. When asked to account for her absence, Dorothy hastily invented a woman called Maria. She was not exactly a friend, she explained to Declan. More like an acquaintance she occasionally bumped into at the playground.

'Her husband is something important in the city,' she lied cheerily. 'She's not interested in a hick like me, but she's a kind lady and her son has taken a shine to the twins. We grab a coffee together once in a while when she's feeling magnanimous, or wants to brag about the new furniture she's bought for her house.'

Declan found this description of the relationship between the two women amusing, and asked no more about Maria. Dorothy's imaginary acquaintance became her alibi on the rare occasions one was required.

When she told the story years later, her real friends could not fathom how her absence from the house most weekday mornings would go unnoticed by her husband for such a long period. 'What about holidays and family occasions?' they used to ask.

The unhappy couple attended events that suited Declan, and put on a show for the families. Dorothy was often congratulated on her choice of a charming husband, which made her feel nauseous. She had to frequently remind herself that anybody can be fooled by an act, and tried not to feel bitter. After all, he had fooled her good and proper, and she had literally walked down the aisle with him.

To Dorothy's everlasting relief, they did not holiday together. Declan would not have dreamt of wasting weeks of his precious leisure time on his wife. He did take vacations, of course, and spent them with a variety of different mistresses, either at British seaside towns, or overseas at Spanish resorts which were all the rage at the time.

Those were the weeks Dorothy enjoyed the most. It was just her and the twins alone, with no chance of being interrupted by an unloving and unlovable spouse.

More than anything else, she was acutely aware that Declan would not willingly allow her to leave him. In many ways, he got a kick out of his persona as a successful man of business who had a house, a wife, a family, and plenty of golf and drinking buddies.

He would never admit to his friends and employees that his wife had abandoned him and taken his children.

From conversations they had shared over the years, she was acutely aware he would actively seek to stop her if she made any such attempt, and might even take drastic measures to prevent her leaving.

Dorothy lived in fear of him getting an inkling of what was on her mind, and subsequently absconding with the children. Knowing how ruthless he was and well aware of her own limited resources, she determined to stick with him until the bitter end, and give him no grounds for suspicion.

She gritted her teeth and learned to live with the horror of it all. Every night, she prayed he would not suspect her actions or motives, or that he was not having her watched. Every day, she put on a brave face and persevered with her plan, determined one way or another to break free of him and the nightmare into which her life had descended.

There's a special place in hell for men like Declan O'Keefe, she often used to tell herself, and it kept her going for one more day.

Once she had the car, she began to post small boxes of possessions to Bel, Simone, Amy, Vivian and Naomi, her particular friends back home. She mainly sent them to Bel, who still lived in her parents' ample property. Every month, she would gather up a bundle of knick-knacks she felt she could not live without. Baby photographs, mementos of a happier time, even ornaments and the odd book or tape.

She would wrap them protectively and place them in an empty carton discarded by the hotel. She would post the parcel to Bel, asking her to keep it safe, not to say a word to her parents and to sit tight and wait for an explanation. By now, Bel was engaged to Gerald and her other friends were also in serious relationships. They were puzzled by Dorothy's behaviour, but were sure its source would be revealed soon enough.

By all accounts, Declan was a partner in a thriving business, and had purchased a beautiful home for his wife and children. When Dorothy called her friends in Ireland, which she did every month, she sounded calm and did not complain of any problems with either the children or the marriage.

When the girls made enquiries of Pat and the sisters, they all said the same thing - Dottie was happy and settled in her new life. When the O'Keefes and Lyles visited the young couple in their stylish London home, they noticed that Declan was civil yet distant, but were inclined to put that down to the stress he was under while trying to create a fledgling business.

They were even inclined to believe it was somehow Dorothy's fault there was tension between them. After all, it was up to a woman to ensure a man did not feel any less loved and supported just because there were children in the house.

Dorothy had a good idea of the way their minds were working, although she did not bother to disabuse them of their notions concerning her husband's character. She was not certain they would believe her, and she knew that, in the face of such disbelief, she would in all likelihood break down. She took the decision to keep quiet for as long as it took to break free.

As she grew older, she often regretted she had left it for so long, although at the time she genuinely believed she was pursuing the proper course of action for all concerned.

Hence, for the three and a half years in which Dorothy lived in London as Declan's wife, she allowed her friends and family back home to believe her marriage, while not perfect, was at least bearable. The only person who had any inkling of the truth of the situation was Simone, and Dorothy begged her friend to keep schtum and wait for the plan to mature.

Dorothy made two foiled attempts to flee Rowntree Avenue before she eventually managed to break free. The first was during one of Declan's golfing trips, when she assumed she would have ample time and opportunity to get away before he returned. Her car broke down, and she was forced to not only abandon her flight plan, but also spend the majority of her precious escape fund getting the vehicle back on the road. The second attempt failed because Josh came down with a gastric bug the day before they were due to leave, and promptly passed it on to his sister.

Dorothy began to feel the universe might be trying to tell her something, and considered the very real possibility of giving up her bid for freedom. One month before the twins' fourth birthday, this defeatist attitude underwent an about turn.

As per her usual habit, she knocked on Karl's door one morning, but instead of being greeted by the stooped figure of the octogenarian, a woman she had never met before opened it. Unbeknownst to her, Karl had been hospitalised the previous day, and passed away during the small hours. It transpired the woman was Karl's ex-wife.

She invited Dorothy indoors and handed over an envelope the old man had left with her name on it.

There was a note inside that read, 'Get out while you still can, Dottie. Be gone by month end. In my younger days, I was a truly appalling husband, as Vera will testify. I am hoping to atone for past misdeeds by helping you now.' Under the short letter was fifteen hundred pounds in used notes and a ferry timetable.

Dorothy was heartbroken by Karl's death, but determined not to squander the opportunity offered to her. She reasoned if she burned her bridges, there would be less chance of failing in her mission. That same day, she told the hotel manager she was moving away, and gave him three weeks' notice.

He was sorry to see her go but said he understood, and promised her a few days' wages as a parting gift. Dorothy almost cried with gratitude. Two weeks before the twins' birthday, she asked Declan for a large sum of money so she could buy them the trampoline they wanted, and arrange some sort of birthday party. As she knew he would, Declan hesitated to acquiesce to the plan. Once again, she was ready for him.

'I know what you mean,' she said, as soon as she spotted the spiteful expression that crossed his face, and knew he was on the verge of refusing. 'It's very odd that none of your family is planning to visit for their birthday. I hope there aren't any health problems at home they haven't told you and Liam about.'

Fear flickered in Declan's eyes, and Dorothy resisted the urge to fist pump the air. Much as he hated to admit it, he knew the mere fact she had even raised the subject indicated his always-boring but frequently spooky little wife was undeniably in possession of information he lacked.

He grabbed the phone and demanded of his father what, if anything, he and Liam had not been told. Billy urged his son to calm down. His mother was fine. The lump in her breast had been biopsied, and was nothing more than a benign cyst. The family had been through an exhausting couple of weeks and were not ready to face a trip to the UK. They would be over to visit during July or August. When Billy asked after his daughter-in-law, Declan reluctantly handed over the phone.

Dorothy told Billy how sad she was about them not visiting for the birthday, and suggested it might not be a good idea to have a party at all. 'Maybe we should wait until you visit,' she said. 'They're only four after all. They might not even notice.'

Billy was horrified at the notion of the twins' not getting a party, as was his wife when she got on the line. They gave the young parents their orders, and said they were looking forward to seeing plenty of photographs of the big day. Accepting he was beaten, at least in the short-term, Declan handed over the price of the fictitious trampoline, as well as enough cash to pay for a lavish spread and suitable cake.

In addition to this, he gave Dorothy one hundred pounds, telling her to have her hair done and buy herself a new dress. This, she correctly surmised, was in case his brother, or any of his cronies, should happen to attend the party, and find Declan's wife less than immaculately attired in jeans that were four years old and boots with worn away soles. Dorothy smiled at her unloving, cheating, loser of a husband, thanked him for the cash, and assured him all would be ready in time for the party.

She had been subjected to many surprises during the years of her marriage. When she looked back afterwards, she decided one of the greatest was that Declan actually believed she knew enough people in the greater Highbury area to invite to a party of any description, even a children's one.

He had successfully driven away the only woman she valued after a most demeaning episode, and since then she had gone out of her way to avoid cultivating friendships. Twice a day, she ran in and out of the nursery like a madwoman, barely pausing to exchange a word with other parents in the same boat.

She knew the twins had special friends at nursery, but it certainly did not follow that she knew those children's parents or anything about them. Now that Karl had passed away, she was truly alone. Party indeed!

Taking into account her final salary yet to be paid; Dorothy was secure in the knowledge she now had almost three thousand pounds at her disposal. A veritable fortune to her back then, although she knew every penny would be needed to get back on her feet.

She spent a week sifting through every item of clothing she and the twins possessed, ruthlessly disposing of anything they had outgrown or which had become ragged. She steeled herself to climb the timber ladder and dragged a very old, large, and tatty suitcase down from the attic.

She packed it with everything they would not require for the final week, and then hid it in the boot of her car. Vera had told her she was welcome to use Karl's drive until the end of the month, but the house would have to be put on the market in early July.

Dorothy spent two days cleaning the house until it shone, ostensibly for the birthday party, but in reality to check if she had left anything behind she would later miss. She found enough items to make up one final box. Not wanting to overload the car, she speedily dispatched the parcel to Bel, grateful the postal rates in the UK were significantly cheaper than back home.

Bel had gotten into the habit of hiding the boxes in her parents' attic and not asking any questions. She was busy planning her wedding, and hoped Dorothy would make it home soon for her bridesmaid's dress fitting, and to explain the great box mystery.

On the morning of the day before the twins' fourth birthday, Dorothy told Declan she would be baking and preparing all day. She showed him the balloons she had purchased for the occasion, and a picture cut from a magazine depicting a lavish pink and blue birthday cake.

She claimed to have ordered the identical design from the local bakery. She spent five minutes fretting over the single cake, and questioning her own judgement in not ordering a separate one for each child.

When Declan began to look irate, she dropped the subject of the cake and suggested he try to eat out that evening, or even stay over at Liam's house. At this time, Declan was seeing a particularly buxom brunette from Camden Town, and was pleased with the excuse to spend the night with her. He promised to be home by the following lunchtime to help celebrate the big day.

When he questioned his wife about the trampoline she had allegedly purchased for the children, Dorothy assured him the shop would be delivering and assembling it on the morning of the party, although the twins would not actually lay eyes upon it until their guests arrived. Satisfied with her explanation, and anticipating a comfortable night away from his pathetic little wife and cute-but-boring children, Declan took himself off to work and from there to Camden Town for an evening of booze, food and casual sex with his not-so-lady love.

The very second his car left the driveway, Dorothy sprang into action. Within half an hour, she had put together a cooler containing a large packed lunch. Bottles of milk and water, a thermos of coffee, blankets, baby wipes, tissues, toys, and anything else she deemed necessary were packed into the car at lightning speed.

The final items she added were Joshua and Diane, carefully strapped into their car seats, tucked up in blankets, and handed their favourite toys and books.

By nine o'clock that same morning, she had reached the M25 ring road and the UK motorway network. She had to make three stops along the way so she and the twins could eat and use the toilets, yet still arrived at Holyhead port before 3.30 that afternoon, in plenty of time for the five o'clock ferry crossing.

The twins were as well behaved as could be expected from any almost four-year-olds, but nonetheless, when Dorothy rolled off the ramp at the North Wall ferry terminal in Dublin, she was close to collapse. Scarcely an hour later, Pat and Joey Lyle opened their front door and discovered their ashen-faced daughter trembling on the step. She was clutching each child by a grubby hand and was in a state of nervous exhaustion.

19

By the time Declan arrived home to Rowntree Avenue the next day, expecting to find a house full of noisy children, his own offspring in raptures over their expensive trampoline and all set to blow out the candles on the luxurious blue and pink cake, Dorothy had been asleep in her parents' spare bedroom for ten hours.

Her mother and sisters had taken over the care of her twins, even going so far as to organise an impromptu birthday party for them. By the time a worried sounding Declan telephoned the house at three o'clock, hoping for news of his children, Joey Lyle was ready for him. Having listened with increasing anger and dismay to Dorothy's miserable recital of her life in London, Joey was taking no prisoners.

After being forced to listen to his father-in-law tearing his character to shreds for five minutes, Declan was informed that if he wanted to see his children again, he had better hire himself a top-notch solicitor.

When he jumped on a plane and arrived in a fiery rage at the Lyle's front door, for all the world like a devoted husband betrayed by a wicked and devious spouse, he was met by the combined wrath of the Lyle clan. Declan stood on the doorstep and ranted until he turned red in the face, but nobody would give up Dorothy to him. In the end, he had no choice but to turn tail and head to his own family in West Dublin, in the hope they might render assistance.

When the O'Keefes showed up on the Lyle's doorstep, demanding to see their daughter-in-law and grandchildren, they were informed of their son's infidelities and general mistreatment of his wife. At first disbelieving, they were forced to take the accusations seriously when they called Liam in London and he admitted the truth.

Ten minutes prior to receiving the call from his hysterical mother and cranky father, the buxom brunette from Camden Town sat in Liam's office informing him of her pregnancy, courtesy of Declan O'Keefe's semen. Liam was in a rare fit of pique at his brother. Not just for taking off to Ireland at a moment's notice and abandoning the business, but also for leaving him to deal with his mistress. As a result, he ratted out Declan to the parents with as much spite as he could muster.

Liam O'Keefe's ire was quickly forgotten and he soon regretted his outburst when he was summoned home for a family meeting, the result of which was that for two days neither brother was on-site to nurture their business. Liam was a mere two years older than Declan and the pair had been close as boys. This bond had waned over the years, although they enjoyed a solid working relationship which was mutually satisfying, to say nothing of convenient.

Liam's nature was considerably softer than Declan's, and he found it difficult to meet his brother's eye when he arrived at the family home clutching a black holdall and a bag of duty-free goodies, which he hoped would go some way towards making up for his lapse in judgement and the subsequent histrionics by his mother.

Declan was seriously peeved with his sibling, and inclined to hold Liam responsible for the current mess in which he found himself with his parents. His feelings on the subject underwent a rapid change when it was forcibly borne upon him that Liam was the only member of the clan with any sympathy for his predicament.

Having initially assumed their son and his young wife were experiencing nothing more than run-of-the-mill marital teething problems, Mary and Billy were genuinely shocked to hear of Declan's philandering. They secretly hoped Dorothy would forgive his transgressions and give him another chance, while simultaneously accepting such an event was unlikely, given the existence of a mistress was bound to add an extra layer of permafrost to what were already bitterly cold relations.

Although this cocktail of infidelity and separation was by no means the trickiest problem the O'Keefes had encountered with their numerous children during their thirty-seven years of marriage, it was certainly up there in the top ten of offspring-related debacles.

As they had done many times in the past, Billy and Mary put their heads together and agreed on a strategy. While they did this and awaited the arrival of Liam from England, a fuming Declan was left to kick his heels and reflect on the ignominy of his spouse. By the time the family conference convened, he had worked himself into a royal rage and was ready to face down anybody who tried to get between him and his quarry.

The advantage of being intimately acquainted with Declan for twenty-six years stood his parents in good stead. They were prepared to do whatever it took to bring him to heel, and to that end had lined up the troops accordingly.

Flanked by their two eldest sons, the senior O'Keefes informed their youngest child that he had shamed them for the last time. He would return to the UK and focus his energies on making a success of the construction business, thereby freeing up and repaying the much-needed capital investment his parents had ploughed into the venture. He would leave Dottie alone and make no attempt to pursue or harass her in any way. The families would work out a way for him to see the twins without any further upset being caused to or by either party.

Declan heard his father out then curled his lip in derision. His green eyes flashed with fury and spite as he regarded their stern faces. Then he informed them he had zero intention of toeing the party line.

He went on to say if they expected him to sit back and allow the bitch he had married at their behest to simply steal his children away from him without making a move to stop her; they were seriously in need of an attitude adjustment.

At this point in the proceedings, Billy looked to his eldest son, a sturdy man of thirty-six who had been married since he was twenty-one and already had teenagers of his own. Noel stepped up close to his brother and, without further ado, hit the young man squarely in the face. Under the force of the blow, Declan dropped like a stone and found himself unable to move for almost five minutes. After a suitable length of time had passed, Liam was permitted to render assistance, and helped his errant brother into a chair.

'Are you receiving the message yet, son?' Billy O'Keefe asked quietly. 'Or shall I ask Ger to pick up where Noel left off? I'm prepared to wait all day if I have to, the choice is yours. The only thing you can be sure of is this. After today, you will leave Dottie in peace. You will return to England tomorrow, and concentrate on ensuring the company prospers so we can be repaid the money we lent you lads. If I hear either of you are bringing disgrace to the family in any way, I will take steps to rein in the pair of you. You have broken your mother's heart for the last time, boy. I advise you not to try my patience any further.'

Declan slowly got to his feet and faced his eldest brothers. He saw a distinctive martial glint in Ger's eyes, and knew the other man would like nothing better than to use him as a punch-bag, the blessing of his parents acting as an additional incentive.

'She's my wife,' Declan spoke sullenly through his rapidly swelling jaw. 'The bitch stole my children and expects to get away with it. Do you lot expect me to toddle off back to London and do nothing?'

'That's exactly what we expect,' Noel almost purred. 'Do as you're told or accept the consequences. If I hear you're harassing Dottie in any way, I will personally put your sorry carcase in the hospital. You won't be chasing many women with two broken legs.'

Declan looked at his mother, curious to see her reaction to this threat. Mary remained silent, her grave expression telling him more than any amount of words ever could. He mulled this unexpected development over for a minute and then addressed his father with, 'You'll make sure I don't lose touch with the twins?'

'Your mother and I will make it our business to see you have regular contact with them,' Billy spoke more gently this time. 'We've known Dottie since she was eighteen. She's a good girl. She won't try to turn them against you as long as you leave the access arrangements to us and stay out of her hair. You can count on us, son, but I need your word you'll stay in London where you belong and keep your nose clean.'

Declan mulled this over for another minute. Then he exhaled a long breath through his hooknose and nodded abruptly. 'I promise, Da,' he said in a low voice. 'Me and Liam will head home tomorrow and get back to work. By the time we're done, we'll make you proud.'

There was a collective sigh of relief from more than one person, and Mary O'Keefe put her hand to heart as if she was about to faint. Seeing this, her husband patted her on the back comfortingly. 'Put the kettle on, love,' he said kindly. 'Let's drink a toast to our lads.'

Once his two youngest sons had been waved off at the airport, Billy made it his business to visit Dorothy and let her know she had nothing to fear from her husband. When she burst into tears and cast herself into his arms, he held her against his solid body and gently stroked her back until she had no tears left.

He kissed her cheek and told her he was sorry things had worked out so badly for her. Then he headed home to tell Mary that Dottie would be staying with her family for the time being, meaning there would be plenty of support available to her.

Pressed to do so by all parties, Dorothy remained with her parents and lived off her escape fund for the remainder of that summer and autumn. Even though she was a long way from feeling normal, she slowly regained the weight she had shed during the previous year, and began to cautiously look forward to a new life. True to his word, Declan stayed away and she began to sleep better, knowing he was unlikely to show up unexpectedly.

Shortly after the twins started school, she began to look around for a job, and also expressed her intention of moving to her own place. She was grateful for all the family support, but never again wished to live in somebody else's house.

Once the children were safely settled in school, she applied for, and was offered, a part-time role with Premier Payroll and Accounting Solutions in Dublin city centre. She was not to know back then it would be the last job for which she would ever apply. Over the course of the following three years, Dorothy and the twins settled into a routine of work and school, very much like any other lone-parent family. She was soon able to increase her working hours and even began to hope that one day, in the not too distant future, she would be able to buy a house for the three of them.

True to their word, Billy and Mary mediated between the warring couple. Sensing she was in their debt and wanting to repay her in-laws for their assistance with Declan, Dorothy agreed to her husband having contact with the children whenever he came to Dublin, providing it was under the supervision of his parents.

It was not that she harboured illusions he loved the twins enough to steal them away from her, although she often wondered if he would try to take them out of a misguided sense of ownership, or possibly out of sheer spite.

Somewhat to her surprise, Declan never attempted anything of the kind, and in 1998, when the twins were seven, the reason became clear. The buxom brunette from Camden Town had brought forth a son for Declan, and the couple had been secretly living together for two years.

There was no way seven-year-old twins would have been welcomed into their cosy nest, especially not the offspring of Declan's legal spouse. The brunette, who went by the name of Lelia, exerted pressure on her lover to obtain a divorce and marry her.

As Declan was the one who lived in the United Kingdom, where divorce was almost run of the mill, he was the one who petitioned the court. Acting on the advice of his solicitor, he not only requested six formal visits with his children each year, but also offered maintenance for their upkeep.

Dorothy was initially inclined to reject his offer out of hand, but her mother intervened, and Mary O'Keefe also took it upon herself to add a word of encouragement. She said Declan was doing well for himself in London and had a duty to his children.

This intercession gave Dorothy pause for thought and she forced herself to sit down and consider the financial aspects of the situation. She came up with an idea which was more palatable to both parties than some of the alternatives, and an agreement was subsequently reached between the estranged pair.

Instead of paying monthly maintenance, Declan created a college fund in the sum of four thousand pounds for each child per annum. This agreement would expire on their eighteenth birthday, by which time they should have enough money accumulated for their continued education. The contact arrangements were also formalised.

Dorothy had to accept the fact that, as the twins grew older, they would travel to London to visit their father and spend time with their stepmother and half-brother.

Initially she found this galling, although as the years went by it grew easier. The twins would look forward to the visits, but always seemed relieved to be home again and certainly were never the worse for wear.

They were fond of their little brother, Roger, and tended to treat him as something of a pet. As long as they stayed out of Lelia's way and did not annoy her, she treated them with civility, and on occasion even showed them a measure of kindness which was unexpected.

As if finding herself newly divorced at twenty-eight years of age was not exciting enough, another life changing event was on its way. Dorothy's paternal grandparents passed away within a year of each other, and left the family home in the much sought after village of Rathmichael to their eldest son.

Pat and Joey sold the Dún Laoghaire house in which they had lived for decades, and moved to the old homestead where the air was definitely cleaner. After all of their affairs were settled, they gave each of their daughters the equivalent of twenty thousand euro, which back in those days was still the Irish punt. In 1998, that was enough for a deposit on a house, and Dorothy had already saved enough to cover the other expenses.

After scouring what felt like the entire southeast for a suitable abode, she eventually purchased a semi-detached house in Shankill, close to the border with County Wicklow. The property was structurally sound, but looked as if it had not seen a lick of paint in two decades. It had three bedrooms, a reasonable sized garden, and a driveway large enough to accommodate one car.

It had the advantage of being situated at the end of the row of houses, which meant the plot was slightly larger than the rest. The only downside was the proximity to the ramshackle laneway accessing the derelict property known as Bluebell Wood, a place which had attracted its fair share of trouble over the years.

Dorothy reasoned that living close to an empty house was better than backing on to a noisy estate with heavy traffic and God knows what other social problems. She shared these thoughts with her parents. They agreed the location seemed quiet and since it was barely half a mile to the DART, the commute to Premier would be straightforward.

Joey speculated about the possible future residents of Old Hen Cottage, which was separated from the prospective new home by the laneway. Pat agreed it would be a disaster if it was bought up only to be demolished in favour of a monstrosity that would spoil the lovely aspect of the area, but reasoned there was no sense in worrying over something which would likely never happen. Dorothy heard her parents out. Then she took a couple of very deep breaths and made an offer on the house.

Financially speaking, she pushed herself to the limit in order to make the purchase. Not only did she never intend to remarry, she never intended to move again. Not for a moment did she fool herself into believing she was putting her foot on the first rung of the property ladder. As far as Dorothy was concerned, she had reached the top rung and was making herself comfortable for the long haul.

By the time the twins were twelve and living in a new millennium had become almost commonplace, Pat and Joey had finished renovating their Rathmichael home, and Joey had started dropping hints about selling his pharmacy and retiring. Bel and Gerald had been happily married for seven years and had two sons.

Gemma and Orla had distinguished themselves, firstly at college and thereafter in their chosen careers. Both women had married and started families. Simone had realised her life-long ambition. She had qualified as an architect and was working at one of the most prestigious firms in Dublin.

During her post college years, but before she got married and became a mother, Vivian somehow found the time to travel the world, telling them all she needed to get the wanderlust out of her system before she knuckled down and made her fortune in the business world.

Amy had been working as a teacher at secondary level for six years, and never tired of complaining about the students' wild behaviour and the parents' overbearing attitude.

Naomi had secured a job with the RTÉ concert orchestra and cherished high hopes for her musical future. Dorothy had forged an unlikely friendship with a British man called Horace Johnson. She had also redecorated the Shankill house, occasionally with the hands-on assistance of Horace, and at other times employing tradesmen to deal with jobs she was unable to handle alone.

She had been promoted to the role of assistant supervisor of the payroll department, and expected another promotion within three years due to the imminent retirement of the existing post holder.

Even though she occasionally felt lonely, especially when she saw the closeness other couples enjoyed, she never regretted leaving Declan. She occasionally dated for a few weeks or months at a time, but always broke it off as soon as she felt things were becoming serious, or as happened in a couple of instances, as soon as she spotted any character trait in the man in question that inspired unwelcome memories of her former husband.

Dorothy had learned a very hard lesson. A lesson she was not likely to forget, and was not about to allow any man past her defences any time soon. Given what life had thrown at her during her thirty-two years, she was as content with her lot as any woman with her history had a right to expect.

20

With the exception of the roast chicken dinner Josh and Deco had enjoyed at Dorothy's house, the O'Keefe twins had scarcely laid eyes upon their mother since the evening they had joined the rest of the family in celebrating her fortieth birthday.

As per her usual custom, she had called them a couple of times each week, but instead of inviting them to their old home for Sunday dinner, or asking if they required any assistance with their laundry, she had been vague and almost distant.

Diane experienced her fair share of guilt pangs over the situation, feeling she was somehow responsible for the widening gap in relations. She suspected her mum had stopped suggesting she visit because it was rare for her to venture into the Shankill area.

When the girl tentatively enquired if all was well, Dorothy reminded her daughter that January was the busiest month in any payroll department, and she had to work overtime merely to keep up. She went on to inform Diane that as soon as the January madness was behind her, she fully intended to get away for a well-deserved break with Bel, and would catch up with her children as soon as she returned.

When Diane passed this news on to her brother, he was delighted. He advised his twin to set aside all her concerns, at least for the time being.

'Mum's busy. There's nothing wrong with her, and she's certainly not avoiding us for some inexplicable or sinister reason,' he said decisively. 'Not everything is about *you*, Di. Mum has her own issues, and that company of hers has been running her ragged for the past couple of years. Let's hope a few days away with Bel helps to recharge the old batteries.'

For all his grown-up talk, Joshua could not help a sigh of relief when he received the phone call inviting him and his sister to Howth for a pow-wow. His gut told him something was going on with his mother, and he was looking forward to seeing for himself that all was well.

When Dorothy went on to say she had a Valentine's gift for him and his twin they would not forget in a hurry, he felt a frisson of excitement run through him. It was agreed that he and Di would catch a DART and meet Dorothy at Howth station. Talk amongst their friends had already turned to festival season, and both young people secretly hoped the gift would be cash, maybe even as much as two hundred euro each.

Pleased the plan was in motion, Dorothy spent a leisurely Saturday unpacking her cases and visiting her family in order to give them all her news. It had been more than two weeks since Pat and Joey had last seen their daughter, and were surprised at how well she looked, and at how much weight she had lost.

Dorothy was gratified to hear this was noticeable. She could feel the weight loss in her clothes, but as Bel had not commented on it, she assumed nobody else would either. On the contrary, not only did they notice, they thought she looked fantastic, and cautioned her not to overdo it. This amused her greatly, especially as the personal trainer had advised her to lose another thirty pounds for the sake of her health.

~~~

From: Dottie8888@chatulike.ie
To: SRedmond@chatchat.com
Date: February 12th, 2011
SUBJECT: CHAUFFEURS AND TWINS
G'day Simone,
I am safely back in the Emerald Isle and all is well. Luckily, the return trip to Dublin was uneventful. We travelled in a similar jet to the one on the outbound journey, which apparently is called an Astra.

    I didn't feel like such a fraud this time. I keep expecting to wake up from a dream, or suddenly find myself detained and arrested, charged with impersonating a rich person. Needless to say, all the pampering at the spa really helped. It's not so easy to stress out over things after being massaged to within an inch of one's life.

    The pilot on the outbound trip was a ten on the rideometer scale, and Bel totally embarrassed me by prying into his private life. I was grateful a female pilot flew us home. I will tell you more about that when we next speak.

    Eamonn collected us from the airport. That's the same chauffeur who delivered us there. The funniest thing happened. Bel got really annoyed with me, although I had no clue what I had done wrong. I was chatting away to Eamonn and making him laugh with my description of the terrible cramps in my arms and legs during my first few days on the treadmill and rower.

    It was only later the penny dropped when Bel started lecturing me on being overly familiar with the 'staff'. Of course, I didn't take the little rant too seriously. After all, I've known the woman for almost four decades. She might be a little prickly at times, but she has a heart of gold. I was just wishing you were there to hear it, that's all, because she was so funny.

Gerald has whisked her off somewhere fancy for the weekend because it's Valentine's Day on Monday (yawn), which means I won't see her for a while. I am due to meet the kids on Sunday to tell them the news.

I promised I would drop by Saul's house in Swords first, because he wants to show me the designs he came up with for the Dohenys. I am interested in looking at them out of interest, although I feel it would be better to commission my own plans.

Are you sure you don't want to come home and design a house for me? I told the twins I have a special Valentine's gift for them. They are the last of the immediate family to hear my news, and I hope they don't kill me. I wanted to take a little time before telling them. I want to be able to say I have a plan in place for their future, or at least the beginnings of a plan. I will keep you posted. Love ya. Hi to C. Dot xx

~~~

On Sunday morning, as Dorothy set off for Swords, she was conscious she had a difficult decision to make. The existing, and as yet unseen designs for the house, had already received full planning approval. If she liked the look of Saul's ideas and wanted to plough ahead with them, the building work could commence as soon as the purchase of the land was finalised.

If she did not feel the plans would suit, she would have to begin the design process all over again, followed once again by the planning application. All of this could potentially add anywhere between six months and two years to the completion of the build.

She wondered if Saul had included a hot tub in his design for Anna and Phil. She had devoted a full twenty minutes to painstakingly examining a picture of one in a glossy magazine she had picked up while indulging herself at the Champney's hairdressers. In addition to an opening roof, it had its own transparent enclosure that trapped the heat during the day so it could be used even during the harshest of winters.

Dorothy could readily imagine herself lying back in her new tub and admiring the full moon, possibly even sipping a glass of wine and listening to music. She was also looking forward to seeing Saul's ideas for the kitchen. The one in Shankill had always been a source of irritation. No matter how many times she painted it or tried to brighten it up, she could not get away from the fact it was simply too small.

Of course, she did not need as much space now the twins were living away from home, but all the same she would like a proper family sized kitchen and one of those en-suite bathrooms. The ones estate agents on the television adored, and kept insisting every house needed in order to make it sellable.

Dorothy spotted Saul's car as soon as she got within twenty yards of his house. She pulled her Focus in behind it, grateful the substantial drive was more than large enough to accommodate two vehicles. Then she jumped out and rang the doorbell of the large, detached house.

Since it looked ideal for her needs, she hoped the architect was about to show her a set of drawings for something similar. She was sure she could see the pointed roof of a conservatory around the back, but was reluctant to crane her neck like a nosy neighbour.

The front door opened and Dorothy was surprised to discover that in addition to Saul being married to a beautiful and rather voluptuous girl called Ryanna, they had four children under the age of ten. While she was still trying to absorb Ryanna's long dark hair, jet black eye lashes, almond shaped hazel eyes and womanly hips, the other woman had already introduced herself and the children, and ushered the guest into her husband's office. She offered to bring them coffee then made herself scarce.

After they spent ten minutes catching up and comparing notes on their recent activities, Saul unrolled the plans. He laid them out on his custom-made desk and turned his computer screen around so Dorothy could view them in 3D. For a few moments, she merely sat and stared at the monitor. Then she gawked at the drawings on the desk. Then she sat back on her chair and put a hand to her heart.

Saul sustained a severe shock when he witnessed this gesture, and quickly brought her a bottle of water from a mini-fridge beneath the desk.

'Do you want me to call an ambulance?' he enquired solicitously. 'Do you have a heart condition?'

'No thanks, I'll be fine in a minute,' she gasped. 'I'm having a Victor moment.'

'A what?'

'A Victor moment. It's that sort of feeling you get when something unexpected happens and it knocks the wind right out of you.'

'Why do you call it a Victor moment?' he asked curiously.

Dorothy sat up straighter and did her best to pull herself together. 'I'm not sure,' she replied slowly, still rubbing her chest where the Space Ache had briefly flared. 'I find that giving things a name helps me to deal with them better. It's particularly true of emotional reactions. Victor is my ex-fiancé. Alas, he was not the most intelligent of human beings. Every so often, he would say something either incredibly crass or just plain stupid, and it would completely knock me for six. 'Victor Moments' is the name I gave the reaction I had at those times. Bowled over or gobsmacked doesn't even come close.'

Despite himself, Saul looked intrigued. 'What sort of things would he say?' he prodded, and Dorothy mentally cursed herself. She hated talking about Victor, yet she was the one who had brought it up, hence could hardly blame Saul for wanting more information. 'Once, for example,' she said quietly. 'I was telling him a friend's baby had to have an operation, and the doctors administered a blood transfusion.'

'So?'

'He asked me if that was when the doctors drained all the blood out of a person's body, and replaced it with fresh stuff.'

The architect's mouth dropped open and he sat down very suddenly and stared at her without speaking.

'Now *you're* having a Victor moment,' she tried not to sound too gleeful.

'How old was this eejit…thirteen?' Saul seemed quite put out by her little Victor anecdote.

'When we first met he was thirty-three, ergo a tad older than thirteen I'm sorry to say. No excuse.'

'And you were engaged?'

'Yep. For a year. Until I woke up one day and smelled the coffee. I'm ashamed to say it was a long time coming. I kept telling myself I was imagining things, or it was all my fault. Victor used to frequently tell me it was all my fault, which slowed down the waking up process considerably.'

'At least you didn't marry the gobshite,' Saul was looking more cheerful and inclined to see the funny side. 'Think how bad you'd be feeling now if you had to share your winnings with a borderline retard. What was your pet name for him? Rain Man?'

'Saul, that's not exactly politically correct. Please say special needs as opposed to retard,' Dorothy reproved.

He sniggered unrepentantly and pointed to the plans on the screen. 'Ready to try again?'

For fifteen minutes, she remained silent and allowed the architect to talk her through the designs. In his attempts to explain the layout, he mainly used his computer and occasionally the hard copy drawings. When he paused to take a sip of water, she raised her hand. 'Just let me see if I have this straight, okay?'

'Sure, go ahead,' Saul waved to indicate she should start talking.

Dorothy took a deep breath and began to speak slowly, trying to remember everything he had said. 'The property is in three distinct parts. There's a large central residence and two side buildings like wings. The main house faces east/southeast, and is built over four floors. As it ascends, each floor gradually becomes smaller. The lower ground floor will be built inside the hill, and this holds the media centre, the games room, and those sorts of things.

'The ground floor is where the kitchen and reception rooms will be located, and the top two floors are mainly made up of bedrooms. As I look at the front of the house, the left wing, for want of a better word, is what you have named the pavilion. This is essentially an entertainment room for parties and whatnot, although it's only single storey. This pavilion is reached by a glass walkway which is situated somewhere around the study in the main house.'

She briefly hesitated, but as Saul made no attempt to interrupt, assumed she was doing quite well and soon continued.

'The right wing is what you have named the leisure complex. This holds the swimming pool, the gym, the sauna, and things of that nature. Attached to this complex is a triple garage. There is no glass walkway on that side of the house, as it would make access to the back of the property damn near impossible for either vehicle or human.

'To circumvent the problem of possibly having to venture out into the unpredictable Irish elements, you are proposing to build an underground tunnel which will link the lower ground floor to the leisure complex. Somewhere at the back of the site, Phil asked you to add a soundproofed studio with dimensions similar to a two-bedroom apartment. On the southeast end, about a hundred yards away from the house, there will be two tennis courts with their own changing area. Because the changing rooms will also be built inside the hill, the roof will be at ground level and can be utilised as a sundeck. How am I doing?'

'Not bad for a novice,' he replied, watching her face anxiously. 'What do you think so far?'

Looking and feeling as if she was about to burst into tears, Dorothy gazed at him with something approaching horror. 'I forgot Phil was a rock-star,' she whispered dejectedly. 'I thought it would be a normal, five-bedroom, detached house with a double garage and a conservatory. My mother loves a conservatory. I was looking forward to telling her all about it. I thought the pool house would be like one of those cute wooden summerhouse styles with a pitched roof you sometimes see on the TV. I thought it would be normal like *your* house, Saul.

'A lovely house, of course, but nonetheless a normal one. A house I could live in on my own. It's a fecking mansion. No wonder you said I'd need a handyman. I'd probably need two of them just to change the light bulbs. I feel like such an idiot now.'

Saul managed to look both startled and upset at the same time. 'So you don't like it?' he asked, trying to sound detached and professional, but clearly disappointed.

'Of course I like it,' she protested. 'Who wouldn't like it? It's a masterpiece of design. Even I can see that, and I know next to nothing about such matters. It's just it's massive, and I'm only one person. You'd need six children to fill that house, not to mention an extra-large spouse. One who liked to spread himself around and had tonnes of hobbies and interests. The sort of man who's always bringing the local football team home for dinner.'

'Phil and Anna were intending to have four children.' Saul sounded bleak, and Dorothy immediately felt bad for reminding him of the tragic events that had been the trigger for their first meeting.

'Before we go any further, I need to ask you some questions,' she jumped in, hoping to distract him from his momentary sadness.

'Okay. Shoot.'

'I'm used to a square or rectangular house, but this one curves, is that right?'

He smiled proudly as he nodded. 'Usually a square or rectangular design is better suited to the smaller site, where size most definitely matters. Here, there are no such restrictions because you have over three acres to play with. I've chosen a curved style in order to utilise the best possible use of light and space.'

'Does that mean it will feel curved inside?' She hoped she did not sound stupid.

'It won't be like living in a windmill or a lighthouse, although you'll certainly notice the house flows differently, and feels more spacious and open than anything you have been used to before now.'

'Won't the view of the bay be restricted by the leisure complex?'

'No, not at all. Here, check it out on the screen again. The complex is situated slightly to the west of the main house, and it's single storey. The house will be elevated in comparison, which means there won't be any restricted views or light issues. It will be beautiful.' He sighed heavily.

'It's an amazing design. You should be very proud,' Dorothy said, as she stared first at him and then at the plans on the screen. 'It's definitely a house for a rock-star, though.'

'Or a Euromillions winner,' Saul replied in a hollow voice, trying not to succumb to the disappointment.

'A Euromillions winner indeed,' she murmured, thinking about the pool. How was she to explain the dream? A tingle started in her lower back and she shivered. His head shot up and he stared at her in alarm.

'I don't like the location of the garage,' Dorothy felt close to desperation as she uttered the words. She was determined not to allow the tingles to grow any worse, but at the same time was genuinely flummoxed by the scale of the house.

What did the universe want from her? She was only one woman for feck sake! Saul did not come across as the sort of man who would appreciate a story about a dream, yet she had to start somewhere. Besides, despite her worst fears, Simone had not reacted badly.

'In fact, the layout of the leisure complex is my only real gripe. That and the sheer size of the place, of course.' She made a concerted effort to get a grip on herself.

'What were you thinking?' Saul tried not to get his hopes up, although he could sense she was possibly coming around, albeit only a tiny bit, to the notion of living in a mansion.

'I'd like the garage over here,' Dorothy indicated a spot on the drawings. 'Close to the studio, but not too close. It should be large enough to accommodate six cars, and have an apartment built over it. I'd still like the leisure complex kept the same size or made even larger.'

'Why?' he asked, clearly puzzled by this unexpected request.

'The pool is too short and it needs to be a diving pool,' was the calm response.

21

In response to this, Saul began to blink rapidly. At this juncture, Ryanna erupted into the room carrying a tray bearing coffee and biscuits.

'I am soooo sorry for the delay,' she sounded out of breath. 'The kids started eating crayons as an experiment, and then I had to break up a fight. How are you two getting on?'

'Saul has created a magnificent design,' Dorothy beamed. 'You must be very proud of him. We're discussing the small changes I fancy making to the leisure complex. The main residence looks fantastic, assuming the stairs don't open directly on to the front door. That's terrible Feng Shui.'

'No, no,' the stairs are on a curve off-centre to the front, so there's no chance of that.' Ryanna oozed calm, like somebody who spent all day quelling children's high spirits. As the other woman poured the coffee, Dorothy saw her exchanging glances with her husband.

She enjoyed watching the silent communication passing between the couple. 'Seal the deal, Saul,' Ryanna was saying with her eyes. It made Dorothy want to laugh aloud. Poor Saul. He was going to be in deep shit if he did not get a result, that much was clear.

Even if he had received payment from the Dohenys for the house design (which was unlikely, given that Anna would hold legal title to them if he had) the money must be long gone. Chances were, he had lived off it for the past year. Now he was in need of more income, and there was nothing quite like having a multimillionaire sitting across from you to get the financial juices flowing.

What was the worst that could happen if she told him about the dream? Simone had not been shocked. On the contrary, she insisted she and Charlie were fascinated by the story, and urged Dorothy to immediately inform them if she experienced any more unusual occurrences.

Perhaps Charlie is part Aborigine and has a penchant for the supernatural? I wish Simone would hurry up and send a few photos so I can test my theory. Does he have very dark hair and a very deep tan and brown eyes?

Dragging her thoughts away from the Australian outback, Dorothy pretended to sound more pensive and hesitant than she actually felt.

'You know, Saul,' she said slowly, 'if we could agree the changes to the pool and garage, and a couple of small adjustments to the layout of the main house, I might be tempted to proceed with this design even though it is rather large for my current needs. As you correctly point out, I *am* a lottery winner. I might suddenly develop a large circle of acquaintances. I hear that can often happen when one unexpectedly becomes uber-rich.'

Inside her chest, the Space Ache began to hum in earnest. *Stop messing about! You haven't hummed in years so don't start playing up now!*

'Saul will accommodate you in any way he can, Dorothy, you can be assured of that,' Ryanna spoke the words firmly. 'I'll leave you to discuss the details.' As she left the room, she threw a final speaking glance at her husband, and Dorothy imagined her high-fiving her children next door.

Knowing she had him, she smiled brightly at the architect. There was no way he was going to refuse any request she might make, subsequently risking the wrath of his spouse.

'You had better tell me more about this pool of yours,' Saul looked resigned to his fate.

'I had a dream,' she smiled warily.

'Pardon? Are we Martin Luther King now?' he snapped.

'Try to be nice, Saul,' Dorothy smiled sweetly. 'Don't make me call Ryanna. While I was in Champneys, I had the same dream about the pool three nights in a row. Would you like to hear about it?'

He sighed with exasperation. 'Go ahead. Sure why not?'

After taking a deep breath, she told him about the tall man with the Sam Elliot voice, the diving boards, the whale mosaic and the scaffolding tower. Saul listened patiently and tried not to look incredulous. At the end of her recital, he scowled. 'You want to excavate the equivalent of five stories so you can have a diving pool,' he stared at her stonily.

Seeing her baffled expression, he smirked. 'You may well look perplexed, Dorothy Lyle,' he said snidely. 'For your information, a safe diving pool depth is a minimum of sixteen feet. That's the equivalent of excavating four stories. In this case, you can add on at least one more as a precaution, because we cannot risk obstructing the view from the house. Of course, that's only my opinion.

'The engineers might recommend excavating as many as six stories. Dorothy, you're talking thousands of man-hours of construction time and huge...no...colossal expense. You'd need a specialist team to oversee the construction, and I'm breaking out in a sweat here just thinking about the bills. The finished product would be similar to the National Aquatic Centre, and no offence intended, but you don't strike me as a woman who's interested in a place on the Olympic diving team. All this because of some fella in a dream who could swim like a dolphin and sounded like a film star. Are you sure you weren't drunk?'

'Does this mean you're not prepared to accommodate me?' she enquired, as soon as he had run out of things to say.

'Naturally I can amend the plans any way you like,' he sounded borderline hostile now. 'That's not a problem. I only hope when you actually get to the building phase, you don't run into difficulties because of your dreams!'

'I'm not worried about that,' Dorothy maintained her cool, determined to remain calm in the face of his ire.

'Why not?' he barked, making her jump.

Ryanna chose that moment to re-enter. She had been listening at the door and could no longer bear the tension. 'Everything okay?' she enquired brightly.

'We're just getting to the project management part of the conversation.' Dorothy smiled at the other woman, wishing she had a wife like Ryanna watching out for her, yet at the same time accepting it was a ridiculous notion.

'Are you offering the job to Saul?' enquired his worried spouse.

'If he's interested,' Dorothy smiled kindly. 'I certainly wouldn't want anybody else to manage this build for me. After all, it *is* Saul's baby.'

Across the desk, the architect did not seem quite so enthusiastic.

'He's not being awkward.' Ryanna looked embarrassed at her husband's blatant absence of goodwill. 'He's not very good at talking about money, and he can't really commit without a ballpark figure from you. With one thing and another, things haven't been great for us during the past couple of years. Truth be told, Dorothy, they've been pretty dire.' Ryanna sniffed and her voice became watery.

Dorothy's smile grew warmer and she resisted the urge to gather the taller woman into her arms and hug her until she squeaked. She assumed her most grown-up expression and addressed Saul with, 'Considering I'm rich beyond the dreams of avarice, the fee is hardly a problem. Why don't you write down the amount you agreed with Phil and Anna for the design, and also for your services as project manager?'

After a swift glance at his wife, Saul grabbed a scrap of paper and, after scribbling two numbers on it, passed it across the desk. Dorothy peered at it for a moment and ran through some calculations in her head.

She said, 'I have no problem with the cost for the design. However, I think you should add twenty percent to your fee because it looks a little on the low side. I don't know what the Dohenys were expecting from you, but I'm a total rookie when it comes to this sort of thing. I'll need you to devote the rest of the year to this build, and I'll be requiring tonnes of support and advice. How does that sound?'

'That would be fine, thank you, Dorothy,' Saul replied quietly.

She saw the couple exchange another glance and sighed to herself. She lifted her pen and, holding it aloft like Ebenezer Scrooge who has recently awoken and discovered he hasn't missed Christmas after all, Dorothy looked Ryanna Newman firmly in the eyes and said, 'Naturally I intend to pay you a retainer. Heaven forbid you should go running off to Canada as soon as my back is turned.'

She made an effort to sound chipper and found herself wishing for the first time in a month she could indulge in a large glass of wine. Suddenly recalling a pen was no good without the accompanying chequebook, she grabbed her bag and produced the plastic covered item with suitable dramatic flair.

'How much?' she asked Ryanna, still maintaining a hint of the theatrical. 'Ten...twenty...thirty thousand?'

'Could you make it thirty thousand, please?' Despite Dorothy's best efforts to cheer her up, the other woman still sounded subdued. 'As I said before, things are not good right now.'

'I'll make it thirty-five to be on the safe side.' Dorothy speedily completed the cheque, signed her name with a flourish then passed it, not to Saul, but to his wife.

As she took it, Ryanna smiled gratefully and looked a little tearful. Feeling she could do no more for the Newmans that day, Dorothy began to pack up her things, saying, 'I have to head off now because I'm meeting my children, but perhaps we could continue our discussions tomorrow?'

'No problem. Where are you meeting them?' Saul sounded more civil now his fee had been agreed and the down payment in safe hands.

'Howth, strangely enough. I'm planning to show them the general area of the Baily and take them for lunch. I have a Valentine's present for them they won't forget in a hurry.'

'That sounds lovely,' Ryanna sounded envious.

Dorothy smiled warmly and firmly reminded herself that God had sent her the money for a reason. 'Why don't you all come with me? You can meet the twins and have lunch with us. My treat. Some fresh air will do us all good. Saul can bring the keys to the site and we can have a proper viewing. My kids would love that.'

The couple immediately brightened at the prospect of an outing, and she wondered how long it had been since they had been able to take the children anywhere. How long had they been hanging around the house, worrying themselves sick about money, and asking themselves and each other if they should take a chance on emigration, leaving poor grieving Anna to fend for herself.

The children were swiftly bundled into warm clothing and boots. Even though Saul's car was designed to hold six bodies, it was agreed that he and his wife would take the two youngest with them, while the older two accompanied Dorothy.

She had not yet had time to even think about changing her Focus, and Saul teased her unmercifully about it. They agreed that, should the chance present itself, it would be fun to pop into the dealership in Howth, and maybe pick up a few ideas.

~~~

From: Dottie8888@chatulike.ie
To:SRedmond@chatchat.com
Date: February 13th, 2011
SUBJECT: ROCK-STAR PAD
G'day Simone love,

I hope you and Charlie are well. I am dropping you a quick line from my new phone. This one has internet access and does weird things I haven't worked out yet. The camera is much better than my old model, which is why I chose it.

I have decided to build a rock-star mansion on the plot of land in Howth. You are not going to believe the scale of it. I will try to mail you something if I can. I'm not sure if I am doing the right thing, but I feel almost compelled to build the diving pool, and I don't know how to achieve it any other way.

It was either go with what Saul already had (which has permission for a pool), or wait another year for a new design and planning approval. I know I should have waited and asked him to design me something smaller and more manageable, but I am nervous the dreams will start again.

Please don't think I am crazy. Saul is not happy about the diving pool, but his wife made it clear he has to accommodate me. I think they have fallen on hard times. I am sure the widowed sister is keeping them afloat. That isn't an enviable situation for anybody, especially a man like Saul who seems to be the proud sort.

Nothing wrong with a bit of pride, of course, but it doesn't keep a roof over the heads of four children. Back soon. Hi to C. Love Dot x

22

After grabbing the last two parking spaces within easy reach of the station, Dorothy explained to the Newmans that she wanted to take her kids up to the site and break the news to them there.

If they thought it was odd she had not yet told her children of her good fortune, they refrained from comment, and agreed to the plan in an amicable way. Diane and Josh emerged from the station and promptly fell upon their mother in true Lyle fashion, hugging, kissing and tickling her.

Begging for mercy, Dorothy wriggled out of their combined embrace. She stared first at one child and then the other. Josh's hair had grown a fraction and looked unruly and windswept. He had a piercing in his left ear she was positive was new.

She decided not to draw attention to it, and hoped it would be his one and only mutilation, and he had refrained from having any other part of his anatomy punctured in the name of fashion. It was Diane who interested her the most. She turned a piercing stare on her daughter and sent out the Dorothy Feelers.

'Please, Mum,' the girl sounded exasperated. 'There's no need to do the weird alien probe thing. I'm fine, I promise. Just busy at college and all that.'

'Sorry, love,' her mother smiled. 'I can see you're both fine and you're looking particularly lovely today. New coat?'

Diane *was* looking lovely. Unlike her brother, who suffered from the occasional outbreak, her skin was clear and glowed a delicate shade of pink from the cold Howth breeze. Her hair was long, blonde and poker straight, the way she liked it.

On top, she had perched a miniature beanie in dark green felt, which Dorothy was sure Emily had unearthed in a second-hand shop. She was wearing a navy-blue coat with large gold buttons down the front that was almost certainly vintage. It hugged Diane's miniature figure and gave her a very womanly appearance.

Emily was studying fashion design at the National College of Art and Design, and had clearly been busy restyling her best friend, and presumably herself as well.

'Who are those people, Mum?' Josh poked her in the arm to attract her attention, recalling Dorothy to both her surroundings and manners.

She quickly introduced the Newman family, then told the twins they were going to visit a special place as she had something of particular importance to tell them. By now, Josh and Diane had ceased worrying about the state of their mother's health.

Whatever she had been doing in the UK with Bel had left her positively blooming with vitality in a way they had not seen for many years. They would have been inclined to suspect she was seeing the tall, slim man with the long face, except it was obvious he was married to the dark-haired hottie with the big boobs, and had eyes for nobody else.

'Mum's certainly not sick anyway,' Diane whispered to her brother as they made their way towards the cars.

'And she's definitely not with your man,' Josh muttered in response. 'Good thing Deco's not here. He'd make a right fool of himself over the sexy missus. Talk about curves.'

'Boys are disgusting,' Diane just had time to reply before they came to a standstill. Dorothy invited the twins to travel in the Focus with her and the two eldest Newman children.

Before anyone else could beat him to it, Josh abandoned his twin and hopped into the passenger seat. Diane climbed into the back and made sure that Shona, who was nine and Troy, who was seven, were securely buckled in. Saul pulled away first and Dorothy eased her car out of its space and followed him up to the Baily with Saul leading the way in the family car. There was some consternation from her passengers when he stopped on Thormanby Road and opened the gates.

'Mum,' Diane asked urgently from her seat between the Newman siblings, 'are you moving to Howth?'

'All will be revealed in five minutes if you're good kids,' Dorothy replied teasingly, as she negotiated her way down the lane.

Both cars pulled onto the concrete area and the nine individuals who made up the two families clambered out and gawked around. Despite the bleakness of the February day, they were greeted by spectacular views of Dublin bay which resulted in exclamations of pleasure from young and old alike.

'There's nothing here,' Diane sounded disappointed. 'I thought there might a house, or maybe a small apartment block.'

She sounded so crestfallen, Dorothy's heart went out to her. *She looks very well on the outside, but something tells me her heart has a long way to go before it's fully recovered. And her pride as well. Personally, I don't know what's the most painful - feeling rejected, or believing you've made an utter fool of yourself. She only visits Shankill because of me. If I wasn't living there, she would never set foot in the place again. This win could not have come at a better time.*

'Please excuse us for a few minutes,' Dorothy called to Saul and Ryanna. 'I need a private word with the twins.'

For all the world as if they were four years-old again, she took hold of their hands and tugged them along behind her until they were within a few metres of the water's edge. She made sure they were standing on an even patch of dirt not likely to crumble beneath their feet, before facing them squarely.

Speaking quickly and concisely, she broke the news. She also took the opportunity to apologise for them being the last to know. Then she took three steps back and told them they could scream as loudly as they wished. The twins did scream. They hollered long and hard for a minute before once again tackling their mother and almost bowling her over in their excitement.

'Are they happy, Daddy?' asked five-year-old Annabelle Newman, who was watching the scene from a distance, her little face deadly serious.

'They certainly are, chicken,' replied her doting father, as he gently stroked her head.

Ryanna clutched two-year-old Robbie in her arms, her eyes misting up as she observed the scene.

Having ascertained their Valentine's gift was twenty thousand euro each, the twins vigorously high fived each other and demanded to know what she had given the rest of the family. This was the part of the conversation Dorothy had been dreading.

They had not yet reached their twentieth birthday, and she did not know if they would understand, or indeed agree, her plans for their futures. Slowly and carefully, she explained that, apart from an allowance which they would receive while they continued in fulltime education, they would not receive a lump sum for a number of years.

She wanted to create trusts that would mature when they turned twenty-four, but had yet to take advice on the process. She carefully refrained from stating an exact amount, wanting to keep the sum as vague as possible. The twins heard her out then stared at each other for a long moment. Josh was the first to react.

'Mum, are we talking millions when we're twenty-four?'

'Yes, sweetheart, we are,' she replied gravely.

'How much will the allowance be?'

'Eh…how would you feel about three hundred a week?'

'Each?'

'Yes, of course each.'

The twins exchanged another look then promptly launched themselves at each other and did some sort of odd little dance. Dorothy hoped it was not voodoo in its origin as it looked remarkably primitive. She was not at all comfortable with the idea of her children messing with voodoo, and it was just the sort of dangerous carry-on that would appeal to Deco Moynihan, who, quite frankly, was up for anything. Once the ritual was complete, they turned back to her, bubbling over with exhilaration.

'The only thing is, Mum, we might need cars and stuff like that before then.' Josh spoke diffidently, not wanting to hurt his mother's feelings, but at the same time, and in true male fashion, determined to stake his claim to a vehicle at the earliest possible opportunity.

Dorothy smiled happily, feeling an overwhelming sense of relief it was going so well. After all, she had given her friends and siblings two million each. It would be understandable if the twins felt it only fair they receive the same.

'I'm sorry, sweetheart,' she felt her knees weaken with relief. 'I forgot to mention that part in all the excitement. I intend to buy you both your own cars as soon as you find ones you like, and I would like to buy you each an apartment for your birthday. Four months should be long enough to find the right place and get the job done.'

Once again, the twins did their strange little dance, linking arms and twirling each other around in a frenzy. Dorothy sensed their excitement was more to do with the probability of owning their own cars than it was about getting their own apartments.

She was glad she had trusted her instincts and not given them more. While twenty thousand euro was a substantial sum to most people, it did not have quite the same impact, or potential for trouble, as two million might have in the hands of a pair of highly excitable nineteen-year-olds.

They walked back to re-join the Newman family. Ryanna promptly congratulated the twins on their good fortune, while Saul thumped Josh on the back and said he was delighted to meet a man of substance. 'What do you guys think of your ma's plans to build a house on this site?' he enquired genially.

A pair of startling green eyes and a pair of soppy brown ones simultaneously turned in Dorothy's direction.

'Oops,' she grinned. 'I forgot to mention it because I was so busy watching your dance. Saul is an architect, and I've purchased a rather impressive design from him. He's going to project manage the whole thing from start to finish, which means you don't have to worry about me having a nervous breakdown over the depth of the foundations or anything of that nature.'

The twins listened carefully to this little speech.

'When you say impressive, what exactly does that mean?' Josh asked slowly.

'My daddy designed a mansion fit for a queen,' Troy Newman piped up. 'If Dorothy is your mammy, that makes you a prince.'

Diane grabbed her mother by the arm. 'You're building a palace?' she sounded frantic. 'Will that not take a long time?'

Dorothy smiled understandingly and reached into her bag for her phone. 'I also purchased a beautiful apartment in Dublin 4,' she said gently. 'The paperwork will be complete in about...' She trailed off and looked to Saul for more information.

'Another week should do it,' he supplied helpfully. 'Your ma will be on the move to Charlotte Quay before you know it.'

Dorothy extended her phone and showed Diane the same photographs she had shown Horace only a month earlier. With Josh looking over her shoulder, the girl stared hard at the image of the Falcon drawing room and sun terrace. 'Dublin 4,' she whispered in awe, and promptly burst into tears.

An expression of fear crossed the faces of Josh and Saul, and they recoiled in horror. Ryanna calmly handed

Robbie to her spouse and stepped up. 'I feel like crying myself,' she said kindly, as she gathered the girl into her arms. 'I know money doesn't make you happy, but it certainly solves any number of problems.'

Diane allowed herself to be rocked in the older woman's arms, while Dorothy felt a tear making its way down her own cheek. Josh edged up to her and put his arm around her shoulders. 'Good job, Mum' he murmured. 'I don't know how you managed it, but job's a good un.'

She put her head on his shoulder and emitted a little sniff. 'It was Ganesh,' she said.

'If you're going to get a boyfriend, could you at least find one with a normal name?' he sounded plaintive. 'I don't want a stepdad called Ganesh.'

'He's a Hindu God,' Shona Newman sounded disapproving as she overheard and responded to this remark. 'We learned about him in school. You're very tall compared to your mammy.'

'I'm normal sized,' Josh told her solemnly. 'My mother is a leprechaun.'

'It's mean to call your mammy a leprechaun,' Troy piped up.

'Especially when's she's incredibly rich,' Saul teased. 'She might change her mind about your Valentine's Day prezzie.'

Diane emerged from the comfort of Ryanna's arms and glared at her brother through red eyes. 'Yeah, Josh,' she said accusingly. 'I'm sick of you mocking us about our size. You're lucky you're the same height as Dad. How would you like it if we slagged you about your stupid floppy hair all the time?'

'Perhaps we could agree to some sort of detente,' Dorothy reluctantly moved away from the heat her son was generating, and began to search for a packet of tissues in her bag. 'Let's explore the site so Saul can show us where the tennis courts and studio will be situated. No more talk of midgets or floppy hair.'

'A studio?' Josh stared at her, all thoughts of insults forgotten.

'A tennis court?' Diane's bloodshot eyes grew large in her little face.

'Time for the big tour,' Saul declared cheerfully. 'Put your imagination hats on, kids.'

~~~

From: Dottie8888@chatulike.ie
To:SRedmond@chatchat.com
Date: February 13th, 2011
SUBJECT: MOANIE MEN, HAPPY DAYS AND FERRARIS.
Hi Si,
Thanks for the text. You must be very busy with house viewing and all that. I hope you are not overdoing it. I hear Australia is enjoying a property boom similar to the one we had during the Celtic Tiger years. Let's hope it ends better for you guys.

I broke the news to the twins today, and they were in raptures as you can imagine. I was dreading it at one level, because I had to tell them about my idea for the trust funds. In fairness to them, they accepted my plans without a murmur of dissent, and don't seem remotely put out about only receiving an allowance for the time being.

Perhaps it's the comfort of knowing that in a few years' time they will be multimillionaires. I think it's safe to assume that would be a comforting thought for most youngsters.

So far, nobody in the Howth area appears to be aware it's the mystery Euromillions winner who is in the process of buying the old Doheny site. I'm happy to keep things that way because I don't want to rub it in people's face.

Saul thinks I should let the information leak out in case any problems develop with the amended plans. I don't see how me being a lottery winner would influence the residents or planners in any way.

When I mentioned that to Saul, he raised his eyebrows at me in what I can only describe as a cynical manner. He also suggested (in a cryptic tone) that I'm being naïve. He is still being bitchy about my ideas for the pool. I don't think he quite appreciates what's at stake here.

What am I to do with the man? So what if it takes longer because there's more digging to do? It's not as if I'm homeless, is it? It's not as if I can't afford it, is it? I'm beginning to suspect he's one of those men who enjoys a good moan. Do you remember how Victor (hiss, boo) used to moan all the time, and do you remember how he ALWAYS blamed somebody else for everything. Nothing was EVER his fault. What a twat!

I read somewhere that always blaming others is a sure sign of being a psychopath. I suppose there are incredibly stupid psychos out there as well as master criminals. Have you ever heard of a psychopath who could barely find his own arse? Apologies, madam, I digress.

We had great fun showing the site off to the twins, and after that we went for a walk on Claremont beach. Then we went to the local hotel for lunch. You should have seen the twins' faces when I began to order like a woman on death row.

Of course, they haven't had time to get used to the change in circumstances. I told them they will be fine once they have a chance to absorb it all. It's not that we ever lived in poverty, but we've always had to be careful. I hope they don't go too mad the other way now they have spondoligs. (What's Oz slang for money?)

We had a bit of a chat about cars over lunch (at least Saul and Josh did, I find it all a tad boring tbh). They were all slagging me just because I still have my old Focus.

Do Australians know that slag means tease, or do they think it's something horrible? Do you have to watch everything you say? After lunch, we went to the car dealership looking for inspiration. What do you think my beloved boy fell for on the forecourt??! Only a Ferrari 612 Scaglietti Formula 1 special wallpaper edition, whatever that is when it's at home.

I wasn't bothered the price tag read €150,000, but I certainly cared that my darling boy wanted me to buy him a very fast and dangerous machine. Fortunately, Saul intervened before Josh became too carried away.

He said it would be impossible for him to get insurance due to his age and status as a newly licensed driver. Josh only passed his test last year. I don't know if that was true or not and I don't care. Joshua O'Keefe needn't think he'll be getting his hands on one of those sporty yokes any time soon. I was very grateful to Saul for averting a disaster.

Ryanna suggested I go to one of those auctions where they sell off the prestige motors at knockdown prices. I thought she made a good point, and I might go to one of those another time. I genuinely wanted to buy something from the garage, because I'm mindful I'll be living in the area in the not-too-distant future. I certainly don't want to be perceived as one of those residents who never shops locally.

It was the stock that was the problem. There's no getting away from the fact that I am not, and never will be, in the market for a used BMW convertible in a particularly lively shade of scarlet.

Luckily, we spotted a beautiful teal green Range Rover Sport. Josh said it would be ideal for navigating the winding lane up and down to the site. Saul loves it. Not only is it the supercharged 5 series HSE edition, but the original owner splashed out on masses of extras.

I thought it would be a good idea to buy it so Saul can use it during the build. Once the house is finished, it can take its rightful place in the brand new six-car garage. The boys stayed cool for about five seconds, but then they got uber-excited about the whole thing. Long story short, I am the proud owner of a swanky, nearly new Range Rover, with barely ten thousand miles on the clock.

Oh! And guess what? They all gave out to me (what's Oz for give out/scold/tell off?) just because I paid the deposit in cash. It was only two thousand euro for feck sake. The way they were carrying on, you would swear I was walking around town carrying millions.

I like carrying cash, and I intend to keep right on carrying it. I don't want to be like the Queen of England. She never carries money; did you know that? I told them the Archangel Michael watches over me and that shut them up. I could see Saul and Ryanna glancing at each other as if to say, who is this nutter? They obviously never needed the services of the warrior angel. Lucky them.

After a little persuasion from Ryanna (she is one of those women who gets her own way by virtue of being incredibly nurturing and generally irresistible) I agreed to the twins taking tomorrow off college so we can spend some quality time together and go shopping.

Diane wants to get a few toys for the Newman children as well. They are such good kids and so funny. She is very good with children, although I hope she doesn't make me a granny too soon. She is looking very well, although she became very emotional when she realised I plan to leave Shankill for good and she will never have to go back.

I'm not sure what to make of that, but I am determined not to over-analyse. We have been presented with an opportunity to better our lives and get the family back on track, and I don't intend to squander it on speculation. Back with the update shortly. Hi to C. Love ya. Dot xx

~~~

Dorothy made enquires of the twins regarding their plans for Valentine's Day. This caused much merriment and abuse between the pair, to which the adults listened with relish, and the Newman children open-mouthed.

It transpired that Diane had finished with her latest beau, having discovered him in the arms of another (as Josh put it). Josh, in his turn, was suffering the pangs of unrequited affections, after wasting six weeks hankering after a girl who refused to give him the time of day. 'She only dates the rich lads,' he told his mother sadly.

They had been subjected to frowns from a number of other diners when they all fell against each other, laughing at what they considered Joshua's joke. The young man had indeed fallen for a girl who only dated wealthy men. He was advised by every occupant of the table, even nine-year-old, Shona Newman, not to get involved with the money-grabbing specimen and 'find himself a nice girl'.

Dorothy studied him from across the table. Unlike his father, Josh had, thus far, shown no real inclination to be a ladies' man. That said, he was not above using charm to get his own way. She could not help but wonder what effect the combination of charm and money would be as he grew older.

Diane was once again looking stunning, having administered eyes drops Ryanna found in her own handbag, and reapplied her makeup. With the exception of her eyes, she was the living image of her mother at the same age. She certainly did not resemble the girl who had sobbed her heart out on the Baily scarcely two hours earlier.

Dorothy detected a bright glint in her daughter's eyes, and hoped it was based on determination to carve out a new life for herself and put the ghost of Horace Johnson behind her once and for all. Her tiny stature was inclined to make her look fragile and vulnerable.

Nonetheless, Dorothy was well aware that of the two, it was her son who was the most sensitive and her daughter the more resilient, a trait she had inherited from Declan. Watching their beloved faces over the lunch table, Dorothy sent a silent entreaty to Michael to watch over and protect her babies during this new phase of their lives.

~~~

From: Dottie8888@chatulike.ie
To: SRedmond@chatchat.com
Date: February 14th, 2011
SUBJECT: HEARTS, ROSES & HALLMARK MOMENTS
Hi Si,
Happy Valentine's Day to you and Charlie. I hope you did something seriously romantic. I found myself back in Dundrum today. It was more relaxed than the last time because we were not in a mad rush. Bel would not have been happy with some of the places we visited. LOL.

I had the presence of mind to return some of the pieces I purchased before. Luckily, I kept all the receipts. Some of the outfits I chose the last time were just plain silly, and I don't know how I ended up with them. Never shop in a hurry!

The size eighteen trousers were never worn (hurrah) and still had their tags on, hence I was delighted to be able to return them for a refund, as they are now too big (hurrah again).

The twins are very impressed with my weight loss but kept making noises about me overdoing it! Do you think they like the idea of a cuddly mummy? I found a white bikini in the shopping bags when I got home, which has also been returned. For the life of me, I don't know how it got in there. Bel in a fit of madness perhaps?

Diane wanted me to buy a beautiful, green silk dress, but when I explained about my fitness program, she agreed it would be better to wait for a while before making any significant clothes purchases. The relief of it all!

Not to have anybody coerce me into spending money on something I will end up giving away in two months. I was extremely grateful for her understanding, and proceeded to shower her with anything that caught her eye. For the first time in our lives, I was able to buy anything I liked for them without fear of running up an overdraft.

We finished the day with a trip to the dining hall in Harvey Nichols, where the twins fell on their food like a couple of boot camp inmates, exhausted from all the spending. I was starving and was very proud of myself because I managed a measure of containment with a small bowl of soup followed by a salmon salad.

I had to finish off with a cup of tea. I cannot imagine life without tea, cellulite or no cellulite. The twins desperately wanted to go and see the apartment, but as the purchase is not expected to be finalised for another week, I told them they would have to be patient for a while longer.

I don't know where they find the energy, Si. I dropped them home, and they were already making plans to meet friends for drinks; the single friends, of course. Ha ha. I swore them to secrecy about the lottery. They are only allowed to tell their closest pals, and they have to warn them not to go blabbing. Once they considered the implications of the news leaking out, they saw I was right and agreed to be discreet.

I made a quick dash to the Newman household to deliver the bags of toys and have another meeting with Saul about my rock-chick mansion.

There were a dozen red roses in a vase, and Ryanna was looking mightily pleased with herself. Saul was definitely more relaxed, which I thought was a good sign. Then I headed home and took a long hot bath, before hopping into bed with my new book. Without a doubt, it was the best Valentine's Day in twenty years. Love Dot x

23

In anticipation of her impending move, Dorothy devoted an entire week to sorting through her possessions. She set aside two boxes of towels, sheets, crockery and cutlery she hoped Horace might find useful.

She reasoned if he did not want them for his own use, he could always donate the contents to a charity shop. She was determined to make a fresh start and, to that end, mercilessly decluttered. She examined every item she owned and ruthlessly judged its fate.

She laundered any of her new clothes that were washable, and had the remainder professionally cleaned. Every pair of shoes older than six weeks found a new home in the local shoe bank.

When she was satisfied that everything left in the cupboards was either new or almost new, and she definitely wanted to retain it, Dorothy carefully packed her new wardrobe, together with all of her recently purchased boots and shoes, into her Louis Vuitton.

The only items she omitted were a couple of pairs of jeans and casual tops she deemed suitable attire for a house move. She dropped the last of her old clothes into banks conveniently situated in every car park for miles around, and packed virtually her entire collection of CDs and DVDs into yet another box for Horace. There was always the possibility he might treat himself to a stereo or television with the money she had given him, and it did not seem right to give it all away without checking with him first.

She was fairly confident none of the fiction paperbacks from her old pine shelf would appeal to a man who had a working knowledge of seven languages including Latin, hence the majority of these found their way into the cage at the recycling centre. The only ones she kept were those related to energy healing, manifestation and other spiritual matters. When that was done, she methodically bubble-wrapped her small collection of crystals and angels, and tenderly placed them in a storage box.

When the heavier items were safely stowed at the bottom, she wrapped the collection of woodcarvings Horace had made for her. About two years after he took up residence in Old Hen, Dorothy paid him a visit and discovered him whittling away at a piece of wood. The next time she saw him, the piece had been transformed into a curled-up kitten.

When she expressed admiration for his talent, he presented her with the ornament and insisted she keep it. Every year since then, he presented her with a different creation. She wrapped her little collection with care and added them to the box. There was a study at Falcon which she intended to put to good use, and had already decided to display them there. That way, when Diane visited, she would not be thrown by the sight of the miniature creatures Horace was renowned for carving.

Dorothy frowned when she remembered the last conversation between her and Diane. Her daughter felt it would be practical to sell the Shankill house and be done with it for good. Saul disagreed. He said Shankill would always be a popular area of the commuter belt, and recommended she keep the house as an investment for the future.

When the subject was broached with Josh, he expressed indifference to the fate of the house. He said the important thing was that she was moving, and it mattered little what happened to the house after that. Knowing how Diane felt about it, Dorothy had taken a couple of days to mull the problem over, and also discussed it with Bel and Gerald.

They had come down firmly on the side of Saul. Bel had even gone as far as to say that an unfortunate crush of Diane's should not be allowed to dictate the outcome of what was essentially a financial decision. Dorothy knew her friend was right, although could not shake the feeling that in some way she was betraying the girl by retaining the property next door to Horace.

Finally, after much internal debate, she had chosen to follow Saul's advice and rent it out instead of selling it in a collapsed market. As soon as she left for good, the local decorators would be in to paint it from top to bottom. When that was done, the contract cleaners would be in to spruce it up and steam clean the carpets. Horace had promised to do some work on the garden and ensure it was in good order for the new tenants.

He seemed relieved she was not selling up, and eager to help with the transition. He said there would be no need to pay him for the work, since thirty thousand euro bought a lot of gardening. Once these jobs were complete, the management agency Saul had recommended would commence viewings with prospective tenants.

When the bulk of the decluttering was finished, Dorothy felt ready to face Amanda, and subsequently invited her around for coffee. The other woman lost no time in popping across the road, her internal antenna telling her something was well and truly up with her friend.

Amanda Flynn was four inches taller than Dorothy and five years her senior. She had married young and she and her husband had purchased the house on Bluebell View during the second year of their marriage. Alas, scarcely ten months later, she lost her twenty-five-year-old spouse in a tragic motor accident. The insurance company paid off the mortgage on the property, thereby ensuring she was in a position to remain in Shankill where she had made some good friends.

Amanda grieved for her spouse for seven years. When she turned thirty, she decided the time had come to give love a second chance. Since then, she had been involved in a number of relationships. None of them had come to anything because, as she freely admitted, every single one of the men had systematically failed to live up to the high standard set by the love of her life.

After years of trying and many failed attempts, Amanda eventually gave up on the idea of true love and decided to become a cougar instead. The problem with that lifestyle choice, she said, was you really needed an air of glamour and sex appeal in order to attract younger men.

Those adjectives simply did not apply to her. For all her kindness, good nature, and sense of humour, she did not have the sex appeal that clung to some women like dust to a television screen. Her hair was a mixture of grey and brown, and was inclined to be frizzy.

She had a great smile, but her teeth were crooked and a never-ending source of annoyance. Her eyes were round and bright blue, but the skin around them had not aged well because she spent so much time either walking or working in her garden. She had a very good figure for a woman of forty-five, although she tended to dress down and not draw attention to herself.

When Dorothy admitted her to the house, Amanda was wearing one of her favourite outfits, a blue fleece over a pair of denim jeans that were too baggy, and a grey shirt that was too long. She had tied her frizzy locks back off her face, which only served to highlight the sagging skin around her jawline and the wrinkles around her eyes. She took stock of the sitting room and immediately noticed the three boxes stacked in the corner with labels that read: Horace to investigate.

'Oh, my God,' she put her hand to her heart. 'Either you and Horace are having an affair, or it's something much worse. There's been a real buzz about you lately, and don't think I haven't noticed you've been avoiding me.'

'I don't blame you for being annoyed,' Dorothy grimaced guiltily, as she gestured towards the sofa and invited the other woman to sit down. 'I *have* been avoiding you, but only because I've been so overwhelmed by my change in circumstances I didn't have the energy to tell you before. I'm hoping in about ten minutes you'll forgive me.'

'That all sounds very mysterious,' Amanda was wide-eyed as she slowly took a seat on the sofa. 'The new diet is definitely working by the way. You look great so I'm going to assume it's not cancer or anything hideous like that.'

'I won the lottery,' Dorothy informed the other woman flatly. 'I have a piece of paper to show you. Please don't freak out.'

She rummaged in her bag and found the well-used photocopy of the winning cheque. She allowed Amanda to peruse it for a few minutes and gather her thoughts. In the meantime, she went into the kitchen and made two cups of coffee.

There were no biscuits in the house which might lead her into temptation, so instead she put a couple of chocolate covered rice cakes on a plate. Then she put the whole lot on a tray and carried it into the sitting room where she set it down on the coffee table.

'It was you,' Amanda uttered the words croakily, as she clasped the photocopy against her chest. 'The mystery winner was *you* all the time. How the hell have you managed to keep it so quiet?'

'I have no idea,' Dorothy grinned. 'A combination of discretion and luck. Please don't say a word to a living soul. If the news leaks out, I don't know will happen to me.'

Amanda's eyes opened even wider. 'Oh, Dottie,' she whispered. 'If the press gets hold of this piece of news, your life won't be worth living. You'll have to go into hiding because they'll never give you a minute's peace.'

'Don't start worrying about me,' Dorothy smiled at her. 'I have a little gift for you here.'

She took an envelope off the mantelpiece and pressed it into Amanda's hands. With trembling fingers, the other woman opened it and withdrew two cheques.

'The smaller one should be enough to cover the tax liability on the big one,' Dorothy told her earnestly. 'If you lodge it into a fixed term account, you'll be earning interest on it between now and tax season.'

Amanda made a few moaning sounds in the back of her throat and began to rock backwards and forwards on the sofa. Dorothy quickly brought her the cup of coffee and insisted she drink some of it. The hot beverage had the required effect, and she rapidly came to her senses and thanked her friend for the gift.

'It was a bit of a shock to the old system,' Amanda gasped. 'I don't suppose you have a drop of the hard stuff in the house?'

'I think I might have a half bottle of scotch in the press. I keep it in case Mum drops by on a social call.' Dorothy shot off and soon unearthed the remains of a litre bottle. She noticed there was a bottle of port tucked away behind it, and resolved to pass it on to Horace.

I need to stay as alcohol-free as possible for the next six months. Horace won't object to the port. I'm beginning to suspect the man would eat and drink anything.

When she returned to the sitting room, she tipped a solid measure of the spirit into both cups, then sat in the recliner, clutching her own mug. 'Sit back and drink that,' she ordered. 'You've had a shock and need time to adjust. Don't worry, you're not alone. Mum fainted when I told her, and Dad looked as if he was about to have a heart attack. Viv did some weird, freaky pacing thing, and the twins danced a voodoo jig. I'm exhausted just thinking about it all.'

She kept up a steady flow of mundane chatter for the next five minutes until Amanda began to relax and see the funny side. She was soon sitting up straighter and listing off the plans she had for the money. These included having her crooked teeth fixed, her frizzy hair straightened and highlighted, and her thirty-year-old tattoo lasered off, regardless of how much it might hurt.

She said as soon as she had shed a couple of pounds and filled her face with wrinkle reducing chemicals, she intended to treat herself to a new wardrobe of designer clothes, then set about finding a toy boy.

When Dorothy asked if she was likely to sell up and move, Amanda replied she would almost certainly continue to live in Shankill because she had so many friends there, but would treat herself to a new car and remodel her house.

Dorothy apologised again for keeping her in the dark for so long and her friend laughed. Now that she knew the truth of the situation, she was not at all offended. She had been curious because Dottie had been acting so strangely, and had convinced herself there was a man involved.

She unequivocally informed her friend that if she had been the one to win the Euromillions, she would not have told anybody except her parents for at least three months to give herself a chance to adjust.

Dorothy was relieved to hear this, and quickly recovered from her guilt. The two women spent a cosy couple of hours poring over holiday destinations and pictures of garden rooms on the web, and polishing off the last drop of scotch. Amanda was delighted with the photographs of the Falcon apartment and promised to pay a visit as soon as Dorothy was settled.

'How did Horace react to the news of your move?' she asked.

Dorothy grimaced. 'He's putting on a brave face, although I know he's not happy about it. First the twins and now me. We're pulling the rug out from under him.'

'He's ridiculously set in his ways for a man of twenty-nine,' Amanda exclaimed in exasperation. 'This might be the best thing that's happened to him for a long time. I hope he pays you the occasional visit and doesn't pine away in his little house, whittling his animals and scribbling his poems. He's such a sap sometimes.'

'Whatever happened to him when he was young really affected him,' Dorothy said sadly. 'Do you think he might have spent time in prison?'

'I seriously doubt it,' Amanda pulled a face. 'He may have received a caution, and I'm sure the whole thing was horrible for him, but I seriously doubt he has a record of any kind. The school would have wanted the scandal hushed up.'

'He must have gotten a terrible shock when it all blew up in his face,' Dorothy sighed sadly.

'It was almost a decade ago,' Amanda exclaimed. 'It's about fecking time he got over what happened and moved on with his life. Would it kill him to behave a bit more normally?'

'Please keep an eye on him,' Dorothy begged. 'And encourage him to visit me at least every couple of months. The new apartment is only a couple of minutes' walk from the DART, and he's welcome to bring Trotsky.'

Amanda agreed that in between her makeover and home improvements, she would cook the occasional meal for Horace and remind him there were few benefits to living the life of a recluse. After that, the ladies put Hairy Horace out of their heads, and went back to reading glossy magazine and planning their futures.

Three hours later, an ecstatic Amanda weaved her way back across the road and, after two failed attempts, successfully inserted the key into the lock of her front door. Unseen by her, Horace observed her antics from his kitchen window.

When she was safely indoors and the door had finally closed behind her, he dropped the curtain. Just for a moment, he buried his face in his hands and willed himself not to cry. After the crisis had passed, he threw another log on the fire, then went to see what alcohol he had left in his dresser.

He was pleased to discover a half litre of vodka hidden behind a large bottle of olive oil. There was a five-inch gap at the top of the bottle, and he decided to fill the space with an appropriate mixer. In the fridge, he unearthed what remained of a carton of orange juice. He gave it a vigorous shake, then carefully tipped the contents on top of the vodka, taking care not to spill it down the sides.

When the carton was empty, he rinsed it out and threw it into the recycle bin. Then he screwed the lid back on the bottle and energetically shook the concoction up and down in order to mix the cocktail. Trotsky had been observing all of this from under the kitchen table and barked to encourage his master.

'To see me in action, one might be forgiven for assuming I trained as a barman,' Horace told the dog drily.

Satisfied the blend was as perfect as he was likely to get it, Horace walked around the fireplace and settled himself in his chair. Trotsky followed and made himself comfortable as close to the fire as he could bear. Horace unscrewed the cap and took a long swig from the bottle.

His gaze roved around the room, taking in the photographs, the books, and the general bric-a-brac strewn around. 'Maybe it's time to buy a TV, Trotsky boy,' he said softly. 'I have a feeling that pretty soon, you and I are going to need something other than literature and a few sticks of charcoal to keep us sane.'

24

Now that Amanda knew about the lottery and had been sworn to secrecy, Dorothy felt more relaxed about the move. Horace carried the three boxes she had set aside for him to Old Hen, and stored them away in one of his many sheds. He assured her he would sort through them at his leisure, and donate anything not required.

Then he advised her to stop worrying about her old stuff and start focusing on the big move. She was grateful to him for putting on a brave face and being so supportive, especially as it was obvious he was deeply unhappy at the idea of the impending changes.

The cleaners were already booked to give the Falcon apartment a thorough overhaul. As soon as Dorothy heard that Tuesday, 22nd February, would be completion day, she confirmed they would be able to gain access by ten a.m. After receiving word from the family lawyers that all was well, Saul obligingly turned up to let them in and show them around.

Once he was satisfied they knew what was expected, he drove over to Shankill to present Dorothy with her two sets of keys. He was driving the new teal coloured Range Rover, and seemed somewhat embarrassed to be pulling up outside of Dorothy's house in a car she owned but had never driven. She knew such an attitude was unlikely to last and was fairly confident that, within the month, he would be treating the Range Rover as if it was his own, and would be loath to return it at the end of year.

Dorothy was on the watch for him and opened the door as soon as he pulled up at the gate. Saul untangled his long legs from the car and waved casually. He slowly sauntered up the drive, taking in the small front garden, the rough track down to Bluebell Wood, and the long wall running perpendicular to the laneway. He stopped at the front door and gestured towards Old Hen. 'What's behind the wall?'

'A garden, which I am reliably informed is one hundred and twenty feet-long,' Dorothy smiled at him. 'It's the reason my neighbour bought the house in the first place. He has four sheds for his hobbies, and twelve species of mature tree.'

Saul whistled through his teeth, clearly impressed by this piece of neighbourhood trivia. 'Was he never tempted to sell up during the boom? He was sitting on a fortune back in the good times.'

'Don't let Horace hear you talking like that,' Dorothy giggled. 'He abhorred property developers long before the rest of the nation did. I think he may even have written a condemnatory and scathing attack on them back in 2006 in the form of a sonnet or some such. I was never too hot at English, although I always enjoyed home economics and history. Is it any wonder I didn't get the points I needed for Uni? Come on in and have a coffee.'

Saul cast a final look at the walled garden before crossing the threshold into Dorothy's house. It immediately became apparent that he was taken aback at the modest surroundings in which he found himself. She saw the thoughts flitting across his mind and supposed that, based on the few suggestions she had already put forward for the new house, he had previously assumed she was a woman of both expensive and elaborate taste. One who only considered using a tile if it had recently arrived on a tall ship from Constantinople, having first been hand-carved by virgins, whilst mounted on the backs of unicorns.

Certainly, one or two of her ideas (borrowed from Image magazine) were stylish in the extreme, but that was because she was going with the flow. She could hardly build a palatial style property and then furnish it from IKEA. She still had to regularly remind herself the foundations were not yet complete. Neither had the amended designs for the pool and garage been agreed by the planning department, hence she was possibly getting a little ahead of herself with her notions of glass staircases and lifts.

Saul had spent the last couple of weeks revising the plans for the garage and leisure complex, and said he was all set to submit them as soon as Dorothy gave him the cheque to cover the necessary fees. If all went well, and she sent up a daily prayer it would, work would begin on the leisure complex within six weeks.

The purchase had been pushed through by all parties in record time, mainly because only minimal queries had been raised by either side. Dorothy had asked her own solicitor to make it his number one priority, which was why it had taken a little longer to complete on Falcon. It had been worth it in the end, as work had commenced on the build in early February.

By the end of January, Saul had successfully lined up a quantity surveyor called Lauren Ashgrove to oversee the financial side of things, as well as his friend Jake Doherty as the main contractor for the build. During the boom years, Jake had owned and run a large building firm, but now only kept a dozen men on his books.

When he heard about the scale of the proposed property, he happily agreed to undertake the role of foreman for Saul's latest project. He was grateful for the opportunity, since the build would provide him and his team with employment for the remainder of 2011.

All of this and more, Saul explained to Dorothy over a cup of coffee and a rice cake. He said he was looking forward to introducing her to the team, but it could wait for another week or two. The site was bedlam at present, he explained, as the men dug into the hill to create the basement for the house. Dorothy assured him she was more than happy to delay her first visit to Howth, giving her time to settle into Falcon and find a financial adviser.

After Saul had poked around the house for a few minutes and made a few critical comments about the absence of light in the rooms at the front, he ceremoniously handed over the keys to her new pad. Then he spent five minutes advising her on how best to present the house to prospective tenants.

Dorothy accepted all his comments, advice and criticisms with good grace, grateful he cared enough about her to express an opinion. After ascertaining she did not need him for anything else that day, the architect said he had better head over to the site pronto, before the lads accidentally dug up the orchard in their enthusiasm to get the foundations laid. With a cheeky grin, he jumped back behind the wheel of the Range Rover and drove off with a slight squeal of tyres. Dorothy waved him off, smirking to herself. *Boys and cars, eh? What ya gonna do?*

She was just about to close the front door when she saw Horace and Trotsky standing on the corner watching her. It looked as if Horace had been waiting for Saul to leave before he ventured out of Old Hen. He walked towards her and when he caught sight of the keys she was still holding, could not mask the grimace of pain that crossed his features. She pretended not to notice and told him she was intending to pack the car and move her essential items while there was still a little light.

'I can always come back tomorrow for anything that doesn't fit today,' she grinned at him. 'I'm so excited.'

'I had better come with you,' he said morosely. 'The Lord only knows what might happen to you over there on your own.'

Dorothy sniggered at him. 'It's Dublin 4, not Sodom and Gomorrah,' she scoffed. 'There's a concierge desk, CCTV, and a lift. There's even an underground car park and an entry phone system. What exactly do you think will go wrong?'

Horace refused to be drawn on the perils of Charlotte Quay and, after settling Trotsky in the sitting room, proceeded to remove the parcel shelf from the Focus before cramming the car full of boxes and suitcases, determined to fit in as much as possible so there would be very little for her to transport the next day. Less than an hour later, they were ready to set off.

Horace took Trotsky home and secured him, causing Dorothy to assure him if there was more space in the car, she would gladly have taken the dog to see the apartment. Horace's reply was that Trotsky was not a fan of high-rise living, and would not appreciate the gesture. He soon returned and slipped into the passenger seat next to her. Up close to him, Dorothy noticed he had started to grow sideburns and a moustache.

Clearly the bushy hair and out-of-control-beard are not enough for the Hairy Bear. I hope none of the neighbours see us because they'll think I've picked up a tramp.

Horace was quiet during the journey and she guessed he was doing his best to adjust to the separation. The traffic was not too heavy, and she was soon pressing the button on the key fob that opened the gate to the underground car park. It was a little claustrophobic, although she was grateful to have the extra facility. Horace did not comment on his surroundings, except to point out the efficient way the rubbish bins were neatly tucked away into wooden cages.

As soon as the car came to a halt in the appropriate space, he jumped out and opened the boot. It took six trips to transport the boxes and cases between the basement and twelfth floor, but since Horace carried most of stuff to the lift, and from there to the apartment, Dorothy was put to very little trouble.

In comparison to any house move she had made before, it was a dream. After the first trip, Horace suggested Dorothy begin the unpacking process while he finished unloading the car and, repressing a flicker of guilt for treating him like a pack mule, she readily agreed to the plan.

Leaving him to it, she went into the master bedroom where she unpacked the luggage, then stowed away the empty suitcases on the top shelf of the storage cupboard. There was a large wardrobe and she soon discovered her recent purchases only filled one quarter of the available space. It did not take her long to organise her clothes and shoes, and she was soon able to move on to the bathrooms. When she was satisfied she had equipped them with the necessary accessories, she moved to the kitchen where she stowed the groceries away in the maple coloured cabinets.

The only newly purchased piece of furniture in the duplex was an extra-large bed for the main bedroom. The cleaners had already assembled this item, but had omitted to attach the headboard.

Horace tutted over this oversight, but after locating a screwdriver buried deep in the pocket of his old raincoat, speedily rectified the oversight. When the bed was fully assembled, he washed his hands and helped Dorothy to make it up with the new lilac and silver bed linen Diane had helped her choose on their Valentine's shopping expedition.

When Dorothy was satisfied with the bedroom, she opened the box of ornaments. The carved miniatures looked very well on the windowsill in the study so she left them there. There was a modern version of a sideboard in the small drawing room that matched the oak coffee table. She chose this as the ideal location for her china and ceramic pieces. They would be safe there and she could always rearrange them when she had settled in properly.

She giggled as she placed a large framed photograph of the twins as babies on top of the piano. It was a beautiful instrument and took over the corner of the smaller living room. She had initially expected Anna to ask for it back, as surely it had belonged to her late husband. When the request had not been forthcoming, Dorothy resolved to safeguard it for her at Falcon.

She was sure the other woman would change her mind once she started coming to terms with her loss. Dorothy was determined that, when that time came, the piano would be exactly where she had left it. After everything that had happened over the past few months, she felt it was the least she could do for Anna Sadler.

Horace admired the piano but did not comment on the photograph. She was certain if he had been alone, he would have placed it face down on the instrument so he would not have to look upon the twins. Well aware he was upset, but determined to keep moving forward for everybody's sake, Dorothy suggested a full tour of the apartment. Horace had hardly looked around at all, so intent was he on emptying the car and putting the boxes in the correct rooms. He readily agreed to this and, wary of slipping on the stairs, she changed into a pair of trainers with extra grip on the soles.

Together the pair methodically worked their way around the apartment. At Horace's suggestion, they then repeated the exercise. At the end of the tour, Dorothy concluded she preferred the more traditional layout of the twelfth floor. In addition to the three largest bedrooms and a small study, it was also home to the kitchen and the smaller of the two drawing rooms.

Phil and Anna had remodelled the apartment on the eleventh floor, removing not only the kitchen but also some internal walls. Even though this level housed the two smaller bedrooms and the gym, its main function was as an entertainment area.

Mainly due to the sheer scale of the space, Dorothy could not quite reconcile herself to this area of the apartment, and Horace agreed with her wholeheartedly. He said the room could easily accommodate sixty people comfortably and was not suitable for an apartment. 'Were they intending to hold some sort of regency ball here?' he demanded impatiently.

'Phil was a rock-star,' Dorothy replied thoughtfully. 'According to Saul, he was quite the party animal. If you think this is OTT, wait until you see the pavilion in my new house.'

Too late, she snapped her mouth shut and stared at him guiltily.

'You never mentioned a house,' he glowered accusingly.

'I haven't built it yet, but this time next year I expect to be living back at ground level. Assuming everything goes to plan and we can work around the Irish weather.'

He grunted. 'Dare I ask where it's situated?'

'It's in Howth. If you're out that way over the next few months, you should check out the Baily. If you see a large construction site about half a mile south of the lighthouse as the crow flies, you've stumbled across my new abode.'

He was nodding. 'That's a good area,' he said approvingly. 'A tad wild in the winter, but a damn sight better than this bird cage.'

'It's almost three thousand square-feet,' she protested. 'Millions of people would give their right arm to own a place like this. You're such a snob.'

He snorted. 'That's not the first time I've been called that. What are you going to do with the peculiar partition?'

He was referring to the barrier that could be concertinaed closed at the push of a button, and used to split the entertainment area into two separate rooms. Dorothy was not surprised he was enquiring about it because she found the contraption quite off putting, and had toyed with the idea of having it removed.

When she had shown a photograph of the offending item to Bel, her friend had been in raptures over it. She said with a house full of teenagers it would be fantastic to have the option of dividing the space, possibly even separating the girls from the boys when they wanted to watch different things on TV.

Dorothy conceded that Bel made a valid point. When she explained her pal's reasoning to Horace, he shrugged and said it was probably best not to rush into any expensive renovations she might regret later. She took on board what he had to say and made the decision to live with the slightly odd partition until such time as she was absolutely positive what she wanted to do with it.

She also resolved to save the lower floor for entertainment purposes only (or for the twins' use if they had friends with them), and stick to the upper deck as much as possible. This would also be more practical for logistical purposes, as the main door on the eleventh floor was a fake. The only real access to the outside world was in fact on level twelve.

At the end of an hour, she was pleased she had taken the time to explore the apartment thoroughly, and grateful for the second pair of eyes. Even though wandering around the 2,975 square-feet of living space with only Hairy Horace for company felt strange, Dorothy was sure she would soon grow accustomed to her new living quarters. After all, wasn't this something she had always wanted?

When she was satisfied very little else could be achieved that day, she insisted on making some food for the two of them. She prepared a light nutritious snack as per her diet sheets for herself. Luckily, Amanda had given her a fish pie the previous evening and she had saved half for Horace. She warmed it up, then served up both meals on two of the brand new plates she had purchased during the week. She had left the house fully equipped for the tenants, and bought a couple of essential items for Falcon.

She intended to fully equip the kitchen over the course of the following week, and was looking forward to it. She did not mention this to her helper, as she doubted he would be interested in small kitchen appliances and dishes. Her assistant seemed pleased to be offered a hot lunch, and readily took a seat at the kitchen table. Dorothy used an opener to flick the cap off a bottle of light beer and casually set it down on the table next to him.

'A remnant of Christmas,' she said lightly. 'It's amazing the amount of food and drink you accumulate over the festive season.'

'Thanks,' he said gruffly and drank a quarter of the bottle down. 'I'm going to miss your cooking.'

Dorothy was reluctant to allow the conversation to drift into dangerous territory. Instead, she spent the next forty minutes telling him about how she had come to the decision to build such a large house.

On impulse, she shared the story of her dream with him, and he listened to the tale with a riveted expression on his hairy countenance.

When she had finished the tale, he stared hard at her and said, 'Americans are cocky, loud and annoying, Dorothy. I hope to God you don't end up married to one.'

She scooped up the last forkful of cous cous and chortled happily. 'Is it normal for a husband to refer to his wife as Boss?'

'That very much depends on the relationship,' he replied gravely. 'I distinctly remember my own father stood very much in awe of my mother, and often referred to her as the boss behind her back. Of course, that didn't stop him treating her like shit whenever the mood took him, but I suppose that's the beauty of marriage.'

'Gosh,' Dorothy stared at him wide-eyed. 'Was it not a good marriage?'

He shrugged indifferently. 'She used to tell me she was happy, although I was never entirely convinced. She was old school, you see. The sort of woman who would never dream of leaving her husband.' He shook his head as if to clear it of bad memories. 'Speaking of dreams, it's a shame you didn't catch the name of your future lover.'

'None of it means anything!' Dorothy protested. 'Just because I dreamed about a man swimming in my pool, doesn't mean I'm getting married. Besides, the dream was about the pool, not the man.'

Horace surveyed her over his bottle of beer. 'Are you quite certain about that?' he sounded deadly serious.

Dorothy opened and closed her mouth a couple of times and gazed at him helplessly.

'I think it's fair to say I'm not sure about anything right now,' she replied slowly. 'But I'm certainly not jumping to any weird conclusions or bizarre assumptions, based on my dream. As soon as I said aloud I would speak to Saul about building the pool, the dreams stopped. To me, that says it was all about the pool and nothing to do with the man.'

'We'll see,' Horace replied in a voice as dry as a bone. 'Americans are obnoxious; ergo for all our sakes I hope you're right.'

25

Horace refused to stay for the afternoon even though Dorothy begged him. He said it wasn't fair to leave Trotsky to his own devices any longer. She escorted him to the main door of the building and, under the watchful and rather perplexed eye of the concierge, bid him goodbye.

Horace dropped a light kiss on her cheek. She held him for a minute, and felt the scratchiness of his beard against her skin, and inhaled the combined odours of wood smoke and mint. For a full thirty seconds, he made no attempt to pull away from her embrace. Then he gently extricated himself and smiled sadly. 'Good luck with everything, Dorothy,' he said quietly. 'Don't be a stranger.'

With that he walked away, striding in the direction of the station as if he was being chased. Dorothy stopped for a brief chat with Brian, the concierge on duty, and explained to him that her former neighbour was endearingly eccentric. She estimated Brian's age to be close to her own, although he tended to be rather officious, a trait which lent him a rather sombre air and prematurely aged him.

He did not look convinced, but assured the newest resident if the hairy fella showed up again, he would not be turned away. Dorothy graciously thanked him then returned to her apartment to change. She did not wish to spend her first afternoon in the new pad alone, and resolved to do something worthwhile instead.

She tested the shower in the en-suite bathroom of the master bedroom. The overall quality was excellent, and reminded her she had to speak to Saul about her private bathroom in the new house. She wanted him to install one of those multi-jet showers that sprayed you from all angles simultaneously. She had also set her heart upon a full-length body dryer she had spotted in yet another magazine at Champneys.

She supposed she would have to employ an interior designer at some point. Whereas she would not mind tackling one or two rooms on her own, she certainly did not feel qualified to decorate the entire palace, as she liked to think of it. Dorothy was not certain how many rooms there were in total, but was confident the number exceeded twenty.

She sang *She Works Hard for the Money* to herself, as she wandered around her new bedroom getting dressed and applying cosmetics. As she applied blusher to her cheeks, she mulled over the possibility of installing a second body dryer in the leisure centre. *Perhaps that would be a shade extravagant.*

Twenty minutes later, clad in a pair of Jaeger trousers and a Ralph Lauren sweater, and wearing some very expensive cosmetics and scent, Dorothy slid her arms into her black overcoat. After a quick glance at her own reflection, she grabbed her bag and keys and took the lift down to the underground car park. It was her intention to pay a visit to the Crow Street shelter.

The trip to the far side of town was blessedly uneventful, and she was soon searching for a parking space. A passing pedestrian recommended she not try to get too close to the building since the road was very narrow. Heeding the advice, she parked a hundred yards away from her destination and fed some coins into the meter.

It was a cold day, and even though she was wearing a scarf and gloves with her Tommy Hilfiger coat, she was chilly when she arrived at the mission. With an accompanying shiver, Dorothy requested an interview with the manager, Brother Damien.

Mainly due to embarrassment, she had deliberately not made an appointment, and was initially concerned she might be mistaken for a needy person. It soon became apparent she was worrying fruitlessly. The kindly looking volunteer who greeted her, took one look at Dorothy's expensive coat and accessories, and correctly pegged her as a wealthy woman looking to make a donation.

Brother Damien was out back in the storeroom counting the depleted stock, and was quickly apprised of the situation. After the visitor had been described to him, he chose to make a speedy appearance.

The mission was doing well in terms of its number of volunteers. In many ways, Damien felt things had never been better. Dozens of men and women assisted at the shelter over the course of the month. Folks who, five years earlier, would have been far too caught up in the way of life offered by the Celtic Tiger to have time to even think about rendering assistance to their fellow man. Contributions had remained fairly static, both from home and abroad, mainly due to the publicity the shelter had received since the downturn began.

Many of the diaspora who were doing well for themselves overseas had taken the trouble to click on the *Make a Donation* button on the website. As a result, by the beginning of 2011, the mission was in a position to help three times the number of homeless and struggling it had helped in 2005. Damien's problem was the numbers who required help just kept growing.

The soup kitchen was providing more lunches than it had ever done in the past. Every Wednesday morning, the volunteers handed out anything up to 1,000 food parcels, and Damien desperately wanted to increase that number to 1,250. The care-parcels were the one thing keeping many families from the brink of starvation while they awaited their next social welfare payment.

The free lunches and blue plastic bags of provisions were the only thing preventing those who were not entitled to state benefits from literally starving on the streets. Due to the straightened economic times, their government funding had been slashed in the recent budget, and this circumstance weighed heavily on Damien's shoulders as he went to the front of house to greet his guest.

He made it a habit never to give anyone the brush-off, especially when he received a tip-off indicating a particular person had a wealthy appearance. As Damien often said, 'God has been very good in sending amazingly good people who have helped in so many ways.'

Dorothy had been rich for less than seven weeks and did not want to lose the run of herself. She was mindful she had not yet appointed a financial adviser, although she did have an appointment to meet one recommended by Gerald Kinsella.

She had never given much to charity over the years, except by way of the Lenten fundraising campaigns, and by sponsoring friends who were involved in events. Whenever she passed a collection box, she would always drop something in as a matter of habit. Nonetheless, until now, she had never been in a position to donate a large sum to a worthy cause.

When Dorothy first laid eyes upon Damien, she saw a slim man of advancing years who looked kindly yet burdened. He had the vaguely stooped appearance of the elderly, and his hair and beard were snow white. In many ways, he reminded her of a little Santa Claus. He was smiling in a welcoming way and holding out his hand to shake hers, all of which served to ease her nervousness.

In his turn, Damien saw a small, fair-haired woman with enormous brown eyes. She looked kind-hearted but ill at ease, as if she had stepped outside her comfort zone. When Dorothy requested a private meeting, he readily agreed.

The care-parcel distribution had finished for the day, and he would not be required at the noisy end for another hour. Sending up a little prayer of hope to his creator that he had been sent a lottery winner with a heart of gold, but not really believing it, Damien ushered the visitor into his office.

Dorothy had found the mission's website reasonably informative, and conducted her own piece of research into the day-to-day activities of the shelter. Discarding all facts and figures about government grants and fundraising as irrelevant, she found the one piece of information that interested her.

For this mission, the cost of feeding the needy of Dublin was €50,000 per month. As she considered €600,000 a nice round sum, this was the amount of the cheque Dorothy handed to Damien. She followed this with a concise run-down of her personal circumstances, and the events of her fortieth birthday.

When Damien recovered from the shock, he asked her if she would object to them saying a prayer together. Here, Dorothy hesitated. She explained that not only did she no longer consider herself a catholic; she did not have any time for the Catholic Church. She categorically stated she regarded it as fatally flawed, unnecessary and antiquated. In her opinion, it was an out of touch institution managed by individuals whose skills would be better suited to a life in organised crime.

Damien solemnly digested everything she had to say. Then he carefully folded the cheque and, after slipping it into his breast pocket, asked her how she would feel about saying a non-Catholic prayer. Unsure if he was teasing her or not, she readily agreed. To her surprise, Damien closed his eyes, folded his hands and uttered only nine words, 'Dear Lord, thank you for sending us Dorothy Lyle.'

When they emerged from Damien's office, a cup of tea was ready and waiting. Dorothy gladly accepted hers, apologising to the volunteers for delaying them as she did so. Clusters of individuals were busily preparing enormous containers of what appeared to be chicken stew. Based on the variety of accents she could hear as they shouted jokes and comments to each other, it seemed the helpers were comprised of numerous nationalities.

The volunteers could sense by Brother Damien's demeanour that things had gone well within the confines of his office, therefore were quick to reassure the visitor that she was being no trouble, no trouble at all. One of them solicitously enquired if she was heading home before it grew even colder or worse still, began to rain. In response to this, Dorothy reluctantly admitted she had intended to visit the Rape Crisis Centre, but as she did not have an appointment, was now questioning the wisdom of simply turning up on their doorstep.

The men and women standing around watching her oval face and brown eyes instinctively sensed the petite, fair-haired woman was not planning the visit due to any tragic personal circumstances. This suspicion was borne out by Damien when he offered to call ahead on her behalf and alert the staff to her imminent arrival.

Like a rocket exploding inside her head, Dorothy clearly saw just how small the Dublin charity scene really was. Damien had contacts at the DRCC, and was not afraid to use them. She gratefully accepted his offer and, ten minutes later, was back in the car and heading in the direction of Lower Leeson Street. She noticed there were some lovely apartment blocks in the area, and wondered if the twins would be interested in living in this part of town, or if they would prefer to remain on the North Side close to college.

~~~

From: Dottie8888@chatulike.ie
To: ANorris@talkalot.com
Date: February 22nd, 2011
SUBJECT: SOUKS AND JODPURS.
Hi Amy,
Stop thanking me for the money. You are most welcome. How are things with you and Donal? Better, I hope. Of course, I will come to visit when the conversion is finished. I'm looking forward to it already!

I was at the Crow Street mission today making a donation, and they called the Rape Crisis Centre and arranged for me to go over there straightaway. It was actually quite funny. It was as if they sensed I had a cheque in my bag, and there was no way they were letting me go home without handing it over. It was a bit like shopping at a souk in Egypt, when the traders see you still have money in your wallet, and refuse to let you leave until you spend it all. Not that I blame them. They knew I was making donations and the Lord knows they need the dosh.

A girl called Rhona met me at the DRCC. She looked to be about 30, but she is one of those shiny people so she may have been fifty. I suspect she is a pal of Brother Damien's and he deliberately gave her the heads-up about me. She is an unusual looking girl, part Mozambique and part British. She speaks in a very upper class British accent and is very striking. She has a magnificent head of jet-black hair and a very grabbable arse (as Joey would say), although she was wearing the oddest clothes.

I almost felt as if I was back in the eighties again because I am sure she was wearing a pair of jodhpurs and a hacking jacket. She kept wittering on and I couldn't get a handle on her so I had to ask her to be quiet. She didn't seem to take offence at this. Perhaps she assumed I was bone weary from being so rich. LOL

So I'm sitting there, and I send out the Dorothy Feelers so I could get some sort of sense of her. I didn't have to do that with Brother Damien because he wears his heart outside his chest. A surprising number of people do that, although Rhona Sinclair isn't one of them.

She's not a secretive girl, although she is inclined to be reserved and lacking in self-esteem. I don't know why, because she is one of those people who are made for love. She is all heart and very pure in spirit, but ridiculously honest. I could see her watching me so I had to ask whether or not she found it exhausting being so honest the whole time. "Oh yes," she says, "but I don't know how else to be."

"It must be very hard keeping a boyfriend, what with men being so needy," says I (before I could stop myself).

"Totally," says Rhona, "but I'm hoping as I get older they will get less needy, or else I'll become less honest."

She had me in stitches laughing. Then the two directors came in and we had to get serious about money. They tried to sideline Rhona, but I insisted she get involved in the meeting. I had already looked at their website, which shows their total income for the year is generally in the region of two million. I wasn't prepared to give them that much as it is still only February after all, but I was prepared to give them a chunk of moola.

I handed over a cheque for €500,000, and they made all the grateful noises. Then they asked me if I would consider becoming a patron. I had to say no. I told them the story of my birthday and they understood I've barely had a chance to get used to my new life. I don't have time right now to become the patron of anything, although it was nice to be asked.

I also swore them to secrecy about being the mystery Euromillions winner. I don't think there is much chance of them telling anybody else, because they will be hoping to receive another cheque next year, if not sooner. After that, I headed home because I was freezing cold and exhausted from the move, even though Horace (bless his heart) did most of the lifting and carrying. Rhona will stay in touch and send me regular updates. I would like to see her again because we got on well.

Election Day is looming here and you are lucky to be missing it. I have received my voting card and am looking forward to doing my civic duty, mainly because I can't wait for it all to be over. The sheer numbers of politicians going door to door is extremely tiresome. Bye for now. Love Dot xx

26

As a dank and miserable February limped out, and a more refreshing March bounced in with a sharp breeze to help carry it over the threshold, St Patrick's weekend loomed on the horizon. It brought with it, at last, the opportunity to celebrate. Feeling guilty for having left it so long, Dorothy made plans for an apartment-warming party.

~~~

From: Dottie8888@chatulike.ie
To: SRedmond@chatchat.com
Date: March 4th, 2011
SUBJECT: NEIGHBOURS AND ITALIAN
Hi Simone,

How are things down under? Good, I hope. Amy says things are much better between her and Donal now the financial pressures have eased. They are revising their plans for the barn and holiday accommodation to make the complex as luxurious as possible. They want to corner the top end of the market in the Lot Valley. That sounds interesting!

Guess what? I met one of my neighbours from the tenth floor today. Her name is Helen Mulvey and she is in her late fifties. Her husband used to be a successful banker. Like most bankers hereabouts, he ain't quite as successful as he used to be. That hasn't stood in the way of him leaving her for a thirty-four-year-old airline hostess with big tits and a tiny ass.

It will be years before she can petition for divorce, but in the meantime, she can live at Falcon while her ex has use of the house. Helen says she doesn't mind the arrangement, because maintaining a large house was very difficult for her on her own.

She would remind you of Mrs Moynihan, our Geography teacher at school. She has quite fierce eyebrows and a penchant for long beaded necklaces and tweed suits. Her hair is dark and really long, down past her waist, although she usually wears it in a bun like the one Princess Anne used to have before she became all 21st Century.

She told me she receives a small pension from her previous employment as a lecturer at Trinity College, and supplements her income by teaching foreign languages to idiots like me. I've always wanted to learn conversational Italian so I've offered her the job of language coach. We start our lessons tomorrow. I am very excited.

I haven't told her about my big win yet because I think it's a tad early in the relationship to be discussing such matters. I could see she was itching to know how I could afford to buy the apartment on my own. I am not sure how Horace will react when he discovers a woman I just met is giving me language lessons, hence I may defer telling him for a while. Italian is his favourite language after Latin...bet ya didn't know that!

I received sad news from Joey. Robert McCaul, that's my solicitor, had a stroke last week, and will be out of action for a long time. Dad says it's possible he will make a full recovery in due course, but for now the poor man can barely move or speak. I know it's incredibly selfish of me to be relieved he sorted out the paperwork on Falcon and the site before he got sick. As penance for my shocking behaviour, I told Dad to let me know if there is anything of a practical nature I can do for him, like hiring a physiotherapist. Gotta run. Hi to C. Love Dot xx

~~~

Dorothy initially had the notion of catering the party herself, as she would have done in the old days. After thinking it over for a couple of days, she decided to take

Helen's advice, and consequently went in search of a professional catering company.

Alas for Dorothy, she was the first to admit that Helen was a shocking influence on her. Even though the lady from the tenth floor instilled a significant amount of Italian into her pupil's brain, she also distilled copious amounts of Chianti into her bloodstream. Dorothy became so distracted learning to say things like *buona giornata,* and *non c'è problema,* she inadvertently started drinking heavily again, and consuming highly calorific food.

This situation changed almost overnight with the advent of another arrival. Two weeks after taking up residence in Falcon, Dorothy encountered Jamie near the roof garden, where in a brief moment of distraction she had gotten off the lift at the wrong floor. Standing there, cursing herself for her own stupidity and vagueness (her mind had been full of bonds and gilts), she saw a young man in his twenties also awaiting the lift.

He had a shock of white-blonde hair, a receding chin and a pair of bright blue eyes. For an attractive specimen, he looked extraordinarily crestfallen. He was carrying a large sports bag and was disgustingly fit and tanned so she took a chance and enquired if he was a fitness instructor.

Being of a naturally garrulous disposition, Jamie was happy to share his story with the small lady with the kind eyes. It transpired he was indeed a personal trainer and nutritionist, but had just suffered the misfortune of losing his biggest client. Mr Brooks from the tenth floor had been a regular for the past year. Alas, due to the straightened economic times, he had been forced to rent out his apartment. He was currently awaiting the required visa before jumping a plane to Canada, where he had an excellent job lined up with a major manufacturer.

After hearing the news, Jamie had gone up to the roof garden in a desperate bid to man-up and not cry. He planned to return to his native New Zealand before the end of the year so he and his brother could open their own fitness centre. If he was unable to find gainful employment in the meantime, he would not even be able to cover the price of his flight, never mind be in a position to provide his share of the much-needed start-up capital for the new venture.

After inviting him to her apartment for a drink, and extracting every last detail of his life, Dorothy offered him a trial as her personal trainer, on condition he rescue her from Helen, her newfound friend. Jamie Irwin gratefully accepted the role, together with the use of one of the bedrooms on the eleventh floor. Dorothy would gladly have accommodated him on the top floor in one of the rooms close to her own, but Jamie assured her the relative peace of the lower apartment suited him better. He added that his preferred room had the added advantage of being situated next to the gym.

Dorothy was secretly pleased when her chance-met acquaintance jumped at the idea of a live-in post; because there was no doubt she would enjoy the company. She still suffered the occasional pang of loneliness, although life without the twins was becoming easier.

Before she had time to blink, Jamie had given notice on his rented studio flat and taken up residence at Falcon. In return for room and board, as well as an appropriate salary, he not only trained with Dorothy every day, but also took over the shopping and cooking duties. He created a fitness and diet regime she would find easy to follow once he had moved home to sunnier climes.

He had been living in Ireland for eighteen months and Dorothy was delighted when she discovered he was au-fait with much of the local lingo. It was not just the basics he was aware of, like jumper meaning sweater and runners meaning sneakers. He had found out during his first day in Ireland that crack was usually spelt craic, and did not refer to hard drugs, but instead to fun. So, if you were greeted with 'howaya head, any craic?' it simply meant 'hello, mate, any fun or news happening?' It did not mean: 'Would there be any chance of some crack cocaine?' At least, not that often.

Relieved to have stumbled across this piece of information before he made a total fool of himself, Jamie made the commitment to persevere with his education. He soon discovered the terms 'deadly' and 'savage' meant 'good' and were generally regarded as complimentary. 'Feck off' had totally flummoxed him, until he learned that it was considered a very mild version of 'fuck off', and was a term most citizens would not hesitate to use in front of their grandmothers. Gas was another unusual part of the Irish vernacular the young man enjoyed using regularly. Gas simply meant funny, as in 'your man is gas.' It did not refer to any bodily functions or to fuel.

By the time he met Dorothy, Jamie had mastered the essentials of Irish slang and considered himself quite the aficionado. When she congratulated him on his know-how, he cheerfully replied he did not begrudge the effort because it had made his life so much easier, and consequently he had not looked back since stepping off the plane.

~~~

From: Dottie8888@chatulike.ie
To: SRedmond@chatchat.com; ANorris@talkalot.com
Date: March, 8th, 2011
SUBJECT: SMOOTHIES AND TOY BOYS
Hi Si and Amy,

Life as we know it has changed beyond all recognition. Jamie is giving me cooking lessons and all the dishes are healthy. You surfers would be proud of me. He goes shopping almost every day for fresh fruit and vegetables. So far this week, I bought an electronic soup maker, a smoothie-making gadget, and a professional juicer. You should see me making soup from scratch, girls, you wouldn't recognise me.

We have a small gym downstairs and he created a routine for me that is easy to follow. Yesterday, he introduced me to Pilates, which I must admit I love, something I never thought I would hear myself say about any form of exercise. We didn't do it in the gym. We took the exercise mats out to the big drawing room instead. Nice to know it has its uses! He's talking about us going running, although I have misgivings about that one. I hear it's hard on the knees. Ouch.

I couldn't find a catering company for my St Patrick's Day party, but Jamie has friends who are interested in the job, so I am meeting them later. Bel is hilarious. She was rather suspicious of him at first, until she realised he's gay. I am not sure what difference that makes. Did she honestly believe he had designs on me? He's only 27, for feck sake.

My mum on the other hand is delighted a man has moved in. You know how she believes nobody should live alone, especially women? She was disappointed when she discovered Jamie's sexual preference. In fact, I get the distinct impression she wouldn't object to me having a toy boy. You can't win!

I suspect Jamie chose the bedroom downstairs so he can bring men home for sex without running the risk of disturbing me. At least somebody will be getting some action in this apartment. Ho hum. Back soon. Love Dot xxx

~~~

Dorothy dedicated those early days at Falcon to getting in shape and throwing off her remaining bad habits like an itchy gansey. Except for when they had company, she and Jamie banned all refined sugar, saturated fat and alcohol from the premises. Unless one or both was going out for dinner, they cooked together, using the specially designed meal plans Jamie had created, and adding to their repertoire as they discovered new favourites.

~~~

From: Dottie8888@chatulike.ie
To: SRedmond@chatchat.com; ANorris@talkalot.com
Date: March, 13th, 2011
SUBJECT: HAIR AND OUCH
Hi Guys,
Can you believe I was up at 7 a.m. jogging with Jamie? He and Bel get on much better now, which is nice. Bel thinks we should run the Women's Mini Marathon in June, and I have promised to think about it.

The running nearly killed me, although I may get used to it in time. Amanda has been really good about staying in touch and is also keeping an eye on Horace. She tells me he and Trotsky are going about their business in their usual way, although his moustache and sideburns have completely obliterated his face. Apparently, all you can see now are his eyes, a patch of forehead, and a small corner of face around his cheekbones.

She is hoping we will have an exceptionally warm summer and he will be forced to shave it all off. Back soon. Love Dot xxx

~~~

Dorothy was amazed at how incredibly healthy she soon felt. She almost did not recognise her own body because it felt so strong, fit and toned. Nevertheless, when she weighed herself a few days before the party, she was shocked to see she had lost another ten pounds.

Many of the clothes she had bought in January were beginning to feel loose, especially around the waist, and one or two of the outfits totally swamped her. When Bel and Jamie offered to take her shopping, Dorothy insisted she would only be buying one dress for the party and nothing else until she lost more weight. As it happened, she purchased two outfits plus a few treats for Bel and Jamie, although in general she was pleased with her willpower and overall thriftiness.

~~~

From: Dottie8888@chatulike.ie
To: SRedmond@chatchat.com
Date: March, 15th, 2011
SUBJECT: SPLITSVILLE
Hi Simone,
Am I the last to know about Vivian and Garry are splitting up?? Did you know? I bet you did! When Viv said she couldn't come to Champneys with us because she needed to 'discuss the future' with Garry, I naturally assumed they would be debating the merits of Bali versus Hawaii.

I didn't realise they intended to spend time discussing how best to dissolve their marriage, for feck sake. Viv is refusing to discuss it over the phone, but I will be seeing her soon and then I will be back with the update. Dot xxx

~~~

Jamie's friends turned out to be catering graduates called Mia and Patsy. They were both twenty-five years old. They both had long blonde hair, which they kept poker straight. They both had big blue eyes and peaches and cream complexions. They looked like sisters, although they assured Dorothy they were in no way related.

They were struggling to set up their own business. It was not so much due to lack of clients. There were plenty of those to be had in Dublin despite the downturn. It was the lack of resources causing the problem. Their premises were too small because they were using a friend's annex. They needed a larger van. They needed stationery, business cards, a new computer, a new oven and kitchen equipment. The list went on.

They explained all of this to Dorothy while they were setting up for the party. She had opted for a buffet-style arrangement due to the number of guests expected. As she always tended to associate buffets with a warm slice of quiche and a spoonful of limp coleslaw, she was left open-mouthed at the fantastic variety and quality provided by the girls. Carved stuffed pork loin, grilled salmon and stuffed chicken breasts sat on platters alongside such delicacies as roasted corn on the cob, red potato salad, and broccoli au gratin, to name but a few.

Even Joey Lyle was impressed. Not by the food alone, but also by the apartment itself. As it was built over two floors, had five bedrooms, two reception rooms, three bathrooms, a study, a kitchen, a gym, and two sun terraces, it was difficult to fault the place, although Joey had a reputation for doing just that. It was sort of his thing.

He took a fortuitous shine to Mia and Patsy. Once they discovered his relationship to Dorothy, they were happy to flirt with and generally indulge him all evening, having quickly realised he enjoyed attention from pretty girls and was essentially harmless. Pat was delighted to see her spouse so well entertained, and congratulated her daughter on her choice of caterers.

'I think I'll ask those two hotties to cater Gordon's birthday party,' Gemma sidled up to her sister at the buffet table. 'Daddy got his moanie hole on the last time I had a little soiree at my place. The food was not up to his ultra-high standards. What a find. Well done, sis.'

Considering it was Dorothy's first attempt at playing hostess since her change in fortunes, the party was decreed a success. Josh brought along an extremely talented duo of musicians who attended college with him. They proved very popular and even had the older guests getting their groove on.

Bel and Gemma had successfully tracked down a number of old friends Dorothy had not seen for a while. Once they had all consumed enough alcohol to feel relaxed about the process, these pals were whisked off to the privacy of the study and handed cheques. Dorothy still found it difficult to give her friends money. It was not like making a charitable donation. Charities actively sought contributions and welcomed them with open arms.

Not one of her friends had ever asked her for anything of a monetary nature. Yet here she was, dispensing cheques for fifty thousand here and one hundred thousand there, for all the world as if she was Donald

Trump in a philanthropic mood. There was no evidence to suggest anybody objected to what was occurring.

Without exception, they readily agreed to keep her secret, and pocketed the cheques with accompanying grins. When she mentioned her misgivings to her mother, Dorothy was advised, kindly but firmly, not to worry about it. In Pat's opinion, folks rarely took offence at receiving a large sum, regardless of the circumstances.

Once again, her family were amazed to see how slim and healthy Dorothy looked. They were inclined to feel that Jamie should become a permanent fixture in the Lyle family, thereby providing the necessary regime which would inevitably lick them all into shape. They kept insisting there was no way he could possibly wish to return to horrible, lush and fertile, lamb-ridden New Zealand, when he could just as easily remain in damp old Ireland with them.

Jamie seemed only mildly taken aback by their insistence he remain with them indefinitely. Dorothy saw he had been in Ireland long enough to realise that essentially being kidnapped and held captive by an Irish family was a terrific compliment to the hostage.

When they heard Bel's idea for the mini marathon, Gemma, Orla and Viv expressed an interest in taking part. Amanda offered to rearrange her hectic schedule so she could join the group, hypothesising that running miles every day might be a good way to meet fit young men. The six women agreed to meet up in a week's time in order to plan their strategy and training schedule.

~~~

From: Dottie8888@chatulike.ie
To: SRedmond@chatchat.com
Date: March 19th, 2011
SUBJECT: CRAZY DADS AND PARTY FOOD
Hi Simone,

The party was a great success thanks to everybody helping out and the wonderful caterers Jamie found. The food was fantastic. Even though the girls only left college two years ago, they are excellent at what they do. We opened up the partition in the largest drawing room. Even though it is a very big room, there was a perfect amount of space.

The girls laid out the food on three long tables and the spread looked very impressive. I have attached a few pics of Mum standing next to it all. That's the baked ham she's pointing at with the tongs. Yum.

There was one awkward moment when Bel and Gerald were talking about how wonderful it would be for me to buy an apartment near them in Edward Place, and Joey overheard. You know how 'prudent' he is. I don't believe he has spent any of the million I gave him. He may have spent the interest earned on it, but I have a feeling he hasn't touched the capital. I have no way of verifying the situation, although I am deeply suspicious. He definitely hasn't changed his car yet.

When we asked him about it, he said there was plenty of wear left in the old one. Anyhoo! He told B & G that anybody who spent two million on an apartment before they even bought a stick of furniture or a cup and saucer was a desperate fucking eejit who had more money than sense. You know how he has this habit of waving his arms around dramatically while stressing a point? Well, he kept doing that while his bald patch turned bright red, his blue eyes flashed, and his thin lips became even thinner.

I didn't know whether to laugh or cry. I don't think they were offended because they've known him for so long, but I do wish that sometimes he would just shut up. Does he have to be so opinionated about everything? BTW, I am almost certain that six months before the bubble burst, those apartments were being marketed in or around the four million mark, although we didn't mention that fiscal titbit to Daddy. LOL

The best news of the evening is that I am investing in Mia and Patsy's catering company. They are great girls and fantastic chefs, although they don't have wonderful business sense. I will probably become a 75% shareholder. Their sweet potato pie is to die for, btw. They will be able to buy me out at some point in the future, assuming they can afford it. That could take years the way things are going around here.

The banks are still not lending. On the contrary, there is very little hope for any start-up enterprise unless they can attract private investment. Gordon thinks it's a good idea, although he says a person as rich as me should be looking at something bigger than a little catering company.

He also thinks I should be thinking about hiring a business manager or an assistant. The sort of person who will oversee these types of investments for me, although he is happy to do it temporarily. He suggested advertising, but I told him the universe will provide the person I need when the time is right. He looked a tad disgusted at that, but he is an accountant after all and cannot be expected to embrace the idea of cosmic ordering.

I think he is worried about me. I overheard him saying to one of the other men he is afraid somebody will try to take advantage of me because I am too trusting. He said it didn't matter the crazy things I believed when I was a middle-income lone parent, but now I am one of the richest women in the land, it could be a problem. I think he must be a closet atheist for him to say such a thing. Is he one of those men who takes his children to mass every Sunday, but doesn't actually believe in God?

I have to go now, so much to do. Oh, did I tell you I am trying out another financial guru this week? The other one was horrible. I am also on the hunt for new lawyers. I spoke at length to Viv and now have all the dirty details. Yikes and shit. Take care. Oh btw, the Space Ache is bearable thanks, no need to worry about me. Hi to C. Miss ya. Dot xxx

27

Based on a recommendation from one of the directors of the Rape Crisis Network, Dorothy had been lucky enough to schedule a meeting with a seriously impressive financial guru.

Claudia Healy was her second attempt at retaining an adviser. Gerald had recommended one to her some weeks earlier, and had even gone so far as to set up the appointment on her behalf. Alas, when Dorothy came face to face with Diarmuid O'Callaghan, she was less than impressed.

After ten minutes of face time with the man, she began to wonder if Gerald had told him she had learning difficulties. He was so incredibly patronising and condescending, she was forced to plead a headache and bring the meeting to a premature halt.

By the time he called the next day, she had collected her scattered wits and was able to coolly inform him she would not be requiring his services. She followed this by saying she did not feel their personalities would suit, nor would they work well as a team. Diarmuid had been staggered by this brush-off, and Dorothy could only assume Gerald had given him assurances not his to give.

As she did not see Gerald very often, it was a few weeks before they met up. He was clearly irritated and embarrassed by her rejection of his pal. He soon backed off when Dorothy angrily described the other man's attitude, seeing she has been genuinely offended by the encounter. By then, she was able to triumphantly inform him that she had secured a meeting with none other than

Claudia Healy. Despite himself, Gerald was impressed. *And so he should be,* she thought smugly.

It was unusual for Claudia (who often appeared on current affairs programs, and was generally regarded as having a brain the size of a planet) to take on new clients, as she was fully committed. However, when she heard the record-breaking Euromillions winner was interested in retaining her services, she could not resist taking the first meeting in order to satisfy her curiosity. Initially, she fully intended to pawn Dorothy off on one of her colleagues with a slightly smaller brain. That was before she came face to face with her.

There was something about the other woman that made Claudia want to collect her as if she was an endangered species. Dorothy came across as incredibly grounded for somebody who had literally been catapulted into an alien world. Unlike others of her acquaintance who had achieved unexpected wealth, many of whom Claudia had advised during her reign as queen of the financial markets, Dorothy was prepared to neither throw her money around, nor hide it away. She was willing to spend as much cash as required on things that interested her, yet had an abhorrence of excess merely for the sake of it.

Claudia could not imagine Dorothy spending four thousand euro on a bottle of champagne she did not really want, simply because she had the means to do so. She certainly did not come across as a woman who felt she had anything to prove. When Claudia discussed it with her husband later, she told him it was this aspect of Dorothy's personality which drew her to the smaller woman. Dorothy did not seem to be seeking anybody's approval.

She intended to do what she wanted with the money, and trust to the universe for the rest.

Dorothy explained all of this and more during their initial meeting. Claudia was a little surprised to hear how much the lucky winner had already given away, but was impressed when she learned she had done her best to take care of the tax side of things as well.

Privately, Claudia felt that, while Dorothy had been well intentioned in her actions, she had effectively put temptation in the way of her friends and family when she handed them the second cheque to cover the tax, but did not voice her opinion on the subject.

Partly because it was too late to do anything about it, and partly because she did not want to upset the other woman by suggesting some of the recipients might be tempted to blow the money in the hopes of a financial bailout further down the line.

She took the decision not to mention it at all unless Dorothy brought it up first. She was appalled to discover that, for the past ten weeks, her latest acquaintance had left over one hundred million euro resting in a ninety-day deposit account with the Irish Citizens' Bank. Speaking slowly and carefully, Claudia began to explain the dire consequences which could potentially befall funds abandoned to the mercy, and somewhat dubious integrity, of the Irish banking system.

'I know it's a disaster waiting to happen,' Dorothy interjected cheerily. 'The bank guarantee scheme only covers a tiny fraction of the deposits. If the bank should happen to go belly-up tomorrow, I might lose everything. And if I left the money sitting there, it would be worth less in real terms in a few years' time due to inflation eating away at its value. I remember you talking about it on the *Late Night Show* a few months ago. What did you think of Marty Lovegood, by the way? Is he as attractive in real life?'

'Eh...as a matter of fact, Marty is a friend of mine. Perhaps I might get the opportunity to introduce you to him one of these days,' was Claudia's careful response.

Not for the first time, a little rocket of light went off inside Dorothy's head. There was no doubt this was not a dream. She was indeed rich. Her life had indeed changed beyond all recognition. She had had a crush on Marty Lovegood for years. Yet here was this tall, sophisticated, highly intelligent woman, with her calm grey eyes, sitting behind a desk that probably cost ten grand, offering to introduce her to the presenter as if it was the most natural thing in the world. She could not wait to tell Bel and Si.

Claudia smiled knowingly when the smaller woman faintly agreed that, yes indeed she would be very interested in meeting Marty one of these days, then returned to the thorny subject of money. Claudia was relieved to discover the winner at least understood she could not leave over one hundred million sitting on account, but of course that was just the beginning.

'At this juncture,' Claudia looked directly into Dorothy's eyes as she spoke, 'perhaps you'd like to share me with me your reasons for not adding your children's names to the winning ticket. Presumably the appropriate person at the lottery office explained the claims process to you in detail. If you had put them down as ten percent claimants, for example, they would have received a significant tax-free lump sum. The way things stand now, they will end up with large tax liability, even with the best minds in the country doing their best to mitigate the bill.'

Dorothy's heart began to pound, and her temperature elevated so much, she felt her antiperspirant beginning to fail. She was wearing a lacy gold cardigan over a pretty cream blouse, and prayed Claudia would not detect the sweat marks under her arms. Striving to appear normal, she made an effort to keep them pressed closely against her body. The guru noticed she was uncomfortable and smiled benignly.

'If the twins have given you reason to believe they are incapable of handling large sums of cash, now would be a good time to tell me,' she said gently. 'Have there been incidents in the past? Are one or both of them involved in the drug scene?'

This question shook Dorothy out of her self-induced panic attack. 'No, no!' she replied hastily. 'It's nothing like that. It's just that neither of them has ever really learned to say no, and I'm concerned others might take advantage of them. Besides, I only had a couple of days to make a decision regarding my official claim. After a couple of sleepless nights, I chose the simplest option and left my name as the only one on the ticket. Do you think I made the wrong choice?'

'Not at all,' Claudia replied soothingly. 'If you're in any way concerned about your children, then it's only right you tie up your fortune until they're older and wiser. Almost fourteen million tax-free euro in the hands of a soft-hearted teenager is a highway to disaster by anybody's standards. I simply wanted to ascertain the facts of the case before we went any further.'

Dorothy slowly exhaled and felt her heart rate and temperate reduce accordingly. Claudia was not judging her. The guru did not think she was a mean or bad parent. She was merely curious about the twins, and what sort of people they were. She risked a sip of water and sat up straighter, determined to give her full attention to the advice on offer.

And so began the first of literally hundreds of meetings which Claudia and Dorothy were destined to have about a subject close to both of their hearts, Dorothy's investments. Naturally, she would have as diverse and global a portfolio as possible since she would be able to access markets that were out of the reach of many others.

Claudia was pleased to hear Dorothy had invested in a catering enterprise, but did not understand why she had chosen such a small business when the world of investments was essentially her oyster. If she was interested in the service industry, then why not look at a hotel, or possibly even a restaurant? Why not get involved in a large, established catering company?

Dorothy deliberated for a moment as she watched Claudia's pale, elegant face, with its understated makeup. 'I understand what you're saying,' she smiled warily, 'and I may get involved in something larger in the future. What you have to remember, Claudia, is God sent me this money so I could help others. I don't have to tell a woman like you that funding for small businesses has dried up. Ergo, who is going to help these start-ups, if not me and others of a similar inclination? I saw an item on the news last year about a group of business people who got together and formed something called the Angel Investor Network.'

She paused and gazed into the distance while Claudia watched her in fascination. 'It's a good name, isn't it, the Angel Investor Network?'

This time, it was the guru's turn to agree in a faint tone that indeed it was a very pretty name. Dorothy grinned. 'You'll get used to me, I promise. You *will* take me on as a client, won't you?'

As Claudia assured her new acquaintance that she would most definitely be welcomed into the Feather Street fold, she privately wondered if anybody ever refused Dorothy Lyle anything she had set her heart upon. They came to a very amicable agreement on how much gold Dorothy would purchase, by the simple expedient of Claudia saying, 'I think you should put 10% into gold and 5% into silver. For now at least. This high won't last forever. What goes up must come down. Never forget that. Maybe we should look at some art investments as well. Real assets are the way to go. At least until the global market improves.'

Her latest client's response to this was, 'Righty ho, Claudia, whatever you think is best. This coffee is delicious, by the way.'

Claudia set in motion the arrangements to open a number of offshore bank accounts which would help to protect the cash deposits from the domestic banking system. Dorothy had no problem with this course of action once she realised that, despite their somewhat tawdry reputation, international bank accounts were not only perfectly legal, but were a standard financial tool regularly used by thousands of folks who did not possess anything close to one hundred million.

Dorothy perfectly understood why Claudia wanted her to keep the cash deposits at a low level. Nonetheless, she was conscious she had the expenses pertaining to the impending house build to cover. Saul's calculations indicated the cost would be in the region of three million, not including furniture and other contents.

There were a number of other projects which also appealed to her. She was wary of finding herself in a situation where she would be forced to liquidate assets because too many of her resources were tied up in the brilliant, yet highly complicated investment portfolio.

She explained this to Claudia, who, as a long-term resident of Sutton in North Dublin, was most interested to hear about the property in Howth. When her new client confided she had purchased, not only the site, but also the house plans previously commissioned by Phil Doheny and his wife, her eyes opened wide.

'But, Dorothy, I heard it took a year to get planning for that house, due to the sheer scale of the place. And now you're going to build it?' Claudia tried hard to keep her cool.

Not fooled for an instant, Dorothy grinned in triumph, thrilled to have shaken the guru. 'Construction started six weeks ago,' she told the other woman with relish. 'You should drive up there and check out the vast numbers of men and women who are employed. I'd gladly offer you a full tour, but it's madness up there at the moment, so it would be better to let things settle down before you risk it. The builders are making fantastic progress on the main house, and they tell me the studio will be finished by June.

Work will officially begin on the leisure complex and garage block next week. There was a short delay because we had to reapply for planning. The pool on the original drawings wasn't big enough.'

Temporarily lost for words, Claudia gaped. This made her client snigger. 'You look just like I did when my architect first showed me the plans. I had a Victor moment. I honestly believed he was going to show me a design for a five-bedroom, detached family home, with a garage and conservatory. You should have seen my face when I realised he had designed a fourteen and a half thousand square-foot mansion.' Dorothy gave into a fit of the giggles as she remembered how flabbergasted she had been that day.

'What's a Victor moment?' Claudia asked curiously.

'Oh, he's my horrible ex. He used to drive me nuts and leave me speechless.'

'What sort of things did he do?' Claudia persisted.

As usual, Dorothy had no desire to discuss Victor, but was pleased to see the more human side of the guru emerging. It was fair to say most people enjoyed a good breakup story, regardless of their own personal circumstance.

'He used to say weird things,' she admitted a little sheepishly. 'Once we were going to stay with old friends in the UK for the weekend. He asked me if they would 'allow' us to share a room, or if they would be 'strict' about that sort of thing 'like his parents'. As if we were going to visit a pair of fecking octogenarians from an Amish family instead of going to London for the weekend!'

On the other side of the desk, Claudia chortled. 'Did he do weird stuff as well?' she enquired eagerly.

Dorothy sighed mournfully as she recalled the hundreds of weird things that Victor had said and done during the eighteen months she had wasted upon him. Time that was gone forever, never to be regained. 'He had a Toyota Sera. In case you don't know, that's a sort of limited edition car most people have never heard of. It has something of a cult following. It has an owners' club and an internet forum devoted to it. Victor was the president of the club. He used to refer to the car as 'his baby' and attend all the meetings. He was pushing me to let him move into my place in Shankill almost from the first day I met him, even though he had his own apartment. Against my better judgment, I eventually agreed to let him move in with the twins and me.

'Don't stop now,' Claudia urged when Dorothy paused to draw breath.

'One of the first things he did was start insisting I park my own car on the road so he could park his 'baby' on the driveway in case somebody might steal it. He kept saying my car was perfectly safe and nobody would dream of touching it. Then, to add insult to injury, every night he would get out his laptop and spend hours on the Sera forum exchanging advice and so-called witticisms with his fellow Sera lovers. That went on for a year. It never seemed to cross his mind even for one moment that it might be inappropriate to ask me to give up my own driveway in a house I almost bankrupted myself buying. Or that ignoring me every night until he wanted sex might not be the soundest basis for a relationship.'

Dorothy lifted her eyes from contemplation of the fancy letter opener and discovered Claudia regarding her from across the desk with a mixture of understanding, compassion and merriment. The guru's eyes were most definitely sparkling. 'Wow, Dorothy,' she said, clearly delighted with the story. 'Victor sounds like a first-class loser. Isn't it pure fab you got rid before you won all the loot?'

28

When she left the offices of the Feather Street Group, Dorothy was in a self-congratulatory mood. As the building was situated close to St Stephen's Green in the heart of the city, and nowhere near a place called Feather Street, she decided to have a wander around.

It was a long walk to the main post office, but as she was wearing low-heeled boots and was supposed to be in training for the mini marathon, she decided to give it a go.

When the subject of the National Solidarity Bonds arose during the meeting, Claudia dismissed them as a practical investment vehicle for her client. The absolute maximum Dorothy would be able to invest in an individual bond was two hundred and fifty thousand euro.

In comparison to her overall wealth, this paltry sum was a drop in the ocean. Nonetheless, Claudia was of the opinion the bonds would be a good alternative to trusts for her underage nieces and nephews. She also disappointed her new client when she pointed out the type of trust fund she had in mind for the twins did not make financial sense. Since discretionary trusts had becoming increasingly expensive to run in recent years, they were really only suitable for minors or vulnerable adults. As the twins were neither of these things, Claudia advised against their use.

'When you begin the estate planning process with your legal team,' she told Dorothy earnestly, 'it's highly likely they will recommend what's known as a will trust. But that's a very different financial tool, whose main purpose is to limit inheritance tax. The only circumstances under which I would recommend creating a trust for the twins is if you wish to tie up their money until they turn thirty. Following our earlier discussion about the children, is this the way your mind is working? Because if tying up the funds for the long term is the way you're leaning, we should certainly discuss doing that as a matter of priority.'

Dorothy was startled by this unexpected change of direction. 'Gosh, no,' she said hastily. 'I want them to have at least two million each as soon as they finish their third level education. I'm trying to avoid them going crazy while they're still at college, but they're good kids. Making them wait until they're thirty would be overkill, and might make them resentful. Especially as I gave the rest of the family large amounts.'

'That's a very sensible attitude,' Claudia nodded approvingly. 'You'd be surprised how many parents and grandparents don't appreciate the bad feelings they generate when they set up these highly restrictive trusts. About five years ago, I had a client who created one for his granddaughter. The girl stood to inherit the best part of two million euro, but the trust only matured on the day of her wedding.'

Dorothy gasped in shock. 'You mean the girl had to get married before she could get her hands on the dosh?'

'That's right. The man in question had some outmoded notion that women are not good at handling money. Needless to say, the girl outsmarted the old fart in the end.'

'She married young?'

'On her eighteenth birthday. The stupid old codger didn't stipulate what nationality the spouse had to be, or whether or not he had to be of good character.'

'You mean she married a crook?'

Claudia smiled like a shark. 'She moved to America and had a quickie wedding in Vegas to a man who had already served time for fraud. As soon as the granddaughter had the money safely in her bank account, she paid the fella off handsomely, and they divorced six months later. She's still in the States and loving it. I hear she opened a chain of tanning salons and turned her grandfather's lump sum into tens of millions.'

'That's a cautionary tale,' Dorothy replied thoughtfully. Once I'm confident the twins can handle large sums, I'll loosen the purse strings a little. The last thing I need is a couple of rebels on my hands. I feel the need to be cautious at present, but I don't want them to end up hating me!'

Dorothy mulled this conversation over as she walked to the post office. Claudia certainly saw a broad spectrum of life and human nature from behind that fancy desk of hers. She had put forward a bevy of different options for the twins' financial future. From the extremely simple, to the eye-wateringly complicated. She suggested her new client spend a few months thinking about how to proceed.

During the time it took to reach her destination, Dorothy concluded a good place to start would be with a simple yet effective financial tool which would generate a solid return. Pleased she had made one small yet vital decision, she entered the post office with a lighter heart.

In total, she collected twenty-two National Solidarity Bond application forms from the large rack. In addition to her six nieces and nephews, she also collected two each for her own children, two for Viv's daughter, Yvonne, and two each for Bel's boys, Justin and Freddie.

She tucked the forms safely into her bag and left the building again. She jumped into a taxi that had just discharged an elderly lady, and asked the driver to take her back to Grafton Street. Jamie had recommended a beauty salon, and today was the first opportunity she had to search for it.

Since returning from the spa, she had experimented with a variety of treatments. So far, the most intensive had been the acid peel, which fortunately did not feel acidic at all. Reassured by Bel she would not feel any pain if she chose the mildest version, Dorothy had gone to a large fashionable salon and given it a go.

The treatment had definitely improved her skin. She felt she was looking younger and fresher than at any time since her breakup. There was no doubt the anger she felt, not only towards Victor, but also towards herself, had left her looking grey and washed out. It had also led to comfort eating and drinking which had resulted in her piling on the pounds. Pounds that were now slowly but surely melting away, thanks to her willpower and Jamie's support.

While the peel itself had been a success, Dorothy had not exactly taken to the salon. She could not quite put her finger on why this was. Her visit there brought back youthful memories of eating in the type of restaurants where the waiters looked down their noses at the diners. She had not exactly been made to feel small, because Dorothy was made of stronger stuff than that, but she received the distinct impression the staff of the trendy salon felt they were doing her a favour merely by allowing her through the front door.

As a rule, she made a habit of not frequenting restaurants with that sort of culture, and did not see why she should not apply the same rule to salons. This was especially important since she intended to spend a considerable amount of time in them for the rest of her life, now she had the means to fulfil her wish list.

In due course, she located the place Jamie had mentioned. It was situated on one of the side roads near Trinity College, and based over a shop selling cigars and spirits. As Dorothy climbed the stairs to Divine, she wondered what the demand for expensive cigars was like in these recessionary times.

The salon was not as large as the other one. Nonetheless, it offered a full menu of treatments, some of which sounded positively exotic. Most importantly, the atmosphere was friendly. When Sharon the proprietor greeted her warmly, Dorothy immediately relaxed and knew she had come to the right place. As luck would have it, a client had just called to say she had been unavoidably detained, and Sharon asked Dorothy if she would like to have a manicure while they discussed the various therapies on offer.

While she was having her hands dipped in paraffin wax, Dorothy explained to Sharon that she had been to a specialist laser clinic for a consultation, and had already set up a schedule of appointments. She was dying to try a spray tan, but had been disappointed to hear that laser hair removal worked best on pale skin and dark hair. Sharon assured her she had a number of clients with the same problem. They were still able to get their tans, as long as it had faded in time for the next laser session.

Dorothy was delighted to hear this piece of news as she was looking forward to starting the laser treatments. It wasn't that she was ever likely to be mistaken for a gorilla, although she had a few stray hairs on her neck which were fairly dark, and drove her demented whenever she spotted them in the mirror.

Her underarms had caused her a myriad of problems over the years. Any method she used to de-hair them either made her eyes water with pain, gave her a rash, or worked for no more than two hours. Since she was having those two areas treated, she decided she might as well go for the whole enchilada and have her legs and bikini line done as well.

Joan, the laser specialist, had initially hesitated to sign Dorothy up. She informed her that natural blondes only ended up with first-class results in approximately ten percent of cases.

'I wouldn't want you to waste your money,' she told her prospective client earnestly. 'It wouldn't be fair of me to get your hopes up. I don't recommend it for somebody with your colouring unless you literally have money to burn. Laser therapy is an expensive business.'

Dorothy forbore to share this nugget with Sharon, although Jamie had gotten a huge kick out of it when she relayed the story to him. Needless to say, she assured Joan the cost of treatments was the least of her worries, and faithfully promised not to hold the therapist to account if the experiment failed miserably.

'I tend to be a very lucky woman,' she grinned impishly. 'Why don't you sign me up and we'll see how it goes? I think you'll find I'm one of the fortunate blondes who gets amazing results.'

Seeing the small woman's mind was made up, Joan consigned any lingering doubts to the wasteland where all such doubts inevitably go to die, and happily set up the machine for a patch test. She refused to book the initial appointment for all four areas, saying if Dorothy had all parts zapped in one session, she might find it uncomfortable. The treatment was described as similar to being flicked with an elastic band; hence Dorothy was not sure what the big deal was. In the end, grateful Joan had taken her on at all, she allowed herself to be guided by someone who was clearly an expert in her field.

A further revelation was that the hair removal would be a long-term project because the hair could only be blasted while it was in the growing phase. Even a relatively hair-free person such as she could not reasonably expect to see a good result with fewer than six treatments.

As the hair could only be treated every three to five weeks, it was foreseeable it would be the end of 2011 before the sessions were done. Joan assured Dorothy that after the initial course of treatments, she would only require the occasional maintenance zap to keep the hirsute side of her nature at bay.

When Dorothy (as delicately as she could) enquired about treatment for the female genital region, Joan was quick to reassure her that because she used only state-of-the-art equipment, her new client could have as much removed as she wished, without any threat to her health. When the therapist recommended a 'landing strip', Dorothy was quick to agree. She was delighted with the prospect of ending up with something inside her knickers, hitherto only read about in magazines, or seen on the *Fashion & Gossip Show*.

After having her nails painted a deep purple shade for a change, Dorothy and Sharon set up the first appointment for her tanning. Sharon obligingly wrote the details in Dorothy's diary so her nails would not get messed up. At her client's request, she also fished the necessary cash payment out of her bulging wallet. If Sharon thought it was odd that a lone woman should carry such a large amount of ready cash on her person, she forbore to comment.

~~~

From: Dottie8888@chatulike.ie
To: SRedmond@chatchat.com
Date: March 26th, 2011
SUBJECT: DEBT CRISIS AND DIVORCE
Hi Simone,

Viv says it's okay for me to tell you what's going on between her and Garry. Obviously, Amy as the BFF has known about it for some time, although you and I have been left in the dark. Bel had no idea either. She is quite upset with Viv for not saying something sooner, but in all fairness it was a similar case when I was breaking up with Victor. I could just about talk to you about the situation, but not anybody else.

Bel hasn't broken up with anybody since she was fifteen, and I think she may have forgotten how heart wrenching it can be, and how ashamed it can make you feel, as if you've somehow failed. Anyhoo!

You know Viv and Garry have the garden centre and Viv's tile shop and the DIY store near Gorey in Wexford? Well, since 2008, things have been getting steadily worse for them, and the shops are losing money hand over fist. They took out a huge mortgage on their house at the height of the boom and used it to expand the business. Needless to say, it hasn't held its value and is now in negative equity.

They also bought two investment properties back in 2006, and haven't been able to either sell or let them for almost a year, which means they have fallen behind on the repayments. Between the taxman, the business loans, the overdrafts, the credit cards, the car finance, the mortgages and the trade creditors, they have debts exceeding one and half million euro. Yikes and yikes again.

Two years ago, Garry had an affair. Viv says she had fallen out of love with him by then, so although she wasn't exactly over the moon about the situation, she was not heartbroken either. They have wanted to separate since then, but their finances are so tied together they felt they had no choice but to stick it out forever more. There was no foreseeable way to extricate themselves from each other. What a state! The poor things. Isn't it awful?

Enter yours truly with her two million yo yos and the problem is a long way to being resolved. They have put the family home on the market, and will accept the best offer that comes along. They have each taken over one of the rental properties and are now living separately, although Yvonne is living with Viv.

They had a massive sale at the tile shop and DIY store. They sold nearly 75% of the stock and generated enough ready cash to pay the creditors and the wages. They have closed both shops, which is sad, but not unexpected under the circumstances. They had already let loads of staff go, but it was still very difficult for the few who were left when they were told it had all gone to the wall.

Garry is keeping on the garden centre as he thinks he can make a go of it now he is debt free. He is probably right. He will be able to give it his full attention now he doesn't have so many troubles dragging him down. I am relieved to hear the news. He has owned it for twenty years, and it would be a crying shame if he lost it now.

Viv thinks he will choose to live in his investment property long-term. She says it's a small townhouse that's perfect for a single man. She wants to move back to Dublin to be close to her mother, and says Yvonne is okay with the idea. At least they only have the one child to worry about. She will be starting secondary school in September. I don't know how it's all going to work out for them. I am in shock over the whole thing.

Splitsville for Viv and Garry of all people. It doesn't seem that long since we went to their wedding. I almost forgot! Viv has had her long hair chopped off really short as some sort of affirmation or something. She has also gained eight pounds, which is not like Viv at all. She says she is fed up having to watch her weight all the time, and has taken to wearing jeans and sweatshirts instead of her lovely suits and high heels.

OMG. I don't mean to be bitchy about our friend, but she looks like Ellen DeGeneres. All she needs now is a pair of dungarees and an equally shorthaired girl on her arm, and she will be fully equipped to join the local muff-diving club. What next? Hi to C. Love Dot xx

29

Dorothy reeled in shock and her jaw almost hit the desk as she absorbed the photograph of her best friend's lover. Was it any wonder that, thus far, no pics of the much-lauded Charlie had been forthcoming?

She was well aware it was the twenty-first century and all that modern business, but, notwithstanding modern times, the boy could not be a day over twenty. What the hell was Simone playing at? Was she experiencing some sort of midlife crisis? She had become one of those cougar women, like on the television. At least it explained why she appeared reluctant to pay them a visit. How would her elderly parents react to the sight of a boy young enough to be their grandson, with their precious only daughter on his arm?

Simone had made it crystal clear she was intending to spend a large percentage of her gift from Dorothy on a house for her and Charlie. Despite being more than a three-hour drive from Sydney, this love nest would be situated on Boomerang Beach, where Charlie had been living with his uncle for a number of years.

The couple had already begun to view any house that became available in such a limited geographical space, and had mailed her a number of links to some spectacular beachside properties. Simone seemed to be completely immersed in her new life on the beach, and there was no hint she was even considering returning to her career in architecture.

Dorothy instinctively felt her friend was asking for trouble. Not just in giving up her old life and career path, but also in setting up house with a boy young enough to be her son.

Not wanting to hurt Simone's feelings, but at the same time unsure of how to react, she decided to play it cool and see how things progressed. After all, there was always the faintest hope Simone would grow bored with Charlie and the surfing lifestyle, and go back to playing with the grown-ups.

~~~

From: Dottie8888@chatulike.ie
To: SRedmond@chatchat.com
Date: March 30th, 2011
SUBJECT: GIANTS AND SURF
Hi Simone,

I hope you are all well there. Thanks for your last mail. I love the pic of you, Charlie, and your friend, Ali. Charlie is younger than I was expecting, you dark horse, but very handsome with all that dark hair and tanned skin. Poor Ali is dwarfed by the pair of you with your long legs. She must find it annoying to be surrounded by giants. I know what that feels like so I can certainly empathise.

I have a very busy week lined up. I promised to join the Druid's Glen Golf club where Bel and Gerald have been members for years. I told Bel I wouldn't have a clue, but apparently there is a lovely pro there who will give me as many lessons as I need. I've decided to have two laser treatments this week just to get the ball rolling, with a trip to the golf club in between.

After that, I'll have an appointment every two weeks. I'm still not certain if I've planned it all correctly. I had a patch test done on my leg a few days ago. Although the shaving part is a tad weird, I didn't have any problems or side effects. I'm sure I could cut down on the number of visits by having all areas done at once. Bye for now. Love to all. Dot x

~~~

Dorothy smiled as she opened her email account. Then she remembered her best friend had a toy boy, and it quickly changed to a frown. Chastising herself for being such a stick-in-the-mud, she put all thoughts of Charlie's age out of her head and started to type.

~~~

From: Dottie8888@chatulike.ie
To: SRedmond@chatchat.com
Date: April 3rd, 2011
SUBJECT: OUCH, FECK, AND SHITE
Hi Simone,

Remember when I said I wasn't sure I had planned the laser treatments correctly? Well, forget it. It wouldn't be possible for me to have all areas done on the same day! I cannot believe that under the Sale of Goods Act, or whatever it's called, these clinics can get away with describing the sensation of having one's hair follicles destroyed by a laser, as similar to that of being flicked by an elastic band.

I was lulled into a false sense of security by the patch test, which only covers a square inch. Joan assured me the first few sessions are always the most difficult due to the sheer amount of follicles that have to be zapped, so I am determined to grit my teeth and endure it. When I got home, I felt quite sorry for myself because the whole experience was entirely unexpected.

This was not helped by Jamie laughing at me. I'd like to take a laser to his underarms and see how he enjoys it! Once he realised I was genuinely upset, he turned sympathetic and nipped out to procure a usually forbidden bottle of wine. We shared the vino in great accord and it took the edge off nicely. We drew the line at takeaway food. As Jamie pointed out, I hadn't undergone major surgery.

We settled for his homemade carrot soup, followed by grilled salmon cutlets and a few little potatoes and roasted vegetables. I'm learning all about portion control, and am officially amazed at how tiny my meals now are compared to what they were six months ago. Of course, I still don't eat saturated fats, but Jamie says, in time, when I reach my target weight, I'll be able to indulge in those things occasionally.

I've been so strict with myself, it's hard to imagine a time when I'll be able to look at a plate of chips or a piece of cake without feeling guilty. I suppose in time, I'll start to feel more relaxed about the subject of food. Love the latest pics of the swanky beach houses. Hi to C. Dot xxx

~~~

By the time Dorothy met up with Bel, she had seen the funny side of the incident at the laser clinic, and reduced her friend almost to tears when she described her reaction to it, and how Jamie had to placate her with wine when she arrived home feeling so sorry for herself.

She also took the opportunity to put the four National Solidarity Bond forms into Bel's handbag. She explained the plan for the boys, and asked her to take them home. As Justin and Freddie Kinsella were only fifteen and thirteen-years-old respectively, their parents would have to give consent on their behalf. Bel was very touched by Dorothy's proposal. As soon as they parked, she hugged her friend tightly, then dashed off to call her husband.

'Gerald is so grateful to you Dottie,' Bel was gasping for breath when she returned. 'He says to say thank you so much. Will you come to the house next week for a little dinner party so we can thank you properly?'

Dorothy was touched by this, but knew from experience that parents were often considerably more grateful for things done on behalf of their offspring, than they were for anything done for themselves. She had no objection to attending a dinner party at the Kinsellas. She hoped they would not be tempted to invite lots of available men, in the expectation she might take a fancy to one of them.

She was loath to spoil the good mood by mentioning this, and eagerly accepted the invitation, telling Bel she would bring wine. She knew Jamie would happily help her choose a mixed batch at the wine shop Helen frequented. It would be a fun little outing for them. Maybe they would check out a showroom or two while they were out, since she was no further forward in her mission to find a new car.

The purpose of their visit to Druid's Glen was to officially complete Dorothy's membership forms, pay the necessary fees, and schedule her first lesson. After signing up and arranging payment, she was introduced to a couple of Bel's acquaintances, who all seemed very elegant and friendly.

She left her friend chatting to them and happily wandered off alone to the shop. She was fortunate enough to find Georgie, the golf pro, on duty. He was a heavyset man in his late forties, with a pair of twinkling brown eyes and a kind smile. Having explained her requirements, he readily signed her up for her first lesson. As she had never played before, she did not even possess a suitable pair of shoes, and asked him to help her choose an essential starter kit.

At first, she noticed the pro was steering her towards the more moderately priced clothing and clubs. Seeing what he was doing, she matter-of-factly informed him this thriftiness was unnecessary as she had recently come into a few bob, and did not mind investing in the more expensive lines.

After that, the duo spent a contented hour choosing a range of goods. By the time Dorothy left, she was the proud owner of two full golfing outfits, as well as a lovely pair of white and pink shoes. Georgie undertook to order the expensive clubs she liked, which he did not currently have in stock in a ladies' size. He assured her they would be ready and waiting for her when she returned for her first lesson. He also said that, if she preferred, she could have a customised set made.

After discussing it with him for a few minutes, Dorothy decided to defer that treat until she was a more experienced player and better able to judge her requirements. Georgie agreed it would be sensible to do that. He also confided that men often demanded customised sets from day one, but women rarely did. She left the shop with a smile on her face.

After a delicious lunch in the club's dining room, Dorothy and Bel tore themselves away from the allure of the comfortable surroundings and went to visit Gemma, who lived in Blackrock. Dorothy had the bond paperwork for the children in her bag, and wanted to distribute the forms to all relevant parties as soon as possible so they could be completed and returned.

As luck would have it, when they arrived at Gemma's house, Joey's four-year-old Saab was parked in the drive. The senior Lyles were busy chatting with their eldest daughter about the proposed extension to her house.

After lengthy debate, Gordon and Gemma had decided against selling their home in a collapsed market. Instead, they had big plans to extend and improve their existing property, and had recently retained an architect. They also intended to invest in, and expand, Gordon's accounting practice.

They had treated themselves to new cars, and were considering taking their three children to Disney World in Florida. Gemma happily relayed all of this news as she rushed around making coffee and trying to force-feed the guests chocolate cake, despite their protestations.

Pre-empting her pal, Bel proudly announced they were on a mission, bringing application forms for bonds for the six nieces and nephews. Unlike their sister, Gemma and Orla had not rushed into marriage. As a result, none of their offspring had yet attained the age of 18, meaning their parents would have to give permission for the bonds. Gratefully accepting the paperwork, Gemma gladly undertook to deliver the remaining forms to Orla and Peter's house, as she knew they would be out all day viewing houses.

It was perhaps rather unfortunate for Dorothy that she noticed her parents' faces while Bel was showing a widely smiling Gemma which section she would have to complete. It was not just that they looked proud. They also looked relieved.

Like being hit by a meteorite, the realisation struck her that the family must have been discussing what, if anything, she intended to do for the children. She was torn between aggravation, hurt and anger. Aggravation that nobody had thought fit to drop a hint, something she could normally rely upon her mother to do. Hurt that they had apparently discussed the situation behind her back. And anger at herself. This was just the sort of situation she had been hoping to avoid.

The bonds had been a spur of the moment decision because she needed to get the ball rolling for the twins, who thus far had received very little of a monetary nature. As the bond rules allowed for a total investment of half a million euro on behalf of each child, she had naturally enough taken the decision to do the same for them all.

She had expected the family to be pleased and grateful. What she had not expected was to find them waiting with bated breath for their next hand-out, and speculating over the reason for the delay. Had she been naïve in assuming the two million she had given each of her sisters would be enough to compensate the entire family? If her parents' reaction was anything to go by, she clearly had. Dorothy learned a valuable lesson that day. As she and Bel drove home, for the first but not the last time that year, she asked the question, how much is enough?

I'll watch what I do from now on. They needn't think I'm a source of unending wealth for them and their children. The cheek of them! Part of me wishes I had only picked up the forms for the twins, and not said a word to anybody.

30

Because Dorothy knew what to expect on her second visit to the laser clinic, the treatment was less of an ordeal for her. Naturally enough, the closer Joan got to her 'lady parts' the more her client tensed up.

At one point, she found herself clenching her fists, gritting her teeth, and praying to both the Archangel Michael and Archangel Raphael for intervention, protection and anaesthesia. That did the trick, because even though Joan, using her specialist laser, ventured into places no man had ventured for some time, it was, for the most part bearable, and over pretty quickly. In fact, very much like sex with Victor.

The knowledge she would have a break before the next session was of considerable comfort. Dorothy wondered at herself for being such a wimp. After all, by the time Joan had done with her, she would be gloriously hair-free and never have to shave or wax again.

Whenever she noticed the nasty little critters rearing their ugly heads, she would simply pop back to the clinic for a quick blast of Joan's magic, laser hot poker. When she arrived home, Jamie had a bottle of wine waiting. Seeing this and hoping to elicit sympathy and half the bottle, she played up and told him it had been much more painful than it actually had.

Her next visit to Divine was more pleasant, if somewhat embarrassing. At Sharon's recommendation, she had booked a body scrub that would help keep the tan even. Apart from the occasional squeak of discomfort as her more sensitive areas were sandblasted, the treatment went well.

She made a mental note to have her body exfoliated more often, since it clearly needed it. Once her skin was sufficiently smooth, she was ushered into the special tanning booth where she was offered a pair of disposal panties, then left alone to disrobe. When Sharon returned, Dorothy was standing self-consciously in paper underwear, feeling extremely exposed.

The tanning itself was not unpleasant, and Sharon chatted away while spraying the entire rear side of her body from neck to ankle. Dorothy was just starting to relax and was looking forward to being tanned for the first time in five years, when Sharon announced the rear was finished and asked her to turn around.

Dorothy had endured a colonic irrigation while at Champneys. After that experience, she felt she was equal to anything. That was before Sharon began to spray her boobs. It seemed so unreal to have this woman, who she had only met a couple of times, standing in front of her, spraying her baps for all the world as if she was Leonardo Da Vinci working his magic on a canvas.

Despite her recent weight loss, Dorothy, like her mother and sisters, had quite large breasts for a petite woman, and simply did not know whether to laugh or cry at her current predicament. Especially when Sharon asked her to hold them up so she could spray underneath. Consoling herself with the thought that it was yet another new experience in her improved life, she tried to relax and, if not enjoy it, then at least not feel quite so self-conscious.

After dressing in loose fitting clothing, Dorothy bid Sharon a vaguely relieved farewell, in many ways pleased she would not be returning to Divine for a couple of weeks. On impulse, she popped into the cigar shop downstairs and, for the craic, bought Gerald, Gordon, Saul, Peter, Joey and Jamie, a giant Cuban cigar each.

She hesitated at the register, wondering if Horace would also like one. He had never been a smoker but who knew what a man would enjoy? They seemed to have the most peculiar taste in things.

'I'll take one more of those giant cigars,' she told the young man behind the counter. 'And I'll take a bottle of that swanky single malt over there. I have a friend who will appreciate it.'

'An excellent choice, madam,' the assistant replied gravely, as he rang up the final items and carefully bagged her purchases.

The bag was a comfortable weight in her hand as she left the building. She had deliberately not invited Horace to the house-warming party. Partly because an event like that would not appeal to him, but mainly because Diane was going to be there. Even though Amanda assured her she was worrying unnecessarily, Dorothy could not help feeling guilty at her behaviour. At the very least, she should have invited him, but made it clear she did not expect to see him at Falcon.

It had been petty and small-minded of her to deliberately exclude him. She resolved to make it up to him by ensuring he received the cigar and single malt at the earliest opportunity. Josh and Deco would probably deliver it to Shankill on her behalf, as they still dropped around to visit him most months. Dorothy fired off a quick text to her son on the subject before making her way up Grafton Street, checking out the latest fashions in the shop windows as she walked.

~~~

From: Dottie8888@chatulike.ie
To: SRedmond@chatchat.com
Date: April 7th, 2011
SUBJECT: BOOBS AND GOLF
Hi Si,

Have you ever had a spray tan? If not, be warned the part where the girl starts spraying your boobs can be quite embarrassing. Although the end result looks fabulous, if I do say so myself. Do you think it would be possible to have a spray booth in a private house? I'm sure there would be plenty of room at the palace for one. That's what I call the Howth house, due to its sheer size.

I went back to Druid's Glen today and my clubs had arrived. I was good to go in my new shoes and professional outfit, and luckily it wasn't raining. Bel was supposed to come with me, but Justin has a bad cold so I ended up going on my tobler (own).

Georgie gave me a copy of the rules because etiquette is very important, and it's not just about hitting a white ball around a field. He took me through the various clubs and gave me a basic rundown on the function of each one. He said for the next few lessons, we will be focusing on the essentials. Grip, stance, posture, and swing mechanics.

Once I master the rules and the basics it will simply be a matter of practice, practice, practice. It's a bit different from watching old Tiger Woods doing it, I can tell you girl. I was very uptight at first, and I gripped the club too hard and sort of attacked the ball. Georgie is a very good instructor and I soon relaxed and actually started to enjoy taking a swing. I'm still not very good, but I definitely started to enjoy it.

I was talking to Georgie about the golf championships, just to be polite. He thinks Rory McIlroy has a good shot at winning the U.S. Open, even though he had a meltdown at the masters. I told him no way, Georgie, even a novice like me knows that's unlikely. Then he floored me by saying it's the 111th U.S. Open.

Remember I told you about the number 111 in the angel book on my birthday? You know it's the wishing number, right? G says he has no inside knowledge, but will definitely be putting one hundred euro on Rory to win. I asked him how much he would bet if he was rich, (not Dorian Ganley rich, just normal rich). He said he would be tempted to bet ten grand. Can you believe that?

Did you see Dorian Ganley on the news, buying out that food manufacturer in Belfast? He is still Ireland's richest man and extremely handsome if his photo is anything to go by. They say he's worth twenty billion, although I don't believe that for a minute. You would need oil or diamond money to be worth that much. I'd say his fortune is closer to ten billion.

Hark at me the expert! I am so poor compared to him. My win is like his beer and shirt money. Anyway, we were chatting away about Rory and Dorian when I suddenly saw lots of little purple lights dancing around Georgie's head and I got the old tingling in the lower back as well. I received the distinct impression the angels were trying to tell me something. Gambling eh? Whatever next? Bye for now. Love to all. Dot xxx

~~~

As she was already out that way, Dorothy decided she might as well drop by her parents' house on the way home from the golf club and beg a cup of tea off her mother. When she arrived at the house, she saw Gemma's car in the drive and hoped she wasn't interrupting anything. Wendy, Gemma's eldest, was with her mother, having finished school early.

After the initial greetings, their middle child was plied with the required beverage. Then Pat and Joey set about extracting the full details of the golf lesson. They bullied Dorothy into standing in the middle of the kitchen floor and demonstrating her swing for the sole purpose of laughing at her.

She was beginning to wonder if it had been a mistake to take up golf and another mistake to drop by, when Wendy deftly changed the subject by asking her aunt if she had considered investing in a holiday home.

On any other day, Dorothy would have replied in an offhand manner that she would think about it in due course. On this occasion, she was wary of dismissing the girl's question and possibly hurting her feelings. Especially as Wendy was her favourite niece and inclined to be a little reserved at times. She smiled kindly at the girl and said, 'I haven't given it any thought, Wendy love, but that's because I've been so busy with the move to the apartment and having meetings with my architect about the new house.'

'Maybe you *should* give it some thought, Dottie pet,' interjected Pat Lyle. 'It would be lovely if all the grandchildren had somewhere to go during the holidays. Daddy and I would love it too. As long as it wasn't in one of those nightclub spots the young people go mad for. Daddy wouldn't like that at all.'

It was on the tip of Dorothy's tongue to suggest her parents take a small percentage of the millions she had given them back in January, and use it to purchase their own damn holiday home, but alas, she felt unable to say anything of the kind in front of her niece. It was one thing to be rich. It was quite another to be a rich bitch.

She could see her sister was a little uncomfortable, and had very likely guessed the turn Dorothy's thoughts had taken. At the same time, Gemma had a hopeful glint in her eye. She knew now that Pat had asked, her sister was unlikely to refuse the request, and it was not as if she was strapped for cash.

'Eh, yes, you're right,' Dorothy chose her words carefully. 'I should give it some thought. I might take a look on the web later this week.'

'I already did that, Auntie Dottie,' Wendy jumped in eagerly. 'As part of one of my transition year projects at school. I have a few printouts here, if you'd like to take a look.'

'Of course, I'll take a look,' her aunt replied, secretly wondering if the transition year project was entitled 'Lifestyles of the rich' or possibly 'Other people's money and how to spend it.'

Even Pat was a little taken aback at some of the details her granddaughter had printed off the web. Most of the properties were elaborate, architect-designed villas in the South of France, Lake Como and the Algarve. There was even one in Saint Barts. Over the years, Dorothy had discovered it was at moments like these when Joey Lyle's nature really came into its own.

He categorically stated that neither he nor his wife would be flying long haul, either now or at any point in the future. At their time of life, he said, they had better things to do than spend twelve or thirteen hours stuck inside a metal tube cruising at thirty thousand feet.

As Pat was inclined to agree that six hours' flight time would be her absolute maximum, the villa in Saint Barts was regretfully added to the NO pile. Dorothy liked the look of that particular one, and wondered if she would end up with any say in the matter at all.

The two impressive residences in Nice were the next ones to be discarded. This time, Joey stated he did not care if Bono and the Edge would be her neighbours. No daughter of his was spending twenty-five million on one house, just because it was situated in close proximity to a couple of pop stars. Smirking to herself, and wondering how Bono and the Edge would feel about being classed as pop stars, Dorothy dutifully placed the two Nice villas on the NO heap.

31

It was at this point Orla made an entrance, having just come from the hair salon. Her light brown curls had been straightened and highlighted and because she was sporting a tan, her blue eyes really popped in her face, making her look healthy and fresh.

She was delighted to have caught both her siblings together, and regaled them with the story of her and Peter's search for a new home in a market where the housing stock was sparse at best. As she talked, Dorothy scrutinised her sister's face. Orla was more like Joey than the other two and therefore found it difficult to mask any feelings of irritation. As soon as she paused to take a sip of her tea, Dorothy jumped in.

'Is there something going on between you and Peter?' she asked calmly. 'Every time you say his name, you clench your jaw. Do we need to send Daddy around to sort him out?'

Orla rolled her eyes and grimaced all at the same time. 'The physiotherapy practice where I run my Wednesday clinic has an opening for a partner,' she explained. 'I'd love to buy into the place, and the manager said he'd give me first refusal because he's known me for ten years. I would never have been able to afford to do something like that before, but now we have your lottery money it's a fantastic opportunity. The problem is, Peter's not in favour of it. He says if I become a partner, I'm bound to end up working long hours. He doesn't want me to spend so long away from the house and the children. That's why I'm a bit cross today. We discussed it again over breakfast this morning and he's being incredibly stubborn about it all.'

A heavy silence greeted this explanation.

'Gosh,' Gemma felt obliged to say after a minute. 'What do you think, Mum?' she cast a glance of entreaty in her mother's direction.

Pat sniffed and her mouth thinned with disapproval. 'Daddy didn't work his fingers to the bone in the pharmacy for all those years, and spend a fortune putting you girls through college, so you could end up sitting at home like housewives from the nineteen fifties,' she uttered the words in a tight-lipped fashion.

'You used to work there too, Ma,' Dorothy pointed out reasonably.

'Indeed, I did not!' Pat sounded vexed. 'I occasionally helped out during flu season and suchlike when I could be spared from the house. You girls were always my priority when you were growing up. It's your daddy you have to thank for your excellent brains, to say nothing of all the financial support you received at third level. At least, Gemma and Orla have him to thank. Dottie fended very well for herself without our help, although I'm sure she knows if she had taken up that place in college she was offered, we would have been more than happy to support her as well.'

'You would have made a fantastic nurse, Dottie,' Gemma said slyly. 'Any regrets about turning down the place? I still think it was a shame you didn't repeat your final year and reapply for veterinary. I'm sure you would have been successful the second time around.'

'Never mind all that,' Dorothy said in exasperation. 'How many times do I have to say it? I lost heart when I didn't get the points I needed for veterinary. I couldn't face another year at secondary school, and it didn't seem right to study nursing when my heart wasn't really in it. As it happens, I disagree with you, Gemma. I'm not sure I would have made a good vet, and when I look back now I wonder if perhaps it was a blessing I wasn't offered the place.

'Can we please stay on topic and stop harping back to things that happened twenty-three years ago? The last thing I want to do is come between husband and wife, but I don't see why Orla shouldn't buy into the practice if it's what she wants. After all, I gave *her* the money, and it's not for Peter to tell her what to do. Fecking men and their highhanded ways. I am so glad I am single.'

'You might be single at the moment, Auntie Dottie,' Wendy said reassuringly, 'but you're bound to meet a man now you're so rich.'

'Thank you, Wendy,' Dorothy replied sarcastically. 'I can't tell you how that prospect thrills me to the very core of my being.'

'One of the other radiologists at the hospital has just split from his long-term girlfriend,' Gemma was regarding her sister thoughtfully. 'He's quite attractive in a nerdy sort of way, and the ex has him pretty well housebroken. Would you be interested at all?'

'Have you all run mad?' Dorothy cried hotly. 'Poor Orla is being bossed around by her husband, and all you can think about is setting me up with one of your colleagues.'

'I doubt he'll be on the market for long,' Gemma shrugged. 'You're probably right. It might be a bit soon to start dating. You need time to adjust to your new life before you introduce a man into the mix.'

'I've never know Orla to be bossed around by anybody,' Wendy ventured timidly. 'Least of all Peter.'

'That's very true,' Pat Lyle regarded her youngest daughter suspiciously. 'Is there something you're not telling us, Orla? You haven't been messing around with one of those male therapists from the practice, have you?'

Dorothy was all set to scoff at the suggestion, until she saw her sister colour up to the roots of her newly styled hair.

'It was nothing more than a bit of harmless flirtation at the Christmas party,' Orla hissed, when she saw the appalled looks on her parents' faces. 'Peter got this bizarre notion there was something going on between us, which is complete and utter nonsense. He hasn't mentioned it for months, but as soon as I said I wanted to become a partner, he flipped.'

'The poor man,' Pat sighed sorrowfully, and looked at her spouse. The light shining through the kitchen window accentuated the deep lines on Joey's rather careworn countenance. His eyebrows were a bushy white over his sharp blue eyes, and Dorothy itched to tweeze them into submission.

Not realising how offensive his brows were to his daughter, Joey shook his head from side to side and gave all the appearance of a man utterly downcast by Orla's admission.

'Is it any wonder Peter's against the idea,' he told her gravely. 'What sort of carry-on is that? Flirting with another man and you a married woman with three children.'

'Hussy,' Gemma's mouth twitched.

'Jezebel,' Dorothy added with a sly grin. 'You have your work cut out there, girl. The man requires considerable reassurance before you have him back in his usual spot.'

'The palm of your hand,' Gemma quipped, and winked at Dorothy.

'Your sisters are right,' Pat said firmly. 'You need to make sure he knows you love him. Make a fuss of him. Why don't you leave the children with us and go off on one of those dirty weekends?'

'Do you think that might work?' Orla looked doubtful.

'Go shopping for lingerie first,' Dorothy told her. 'And pack one of those containers of squirty cream. He might take some convincing you're not about to leave him for a fellow physio.'

'Don't try anything too kinky though,' Gemma advised. 'He might think you learned it from the other fella.'

As the women dissolved into sniggers, Joey shook his head sorrowfully once more. 'You girls are very like your mother,' he said mournfully. 'If I had a euro for every man she flirted with over the years, I'd be as rich as Dottie now.'

The sniggers became a wail of laughter, and Gemma literally held on to Wendy for support as her body convulsed with mirth. Dorothy and Orla wiped the tears off their own cheeks as they tried to contain their humour.

After telling them all not to be so foolish, Pat went to make another pot of tea and slice some cake. Dorothy watched her mother pottering around the kitchen. There was no denying Pat Lyle was small. Dorothy's childhood memory was of a woman who had been well in excess of five feet tall. Even if it had been true back then, it was no longer the case. Pat could not have been any more than four feet eleven, and she looked every inch of it as she carefully sliced up a carrot cake.

Her naturally wavy hair had been blonde in her youth, although she now kept it a light brown shade. All her girls had inherited her oval face and upturned nose. Whereas Gemma and Orla had Joey Lyle's piercing blue eyes, only Dorothy had her mother's large brown orbs which on occasion gave her a sad, monkey-like appearance.

Pat was one of those women who genuinely looked like a grandmother. She had that not-too-skinny, not-too-fat, Granny look about her, always wearing comfortable trousers or long skirts and sensible heels. She shook her head at her still-chortling offspring and advised her eldest daughter to stop making a show of herself, and show Orla the pictures of the prospective holiday villas.

Orla immediately stopped laughing and demanded to know what was going on. A slightly bemused Wendy explained the mission on which they were engaged. All thoughts of whipped cream and lingerie forgotten, Orla eagerly accepted the first pile of documents and examined the NO pile.

After careful perusal, she agreed the distance was too great for the Caribbean, and Nice represented very poor value for money unless it was your ambition to rub shoulders with the jet set. She then turned her attention to the MAYBE pile.

Dorothy had demolished two cups of tea in quick succession, and now popped out to the bathroom for a little light relief. She admired her reflection in the mirror as she washed her hands. The acid peel had done wonders for her skin, and there was no doubt she was looking younger. The fresh air from playing golf had not done any harm either.

She wished she had blue eyes like her sisters that sparkled in a tanned face, instead of the dopey orbs with which she had been blessed. She accepted she would never be as good looking as Orla, but then there was always one prettier sister, ergo there was no sense in worrying about something that could not be changed. Orla might be the looker of the family. She might have men queuing up to flirt with her at parties, and a husband who loved her enough to be crazy with jealousy, but she wasn't worth one hundred million, was she? Huh!

Dorothy cast a critical eye around her parents' bathroom, which was starting to show its age. The house her paternal grandparents had bequeathed to Joey was a four-bedroom dormer bungalow set on an acre of ground. Morty and Bridget Lyle had somehow found the funds to build the family home back in the fifties, little realising Rathmichael would one day become such a sought-after area.

When Pat and Joey had taken up residence in the nineties, they spent a considerable sum modernising the property and landscaping the substantial gardens. Apart from the occasional lick of paint or new set of curtains, they had done very little with it since then. The décor remained firmly stuck in the nineties.

Dorothy understood why they had not spent much money on it in recent years. Since Joey had retired and sold the pharmacy, her parents had lived on a fixed income. They chose to spend any surplus cash on holidays, days out, and treats for the family. Facing into their twilight years, they had been loath to fork out thousands on new kitchens, bathrooms and designer wallpaper. But that was then and this was now.

These days, they had plenty of spare cash, and would not have to do a scrap of the work themselves. They could employ a team of tradesmen to tart up the whole house, and would only be required to sit back and wait for it to be finished. They could even employ a project manager and avoid the majority of the stress often attached to such endeavours.

Dorothy resolved to mention this when the moment presented itself. Better yet, she would ask Gemma to do it. As the eldest child, she could naturally get away with things the younger daughters could not, and could always be relied upon to initiate the awkward conversations or break the bad news.

Perhaps the senior Lyles had simply failed to notice how dated the house was beginning to look because they had been living in it for so many years. Yes, she would definitely ask Gemma to broach the subject of redecorating the house. The twelve-year-old conservatory urgently needed to be replaced with something more befitting the parents of a lottery winner.

Pleased at her devious scheme to enlist Gemma's aid, Dorothy returned to the kitchen where she fully expected to be greeted by a scene of familial bliss. Instead, she was astonished to discover a battle royal in progress. The fight was not limited to her siblings. It also included her niece and parents.

It quickly became apparent the dispute was over the proposed location of the holiday home. Gemma and Orla, their little oval faces suffused with irritation, and their blue eyes flashing, were facing each other down like a couple of stags about to paw the ground and charge one other.

Pat was attempting to calm her daughters, while at the same time vigorously voicing her opinion in favour of a house in Italy. Joey's thin face was screwed up and his eyes were also flashing, as he shouted at them to keep the noise down, while simultaneously bellowing his preference for something 'rural and peaceful.'

Wendy, wise to the ways of her grandfather, knew rural equated to cheap and quiet, which meant being far away from both shops and nightclubs. She was desperately trying to make herself heard above the din, as her personal favourite was a spacious, but very affordable apartment in Alicante.

Dorothy took a deep breath and let a roar at them to shut up. Startled, they stopped shouting and turned to stare at her in amazement, not having heard her raise her voice since she had become overexcited during the Wimbledon final of 2006, back in her Pre-Victor days when she had considerably more zest for life. Through gritted teeth, Dorothy snarled, 'If you don't stop arguing like a pack of rabid wolves, as God is my witness, the only holiday home I'll be buying is a bungalow in Westport.'

When Dorothy relayed the story to a deeply enthralled Bel, Jamie, Amanda and Helen a few days later, it was virtually impossible for her to describe the mixed reaction to this threat. Her sisters shut up, but continued to glare at each other as if the slightest spark might ignite their ire again. Wendy blanched and curled her body in a way which indicated she was wishing herself invisible, clearly assuming she would be blamed for the major falling-out the Lyles were currently experiencing.

The senior Lyles essentially ignored their daughter's outburst. Joey's eyes lit up at the mention of Westport, while Pat smiled at Dorothy as if she was the angel Gabriel, for all the world newly arrived in Rathmichael to hail the advent of another Messiah.

'Daddy would love a cottage in Westport for the fishing,' Pat beamed joyfully at her middle child. Westport was a beautiful town on the west coast of Ireland, well known for its scenery, angling and water sports. Joey Lyle had often coveted the holiday homes friends possessed in that part of the world. The idea of actually owning his very own piece of the West appealed to him very much and Dorothy felt her heart melt when she saw his eager countenance.

Once again, she recalled they had two million sitting on account, and asked herself what they were saving it for. If they were intending to have themselves made over by a plastic surgeon, it was safe to assume they had left it a tiny bit late in the day. She shrugged off all negative thoughts and resigned herself to the reality of her parents' thriftiness.

'Okay, Lyles, first things first,' she said in a determined voice. She grabbed her bag and extracted a handy fifty-euro note, which she offered to her niece. 'Your mission, young Wendy, should you choose to accept it, is to come up with a shortlist of properties in Westport in County Mayo for your granny and granddad to view, once they feel up to it. Do you accept your mission?'

Wendy eagerly accepted the fifty, giggling like the teen she was. 'No problem, Auntie Dottie,' she said. 'I'll find

Granddad the best fishing cottage in the Wesht,' she said, deliberately mispronouncing the word.

Her mother half-heartedly tried to intercept the fifty before it reached Wendy's pocket, but Pat was quick to bat her daughter's hand away. 'Leave the girl alone, Gemma,' ordered the girl's granny. 'It's not as if your sister is going to end up in the poor house.'

Gemma rolled her eyes and reclaimed her seat. It dawned upon the rest that they were all standing up and they quickly followed suit.

'Now,' said Dorothy, as she seated herself at the head of the table. 'Why don't we draw up a list of pros and cons of the properties that are left, and see if we can come up with a shortlist? It would help if we could pin down one or two preferred locations.'

Soon they had acquired a number of blank sheets of paper and were happily involved in marking each property out of ten. They based the marks on their chosen criteria. These were proximity to the sea, size of pool, distance to pubs and restaurants, transport links, climate, culture, and of course, price.

One of the more striking properties, a chateau near Lake Como, was quickly vetoed. The asking price was in the region of fifteen million, and Dorothy did not feel justified in spending that sort of money on a house which might only be used for half the year. Besides, Joey had started to turn an alarming shade of purple when he heard the sum involved.

There were a further two or three villas in France and Italy, which, when located on Google Maps, were found to be over two hours' drive to the nearest airport, as well as being fifty-five minutes from the nearest town. Having narrowed the choice of villas down to four, they set about voting for their preferred location.

To Dorothy's complete and utter astonishment, the Balearic Islands came out on top as everybody's first choice. She had fully expected them to vote for Italy, Turkey or Portugal. Even more surprising, the island of Mallorca was the outright winner, as it was deemed to have all the qualities the Lyle family required in a resort - namely, sea, sand, sun and hopefully sex - all within the confines of a very posh villa.

Wendy had printed off the details of two beautiful properties, one in Son Vida and one in Palma. Dorothy told her niece that since they had successfully narrowed down the preferred location, she would like to view a minimum of six potential houses before reaching a decision.

'I could do some more research for you,' Wendy offered tentatively.

'No, honey. What I meant was, I think we should go out there and view some places first-hand,' Dorothy smiled. 'The Easter holidays start on Friday, meaning it would be the ideal opportunity to pay a visit. I suppose you two already have plans,' she addressed her sisters.

'More house hunting for me,' Orla sighed. 'Peter says if he's to take all summer off, he has to work over Easter.'

'We have a holiday cottage booked in Scotland,' Gemma added. 'If you're thinking of something further afield and warmer, I expect I could persuade Gordon to defer the Scottish trip until later in the year. God knows the highlands will still be there in two months' time.'

Dorothy and Orla exchanged an amused look but refrained from commenting on the Scottish Highlands.

Dorothy said, 'If you think it might work out, I'll reserve some hotel rooms before they're all gone. Perhaps now might be a good time to call your husbands. We don't want to upset the little dears by excluding them from the arrangements.'

Gemma and Orla exchanged a look then grabbed their respective phones. They disappeared outside and from the kitchen window could be seen pacing up and down in the backyard on their short legs speaking rapidly into their mobiles.

They looked nothing like a physiotherapist and radiologist, and remarkably like a pair of bond traders or horse trainers. By the time they returned, Wendy had handed over Pat's laptop and Dorothy was already searching for suitable accommodation.

'I'm thinking enough rooms for twenty,' she told her sisters. 'Are we good to go?'

'Gordon is very keen to help you make the right choice, and agrees that Scotland is going nowhere fast,' Gemma smirked. 'We're thinking the nineteenth would be a good day to fly. That should give us enough time to get packed and organised.'

'Peter's delighted the kids will be getting a break,' Orla added. 'He intends to spend long hours at the office while we're away. I married a workaholic.'

'We have to be back in time for the royal wedding,' Pat piped up.

'Righty ho,' Dorothy replied, as she perused the hotel site. 'On the dates that interest us, it looks as if staying in Palma would be the best option, since we're intending to explore the whole island. Is everybody in agreement?'

They all nodded or grunted their assent.

'Good. There's quite a lot of availability for that date, but in a limited number of five-star hotels. One that can accommodate twelve of us in a mixture of doubles and singles. The other one is two hundred metres down the road and can accommodate eight. I'm going to book them all.'

So saying, she quickly ticked all the available rooms in the first hotel then filled in her details, asking Wendy to pass her wallet so that she could use her credit card.

'But, Dottie,' her mother protested, 'even if you book the rooms, what about flights? Shouldn't we be organising that first?'

'We're not flying commercial, Ma,' Dorothy frowned at the screen, wishing her mother would not distract her when she was trying to complete the form. 'I'll charter a plane. Although it will have to be a big one to accommodate the entire family. Maybe even a Jetstream.'

Having completed the booking for the first hotel, she quickly ticked all the necessary boxes on the second then went through the same procedure. She breathed a sigh of relief when she checked her mailbox and saw the confirmation emails for both establishments.

'Excellent, at least that part is done,' she announced with satisfaction and raised her head. They were all staring at her as if they had never seen her before. She pretended not to notice.

'I'm going to contact some estate agents first thing tomorrow. Correction. Not first thing. I'll book the jet first thing then I'll ask Bel if she wants to go. Then I'll contact the estate agents and ask them to set up a minimum of eight viewings for us while we're there. Have I forgotten anything?'

'A gold plated, diamond-studded, stretch limo?' asked her dad in voice heavy with sarcasm.

'Two or three limos would be more like it, what with all of us and the luggage!' Dorothy agreed cheerfully, again refusing to acknowledge his attitude. It had not been her idea to buy a fucking villa in Spain, and now they were judging her because she wanted to take them out there to have a hand in the choosing.

Well, let them judge her, she was fecked if she was going to worry about it! Gritting her teeth and determined not to lose her cool, she took her leave, claiming she had a multitude of things to do. Pat protested this sudden departure and invited her to stay for dinner. Dorothy thanked her mother, declined the invitation, and almost ran out the door. She promised to email the relevant details the next day, once she knew more. With her parents trailing behind her, she jumped into her Focus and took off with one final hasty wave.

Orla and Gemma joined their parents at the front of the house and watched the blue hatchback making its way through the gates of the property. Not a syllable was uttered, although the expressions they wore, a mixture of unease and envy, said more than a million words.

32

Dorothy was as good as her word. By lunchtime the following day, she had booked a Jetstream which would enable the group to travel to Spain in comfort.

She also contacted Bel and begged her friend to make up one of the party, thereby rescuing her from her loving family. Next, she contacted a Mallorcan agent who specialised in high-end properties, and asked him to set up a number of viewings.

When she had completed all her assigned tasks, she sat down at her computer and did some research into the subject of gambling. After an hour in which she mostly stared blankly at the monitor, Dorothy admitted to herself that she had made very little progress.

Feeling that perhaps the personal touch might be better for a novice, she capitulated and called Paddy Power bookmakers. To her relief, she found them extremely helpful. When she explained that she was interested in placing a wager on the outcome of the U.S. Open, they offered her odds of 18-1 on Rory McIlroy.

Dorothy asked if they would be prepared to accept a bet of fifty thousand euro. The pleasant young man at the other end of the phone said he could not possibly accept a wager of that size without the express authorisation of Richmond, his manager.

'Go ahead and discuss the situation with Richmond,' Dorothy told him. 'Make sure you let him know I'm a lottery winner with one of those credit cards that doesn't have a limit.'

Even after Richmond authorised the transaction, it took a further twenty minutes to set up her account and exchange all the relevant details. By the time she hung up, Dorothy felt wrung out, and seriously considered the possibility of leaving it at that.

Fifty thousand was a lot of money, especially for a first bet. *Don't be such a wimp. Try something else now.* Because she had heard so much about online gambling via the media and was curious about it, she browsed until she found a familiar sounding website. Having registered and created her account, she placed a modest bet of two thousand on Rory.

On impulse, she created an account with a second company and placed an additional couple of thousand with them. Lastly, she called William Hill, one of the large UK bookies, and asked the adviser at the other end of the phone what odds she would get on a twenty-five-thousand-pound wager on Rory McIlroy to win.

She was told by the exceedingly polite young British girl that 19-1 was that day's price on the Irishman. Once again, the operator said a bet of that size would have to be agreed by a manager. Dorothy repeated the message she had sent to Richmond, and the operator put her on hold. It was interesting to note that this time it only took two minutes to get the green light. Dorothy filed this nugget away to be contemplated later.

Was it possible the British bookies were more inclined to take larger bets because their market place was ten times the size of the Irish one? Perhaps they were more used to high rollers, and considered twenty-five thousand smackers to be almost run of the mill.

The operator came back on the line and Dorothy plainly heard the hesitation in the young woman's voice. She guessed the general feeling amongst the boffins was that an older and more experienced player would walk away with the winning trophy. The girl was clearly experiencing a twinge of conscience at taking such a large sum from a woman, who for all she knew might not be able to afford it.

The girl's attitude gave Dorothy pause for thought. *Perhaps I should forget the whole thing. Am I being foolish?* Her question was answered by a sudden surge of what felt like butterflies dancing up and down her spine. She took a deep breath, assured the girl she fully understood the implications of what she was about to do, then went ahead and placed the bet.

When she put the phone down with hands that shook from the excitement and adrenalin rush of doing something so different, she asked herself if she was totally off her rocker. *Too late. You've got skin in the game now, or whatever the appropriate sporting metaphor is. Just relax and forget about it for the time being.*

She verified Jamie was not loitering before making herself a cup of strong coffee with full fat milk by way of a small celebration. Then she spent what remained of the day making a list of holiday clothes she would need for Spain, and enjoying a long, luxurious bath with essential oils. By the time Dorothy retired to bed that evening, she was exhausted from not thinking about gambling.

 The group was due to fly to Mallorca on April 19th. They would be returning at the end of the month so as not to miss any of the footage of the royal wedding, namely HRH Prince William marrying the charming Catherine Middleton.

Dorothy spent the week preceding their departure in a frenzy of activity. Apart from her daily runs and exercise sessions with Jamie, she was still receiving a couple of hours Italian coaching each week from Helen. In addition to that, she had a golf lesson scheduled with Georgie which she was loath to miss. She also had a spray tan booked with Sharon, so when she arrived in Palma she would not be pasty and boring.

She had to fit in a site meeting with Saul as well as one with Claudia, who urgently wished to educate her client in the finer points of something called hedge funds. There was also a meeting in the pipeline with Gordon, Mia and Patsy, to ensure they were on target with the catering company.

She did not have time for a massage. Fortunately, she was able to squeeze in a pedicure, because she would be wearing sandals all week and did not want to disgrace herself. Jamie went shopping with her and helped her choose a week's worth of holiday outfits. He offered to take care of her packing while she went to visit M&P Catering, which was a huge weight off her mind.

Dorothy offered him one of the many pre-booked rooms, but he regretfully declined. He had recently met an extremely handsome actor called Jerome, and the two planned to spend some quality time together during her absence. They were considering a tour of Ireland, providing Jerome's work commitments allowed it.

As Jamie did not keep a car, he would be using Dorothy's Focus during her absence. They agreed that, as soon as she returned, they would sit down and find her a vehicle more befitting her new lifestyle.

After the twins' initial excitement on first hearing her news had abated, Dorothy fully expected them to have their own cars ordered by the end of February. By mid-

March she had still not received a request for the necessary funds, and enquired as to the reason why.

She was assured by her offspring that they were enjoying the process of choosing brand new vehicles. They claimed they had no wish to rush the experience and spoil it. She found their explanation for the delay utterly adorable, and was gullible enough to accept it at face value.

That was until the fateful day at the beginning of April when she overheard a snippet of conversation between Diane and her BFF, Emily. She had not meant to spy on her daughter, and it had been sheer chance she walked into the room as Diane was finishing the call. As a direct result of this happy accident, Joshua O'Keefe was summoned to his mother's apartment during the week leading up to the proposed trip to Spain. He was ushered into her study by a sympathetic looking Jamie. There, he came face to face with an enraged Dorothy. She did not even bother to greet him. Instead, she pointed a freshly manicured finger at her son's chest.

'Diane is in the process of ordering a Nissan Qashqai,' she hissed. 'That is a very appropriate car for a girl of her age. When I heard a rumour that you were also interested in a Nissan, I naturally assumed you were looking at a similar specification of vehicle. I have since discovered you have taken a test drive in a Nissan GT-R, and it is your number one choice. Presumably, you thought I would be unaware of what sort of vehicle that is, and give you the go ahead to buy it.'

'Yep,' Josh muttered with a sulky look.

'You were quite correct in your assumption,' Dorothy knocked a box of staples off her desk in a fit of temper. 'I have no clue what a Nissan GT-R is. Unfortunately for you, Joshua William O'Keefe, Jamie Irwin is a petrol head. It has 500 horsepower. I'm not entirely certain what that means, but Jamie assures me it's a beast of a motor. He can't wait to see it! He almost cried when I told him there was no way you were having it. What were you thinking?'

She stopped talking and put her hands on her hips. Josh knew from vast personal experience that she was beginning to calm down. He also knew he had to tread carefully. 'I was chancing my arm,' he replied quietly. 'I knew once you heard the word, Nissan, you'd assume it was a normal car. I was hoping you'd ask Gordon to go ahead and arrange the payment, and I'd get away with it. Deco said something would be bound to happen to fuck it up, but I thought it was worth a shot.'

'You're a chancer,' Dorothy spoke through gritted teeth. 'It's a hundred-thousand euro sports car, for feck sake.'

Josh snorted through his hooknose. 'And the rest,' he said. 'This is rip-off Ireland, Mother. Try one hundred and twenty thousand yo-yos.'

'You are forbidden to purchase a sports car until you are financially independent. Am I making myself clear?' Dorothy replied coldly. 'I suggest you find something more suited to a boy of your age.'

Josh shrugged and said sulkily, 'Maybe I'll get a Mini Cooper instead. The dealership will fit the racing stripes for me. Deco will be happy. He said I should have gone for one of those in the first place and not tried to trick you. He says deceit never pays.'

Dorothy expelled all the air from her lungs and sat down in her office chair. She closed her eyes and willed her heartbeat to slow down. The Space Ache sort of fluttered and she rubbed it distractedly. *Amy drove a Mini Cooper for years before she took off to the Lot Valley and became the Queen of Restoration, so at least I know what the fuck it is.*

'I'm disappointed in you, Joshua,' she said quietly.

'Sorry, Mum,' he sounded dejected.

Dorothy's heart melted at the sight of his wan face. She rubbed her chest again. 'I suppose you and Deco could both have a Mini Cooper. Providing you agree to be sensible and not race around Dublin like Stirling Moss or Michael Schumacher,' she gave her son a half smile.

The spark instantly came back into his eyes. Quick as a flash, he was around the desk and Dorothy found herself pulled up out of the chair and hugged hard. 'Thanks, Mum,' he sounded emotional. 'I'll go and tell Deco. See you soon.' With that, he was gone, leaving her staring after him in dismay. *Jesus, Mary and Joseph. Was I just scammed by my own flesh and blood?*

Close to the Falcon apartment building, Diane lolled against Emily Duncan's Toyota. Her best friend was perched on the bonnet of her car, intent on posting a tweet, so Diane did not interrupt her. She was trying not to worry about her brother.

She knew by Deco's body language that he was concerned, but doing his level best to appear nonchalant. Emily was not even remotely anxious. She brushed her strawberry blonde hair back off the alabaster skin of her face, and readjusted her designer shades. Then she moved on to Facebook. 'State of Kayleigh and Becca in these pics,' she sniggered. 'They were on the cocktails. I hope

Kayleigh's da doesn't see them. Rumour has it he created a profile on Facebook so he can stalk her.'

Having updated all her digital platforms, Emily now untangled her long blue-denimed legs, stood up straight and stretched. Even in ballerina pumps, she towered over Diane by ten inches. 'What's keeping that wingman of yours?' she casually addressed Deco.

'It takes time to receive a proper bollocking from a mother,' the young man replied patiently, 'give him a few more minutes.' He suddenly tensed and looked around. Diane glanced in the general direction of Falcon. Sure enough, a sprinting figure materialised. It took Josh less than a minute to reach the other three.

'Plan C is a go,' he crowed, his brown eyes sparkling with joy.

Deco's mouth dropped open. 'The fuck it is,' he spluttered. 'I thought she was going to kill you stone fucking dead. Don't go winding me up, man. A Mini for both of us?'

Josh grinned. He pulled first Emily's, then Diane's hair. They responded by hitting him as hard as they could in the chest. His grin widened.

'I honestly thought you wanted that GT-R,' Diane said helplessly.

'I *did* want it,' her twin replied happily, 'but I always knew the chances of getting it would be slim. Ergo, we came up with a few backup plans. C worked. Now we're both getting Mini Coopers. Happy Days!'

'That seems a bit unfair,' Emily said in a small voice.

'Your parents only bought you that Yaris in September,' Deco pointed out. 'You love it. You wouldn't change it for anything. The way things are with my family since this fucking recession began, my parents can't even afford to buy me a bike.'

'I don't begrudge you the car,' Emily thumped him on the shoulder.

'Ems is right,' Diane said firmly, 'it *is* a bit unfair.'

'Maybe you could get some Mandalas or Shimmy Shoos,' Deco suggested helpfully.

'They're called Manolos and Jimmy Choos, you big thick,' Emily did not bother to hit him this time. She looked at Diane questioningly. 'A shopping trip to New York would be very nice,' she said hopefully. 'Just the two of us. We wouldn't go mad or take the piss. Your ma knows we wouldn't go to Bergdorfs and buy up the whole store or anything like that. What do you think?'

Diane squirmed uncomfortably. 'Mum knows we wouldn't exceed the budget she gave us,' she said quietly. 'That's not the problem.'

'Well, what *is* the problem then?' Emily demanded. 'Do you not fancy the Big Apple? We could go as soon as college finishes next month. You've wanted to go there since you were ten. Or am I thinking of my other best friend?'

Diane squirmed again. 'It's us going alone,' she admitted sheepishly. 'Mum won't be happy with the idea of me travelling without Josh.'

Emily's mouth dropped open. 'Di, we're not fifteen any more. You're going to be twenty in three months' time, for feck sake,' she protested. 'I'm sure your mother won't mind if you take off with me for a couple of days. It's not as if we're heading to the fecking Congo.'

Diane shrugged. 'I know it's silly but I've never travelled without Josh. Mum gets these weird notions sometimes. She worries.'

'Are you seriously telling me,' here Emily drew herself up to her full five feet nine inches. 'Are you seriously telling me,' she repeated, 'we are effectively joined at the hip to these two losers for the next ten years?' She cast a glance of sheer loathing at Josh and Deco.

'Not that long,' Diane replied with a guilty look. 'Just until we're twenty-four and get our money. After that, we'll be able to do what we like.'

Emily grabbed her bag and began to rummage around. 'And to think I was going to suggest we backpack around Europe next year,' she growled, as she triumphantly produced a tweezers. 'Your monobrow is hideous,' she snarled at Deco. 'Hold still for a minute while I tidy you up.'

Deco obediently stood like a statue as she methodically plucked a few hairs from his forehead. 'It's beyond me how you attract any girls at all,' Emily said crossly, and stepped back so that she could admire her handiwork.

'It's my charm that does it,' Deco's blue eyes twinkled at her.

Emily appeared to be immune to this. 'More like you hang around a college for the visually impaired,' she replied then stared at his lips accusingly. 'Why don't you wear chapstick?' she demanded. 'Your lips are in a terrible state. Would it kill you to try a few grooming products?'

'Maybe you could bring me back a few bits and pieces from New York,' Deco suggested slyly.

Emily moaned and turned back to Diane. 'Come on, Di,' she urged. 'Think of a cunning plan. Josh got two cars for feck sake! You can't even get us to the Big Apple for five days! Call yourself a modern woman!'

'Let me think for a minute,' Diane ordered. Then she closed her eyes and leaned against the car again. Josh watched his twin pondering the dilemma, while Emily got out her concealer and busied herself disguising a few spots on Deco's face. Then she took out her brush and fixed his mop of black hair to her satisfaction. Deco remained impassive throughout the entire proceedings.

Diane's eyes slowly opened. They glinted in a way that reminded Josh very much of his dad. 'She has it,' he announced proudly. 'Atta girl.'

'What's the plan?' Emily demanded excitedly.

'Intervention.' Diane grinned all around. 'New York here we come.'

33

Three days later, Dorothy received two electronic invoices for the Mini Coopers. The cars would be of the highest possible specification, and would be fitted with the optional racing stripes. The sum of money required for both vehicles was enormous, but considering she had blown the best part of ninety thousand euro on gambling, she did not feel in a position to judge.

Besides, she had agreed to the cars, and had no intention of going back on her word. Josh was to have the red one, while Deco had chosen the racing green. The garage had provided full bank details, so she immediately transferred the necessary funds and emailed the details to the salesperson in question. She smiled to herself when she was finished.

Strictly speaking, the twins should not be taking time off college to go to Mallorca as they had exams coming up. When their mother suggested they might want to forego the trip and focus on their studies instead, she had been met with mutiny. They were indignant at the notion she might choose a holiday villa without their input.

As Helen was the only person she knew who had detailed knowledge of life at third level, Dorothy asked her to have a word with Josh and Diane. Helen was happy to oblige, and arranged to meet the pair for lattes and cake one afternoon. She reported back to Dorothy that all project work appeared to be up to date, and there was no reason to suppose either child would fail the final term paper. She advised Dorothy to relax and allow the twins a little more rope. 'They're good kids,' she said gently. 'They both love the courses they're taking. I honestly don't believe you have anything to worry about.'

'You don't think the money has gone to their heads?' Dorothy asked worriedly.

'Not yet,' Helen chuckled. 'Give it a few more years.'

Needless to say, Dorothy capitulated. The twins had completed the majority of their packing, and were looking forward to accompanying the rest of the family to Mallorca. Emily and Deco's parents had raised not the slightest objection to their offspring being dragged along for support.

This was good news for Josh and Diane, who were of the opinion their cousins were simply too young and boring to be worthwhile companions for them. This leniency was not especially surprising in Emily's case, as she adored her course in fashion design at NCAD and was at the top of her class. As Deco's electronics course was tough going, Dorothy would not have been surprised if his parents had objected to him taking time away from his studies.

The next time he dropped by Falcon with Josh, she enticed him into her study under false pretences, and casually raised the matter with him. Deco cheerfully informed her that since his mother and stepdad had lost the mortgage broking business, they were both completely focused on earning enough to keep the family home from being repossessed, and putting food on the table.

'It gets a bit harder every year,' he said brightly. 'They wouldn't even notice if I took off to the moon, they're that obsessed with keeping body and soul together. It's the younger ones, you see. If things don't pick up soon they might not even be able to go to college. That's killing my ma.'

Dorothy was startled by this insight into Deco's home life. 'Are they the proud sort when it comes to money?' she enquired timidly. 'I wouldn't want to offend them by offering to buy up their mortgage. That would remove some of the stress from their shoulders, and give them a bit of breathing space. I would only charge them the European interest rate, which is very low at present. The term could also be restructured to suit them if they're struggling with the repayments. It would all be done professionally through Claudia and Gordon. I would remain in the background so it wouldn't be too embarrassing for them.'

Deco blinked a few times and his jaw flopped open. 'You know what they're like. You've met them loads of times over the years,' he said slowly.

'Yes,' Dorothy smiled, 'but that was socially. There's a big difference between chatting with a couple on sports day, and asking them if they would like you to help them escape the bondage of a high street bank. Besides, Deco, I don't have to remind you we moved in very different circles when you and Josh were growing up. I never had the resources your parents had at their disposal. It's a wonder the two of you remained friends at all.'

Deco leaned back in the office chair and rubbed his right hand through his hair. 'I don't know what to say,' he said quietly.

'How about you take Gordon's number and give it to your parents,' Dorothy suggested gently. 'If they're interested in coming to some sort of arrangement, all they have to do is call him and start the ball rolling. I'll leave it entirely up to them. If we should happen to come face to face socially, I won't even mention it.'

In something of a daze, Deco keyed Gordon's number into his phone, then left the study with a stupefied expression on his youthful countenance.

~~~

From: Dottie8888@chatulike.ie
To: SRedmond@chatchat.com
Date: April 16th, 2011
SUBJECT: SCAMS
G'day Si,

Do you remember the time you told your mother you were going out with Declan's friend, Paddy? Remember how she freaked out because he was very wild, but you kept insisting you were in love with him and wanted to marry him and have his baby?

Then two weeks later, you mysteriously dumped Paddy and your mam was so relieved she gave you the money to go to London with Gemma and me for the weekend?

Try substituting a Nissan GTR for Paddy, and two Mini Coopers for London, and you have a pretty fair idea of the scam my only son pulled. The worst part of the whole thing? I distinctly recall it was my idea. Remember I called it the "Paddy Plan"? Holy Shit. Talk about Karmic Justice.

I had just gotten my head around that insight into my son's character when Mum and Dad dropped by on a little social call. They had somehow come by the information regarding the two new cars for Josh and Deco. They said they were a little worried that Diane and Emily's feelings would be hurt by it all.

They are well aware those four have known each other since they were five years-old. Even though they bicker, they secretly adore each other. There is no way Emily would mind about Deco getting a car, especially the way things have been with his family's finances these past few years.

I told the parents that, but they weren't convinced. They said it's easy for small resentments to grow into something larger and more toxic if they're not addressed. Seriously Si! They have been watching Doctor Phil. Even Dad started muttering about sibling rivalry. What does Joey Lyle know of such things??

Long and tedious story short, they think Emily and Diane should be treated to a little shopping trip to New York as soon as college finishes in May. I said that was fine, but Josh and Deco would have to go as well. Then the senior Lyles started getting their Doctor Phil on again. They implied the twins' relationship would begin to erode in some way if I insisted on them doing everything together.

They said now they are getting older, it would be bound to have a detrimental effect because they might begin to despise each other. Then they reminded me I was married one month after my 20th birthday, and I was well able to take care of myself, even if I did have appalling taste in men. Can you believe it, Si?

I don't mind telling you, they scared the living crap out of me with their crazy talk. In the end, I could take no more of their amateur psychology and gave into their demands. The girls will be heading off on their own to the Big Apple at the end of May.

Diane has promised to call me every day, and send regular texts and emails. She says she will be putting up pics on Facebook all the time she is there, and I will be able to see what she is up to. Jamie has promised to show me how to do all the necessary on my phone, but he says I am not to create a full profile for myself.

He says somebody like me has to be careful. He has offered to create a simple one for me, but says I am not to put up any private stuff or pictures, in case it might give rise to suspicions about the money.

He can't believe I have managed to keep my big win quiet for more than three months. I can't quite believe it either, but am truly grateful. I am looking forward to Mallorca. I will send you links to the villas I like. Bye for now. Hi to C as always. Love Dot xx

~~~

Now the thorny issue of the cars had been resolved, Dorothy suggested to the twins that they might like to start viewing apartments. She wanted to buy them one for their birthday, which was scarcely two months away. They seemed reluctant to commit to even a viewing, and she could not fathom the reason behind it.

The recent excitement of the cars had certainly cast a shadow over everything else. Then there was the pressure she had applied about college, using Helen as her emissary. Perhaps a combination of these events had somehow taken a shine off the apartments. Dorothy put it out of her head and focused on the preparations for her trip. She resolved to get to the bottom of the mystery while she had the twins pinned down in Spain.

Despite Orla's efforts to persuade him to change his mind, Peter steadfastly refused to budge on the matter of Mallorca, and insisted he would be unable to get away from the office due to work commitments. Dorothy privately felt he was looking forward to a week of peace and quiet, but did not utter the thought for fear of giving offence.

Given he was not accompanying them, she was surprised to hear from him a few days before they were due to travel. The reason for the call quickly became clear when Peter expressed concern about the entire family proposing to travel without insurance.

Admitting the fault was hers, Dorothy immediately asked him to rectify her oversight, and arrange everything through his brokerage business. Then she suggested he might like to take over all her insurance requirements as they occurred. She would soon have, not only the twins' cars, but also her own and Deco's. Not to mention the new house and everything that would be involved in safeguarding it.

Peter seemed pleased to be asked and even teased her a little about taking up with a Spanish boyfriend. When Dorothy replayed the conversation in her head afterwards, she was relieved he had called. Putting her insurance business his way was probably yet one more thing she should have done weeks earlier, but had not even considered.

She was beginning to think she should request a wish list from every family member, since it would probably be less complicated that way. If she went on as she had been doing, she would no doubt continue to disappoint them as she failed every one of the tests they lined up for her.

Dorothy was aware she was overreacting and being unduly sensitive. She hoped the holiday would go some way towards smoothing things over. After all, the extended family had to get used to big changes in their lives as well. It was not their fault they were driving her to distraction.

Like Peter, Gerald could not be spared from his legal firm since he was dealing with a couple of very complicated cases requiring his full attention. Fortunately, Bel had not made any plans that could not be easily changed, and agreed to join them along with Justin and Freddie.

Dorothy had earmarked two of the deluxe rooms for herself and her friend. She was looking forward to spending a few days with Bel by the pool, as they had not been on a beach holiday together since they were in their early thirties. They had somehow managed to all get away together in an attempt to help Bel come to terms with Naomi's death from ovarian cancer. Needless to say, they all missed Naomi and had been distraught over her passing, but Bel had been her best friend since they were twelve years-old, and had been traumatised by the loss.

Dorothy rummaged around the top shelf of the wardrobe in the second bedroom until she located her old box of photographs. It was a large box she had bought at a craft fair during her first year back in Ireland. Because the cardboard had been reinforced with wood at the corners, the container had been quite expensive.

She had not begrudged the cost, knowing she would use it for many years to come. She soon located three excellent pictures of Naomi, and set them aside to show Jamie. The trainer had listened sympathetically when she recited the tale of Naomi's cancer and subsequent death, and had already offered to scan as many photos as she liked on to an external hard drive.

As she rooted around in the box, she discovered a padded envelope at the bottom. It was large and full of documents. She wondered what it was until she saw the description on the front, written in her own handwriting: *Photos of Declan, O'Keefe family, and twins as babies and toddlers. Put in album for twins when they turn twenty-one.*

'Another year and bit to go before I have to worry about that,' she said with satisfaction. 'Maybe I'll have an assistant by then who'll do it for me.'

She pulled the photographs out and flicked through them. The vast majority had been taken during the years before the children's fourth birthday. There was a nice one of Viv and Declan standing behind the twins' highchairs at what was clearly some sort of party. Both children were wearing bibs that said: Baby's first Christmas.

As usual, Diane resembled a doll next to her more vigorous brother. She sat quietly, clutching a small clown to her chest, while Josh waved a bright red train at the camera and grinned happily. Dorothy scrutinised Viv's face. You got so used to your friends' appearance it was often easy to forget how attractive they were. Viv had clearly made an effort with her appearance for the party, and was looking stunning in a red dress and full makeup.

Declan's hand rested on Josh's shoulder and he grinned at Viv flirtatiously. *Given how beautiful she was back then, I'm surprised he didn't do more than flirt with her. Especially as I was probably wandering around in an old sweatshirt covered in milk and pooh.*

She put the photo back in what she hoped was the right place and flicked through the pile again. *It must be ten years since I looked at these.* She landed on another one of the twins at three years of age. They were standing on either side of a beautiful brunette, who was smiling at the camera with the ease of a professional photographic model. 'Where are you now, Brenda?' Dorothy asked the photograph. 'Hopefully, happily married to a wonderful man who appreciates you.'

As the picture looked as if it had been snapped with a top-quality camera, she was tempted to keep it out and have it framed for her study. She hesitated for a moment with her hand hovering over the pile of photographs.

A sudden wave of nausea hit her, and she put her hand to her stomach. Moving quickly, she shoved the photographs back into the padded envelope and flung it back into the box. Standing up slowly so as not to upset her stomach even further, she carried the box back to the cupboard and placed it gently on the top shelf. Then she slammed the door on it. Dorothy bolted to the bathroom and only just made as far as the toilet before she threw up.

34

Departure day came around quickly, and brought with it some much-needed sunshine. Six taxis were required to transport the holidaymakers and their luggage to the service centre at the airport.

Not at all put out by the size and multi-generational makeup of the travelling party, the crew of the Jetstream greeted them with cheery smiles and the barest minimum of security.

Despite the excitement, nobody let the family down or disgraced themselves during the flight to Palma. Dorothy was convinced this was mainly through fear of Orla and Bel. Both women were on the watch to make sure all members of the group behaved in a decorous manner and did not, for a moment, act like a family who, until recently, had only ever flown economy.

It was only after they had safely disembarked and their luggage unloaded that the younger members started acting out. Eoin and Kathy, Gemma's younger children, took turns at pretending to be a diva and a rock star. They began to order their cousins around, telling them to fetch their Veuve Clicquot and zebra striped Skittles. The situation was not helped by Justin and Freddie enacting the role of professional footballers, as they demanded a foot rub and lap dance.

Not to be outdone, Josh and Deco could not resist acting out a fantasy as a couple of high maintenance movie stars. They began to make highly inappropriate requests of Orla's children. They demanded, amongst other things, that the children kneel down and allow themselves to be used as footstools.

Adam, Laura and Ben, who were all under the age of ten, were reduced to tears of laughter by such antics, and the scene rapidly dissolved into chaos. Even though most of the adults found it amusing, Orla and Bel soon put a stop to the high jinks and marched the wrongdoers to the waiting limousines.

The children were thrilled with the hotels Dorothy had chosen. They had full air conditioning, two restaurants and three pools apiece. The group settled into their respective rooms on the double. They threw off their travelling clothes, donned their shorts and rushed to meet by the largest pool for a family powwow about the prospective viewings.

Dorothy had an appointment to see the first two villas the following morning. She felt it would be unfair on the agent to take everyone along, but said she definitely wanted Bel with her. The adults agreed it would be unseemly to show up at every villa like a band of gypsies. It was decided they would take turns to accompany Dorothy and Bel on the outings. In a week's time, when they knew more, they would view the shortlist as a group.

Bel was secretly delighted she would not miss out on seeing any of the properties first-hand. Feeling smug about her elevated position in the viewing party, she offered to be the designated photographer. In that way, the others would be able to get a better idea of the potential of each property, which would further help with the assessment process.

A very attractive estate agent called Lita, who had perfect English and made everyone except Diane feel inadequate, was their designated assistant for the week. Dorothy wondered if Helen also taught Spanish. As her conversational Italian was progressing well, she might be as well to add a second string to her bow. It was not as if she had to sit an exam on the subject. She just wanted to be able to converse with the locals without sounding like a total fool or putting her foot in it.

Accompanied by her parents and Bel, Dorothy viewed the first two villas the next day. Later that evening, once they had showered and were settled by the bar, the rest of the gang admired the photos Bel had taken. Using them as a guide, they listed the pros and the cons of both properties, and allocated marks out of ten. The next day followed a similar pattern.

This time, Orla and Gemma accompanied the two pals, while the grandparents watched over the children, giving in to their every demand for ice cream and other treats, while Gordon relaxed with a book by the pool and feigned profound deafness.

As the viewings were conducted in the relative cool before lunch, the group had ample time at their disposal to laze around the pool or head to the beach. At Joey's insistence, they even engaged in a little sightseeing. Diane and Emily wore their skimpiest bikinis, and sashayed along the beach with the sole object of tormenting as many of the male population as possible.

Josh and Deco stalked them, convinced that, left unchaperoned, some harm was bound to befall the pair. Despite bitter complaints from the scantily clad duo, the adults were loath to discourage such chivalry. They told the girls that when they were older they might not have anybody watching out for them, and advised them to enjoy the cossetting while it lasted.

As Emily's mother was an only child, and freely admitted she would have loved a few brothers to fight her corner when she was growing up, the girls acknowledged there might be some truth to this adult wisdom, and stopped bitching at the boys. After that battle of wills, things settled down and harmony reigned. That was until day six, when their peaceful co-existence was unexpectedly interrupted.

They had been unable to arrange any viewings for Saturday or Sunday because it was Easter weekend. Instead, they spent much of the leisure time enjoying the hotel pools and Palma restaurants, where they relished Joey's horror-stricken countenance as he sampled the local cuisine.

By Monday, Lita was back at work by special arrangement. Dorothy and Bel headed southwest with her, this time accompanied by Diane and Gordon. Diane was sporting her newly acquired tan, skimpy shorts and strappy top. Gordon had wisely chosen to wear cargo pants and sandals, since he was in constant danger of burning due to his fair skin and auburn hair. Even while on holiday and sporting a trendy baseball cap, Dorothy privately felt he still looked like an accountant, with a pointed nose that always seemed to twitch like a rabbit whenever matters of finance were under discussion.

Lita had lined up what she warned them in advance were the two most luxurious villas of the week, and Dorothy could hardly contain herself. She had already privately earmarked two properties she liked, but was determined to see everything on the list before reaching a decision.

There was no doubt the first villa in Port Andratx was spectacular. It was built on two fully terraced levels. It had one indoor and one outdoor pool, five bedrooms, six bathrooms, three reception rooms and a study. The views over the bay and Palma city were breath taking.

Lita proudly explained the property belonged to a world-famous singer/actor, who no longer wished to keep it because it held too many painful memories of her third husband. It transpired that during the previous May, the man in question had died tragically while attempting to scale Mount Everest.

It was a real treat for them to explore such a building, especially when Diane did a spot of research on her phone and discovered the 'sleb' owner was none other than Krystal Maze herself. The most influential woman in the world of entertainment, if Forbes was to be believed. The price tag for Krystal's villa was ten and a half million euro.

Even though she would not have missed seeing it for the world, Dorothy did not feel the villa was a serious contender. She was fully aware that, for less than half the sum, she could buy a fantastic place elsewhere on the island. Bel thought differently. She was convinced her friend had found the perfect location, and made her feelings on the subject abundantly clear. Diane was very fond of Bel, who was the twins' godmother, but even she looked at her askance.

'But, Bel,' the girl protested. 'Mum wants a holiday home we can all share. Why would she spend ten million on this place, when she can get a beautiful property for one million on the other side of the island?'

Bel glared at her goddaughter in disgust. 'This is a much sought-after area, Diane,' she replied condescendingly. 'I wouldn't expect you to fully understand the implications of that at nineteen years of age. This is *the* place to buy in Mallorca if you want to be seen by the right people, and be invited to the right parties. I know if Gerald were here, he would be recommending Dottie make an offer.'

Gordon, Dorothy, and Diane gawped open-mouthed at Bel, who was wearing a white halter neck dress and a pair of Gucci sunglasses, and was looking very Audrey Hepburnish in her kitten heels and matching white straw hat.

'Eh...,' Gordon's nose twitched as he spoke. 'I'm not sure the idea behind the purchase of this holiday home is for anybody to get invited to showbiz-type parties or rub shoulders with the jet set. As Diane says, it's supposed to be a family getaway. As Dottie's, albeit temporary business manager, I would have to advise her against the purchase of this villa.'

To everyone's relief, Lita, who had been standing some distance away, chose this moment to approach. She asked if they would like to continue on to the next viewing, or if they would prefer to go around again or possibly take a break.

'I'd love to move on and look at the next one, Lita honey,' Dorothy told the Spanish girl with a hint of desperation, all the while wondering what the hell was going on with her friend. Perhaps she was missing Gerald. Bel was truly devoted to her husband and had been neglecting him somewhat since the lottery had invaded their world. Dorothy hoped her change in circumstances had not been the cause of any marital strife which was manifesting in this odd behaviour.

In order to reach the next property, it was necessary for the group to head northeast. This proved to be something of a double-edged sword. They travelled in the air-conditioned limousine, giving them a chance to cool off and consume some water.

However, being stuck in the car for almost an hour did not help Bel's mood, especially when Dorothy refused to engage in a discussion about the Krystal villa. Instead, she calmly suggested the best way to approach it was to mark it out of ten as usual, based on their normal criteria. Alas, her friend steadfastly refused to let it go.

'But surely, Dottie chicken,' Bel urged, 'you can see how perfect it would be for all of us. Can't you see yourself on those terraces, with a butler in a white jacket serving you a cocktail before dinner?'

Diane was seated directly opposite her mother, and Dorothy barely managed to maintain a straight face when her daughter began to roll her eyes melodramatically. There was no doubt in Dorothy's mind that later on, either Josh or Deco would be coerced into donning a white jacket and playing the part of the butler, as she was presented with an imaginary cocktail on an equally imaginary tray.

She frowned at her daughter, desperately hoping Bel would not notice Diane scoffing. Gordon had no problem keeping a straight face. Dorothy assumed this was because, as an accountant, he heard so many fanciful and no doubt nonsensical assertions from clients during the course of his working week.

Just before noon, they reached the next viewing. This latest offering from the lovely Lita was a frontline property in Costa De Los Pinos with its own sea access. The villa looked normal enough from the front, and offered enough off-road parking for four cars.

Lita told them the house was best admired from the back, and asked if they would prefer to start there or head indoors straight away. As Diane was keen to check out the pool, Dorothy was more than happy to follow the path around to the rear of the property overlooking the ocean.

Diane squeaked with pleasure when she spotted the rear of the site and, for a moment, Dorothy felt tears pricking at the corner of her eyes. The garden was large and beautifully landscaped with trees, flowering plants and shrubs. The long sandy beach was barely a two-minute walk away, and was accessed by a gate at the end of the garden.

Slap bang in the middle of all the landscaping was a substantial pool in the shape of a shell-intact peanut with attached hot tub. The pool was surrounded by a red brick terrace on which half a dozen sun loungers had been laid out enticingly. Diane immediately rushed to the nearest lounger and threw herself into it. She demanded that Gordon take a picture with her phone so she could send it to Emily.

Gordon was happy to oblige, and Dorothy watched him taking the phone and aiming it at the girl. She saw Bel was examining the hot tub and decided to leave her to it for a minute. Now her friend seemed calmer, she did not want to risk another discussion about Krystal's villa.

As an alternative, Dorothy wandered over to examine a wooden structure constructed about ten metres away from the pool. She assumed it was a gazebo but when she peeked inside saw it was a type of wet room complete with two showers. *Impressive*. It would provide an ideal solution for swimmers who came back from the beach covered in sand.

She wanted to show Bel her discovery, and turned back to check on the other woman's whereabouts. She rested her hand on the side of the wet room and scanned the area for her friend. All was quiet. Lita had a small smile hovering around her mouth as she watched Diane dipping her toes into the pool. Gordon had wandered over to Bel and the duo were admiring the ocean view.

In the blink of an eye, the scene changed and Dorothy's grip tightened on the enclosure. Gone was the peaceful vista of the placid Lita and the girl dipping her toes.

Her senses were assailed by the sound of music booming through hidden speakers, while she simultaneously smelled the distinctive aroma of barbeque. The glass doors to the back of the house stood wide open, and Helen appeared carrying a tall glass topped with an umbrella. She was accompanied by a slender woman wearing only a red swimming costume and flip-flops.

Human shapes wandered around the poolside and terraces, although they were shadowy and out of focus. From their midst, a small figure emerged. *Orangutan.* She was sure it was the same man who had been in the vision of the basketball court. His tanned face was framed by black curls, and his black eyes danced with mischief. Wearing only a skimpy pair of pink shorts, he cartwheeled across the lawn in the direction of the pool.

Dorothy glanced around looking for his companion. If one was here, surely the other would be as well. The cartwheeling man came to a standstill and grinned into the distance as if he had spotted someone he knew. Then he raised his voice and bellowed, 'This pool is pure shite compared to the one at home. Let's head down to the sea for a decent swim.'

Dorothy scanned the area for the newcomer. She was sure it was him. The man appeared as if from nowhere, and she received an impression of great height and strength. The Space Ache hummed loudly in her chest and she gasped with shock.

Then he was gone. They were all gone, and she was left holding onto the enclosure with a tingling spine and the same sense of sadness she had experienced after the basketball court vision. Who were they and where were they? Why did she never see the taller man clearly?

'Everything okay, Mum?' Diane's voice broke into her reverie, and she did her best to pull herself together.

'The heat got to me for a minute and I felt a tiny bit faint,' she lied. 'Perhaps we should head indoors where it's cooler.'

Diane was delighted with the opportunity to see more, and quickly rounded up Bel and Gordon who were still dawdling over the vista. Lita led them inside and gave them a full tour. The villa was built over three floors and boasted magnificent views. The open-plan living area had stone floors, large windows and a real fireplace.

There were six bedrooms, four bathrooms and a covered terrace. There was a self-contained guest apartment on the second floor which had Diane squealing in joy. Without exception, every room claimed some sort of sea aspect.

Even without the vision and accompanying tingles to nudge her on, Dorothy knew she had found what she was seeking. Given what had happened at Krystal's villa, she was hesitant to speak, but could not resist elbowing her daughter gently in the ribs. She surreptitiously gave Diane the thumbs-up, before putting her finger to her lips and nodding in Bel's direction. It would be cruel to show too much enthusiasm so soon after the other woman's hopes had been dashed.

Out of the corner of his eye, Gordon caught the gesture. Despite the heat and thoughts of the book and cold beer awaiting him, it spurred him on to take more of an interest.

There was both central heating and air conditioning. Diane wondered at this, until Gordon explained the house could be used as an all-year-round retreat, and not just for the summer holidays. Diane's bright green eyes became round with anticipation when she heard this.

Dorothy knew her daughter was picturing Christmas vacations with her friends around the fire, waking in the mornings to sea views, palm trees and brunch on the poolside terrace with its convenient awning.

At 3,500 square feet, the villa was similar in size to the swanky one owned by Krystal Maze, although it was sadly lacking the indoor pool. Even though the resort of Costa De Los Pinos was quiet and residential, it was located a short drive from Cala Ratjada and Cala Millor, which Lita assured them were lively tourist towns. The price tag on this property was just short of three million euro.

Bel took the customary number of photographs, but spoke little as they examined every nook and cranny of the three floors. She seemed to slip into a light doze on the return journey. Upon reaching the hotel, she pleaded a headache and excused herself. She was not seen again until dinnertime, when the group assembled to catch up on the day's events.

Bel had indulged in a nap and was feeling more the thing. She scarcely reacted when her favourite Krystal Maze property was vetoed within the first five minutes. As it was obvious to all, including Justin and Freddie, that Dorothy had no serious intentions regarding it, and Gordon was not in favour of it from a value point of view, it was speedily added to the NO pile.

By the time their leisurely dinner was over and the older kids had disappeared off to the local hot spots, three properties had been shortlisted. One of them was the house in Costa De Los Pinos with the peanut-shaped pool.

On Wednesday, a tired but gratified Lita led the party in a convoy of limousines around the island, giving them the opportunity to re-examine their top three choices. Diane had already primed her twin about which villa was likely to be their mother's first preference, and Gordon had alerted his wife.

Gemma had warned her sister, who had given her parents the heads-up. By 9.30 on Wednesday morning, all the adults knew the villa at Costa De Los Pinos was Dorothy's favourite. They were all determined to make it their own favourite as well. The other two properties were considerably cheaper, with a price tag of 1.3 and 1.9 million respectively, but there was unanimous agreement that Dorothy's choice was the correct one. She was gratified by their support, especially after the incident on Monday. Even Bel seemed to have come around, and made some excellent suggestions about hiring a local gardener and pool boy to maintain the grounds.

'If everybody is in agreement, I'm going to make an offer,' Dorothy announced, after assembling the gang under a convenient palm tree. 'If anybody has any reservations, now is the time to express them. In about five minutes, there will be no going back.'

Not a word was uttered, although there were a number of excited squeaks, not all of which emanated from the youngsters.

~~~

From: Dottie8888@chatulike.ie
To: SRedmond@chatchat.com; ANorris@talkalot.com
Date: April 27th, 2011
SUBJECT: WEDDINGS AND VILLAS
Hi Girls,
Please find attached the details of my new villa in Mallorca. I got it for €2.7 million, even though they wanted €2.9. Gordon negotiated on my behalf, and I am a cash buyer after all. We also found a highly recommended solicitor to handle the legalities at the Spanish end. She speaks perfect English, which is a great bonus for us.

It has been a pleasant few days and the weather has been amazing, although I will be glad to get home after all the excitement. Mum is worried she might miss the royal wedding. She is convinced if we watch it here, William and Catherine will be speaking Spanish. Mad woman. Love Dot x

35

In the relatively relaxed atmosphere of the Palma resort, it had not taken Dorothy long to put on her interrogation hat and discover the reasons behind her children's apparent indifference to apartment viewing.

Their response to her query was startling. They were happy sharing their current pad in Santry, they said. They did not like the idea of buying a place, then renting it out to a stranger. They could not decide whether it would be better to buy one large apartment or two smaller ones. As they had never lived apart, it was proving to be a difficult decision.

'I'm sure we'll have made up our minds by the end of the year, Mum. When we've had a chance to think about it a bit more. We're just not ready yet,' Josh told her earnestly.

It was like looking into a mirror image of her own dopey eyes when Dorothy stared into her son's brown orbs. She could not help but feel a little surprised and disappointed. Personally, she did not think it was such a big deal. She was quick to point out they could each have a two-bed place, since there was nothing to prevent them renting one apartment and sharing the other.

She deliberately did not mention this had been her plan from the beginning. She was mindful of her parents' warning, and no longer fell into the trap of talking to Josh and Diane as if they were conjoined.

The twins were adamant they would ponder their living arrangements for a while longer, and their mother had no choice but to accept their decision with good grace.

After all, for one reason or another, hadn't she been putting off a few things herself?

She had still done nothing about finding either a piano tutor or a new car. She advised her offspring to take the remainder of the year to consider their housing needs, but found it difficult to put the whole thing out of her mind. When she casually mentioned it to Jamie, he was quick to reassure her.

'I was exactly the same at their age,' he said earnestly. 'A year later, I made a complete U-Turn. As soon as I turned twenty-one, my brother and I bought a tiny little apartment between us. He still lives in it with his girlfriend. When I go home, they'll find a bigger place and I'll move in. Give the twins another six or twelve months, and they'll be begging you to go house shopping with them.' Dorothy smiled at him gratefully.

Perhaps the kids are right. We have so much going on right now, do we really need more house purchasing on top of everything else? I'll focus on finding a new car for myself, and leave them in peace until next year. I wonder how helpful Jamie will be. He's so obsessed by this wedding he's starting to get on my nerves.

I know it's not just a gay thing because the world has gone stark raving mad over it. Anyone would think it was the first royal wedding ever to be broadcast on TV. I hope the dress isn't a mass of wrinkles because that will put him in a bad mood forever.

On the day of the royal wedding, Dorothy and Jamie stayed at home. This was partly because their recent exertions had worn them out, and partly due to the fact that Jamie was an unashamed royal watcher and had been looking forward to the wedding for weeks. As an added bonus, Dorothy planned to use the quiet time to surf the web in a quest for a car that might suit her.

~~~

From: Dottie8888@chatulike.ie
To: SRedmond@chatchat.com
Date: April 29th, 2011
SUBJECT: WEDDINGS AND CARS
Hi Simone,

I hope you and Charlie are well. I think you must be the only person who has not yet expressed an opinion about my new car. Is this an oversight? Bel thinks a BMW 5 Series would be perfect because she loves her own. Gerald is in favour of a Lexus. Joey and Gordon think I should buy an Audi.

Josh cannot understand why I would even consider buying anything except a Ferrari. The little scamp didn't mention the Nissan GTR. Diane thinks an Alpha Romeo would be cute. Justin and Freddie are in favour of a Lamborghini. Wendy saw an Aston Martin in a James Bond movie, and thinks it would suit me down to the ground. 007 has a lot to answer for.

Even Mum started rambling on about something called a Camaro. What is that when it is at home, pray tell? Jamie has two preferences, either a Jaguar XFR, or a Maserati Quattroporte S. Merciful heavens!

I have six different windows open on the laptop and am viewing photographs of them all. Jamie is busy watching the wedding. He can barely tear his eyes away from the screen, alternatively gasping in delight or horror, depending on who is wearing what, and how much he approves of it.

I set myself up at a conveniently situated table so I can surf the web in comfort and still watch the action on TV. I have created a little spreadsheet, and when I spot a car I like, I mark it out of ten. I am off to check out Rolls Royce. Back soon. Dot x

~~~

By the time Catherine Middleton gingerly exited the 1977 Rolls Royce Phantom outside of Westminster Abbey, almost causing poor Jamie to succumb to a stroke at the sight of her dress, Dorothy had narrowed her preference to four cars.

By the time the happy couple kissed on the balcony of Buckingham Palace, and Jamie had flicked through all the channels in search of highlights and yet more glimpses of the dress, she had narrowed her choice to two.

When Jamie took a break from alternatively criticising or praising all thirty-seven of the Philip Treacy hats on show, and came to look over her shoulder, she thought she was going to have to revive him with a glass of the Palo she had brought back from Mallorca. He simply could not comprehend she was contemplating purchasing a Mercedes or Porsche, when she could have a Jaguar.

If something similar had occurred a mere month earlier, Dorothy might have been more inclined to concede to his melodramatic demands. However, she had learned something from her experiences in the Balearics. She had learned when she found something that appealed to her; there would always be somebody ready to take it away.

Even if that person was somebody she loved and trusted. Not because they were being deliberately selfish, hurtful, or thoughtless. But because they wanted her to buy the thing that appealed to *them* the most, and not the other way around. The best way to deal with it, she had discovered - the hard way - was to stand her ground against all opposition, and patiently wait for the other person to come around.

~~~

From: Dottie8888@chatulike.ie
To: SRedmond@chatchat.com
Date: April 29th, 2011
SUBJECT: TIARAS AND MERCEDES
Hi Simone,

I am back. We enjoyed the wedding. Young and in love and all that. Good luck to them is what I say. Jamie loved the dress but if by some miracle I should wed again, I would prefer less lace. I know it's all the rage, but it's not for me. I would also like a tiara like Elizabeth Taylor. Married eight times to seven different men. Some call it madness, I call it courage.

By the way, a Camaro is an American muscle automobile. My mother is a nutter. I have decided against the Roller or Bentley for the moment. Perhaps when I am older and have a uniformed chauffeur to go with it. Ha ha. I am attaching two links. One is for the Mercedes I like and one is for the Porsche. Anyhoo! Cars, eh? A tad boring but a girl has to get around.

Have you watched much CNN during the past few days? That assassin is at it again. The one they call the Conger. He's in China this week, shooting up a storm. I say he, but it could very well be a girl with raging hormones. Or a girl who has been crossed in love. Or a girl who is seriously fucked off with the world.

Did I ever tell you that (s)he was on the news the night I won? I think (s)he must have a few emotional problems. Perhaps (s)he has a really annoying family. I wonder what professional assassins like to drive? Presumably something with a substantial boot for all their guns. That's a spacious trunk should the Conger happen to be American.

Ha ha ha. It's just as well I don't know him/her because my terrific sense of humour would be totally wasted on one of those highly trained killer types. Back soon. Love Dot x

~~~

'Jamie, honey, I'm interested in the Mercedes C63 AMG,' Dorothy eyeballed her personal trainer. 'I'm going to call one of the Dublin dealerships and make an appointment for a test drive. You're welcome to come along if you'd like, although I don't want to put pressure on you if you'd rather not.'

Jamie brushed his white blonde hair off his forehead and regarded her steadily. 'Did something happen while you were away, Dottie babe?'

'Not a thing except for copious amounts of villa viewing, sun, wine and high finance,' she replied steadily, hoping nobody else would let slip the story of Krystal's villa.

As Jamie had no intention of being sidelined from the car purchase, the next day the two of them headed off companionably. They were welcomed with great hospitality by the Mercedes dealership, where Jamie was soon involved in a technical discussion with the salesperson about turbocharged something or other.

Dorothy interrupted them to ask, 'Do you think the steering wheel is a bit fat?'

Both men stared at her.

'Eh...yeah, a bit,' Jamie agreed, 'but you'll soon get used to it.'

She nodded and went back to the colour options, which were, she could not help feeling, a tad boring. An hour later, she had chosen the AMG four-door sedan, which she felt would be more practical. Jamie strongly disagreed. He argued if his favourite client wanted to buy an AMG, then she should at least go for the two-door coupé, which was stylish in the extreme.

As he was not the one paying for it, Dorothy did not allow him to influence her decision one iota. *He can buy his own*, she thought, knowing she was being unfair but past caring.

They eventually settled on the performance pack as well as every conceivable optional extra available on the model that appealed to her, in an exterior shade known as Capri Blue. When the time came to choose the interior trim, Dorothy went for a combination of black cashmere leather and something called silver shadow.

The sales manager assured her she would have her new toy in eight to ten weeks. She did not mind the wait and was grateful the dealership was in the Republic. This meant when the new sedan did eventually arrive from Germany or Malaysia, or wherever it was manufactured; it would be delivered to them promptly at Falcon.

As it was the weekend, she texted Ken, her bank manager, to let him know a large sum would shortly be leaving the current account as payment for the new Merc. Notwithstanding the fact he was at home with his family, he called her back straightaway to hear the details. He was pleased to hear she had taken the plunge at last, although disappointed to learn she had not ordered a Lamborghini.

Her next purchase was significantly more adventurous than a four-door Mercedes. Dorothy initially intended to relax and play a round of golf over the May bank holiday weekend, but after a discussion with Jamie, the plan went out the window. As an alternative to hitting a ball around a field, the pair of them drove to Belfast on Sunday and checked into The Merchant Hotel, which Jamie had stayed in once before and loved. After a fantastic night's sleep followed by a sumptuous breakfast the next morning, they sallied forth and made their way to yet another showroom.

Their instincts were proven correct and they were delighted at the hospitality they received at the Porsche dealership. The boys from Belfast were over the moon when they spotted an expensively clad female, accompanied by a so-obviously homosexual male, strolling through the glass doors of the showroom. They promptly fell over themselves and each other in a bid to reach the duo first, and do everything in their power to assist them in making the right choice.

The salesmen raised no objections to Dorothy taking three different test drives in three different Porsches, then staring at the colour charts for forty minutes before eventually deciding on the preferred shade and trim. Feeling ridiculously extravagant, Jamie and Dorothy returned to Dublin on Monday evening and congratulated each other on a job well done. Now all they had to do was wait for news of the new toys.

They had barely been back a day, when to Dorothy's surprise, Jerome dropped by to say he had found her a piano teacher. He had encountered the man in question at an audition, and had been impressed enough to take it upon himself to make a few enquiries.

When Jerome informed her he had heard nothing but good about the Piano Man, Dorothy invited Patrick Joyce to visit her at Falcon. Straightaway, she understood why he came so highly recommended. Not only was he carrying an ivory-topped cane, he also had a trilby perched on his grey, wavy locks.

When he took off his jacket, he was wearing what could only have been a bespoke suit in pale blue tweed, complete with a cravat of all things. Patrick exuded patience and had a wonderful gentle and kind personality that immediately put her at ease.

Dorothy knew from conversations with Viv that the theory of music was difficult, and had left her friend with a near dread of the piano after years of being pressurised into attending hated lessons. Bel had also taken lessons when she was younger, and still told horror stories about being forced to spend weeks learning finger techniques.

Then there was the time factor to consider. When Dorothy originally conceived the idea of learning the instrument, she had only been living at Falcon for a few days, and her life had been less hectic. She was mindful the chances of being able to practice for an hour a day were slim to none. Patrick was sixty, hence she had no idea how he would react when she told him she really only wanted to learn popular songs. Apart from mastering one or two pieces for the sole purpose of showing off, she had no genuine interest in learning the classics.

Patrick listened to Dorothy's tale of woe with a sympathetic ear. He assured her she would find the classics a wonderful aid to learning, since modern songs tended to be repetitious. That said, once she had achieved a high enough standard, she would be able to play anything she damn well pleased.

He assured her that, far from spending months learning finger techniques, the best way to develop interpretation and expression would be by actually playing, even if it was only *Mary Had A Little Lamb*. Last, but by no means least, he said if she could manage three to four hours per week, every week, this would be more than sufficient practice time. This would give her brain time to recover, not unlike a bodybuilder resting between workouts.

His gentle voice and soothing manner appeased her concerns. She wished she could keep him so she would have a calming influence nearby at all times. Patrick liked her piano very much. He was sad when Dorothy relayed the story of how she had come to acquire the apartment, and how Anna had never returned to claim it.

According to Patrick, it was a Schimmel 169 baby grand in rosewood. This was something of a revelation to Dorothy and Jamie. They tended to think of the instrument as a wonderful platform for a vase of flowers, and not much else.

Dorothy's piano lessons began. During the learning process, a woman was revealed to her of whose existence she had hitherto been aware. At first, she was aghast to discover she had to read two lines of notes at once, while thinking about what her left and right hand were doing, and also master the use of the pedals. As if this was not enough to contend with, there was also the concept of the bass and treble doing its level best to reduce her to tears.

Pretty soon, she began to wonder if she had left it too late in life to start learning. Throughout it all, Patrick was incredibly supportive. During those moments when she was tempted to throw in the towel, she reminded herself that children as young as seven learned the piano every day, and this spurred her on to be less of a wimp.

Even though she was only a beginner, she soon became lost in the process, and wondered why she had not embraced it years earlier. Dorothy discovered that even in learning the most basic piece, she began to slip away into the world of music, losing herself in the sensation of the keys beneath her fingers, and attempting to capture what was in the composer's mind when he originally dreamt up the score. She took Patrick's advice and, instead of buying easy modern pieces right away, stuck with the classics. Sure enough, she soon found she was learning at a rapid pace.

Sensing that Patrick was not as affluent as he had once been, Dorothy offered to pay him a fixed monthly fee, regardless of the number of lessons she was able to fit in. This was, she explained, because lately her schedule had been difficult to manage due to some major life changing events. There might be times when she would suddenly call upon him, while there might be others when he would not hear from her for weeks at a time.

Upon hearing this, Patrick grew alarmed. He asked if she was in the middle of a divorce or had health problems. Dorothy instinctively knew his reaction was genuine, and he was unaware of her personal circumstances. A rather sheepish Jamie later admitted that Jerome had a strict habit of being discreet about his boyfriend's rich employer, in case some avaricious queer might try to put the moves on Jamie.

When Dorothy threw caution to the wind and revealed the true state of affairs, Patrick was flabbergasted, but quickly revived. 'In that case, young lady,' he bowed slightly. 'I accept your offer of the monthly fee. I also intend to charge you slightly more than my usual clients because you have been such a lucky little minx.'

36

By the end of the first week in May, Dorothy was organised enough to yet again pack her bags and leave Falcon behind. On this occasion, she drove to County Kerry in the southwest of the state, where she had arranged to visit her old friends, Jools and Bea Lacey.

Originally hailing from Norfolk in the United Kingdom, the Laceys ran a Bed & Breakfast in the tourist resort of Killarney. Dorothy first met them ten years earlier when she had taken the twins on a break to that neck of the woods. Back in the days when a holiday abroad was a real luxury and a swanky villa in Mallorca was something you only got to see on holiday shows.

She planned the trip carefully in advance. She deliberately scheduled it after the busy bank holiday period so her pals would have more free time to devote to her visit. Over the phone, she told the Laceys she had important news to share. After she arrived and they greeted each other, Dorothy sustained a severe shock when it quickly became apparent they thought her news was that she was getting married.

'Why would you think such a thing?' she demanded incredulously.

Jools and Bea exchanged a glance. 'Well...you've been single since Victor,' Bea replied hesitantly. 'We thought that *might* be it. Then when you turned up looking so tanned and slim and gorgeous, we naturally assumed there was a man involved.'

Jools readjusted his glasses while he perused her face. Dorothy stared at his bald head for almost a minute, not sure how to react. Then she shifted her focus to Bea and regarded the multitude of plaits framing her rectangular face. In their turn, Bea's brown eyes regarded the visitor with avid interest.

After Dorothy had looked her fill, she began to psych herself up to deliver a speech about how a woman did not need a man in her life in order to look good. The ring of her phone interrupted before she could begin her remonstrations in earnest.

Bel was the one who stopped Dorothy in her tracks and saved the Laceys from the threatened earache. It had been brought to her attention that Dublin was about to be treated to virtually a full week of traffic restrictions. This was due to the impending visit of the Queen of England, closely followed by the American President. Bel was of the opinion the two friends could avoid the hassle by the simple expedient of heading off to Rome for ten days.

As they had returned from Spain a mere ten days earlier, and Dorothy was looking forward to spending some time at home, relaxing and catching up with her many commitments, it was on the tip of her tongue to refuse the request. As she opened her mouth to do so, she found herself hesitating. Although the last day or two in Mallorca had been relaxed and enjoyable, she had not been able to shake off the feeling that Bel was still sorely disappointed at her friend's refusal to purchase the Krystal Maze villa.

'What's the matter, Dottie?' Bel sounded peeved at the other end of the phone.

'It's just I was hoping to see Horace on his birthday,' she replied sheepishly. 'He turns thirty on the nineteenth of this month. I'll miss it if I'm away.'

'Why don't you send him a lovely gift and tell him you'll be over to visit him as soon as you get back?' Bel suggested reasonably. 'You can buy him and Amanda a pair of designer shades, and visit them both in early June. You could make a day of it. I bet they'd love that.'

'That's not a bad idea,' Dorothy reluctantly admitted. 'I don't want him to think I've abandoned him. I expect Josh will deliver the gift on the day. He's very fond of Horace.'

'After the cars you bought him and Deco, I should hope he would willingly run a little errand for you,' Bel replied drily. 'So, Missus, are we on for Rome or what? Don't keep me hanging. I'm a woman on the edge.'

Feeling rather overwhelmed by this unexpected turn of events, Dorothy found herself agreeing that a trip to Rome sounded fantastic. She smiled when she heard the answering squeal of excitement at the other end of the line. Still standing in the Lacey's kitchen with the phone pressed against her ear, Dorothy listened to Bel explaining she had been online and really liked the look of the Hotel Cavalieri. It was five-star, and by all accounts the preferred hangout of celebrities whenever they visited Rome. As a bonus, it had no fewer than three pools.

Bel had done a little preliminary investigative work and discovered there were two suites available for the dates she had in mind. The problem was, due to the cost, she really needed Dottie's credit card details. Dorothy was not surprised when she heard the price of each suite. Still reluctant to rock the boat, since Bel clearly had her heart set on the trip, she fished out her wallet and managed to extract her credit card, phone still in hand. As she called out the card number and the usual details, she grimaced apologetically at the Laceys. 'Won't be a tick,' she whispered.

'Dottie chick, is it okay for me to book the plane using this card?' Bel's voice carried into the kitchen. 'Gerald was only saying last night you really should open an account with one of the private jet companies. I bet they wouldn't mind invoicing you, if you asked.'

'Sure, that's fine. Make sure you book that company we used the last time,' Dorothy replied, noticing Jools and Bea were beginning to look at her rather strangely. 'I thought they were very professional, considering they had a planeload of children. To say nothing of Joey giving them tips on flying, bless his heart. Hon, I have to go now. Don't forget to mail me all the details later once you've made the booking. Talk soon!' With that, she disconnected and returned to her friends.

Jools and Bea were in their mid-thirties. They had been married for twelve years but were childless. They had purchased the medium-sized B&B with money Bea had inherited upon the passing of her parents.

They had built it into a very popular establishment, with over 95% occupancy during high season, and 65% during low. This was due to a combination of their marketing skills and an extremely professional attitude to customer service. Dorothy was not a huge fan of Irish hotels or B&BS in general, but on her first visit to Killarney she had fallen in love with The Bee.

Unlike many of the larger hotels that had lowered their prices, but at the same time lowered their standards of service, The Bee had managed to remain competitive while still maintaining a consistent level of quality that put many larger establishments to shame.

Jools quickly carried Dorothy's case up to her room and told her she had exactly forty minutes to freshen up and change out of her travelling clothes. Then he dashed off to continue with his food preparation and other duties. She thoughtfully hung up her two best dresses and mulled over the prospect of seeing the Vatican Museum and Trevi Fountain.

After her shower, she dressed in a T-shirt and comfortable trousers. Then she slipped a neat envelope into her pocket and slowly made her way downstairs. She knew from past experience the Laceys would not mind she had not told them the news earlier. It was the amount of the cheque that was eating at her. She hoped she had judged it correctly. Jools and Bea had always been very good to her and the twins.

Dorothy was well aware that since the bubble burst in 2008, times had been challenging in the hospitality business. In 2009, the Laceys had even hinted they might return to the UK if things did not pick up. They had not mentioned it since then, but that did not mean they were rolling in juice. It simply meant that, like the rest of the nation, they were managing their resources better and cutting their proverbial cloth.

Over dinner, Dorothy broke her news. Then she handed them a cheque for three hundred thousand euro, plus a second one for the gift tax. The couple stared at her mutely for two or three minutes, then at each other. Still silent, they went back to eating their dinner. Sensing something was afoot, and wondering if perhaps Bea was pregnant at last, Dorothy concentrated on eating the delicious trout and fresh vegetables Jools had prepared, and allowed them time to collect themselves.

'So you're not getting married?' Bea asked, as they cleared the dinner plates and Jools served bowls of fresh fruit salad.

'Absolutely not,' Dorothy replied cheerfully. 'Despite recent developments, I'm still very much the single woman. I don't anticipate that changing any time soon. As a matter of fact, on my birthday I took the decision to remain man-less for the rest of my life. A few hours later, I discovered I had won. I couldn't help but think of it as a sign from my angels that I'm destined to be alone.'

The Laceys briefly exchanged a glance, but refrained from comment. Instead, they asked what she had been doing since January, and more specifically, how she had spent her money. Dorothy obligingly relayed the story of how she met Saul and bought the apartment, and because of that, purchased the site in Dublin 13, and how her new rock-star pad was currently under construction. She then went on to tell them about her twelve days in Champneys which was the start of her transformation.

Then she told them how she had discovered, not only Helen and Italian lessons, but also Jamie and cooking lessons, Georgie and golf lessons, and of course, Patrick and piano lessons. Lastly, she filled them in on the ten days she had recently spent in Mallorca on a quest for the perfect villa.

'You didn't mention any investments,' Jools commented gravely, after he had dutifully admired a few pics of the new holiday home with its peanut pool.

'Oh, don't worry about that,' Dorothy replied breezily. 'Claudia Healy is my financial adviser. You know the guru from TV with the brain as large as a planet? She's already created a substantial portfolio for me, and she's trying to educate me in the ways of high finance. Poor woman.'

'Have you considered investing in any businesses?' Bea enquired hesitantly.

'Absolutely. But so far, I've only managed to find a company called M&P Catering. Claudia felt they were rather on the small side for a woman of my means, although I went ahead anyway. My brother-in-law, Gordon, is taking care of my business dealings for the time being, but he says if I continue to invest in other companies, I'll have to hire an assistant. Ideally one with an accounting or business background.'

Dorothy caught her breath and sipped her wine. She wondered if she had forgotten to tell them anything significant. She had deliberately avoided mentioning the large sums she had given her family and close friends. She had genuinely forgotten to mention the Mercedes, which no doubt they would see the next time she came to visit.

Sometimes she found it difficult to remember all the things she had seen and accomplished during the course of the past few months. Not for the first time, she marvelled at how different her life was now compared to how it had been a short six months earlier.

Bea invited her guest into the small family sitting room, where she almost tenderly placed her in the most comfortable armchair before lighting the gas fire. Even though it was May, the night air was chilly. They were not enjoying especially good weather, and Dorothy hoped it would not impede the construction of the house.

She had authorised Jake, the building contractor, to employ as many men as he needed in order to make the best progress in the fastest time possible. During their last meeting, Saul assured her that more men were employed on her site than he had ever heard of before. Indeed, he was growing concerned they would run out of work for some of them.

'I don't want anybody let go until September at the earliest,' Dorothy told him. 'We need to take advantage of every day it doesn't rain. Don't be worrying about money!'

The tennis courts and changing rooms were well underway, while the studio and garage were almost finished. The leisure complex and pavilion were under construction in tandem with the main house. As she relaxed into the chair and admired the dancing flames, Dorothy idly wondered who was going to keep her house clean once it was finished. She had just started to explore the various possibilities, when Jools and Bea returned from the kitchen with more wine and a brochure.

~~~

From: Dottie8888@chatulike.ie
To: SRedmond@chatchat.com
Date: May 7th, 2011
SUBJECT: HOTELS AND STRANGE IDEAS
Hi Simone,

After spending some quality time with Jools and Bea, I suddenly discovered why they were so edgy when I first arrived. A large hotel has come up for sale. It's near the Cork Road in Killarney, about a ten-minute drive from The Bee. It's called the Family Friendly and has been established for many years.

Out of 150 guest rooms, only 50 are currently in use, and the remainder all need a complete overhaul. There are two restaurants, two bars, and an indoor and outdoor pool. It has a small gym, a play area, and there is even a beauty salon which again has not been used for years.

Jools and Bea were turned down for a loan, which is hardly surprising since everybody is turned down by the banks these days, and the asking price is 4 million! That's before the cost of refurbishing virtually the entire property, inside and out. Jools is raging. He's certain that during the Celtic Tiger years, he would have had no trouble securing the finance.

As Bea pointed out, the same establishment would probably have sold for ten million back then, so the two things pretty well cancel each other out. In short, they're looking for an investor. No baby bump to report, which is a shame. By the way, they thought my big news was I was getting married. Strange people. More later. Love Dot xxx

~~~

'No wonder you looked a little odd earlier,' Dorothy leafed through the brochure showing pictures of the swimming pools and hotel accommodation. 'You must have been praying for a miracle these past few months, after the bank turned you down.'

'Are you offended we even suggested it?' Bea asked anxiously.

Dorothy turned her large brown eyes on them. 'On no, not at all,' she smiled brightly. 'In fact, Claudia was only saying recently if I was interested in investing in a business, why not look at something more substantial than a little catering firm. Claudia is very direct.'

'So it's something you'll consider?' This time it was Jools who asked.

'Oh, certainly. But Gordon will have to check them out and see what he thinks. We'll have to make an appointment to view the place. Preferably over the next day or two while I'm here. Then there's the question of ownership. If I'm going to put up all the funding, I'm going to have to insist upon a large shareholding in the new business. You might want to consider that aspect of it before we go any further. It's a huge commitment for us all, and I don't just mean financially speaking.

'The pundits say friends should never go into business with each other. I'll be a silent partner for now, that goes without saying. But what about further down the line? I have two children who will be twenty-one next year. At some point in the future, they might express an interest in the hotel business. They might even want to get involved. How would that make you feel? I think you should give it some serious thought over the next few days. In many ways, the cash is the least of your worries. I have shed loads of that, the Lord knows.'

She finished her little monologue. Jools and Bea traded a look and an unspoken agreement passed between the couple. Before Dorothy got a chance to come up with any more reasons why it might not be a good idea for the three of them to buy a hotel together, they took themselves off to the kitchen for an intense chat. Comfortably situated in front of the fire, and in danger of nodding off, Dorothy heard the clatter of a keyboard. She deduced they had fired up the laptop, and were busy crunching a few numbers.

When the Laceys returned thirty minutes later, they were all smiles and looked considerably more cheery than they had when she first arrived. They tried to return the €300,000 cheque, but she assured them she had given all her friends a gift, and it had nothing to do with their possible future business dealings. Before they retired for the evening, they agreed to contact the agents as quickly as possible to arrange a viewing and request the necessary accounts.

Dorothy promised to contact Gordon and Claudia at the earliest opportunity. Her brother-in-law would be certainly be required to fly to Kerry at short notice, for the purpose of meeting with the hotel's finance director and auditors.

~~~

From: Dottie8888@chatulike.ie
To: SRedmond@chatchat.com
Date: May 8th, 2011
SUBJECT: HOTELS AND ROMAN HOLIDAY
Hi Simone,
Gordon and Claudia reacted very similarly to my news about the hotel. On the one hand, they are pleased I am looking at a substantial business in the heart of one of the best-loved towns in Ireland.

On the other hand, they are not at all sure about the asking price, especially as the American tourist market is not what it was five or six years ago. Claudia says I am not to commit to anything until she makes a few enquires.

Gordon has joined us so he can examine the books. I will be staying for a while to see what develops and get some fresh air. Jamie has volunteered to do my packing for Rome, although both he and Bel are of the same mind. They say we will be doing plenty of shopping while we are there, so not to worry about bringing too much. Back soon. Hi to C. Love Dot.

~~~

Gordon spent a full day in meetings with the Family Friendly management, examining as many aspects of the business as he could. On the first night, he even took the precaution of booking into the Family (as it was known locally), under an assumed name. This was so he could judge the level of hygiene, service, and standards from the point of view of the guests.

He concluded that, in its current format, the hotel simply did not measure up. This was hardly earthshattering news, as it would not have been on the market if it was hitting the right buttons. The Family was mediocre at best. The facilities were extensive but tatty. The rooms were overpriced based on the standard they offered. The food was average and occasionally disappointing.

The staff were polite and helpful enough, although there were too few of them doing too many jobs, meaning they were under constant pressure. While it was not unpleasant or dirty, it was not the sort of establishment likely to receive much repeat business.

When Gordon reported his findings back to Dorothy, she acknowledged the Laceys had their work cut out, and did not envy them the task ahead. They, on the other hand, were relishing the prospect of turning something which was barely three stars into a top end four-star establishment within twelve months.

~~~

From: Dottie8888@chatulike.ie
To: SRedmond@chatchat.com; ANorris@talkalot.com
CC: BelKin100@blogit.com
Date: May 10th, 2011
SUBJECT: YET MORE HOTELS AND BIG MONEY
Hi Girls,
I am attaching a few pics of the Family Friendly Hotel. The asking price is four million. What a dive. Back soon. Dot xx

37

Dorothy was fully aware she was glaring at the screen but, try as she might, could not seem to help herself. Simone had sent yet another group shot showing happy, fit-looking surfers posed for the camera in front of the ocean.

Simone's friend, Ali, was standing on her right-hand side, her short frame dwarfed by the surfboard she held upright. In no way dwarfed by any man, woman or board, a handsome Charlie stood on a radiant Simone's left. He was smiling broadly and his long arm firmly encircled Dorothy's best friend. They did not, by any means, resemble a couple on the verge of a breakup. Dorothy sighed heavily.

~~~

From: Dottie8888@chatulike.ie
To: SRedmond@chatchat.com; ANorris@talkalot.com
Date: May 11th, 2011
SUBJECT: GURUS AND LAWYERS
Hi Girls,
I have a quick update for you (I should say I have a quick update for 'yee' as I am in Kerry). Claudia Healy recommended a solicitor, and I have an appointment to meet him before I fly to Rome. His name is Nicholas Kerrigan from the firm Cushnahan, Cushnahan & Kerrigan, or CCK for short. I hope he is not the condescending type.

Claudia has concluded her investigations into the Family Hotel and you will never guess what! The word in the right circles (Claudia's circles) is it will be included in the next distressed auction in Dublin unless it is sold privately before then. That gives the owners less than two months to find a buyer.

If it goes to auction, the owners (or the receivers) will not achieve anything close to the four million asking price. Gordon and Claudia are ecstatic at the news, and Gordon is looking forward to playing hardball. He says they will be lucky to get two million out of us. Jools and Bea are shocked. If they had been lucky enough to get a loan, they would have ended up paying over the odds.

Viv called earlier and sends love to you both. She says she would like to run a little shop in Dublin, but wants nothing to do with the design business. Maybe a newsagents or bookshop, something like that.

She sounded happy and I could hear Yvonne singing along to the radio in the background. They had just finished baking a cake. I don't think we need to be unduly concerned about their emotional wellbeing for now at least. I cannot wait to have her back in town.

I know I shouldn't say it, but I am sick of all this talk of business and am taking off for a drive around the Ring of Kerry. I will head towards Sneem and then on to Caherdaniel. You are supposed to travel in a particular direction around the ring, but I don't know which way is the correct one. It's a shame I don't have my new Merc. Dot xxx

~~~

Dorothy never made it as far as Caherdaniel because at a point on the map between Sneem and Castle Cove, she rounded a bend and spotted a large sign announcing an open-house viewing. It was due to begin in five minutes' time, and would last exactly one hour.

On impulse, she decided to stop and take a look. Her decision was partly based on the weather conditions. It had been overcast when she left Killarney, but the cloud cover had blown away leaving behind a beautiful spring day with only a hint of a breeze. She felt it would be criminal not to take advantage of the unexpected sunshine.

Furthermore, her curiosity was piqued by the volume of cars already making their way through the gates, indicating a considerable degree of interest in the property. Neither the weather nor the cars were the main reason she stopped. A large iron otter attached to the wooden gate caught her imagination, and she was curious to know its significance.

The gates stood open and a young man with the slick look of an estate agent about him, was taking a note of names, numbers and, where possible, email addresses. As Dorothy paused to tell him her name, the young man cast a rather disdainful glance at her Ford, before making a note of her details and handing her a brochure.

He pointedly asked her to return it at the end of viewing and then looked down his nose at her. She was not sure whether to be amused or irritated by his attitude. If she had turned up in her new Mercedes or Porsche, would he have treated her in the same way, or was he habitually a disdainful person?

The entrance was not especially wide so she carefully nosed the car through the gates, then negotiated the tree-lined winding track on the other side. She enjoyed the back-to-nature feel of the place as she drove steadily along, and knew if Horace had accompanied her he would have been very much taken with it. She assumed the track would lead to an asphalt parking area, or possibly even a paved forecourt.

The agents were certainly pushing the boat out for this one, and she reasoned it must be something special. She pictured a period property tucked away at the other end of the track, complete with landscaped gardens and fountains. She racked her brains and tried to remember if any historical figures had lived in the Sneem area during their lifetime, and if perhaps this had been their home. *I'm sure Daniel O'Connell lived closer to Caherdaniel. I'm sure this can't be his old gaff.*

To her surprise, the track opened out into a small clearing that was certainly not finished with asphalt or anything close to it. Doing her best to avoid the mud, and grateful she was wearing shoes costing less than two hundred euro, Dorothy stepped out of her car and stared around.

She found herself looking out over the clear waters of Kenmare Bay, with extensive views over the south coast of the Iveragh Peninsula. In the near distance, she could see a number of small islands hovering protectively over the land on which she stood. There was even something that looked remarkably like a little private beach, complete with slipway and boat mooring. She took a deep breath then exhaled slowly, the view and fresh air making her glad to be alive. *I wish Horace was here to see this. I can't even text the fecker to tell him about it. I've a good mind to buy him a phone for his birthday.*

None of the other interested parties seemed surprised at not finding themselves outside a stately home, and Dorothy smiled to herself. She must be more tired than she realised from the excitement of the previous weeks.

She looked at the brochure she still clutched but decided against reading it. She may as well take a look around while she had the chance, and save the literature to read later when it was quiet. She had no intention of handing it back to the disdainful chap at the gate.

The rest of the viewers began to emerge from their cars and admire the view over the river. A second estate agent came bustling up to the group. This man was considerably older than his colleague attending the gate. He was wearing a pale grey suit and blue tie and clutched a clipboard and set of keys in a rather officious manner.

The agent was very slim and his hairline had receded to the point where it could no longer be officially called a hairline. *Perhaps he began to lose it on the day he discovered the arse had dropped out of the property market. He might have been a fattie back in the boom times. That suit is hanging on him as if he's lost three stone.* Dorothy's thoughts on weight loss were interrupted as the newcomer herded her, together with six couples and two families, around the corner to the front of the house.

The house was elevated and, as one, she and her fellow viewers paused and gazed up at it. At first glance, it looked like an ordinary enough abode, except it had been finished in slate and had a beautiful grey exterior that glinted in the sunshine. It was built over three floors and each window was enormous.

Dorothy knew from looking at the designs for the house in Dublin, that Saul had made the majority of the windows floor-to-ceiling to give her the best views of Dublin Bay and the surrounding countryside. Yet that was back in Dublin 13. When she had driven through the otter gates, she had not expected to come face to face with a residence that had clearly been designed as a nature observatory. For that was what it was, she was now certain.

Everything about this property screamed nature. The windows had been chosen for their vast size, meaning there would be zero possibility of the occupants missing any passing wildlife, if they happened to be in the kitchen putting on the kettle. Certainly, the views from the front were amazing, as the waters of the little protected lagoon gave the illusion of almost lapping at the front door. Once again, she found herself wishing Horace was with her, since he was one of the few people she knew who would truly appreciate the property.

The balding agent interrupted her reverie when he pointed out the second house. Sure enough, the building which, at first glance, she had assumed was a garage, was no such thing. It was a small cottage. The large and small houses complemented each other beautifully, particularly as the cottage had the same amazing windows.

As Dorothy made a quick 360-degree turn, wondering if she had missed anything else, she suffered another shock. There was a small hill between the houses and the river. She was glad to see this as it must surely help to protect the houses from flooding if the waters happened to reach a high level. It looked as if an old collapsed wall had been levelled and topsoil laid upon it to create a platform.

It did not restrict access to the front door or block any of the views, although it ran from the corner of the house towards the cottage and beyond. Perched on top of this hill were two hot tubs, currently with their lids in situ.

It was interesting to note that, despite the proximity to the elements, neither tub was enclosed. It was clear the current owners relished any and all opportunities to get close to nature, regardless of the temperature. *Oh, Lord, yes, Horace would love this. Why didn't I bring a camera? I wonder if I could get a few decent shots on my phone.*

She was hoping to be offered the opportunity of examining the tubs in more detail, but the group was promptly ushered inside. The agent informed them in unequivocal terms that the tour would start at the top floor and work its way downwards. Placing his foot firmly on the first tread of the wooden stairs located to the right of the front door, he led the way upwards.

At this point, Dorothy began to wish less for Horace's presence and more for Saul's. She would love to hear his opinion of the layout. She was pleased to discover that, although the house was large by most people's standards, it was significantly smaller than her proposed palace. She tried not to chuckle when she found herself thinking of three thousand square feet as 'compact and manageable'.

All the rooms at ground level had either slate or stone slabs on the floors, but on the first and second levels the rooms had hardwood flooring in either mahogany or maple hues. The top floor was essentially one large space with an adjoining bathroom and a little nook where a single bed currently resided.

The front was entirely glazed and offered a breathtaking view of the river. Despite its magnificent views and colourful coverlet, the bed and the room in general looked rather sad and forlorn. The agent informed the group that the big room had been used primarily as a work area for the 'woman of the house', who was a well-known artist.

Dorothy peered around but could see no residue of either paint or materials. She wondered when the artist had last lived at Otter House, and if she was missing her lovely home and views of Kenmare Bay. *This would be an ideal space for the Hairy Bear if I put a decent sized bed up here. Stop thinking about Horace Johnson, woman! Anyone would think you were in love with the man.*

Once the group had finished admiring the top floor, they obediently trooped down one flight of stairs to the next floor. This was comprised of four, good-sized bedrooms, all with en-suite facilities, plus a large master suite with a small dressing area and luxurious bathroom.

Over the bath a magnificent stained-glass window depicting a family of dolphins astounded Dorothy. *Feck this for a game of soldiers. I'll use what I have.* She pulled her phone out of her bag as discreetly as possible, and took a quick pic of the window. She would ask Saul about it when she next saw him. She would love a stained-glass window at the palace, assuming the right setting could be found.

A couple of the other viewers followed suit and pointed their phones and cameras at the window. Then the agent shepherded his charges out of the bathroom so they could admire the bedroom, which housed a wood burning stove of all things. Dorothy felt her knees go weak at the sight of it, but refused to acknowledge the tingling in her lower back. *I'm not interested in any tingles today, thank you very much. Trace a few of Daniel O'Connell's descendants and torment them instead.*

When they had been given the opportunity to admire the sizes of all four of the bedrooms, the agent announced it was time to move on. Dorothy obediently followed the herd downstairs to the ground floor with its open-plan layout. Although there were doors acting as dividers between the different living areas, these blended into the design because they were made of glazed oak in order to maximize the light.

Even with a veritable army of folks trekking through it, the house had a peaceful feel about it, as if it would not be possible to be unhappy there. Dorothy hoped her vaguely idiotic thoughts were not showing on her face as she followed the crowd to the heart of the home.

At eighteen-feet long and fourteen wide, the kitchen was large without being overwhelming. It was finished in a mixture of slate flooring, stainless steel appliances and granite work surfaces. She took an immediate shine to the American-style fridge freezer because hitherto, she had only ever admired one in a showroom. Seeing the real thing plumbed in was fantastic, especially as it had been set back between the cupboards in what was clearly a custom-made slot.

She wondered how a similar model would look in the new house, and if one would be spacious enough. There were few things more annoying than a freezer that was too small. Taking into account the vast size of her anticipated new home, it would be a mistake to overlook such mundane matters as appliance capacity. Perhaps they should install two, just to be on the safe side.

It was only May; hence it would be three more months before they would have to start making serious decisions about the kitchen layout. *Just as well, because right now I ain't got a clue.* Dorothy pulled her mind back from thoughts of the Howth project and focused on the kitchen at Otter House instead.

At the centre of the room, a quantity of tall wooden stools surrounded a large island with a granite slab acting as its top. Thoughtfully brushing her finger along a vein running through the stone, she pictured herself perched on one of those stools, eating a home-cooked meal and admiring the sun lighting up the river. She might even have Jamie and Bel with her, although she was not sure how either would react to the mud.

Also on the ground floor was a utility room, a conservatory, a family room with another stove, a small bathroom, a library, and a spare room. The house was not empty, although it did have an unlived-in feel about it. There were a few rocking chairs and couches scattered about, yet there was something false about the way they were covered in scatter cushions.

It was as if the owners had dressed the house for viewings, but had not used the furniture for a long time. Dorothy traced a line down the back of one of the rocking chairs (which was not a patch on the two Horace had made) and sensed how lonely the house was for human company. Its loneliness made her feel almost tearful.

Luckily, before she could disgrace herself, the agent threw open yet another door and ushered them into the library. It was still half-full of books, but also had an abandoned air. It was as if the owners had begun to pack them away, then lost heart midway through the process. Dorothy did not want to draw attention to herself by asking any questions of the agent. Instead, she discreetly enquired of the couple next to her if they knew how long Otter House had been on the market.

'Thirty-one months,' whispered the woman, who resembled Bel with her high cheekbones, short hair, and fashionable dress. 'The owners are divorcing, but as the market crashed at almost exactly the same time as their marriage, they haven't had any decent offers. They've already dropped the asking price twice.'

Dorothy murmured her thanks, grateful for any piece of information. One of the other viewers, a heavyset man in his fifties wearing an expensive tweed jacket that did not sit well on his stocky frame, was not so retiring. 'What heating system does it use?' he demanded. 'I can't see any radiators.'

It transpired there were solar panels on the roof which provided energy efficient heating through the underfloor system. Dorothy was not entirely convinced of the veracity of this statement. They had enjoyed some reasonable May temperatures during the preceding week, yet the house felt chilly. She supposed anyone who bought Otter and found it too cold during the first winter would always have the option of installing an alternative heating system the following spring.

It quickly became apparent she was the only multimillionaire in the room. In the space of a heartbeat, the others began to vigorously complain about the solar panels, and question their efficiency. They stated, almost unanimously, that some decent fossil fuel heating would be required to keep the Kerry climate at bay. They demanded to know whose bright idea it had been, not to install a backup system when they had the chance? Who, pray tell, was going to climb the ladder and brush the snow off the panels, come winter?

For a brief moment, Dorothy pictured Josh having to climb onto the roof at the palace and clear the snow off the panels there. Then she reminded herself that Saul had included a number of backup systems in his design.

Unlike this property, solar panels were only one of the ways the new house would be kept warm.

The agent did not seem especially surprised at the reaction of the crowd to the heating system. His long-suffering expression suggested he had been subjected to the same gripe countless times before. He tried to persuade the group the panels were in fact, hugely efficient, and blazing hot sunshine was not required to charge them.

38

While the agent worked the crowd and did his best to assuage their doubts, Dorothy checked out the brochure she still carried. According to the literature, the entire property was on five acres, meaning it was considerably larger than her Howth site.

The mooring and launch pad formed part of the deal, as did the tiny, private beach. What was described as 'woodland walks and substantial fields and grounds' made up the majority of the five acres at the back of the house. Dorothy pursed her lips thoughtfully. There was no denying it sounded impressive.

In addition to all this splendour, there were the two hot tubs and the cottage, which was part of the original farm and had been fully restored. There was a double spread layout devoted to the cottage, and Dorothy read that the second hot tub had been installed because the owners often rented it out to holidaymakers.

One thing she could not fail to notice was the complete absence of gadgets. She had already endured a long meeting, not just with Saul, but also, Dinny, the master electrician, Owen, the electronics engineer and, Lauren, the quantity surveyor, about the home networking and automation system for the new house. It had resulted in Dorothy taking to her bed with one of the worst headaches of her life.

Dinny, Owen and Lauren were of the opinion she might as well stick as closely as possible to Phil's original plans from day one, and go with full automation. Saul had no problem with future proofing the wiring. He agreed that all the necessary cables, sockets and ports should certainly be fitted. Yet, unlike the others, he felt it would be better for her to start small and upgrade over time.

He thought it would be unnecessarily confusing for Dorothy to have the lighting and heating automated, in addition to having every electronic gadget in the house linked into the network. He advised her to patch in the essentials at first. Once she was comfortable with that, he argued, she could consider adding other devices, and exploring full automation.

Dinny and Owen wanted her to have a dedicated room for the hubs and other gadgets required for the system setup, as this would make it more user friendly. Saul was not in favour of an entire room being sacrificed to the technology. He felt a small, dedicated area under the stairs would be perfectly acceptable.

Dorothy knew Saul was right in many ways, and was only looking out for her interests. The idea she might log on to the internet while she was in Mallorca in order to turn on the lights at the palace with the intention of thwarting burglars, was not just laughable, it was quite frankly ridiculous and a little scary. And that was just the lights!

She would also be able to scare potential intruders away by talking to them through the security system, and advising them to leave unless they wished the police to be alerted. When Owen told her that part, Dorothy had not been entirely convinced he was not trying to make a fool of her, and had not pursued the conversation any further. What sort of security system allowed you to talk to potential burglars, and suggest to them it might not be in their best interests for them to scale your wall and enter your house illegally?

Dinny and Owen had shown her pictures of the controllers she would be using, which looked similar to TV remote controls. They had also shown her the mini-LCDs which would be built into the wall of each room so she could access all the available features using the miniature touch screen. There was no sign of any LCD screens, miniature or otherwise at Otter, either within the walls or sitting loosely on tables.

Consequently, Dorothy felt it safe to assume there was no automation system in place. *They must have to get up off the chair and draw their own curtains, the poor wee creatures.* The others had been adamant about full automation until Saul turned on them and snarled: 'She's a woman living on her own. Are you muppets trying to drown her in technology?'

Dinny and Owen abruptly shut up, clearly unimpressed by Saul's attitude. Lauren was on the point of taking up arms in defence of the female of the species, when Dorothy stepped in, not only to keep the peace, but also to make the final decision.

'Saul,' she touched his arm, hoping it would calm him. 'I know exactly what you're saying, and I can see I'll need plenty of training. I might even hire a company to maintain the systems for me, in case I'm hacked or something like that. As for the dedicated room, I think that's a good idea. We always had a server room at Premier, and it made life so much easier. We were able to walk in, instead of scrabbling around in cupboards. There's a playroom on the ground floor that could be used as the gadget room.'

The others stared at her, clearly impressed she had made such a sensible speech to the fuming Saul. The architect sighed melodramatically. 'Have you had any dreams about this?' he demanded.

'Not that I can remember,' she replied coolly, 'but after seeing all those pictures of LCD yokamajigs, I might have one tonight.'

'Okay, you're the boss,' he said rather begrudgingly. 'We'll automate you to the moon and back, and use the playroom as the office. Maybe the neighbours will lend you their teenagers when you run into problems.'

Back at Otter House, Dorothy smiled at the memory of Lauren's outraged face, then obediently fell into line behind the other viewers. They trooped outside and followed the agent over to the cottage. The interior was so adorable, Dorothy could almost picture herself living out the remainder of her days there.

The kitchen was a scaled-down model of the main house, minus the large, steel appliances. There was no way the enormous fridge freezer would even get through the door. There was, however, a professional-looking double oven and a six-ring hob for the enthusiastic chef. The conservatory had been set up as a dining room. This was an ideal arrangement since the area offered extensive views of the river. The conservatory floor was also made of slate.

Dorothy was interested to note the current occupants had plugged in a small, oil-filled radiator. This feature did not go unobserved by her fellow viewers, who all took turns at making pointed comments about the Irish weather and 'fanciful notions of house design.'

Far from being annoyed by their attitude, she was quite enjoying listening to them bitching and moaning. It was vaguely comforting, and reminiscent of sitting around the dinner table at Christmas. With the family taking it in turns to alternatively praise the food and then pick on each other.

The cottage had its own laundry room with adjacent toilet and basin, and a family room, which, luckily enough, had a stove. There was a winding staircase up to the first floor, and at the top was a substantial family bathroom as well as an enormous master bedroom. The cottage was in the region of 810 square-feet and in Dorothy's opinion would make a perfect home for a couple.

Assuming they were madly in love, since there was only a limited amount of space available which would allow them to escape from each other. She felt that merely by wandering around for fifty minutes, she had learned quite a lot about interior design. For that reason alone, she was glad she had opted to stop for the tour.

Once inside the cottage, they were offered a glass of fruit juice and the use of the facilities to freshen up. Five minutes later, she left the little house with a bounce in her step. The group was herded around the back, where, with a measure of pride, the agent showed them the large patio area.

Dorothy estimated it would easily accommodate forty guests and a barbeque. Behind the patio was a type of Zen garden with wooden benches surrounding a small pond. To the right of this area was a two-car garage. Further back still, was the woodland area she had read about in the brochure. The agent enthusiastically informed them this had nature trails laid out within it, and a treehouse hidden in one of the larger oaks.

'The treehouse sounds like fun,' muttered an elderly man crankily. Most of the adults hastened to agree with him. It was indeed an insult to their intelligence, they declared, to expect them to get excited about a treehouse, when there was no decent central heating system. Dorothy smirked.

Next, they were shown the forty foot-long greenhouse, which was the cause of many envious sighings and mutterings from amongst the gardeners of the party. There was also an extensive woodpile in its own dedicated enclosure at the side of the cottage, where vast quantities of logs were piled high.

There was a convenient woodshed built of brick. To the untrained eye, it appeared to house enough fuel for an Alaskan winter. *I would love Horace to see this gaff.* Last but not least, they were escorted around to the front of the property so they could admire the launch pad and tiny beach.

They strolled past the hot tubs as they moved towards the river but, alas for Dorothy, the agent did not offer to remove the lids so they could get a closer look. This irritated her. She wanted to check out the sound system and compare it to the one she had chosen for the tubs in her new house.

After some debate, she had decided to have two hot tubs installed at the palace. The one she intended to keep mainly for her own use was the outdoor one. This would be based in the garden, or at least at the foot of the garden. Even though Saul did not intend to arrange for any actual landscaping to be done until the house was well and truly finished and the weather reasonable, a landscape architect had been retained as an adviser.

This was a precaution in case the builders put any of the outdoor facilities in the wrong place, thereby causing problems for themselves further down the line. Leon had recommended a suitable location for the outdoor tub. He also suggested they camouflage it with foliage in the fullness of time, so as to afford her more privacy. Dorothy felt a flutter of excitement at the much-anticipated treat, and had to forcibly drag her mind back to Otter.

As the group obediently admired the little launch pad, the agent, who had still not lost the will to live, assured them they might often glance outside while enjoying a leisurely breakfast, and be greeted by the sight of a playful otter as it scampered past the tubs on its way back to the water. He reached into his jacket pocket and, with something akin to a flourish, produced his piece de resistance, a small pair of binoculars. He offered them around so everyone could get a proper feel for the surrounding area and the sites they could anticipate enjoying, should they choose to become the proud owners of this magnificent dwelling.

In Dorothy's opinion, the man was not exaggerating in the slightest. Without a doubt, Otter House was a magnificent dwelling. She could sense the love that had gone into making it the house it was today, because it almost seeped out of the slate floors and stone tiles, and flowed through the windows like the light of heaven. She knew she was becoming almost poetical, but despite her best efforts to remain neutral, found herself incredibly drawn to the property, and was finding it difficult not to shout, 'I'll take it! I'll take it! Send the others away. It's all mine!'

Dorothy Lyle was by nature a cautious woman. Since the day she collected her cheque from the lottery offices, she had kept a careful record of her expenditure. This was mainly due to force of habit, as she had always been a budgeter. It was also because she was wary of being lulled into a false sense of security, and inadvertently ending up bankrupt. Like those people she sometimes saw on television shows who won vast quantities of moola, but did not spend it wisely.

She estimated that, taking into account the money she had given her family and friends, the donations, the Falcon apartment, the site at Howth, the designs for the palace, the peanut pool villa, the golf gambling, the various cars, the travelling, the investment in M&P Catering, and the funds she was about to commit to the hotel, she had spent close to thirty-one million since January.

This realisation had come as something of a jolt. She had sneaked into The Bee's brandy supply once she double-checked the numbers and verified she was correct in her calculations. What sort of person spent thirty-one million in less than five months?!

She had not included any of the fixtures or fittings for the new house in that total. The majority of those costs, plus the additional labour for the project completion, had yet to be incurred. More importantly, she had not included the cash deposits she wished to set aside for the twins, or indeed the purchase of their apartments or other assets she intended to acquire for their future.

On top of that, there were a significant number of smaller charities who, thus far, had not received a cent from her. The only one to whom she had sent a cheque were the Pioneers, a famous Irish teetotal society she heard were short of funds and in danger of having to shut up shop. As her maternal grandfather had been a pioneer all his life, Dorothy had sent them one hundred and fifty thousand euro in his memory.

She could not help but feel disgusted at the scale of her expenditure, and wondered if Claudia and Gordon had concerns about it. Perhaps they had chosen to remain silent on the subject because they were wary of offending her by speaking out. She was so glad she had not succumbed to Bel's demands and purchased the Krystal Maze villa. It was bad enough she had spent almost three million on the one with the peanut pool.

For a moment, she almost regretted her decision to invest in the hotel, and had to pause and chastise herself. When all was said and done, she was making an investment for the future. All she had to do was be patient and trust to the universe, and of course, Jools and Bea. Besides, it would be a terrible thing to pull out now when they were depending upon her.

She must have more faith than this. God would not have sent her the money unless he trusted her to do the right thing with it. Doing the right thing did not involve letting her friends down at the eleventh hour. Of course, she had earned something on the cash while it had been on deposit, and this thought cheered her. It was surprising the amount of interest millions were capable of generating merely by resting in the bank. Naturally enough, she would never dream of mentioning such a thing in front of Claudia, who would launch into a lecture about inflation.

The asking price for Otter House was 1.1 million, having previously been on the market at 1.9 million, then 1.4. It was hardly surprising the vendors were finding the property difficult to shift. These days, it was only the lucky few who had money to spend. The majority of lottery winners won three or four million, not one hundred and thirty-eight. They could ill afford to spend half their prize on a (albeit fantastic) property in Kerry, with amenities that really only appealed to nature lovers. Especially when it was situated half an hour's drive from the nearest town, and in an area with few employment prospects.

Even if she did buy it, when would she find the time to stay here? She already had her sophisticated apartment with its two floors and humungous drawing room. By the end of the year, she would have her rock-star pad with its fourteen and a half thousand square-feet of glory.

Within a matter of weeks, she would have the villa in the Balearics. Although the way the family were busy dividing the year into timeshare slots, she would be lucky to get to spend four weeks there annually. Dorothy mentally chided herself again. She really should not be so bitchy. They were only trying to split it up in order to be fair to everyone. They had promised to keep the first two weeks in September free for her use because the children would be back at school by then.

She had forgotten to add the €190,000 cost of the house in Westport to her grand total. True to her fifty-euro mission, Wendy had shortlisted six prospective properties for her grandparents. Pat and Joey, with the assistance of three of their grandchildren, and their son-in-law, Peter, had taken a trip to the West of Ireland and chosen a very pretty three-bedroom bungalow.

It would be ideal as a base for the fishing and easy to maintain. Dorothy knew she would not get to stay there either, as Pat and Joey intended it as a home away from home. They had already promised timeshare rights to at least three other couples of their acquaintance, despite the fact the paperwork had scarcely begun.

Frowning and causing the skin on her forehead to pucker (in a way that would infuriate Jamie if he saw it as, thus far, she had refused to consider Botox because the needles looked scary), Dorothy drew in a deep breath then slowly exhaled. She resolved that, whatever happened, love or no love seeping out of the walls, otters or no otters playfully scampering around the hot tub, she was going to say *No* to Otter House and walk away from it, saving herself over one million in the process.

While she had been busy berating herself for being such a spendthrift, the other viewers had taken a quick peek through the field glasses and made the requisite noises of appreciation. By the time the stocky man in the ill-fitting jacket passed them to her, the agent had glanced at his watch at least twice.

She was the last to take her turn, and some of the others were already drifting off towards their cars, chatting amongst themselves. Dorothy had not used binoculars since she was a child. Her cousin, Martin, had brought some around to the house at Christmastime one year to show off his latest gift from indulgent parents. He had embarrassed them all mightily by spying on the neighbours in what Pat deemed to be a voyeuristic fashion. It had caused a breach in the family between Pat and her sister, Marie, which had taken two years to fully heal.

Sparing a brief thought for Martin, who would be in his thirties now, and wondering what he was up to these days, she placed the glasses to her eyes and twisted the focus adjuster to get a better view. Dorothy had taken biology as a subject in post-primary school. She had not especially enjoyed it, as dissecting frogs was not really her thing. One of the few lessons she *did* remember, involved the human heart.

According to their teacher, Mrs Mannion (who Naomi always insisted was a lesbian because she wore culottes), if you closed your hand and made a fist, the size of that fist would very closely resemble the size of your heart, since by rights your body should be in proportion. The idea had always appealed to her. Her own fist was tiny. Did that mean her heart was tiny too?

As she twisted the focus adjuster and aimed the binoculars at the river, Dorothy's tiny heart swelled inside her chest cavity and threatened to burst out through her rib cage. She saw them quite clearly. What appeared to be an entire colony of seals resided half a mile out from the shoreline and rested lazily on the rocks lying close to the small islands.

She was not sure why she had such a strong reaction to them. It was not as if they were as cute as dolphins or as playful as otters. They were doing nothing but lying around on their perch, looking dopey, with their big sad eyes seeming to stare back at her.

Without warning, the tingle began in her lower back and the view wavered in front of her eyes. This time, she did not see a basketball court or anything close to it. There was no cartwheeling Orangutan with impish black eyes. This time, she felt herself floating in the water, fully aware of the seals on the rocks above her.

She could see the riverbed below, and a fish swimming past which she instinctively knew was a Pollock. The image was incredibly powerful, especially as it quickly became apparent she was not alone. A large companion weaved through the water by her side. For a deeply satisfying moment, Dorothy felt absolutely secure and protected. Both she and her companion were wearing seal coats.

The image disappeared as quickly as it had arrived. It left her dizzy and asking herself what the fuck was going on. 'I don't believe the clairs are at it again,' she muttered, as she lowered the glasses and put her hand to her spinning head.

'Pardon?' asked the agent. Once again, he glanced at his watch, clearly impatient to end the viewing.

'I said,' Dorothy raised her voice slightly, 'the clairs are at it again. They're trying to tell me something. Except this time, there was no basketball court or swimming pool.'

The man looked astounded by her words, but nonetheless was clearly unimpressed by her reference to a woman called Claire. 'What are you talking about, madam?' he sounded vastly irritated.

'Are you the sole agent handling this property?' she enquired tersely.

'As a matter of fact, I'm not. There are three of us marketing it at present,' he sounded defensive this time. 'The vendors took that decision due to the slump in the market.'

'Excellent,' she responded more cheerily. 'I don't like your company. You're all too quick to judge by appearances. Plus, you're borderline rude and cranky.'

With that caustic comment, she threw the binoculars at him and returned to her car. She stopped at the gate to tell the other agent she was keeping the brochure. She also advised him there was plenty of training available in the area of customer service, should he choose to avail himself of it.

39

An hour later, after an incident-free journey, Dorothy made it safely back to The Bee. She took a quick shower and changed into her most comfortable pair of jeans and a cotton top. Feeling refreshed, she trotted downstairs to join her friends, and gratefully accepted a glass of wine from Jools. The others were full of news. Gordon had bulldozed the beleaguered vendors into accepting half of their original asking price for the hotel.

They had initially balked and acted affronted at the notion of parting with their property for a cent less than four million. Gordon heard them out then calmly informed them he had no objection to waiting until July, before popping along to the Shelbourne Hotel, where the auctions for distressed properties were usually held.

He smugly informed the beleaguered hotel owners that he was confident his bid for their run-down establishment would be successful. Three hours later, his offer was accepted. The vendors begged him to retain the long-serving staff, if possible, as some had worked at the Family Friendly for more than thirty years.

Jools, Bea, and Gordon enthusiastically shared with Dorothy every second of the day's events. Bea periodically topped up the glasses, while Jools prepared a delicious dinner of lamb steaks. After a while, Bea noticed their guest was very quiet and grew anxious. 'Dot, you're not having second thoughts about staking us, are you?' she enquired with a tremor in her voice.

Dorothy looked up from her wine and rested her eyes on her friend. She admired Bea's sallow skin and full lips. Privately, she wondered how a bald and bespectacled creature like Jools had snared such a lovely girl. She mentally chided herself.

After all, she loved Jools too, and it was hardly his fault he was not the best-looking man in Kerry. Handsome is as handsome does, as her mother would say. She pulled her thoughts away from levels of attractiveness and smiled reassuringly at the other woman. 'Not at all. I was thinking about something that happened today, that's all. Don't worry about the money.'

'What happened today, Dottie?' Gordon asked gently, his pointed nose twitching with interest.

She had zero desire to share any of it with them. If she did, they would likely think her mad. Despite this, she felt the overwhelming need to talk to somebody. Perhaps they would not try to have her committed or anything horrible like that. Perhaps they would accept what she had to say, and not judge her too harshly. After all, it was only one little vision, and it wasn't as if she had shared the one about the basketball court or the Spanish villa with anybody, not even Simone.

'I went to view a house out in the Sneem area,' she spoke hesitantly. 'It wasn't planned. I happened to be out that way and saw a sign for an open viewing. There was a big otter on the gate I thought looked interesting, and I couldn't resist going in for a look. It's a lovely place, but I don't think it's right for me to spend the sort of money they're asking. I don't know if you guys realise I *have* been the big spender recently.'

She moved her glass of wine in a figure of eight motion without even realising. The others remained silent and waited for her to continue. Dorothy sighed listlessly and said, 'At the end of the viewing, the agent lent me a pair of binoculars. I looked out at the Kenmare River and it was as if God spoke to me. I had a vision of swimming with the seals. The man was there, the same one from the pool dream. We were swimming together in the river. We were both wearing seal coats, and I felt so light and safe with him. It was an amazing sensation. It's a beautiful house, but I feel guilty for even considering it. They want over a million. I've bought a tonne of stuff already since January. I'm a desperate spendthrift.'

For a few seconds, nobody spoke, although they glanced at each other questioningly.

'Why don't you tell us about the pool dream, Dot?' Bea eventually suggested when it became obvious the men had no intention of speaking.

Dorothy looked at the three faces, but could find only expressions of interest there. *Ah fuck it! I may as well give it a go. What's the worst that can happen?*

In between sips of wine, she related the story of the three restless nights in the health spa, and how she had dreamed of a diving pool with a whale mosaic, and a big man who sounded like Sam Elliot. She told them how the dream had finally stopped, but only when she promised God she would speak to Saul about building the pool.

'This Sam Elliot guy was in the vision you had today?' Bea looked stupefied.

'Yes. I could sense his presence next to me. But he wasn't a man like in the dream.'

'Well, Dot, if he wasn't a man, then what was he?' Jools heroically waded in.

'He was a seal. A really big one,' she replied quietly.

They all cast worried glances at each other. Then they stared into their wine glasses as if the answer to the Sam Elliot mystery was to be found within.

'Why don't you buy it?' Bea suddenly lifted her head and spoke. 'It's not as if you can't afford it.'

Dorothy hung her head in shame. 'I've spent so many millions these past few months,' she said sadly. 'I feel guilty about buying another place.'

'Gordon, what do you think?' under the table, Bea nudged the accountant with her foot.

'Well,' Gordon's nose twitched as he chose his words carefully. 'If Dottie really likes the house, I don't see why she shouldn't put in an offer. After all, she's entitled to spend her own money. It's not as if you can take it with you, eh, Dottie? I'd be happy to negotiate with the agents if you like. Maybe they'll accept a cool million. You *are* a cash buyer, after all.'

'You'd do that for me?' Her eyes opened wide with surprise.

Not quite believing her brother-in-law was supporting her like this, Dorothy ran off to fetch the brochure from her room. Soon, they were all happily poring over it and consuming yet more wine. The others were impressed she had stumbled across such a treasure.

They were inclined to think that, even at 1.1 million, she would be getting something of a bargain. After that, they all took turns at reassuring her she had not really spent *that* much, considering how much she had won. Before long, she was feeling far more relaxed and accepted yet another top-up from Jools.

'I wonder if we should we make an appointment for a private viewing,' Bea said, as they were halfway through dessert.

'Would you have time for that? You've been so busy this past week,' Dorothy replied earnestly.

'I'm sure we could squeeze in a little house inspection,' Jools assured her with a wink, making her giggle.

Gordon was the first out of bed the next morning, and lost no time in Googling Otter House. Ensuring he avoided the agents who had annoyed his sister-in-law, he made an appointment to view the property through one of their competitors. The group spent what remained of the day alternatively swearing off alcohol and poring over design ideas for the hotel.

After another good night's sleep, the copious amounts of wine had cleared their systems, and they felt ready for their outing. They took two cars and arrived at the house in convoy. Right away, Dorothy knew Gordon had dropped a hint to the agent. It was a mature woman this time, although without anything even remotely resembling a receding hairline. From the first, she treated them as if they were serious buyers, even though not one of them was driving a car that could be considered prestigious.

The Laceys fell in love with Otter on the spot. Even Gordon was impressed, and with the notable exception of the Scottish Highlands, he was very much the city man. He advised Dorothy not to allow Joey within ten miles of the place. The fishing was bound to be good and she might never get to call it her own again. Dorothy took his advice to heart. She began to wonder if this might become the one retreat she never shared with anybody, not even her nearest and dearest.

Having received an unqualified seal of approval from her friends, she authorised Gordon to go ahead and make an offer. The agent explained the vendors were living apart and on different continents. She apologetically told Gordon it might be as long as twenty-four hours before she had an answer for him.

Determined to wait patiently, Dorothy returned to The Bee and spent the rest of the day wandering around Killarney with Bea, while Jools took care of things back at the B&B, and Gordon pored over yet more cash flow forecasts, content it seemed, to sit alone in the study and work away on his laptop.

That evening, Dorothy wandered out to the small courtyard at the back of the building. It had been designed primarily as a smoking area, and a number of small metal tables and chairs littered the space. It was the time of year when daylight hours typically lasted in excess of fifteen hours, and she pulled one of the tables closer to a patch of sunlight.

She made herself comfortable and placed her book on the table next to a small bottle of water. She felt guilty for having taken Bea away from the business for so long, and was determined to give the Laceys some much-needed peace and quiet so they could catch up with their myriad chores. She had no idea where Gordon was, but suspected he had taken a drive up to the Cork Road for yet another look at the hotel. She was glad he had left the solitude of the study, and hoped he would leave his spreadsheets well and truly alone for the rest of the day.

Her phone beeped and she chuckled as she read the text from Orla. *It took forever, but the whipped cream and slutty lingerie eventually did the trick. I am so excited, Dottie! I never thought I would be a partner in my own business. Gemma says hi and don't let Gordon eat too much high cholesterol food. Orla. xxx*

Dorothy did some mental reviewing of the menus over the past couple of days. Jools was a fantastic chef, and her brother-in-law had fallen on every plate set before him like a man possessed by a hunger sprite. If Gemma discouraged poor eating habits at home, this explained why Gordon seemed pathetically grateful for any scrap of dessert he was offered, and never refused a morsel of anything Jools concocted.

Dorothy chuckled to herself. To hell with it. If asked, she would tell her sister their Killarney diet consisted of green salad, fresh fruit and lean meat. Gordon had been very good to her since her big win, and she had no intention of ratting him out to his wife.

She lifted her head towards the evening sun and felt the rays warming her face. Despite the brightness, the temperature was beginning to drop. She unrolled the sleeves of her cardigan and fastened the buttons at the front. The novel she was reading lay untouched on the table in front of her. Otter House played on her mind and it was difficult for her to focus on anything else while a question mark hung over its future ownership.

I hope I've done the right thing by making this offer. It's all right for Bea and Jools to say I can afford it, hence I should buy it. They aren't the ones eating into their fortune. If the vendors come back with a counter-offer, it might be best if I reconsider and don't take this deal any further.

The thought had hardly formed in her mind when the yard suddenly darkened. She looked up and saw a large black cloud obscuring the sun and casting the area into chilly shade. Dorothy shivered inside her silver cardigan and rubbed her hands up and down her arms. Her whole body began to tremble, and the Space Ache caught her off-guard as it flared inside her chest like the worst kind of heartburn. She gasped and clutched the edge of the table for support.

The Laceys had a small wooden shed in the corner of the yard, which they used as winter storage for the furniture. Out of the corner of her eye, Dorothy saw a shape flickering in front of it. Not certain whether or not she should be scared, she slowly shifted her body in the chair and faced the illusion full on.

This time, the man was neither swimming nor playing basketball. He was certainly not smiling, or anything close to it. He was dressed from head to toe in dark clothes, and his face was coated with a thick layer of dirt as if he was trying to disguise it. Even his hair was matted with mud, making it impossible for her to judge its true colour.

He was tall and broad shouldered just as she remembered from the swimming pool dream. His head was bent at a slight angle as he examined the item he held. Even to Dorothy's untrained eye, it was obvious the object was a sawn-off shotgun. The man ejected the one remaining cartridge and pocketed it. She clearly saw how his eyes glinted with barely suppressed rage, and felt her heart rate escalating.

He seemed to lose interest in the weapon and shifted his stance. He glanced down at the ground near his feet, and Dorothy heard the squeak of terror that issued from her mouth. A still form lay lifeless on the ground and, as she watched, the man nudged it contemptuously with his booted foot.

Dorothy forced herself to get to her feet and move a step closer to the shed. She watched intently as he leaned the shotgun against a wall. In one graceful movement, he bent down and grabbed the body, then hoisted it onto his shoulder in a fireman's lift. He began to stride away from her, and Dorothy instinctively took another step closer to the shed. Then she saw something that halted her in her tracks.

It was the Zen garden at Otter House. There was no mistaking it because the fountain was designed in the shape of a mermaid. The man did not pause to admire his surroundings and continued to walk. He suddenly paused, as if he knew he was being spied upon. He slowly turned around and faced her. Dorothy held her breath and edged a few steps closer to the vision. The man narrowed his eyes and scanned the area, searching for the voyeur.

'I'm over here,' Dorothy heard the words leaving her mouth. 'Look this way.'

He frowned and dug a hand into the pocket of his jacket. When it emerged, it was clasping a handgun. He checked the ammunition then slowly turned away from her again. He walked in the opposite direction with the corpse slung over his left shoulder and the gun firmly gripped in his right hand.

'Come back and see me,' Dorothy called after him. 'Who are you? What's your name? I'm Dorothy Lyle.'

The vision wavered and disappeared while the sun simultaneously came out from behind the cloud and flooded the courtyard with warm, comforting light. On trembling legs, Dorothy made her way back to the table and almost fell into the chair. What did it all mean? Who was the man, and what was he doing at Otter House with a dead body?

She managed to get the bottle of water open and knocked back half the contents. The liquid grounded her, and thankfully steadied her shattered nerves. 'This is all getting very weird,' she told the still-untouched book. 'Am I supposed to deduce something from all that? Why do I never get to see his face properly?'

Gordon unexpectedly appeared in the yard. He had indeed taken a drive up to see the hotel, but was back and urgently needed to speak to his sister-in-law. As soon as she clapped eyes on his face, Dorothy knew the news was bad.

'They turned down the offer,' she said flatly, before he had a chance to speak.

'Their divorce is getting very acrimonious,' he nodded grimly. 'By the sounds of things, only the husband is prepared to accept. The wife will only agree to sell Otter House if she gets the full asking price. Personally, I think she's trying to scupper the deal because your man has gone off with a bimbo. Maybe you should rethink your position for a few days and let them sweat. I'm not comfortable with the notion of you being bullied.'

As she listened to the words, a great sense of calm and wellbeing settled over Dorothy, and she smiled warmly. Gordon was expecting her to be disappointed, and looked startled at this unexpected development.

She said decisively, 'Tell them I'm prepared to pay the full asking price, but unless the paperwork is signed by the warring parties within six weeks, I shan't hesitate to pull out of the deal. Make sure the agent understands I'm not prepared to be messed about by the vendors just because they're divorcing.'

Gordon nodded and, pulling out his phone, took off around the corner with a determined look on his narrow face and a definite twitch to his nose.

Dorothy relaxed back into her chair. Whatever happened, Otter House was destined to be hers. She knew that now. So many things had occurred recently which defied logic or made little or no sense. Nonetheless, in her heart she knew another piece of the jigsaw which was fast becoming her new life had fallen into place.

She may not understand it, but she was prepared to accept it. As she sat in the sun-drenched courtyard, Dorothy sensed within these confusing moments and dizzying sensations a message from a powerful force. A force she was positive had her best interests at heart.

'That makes thirty-two million spent so far,' she informed the shed in the corner. Then she picked up her book and water and went to see how Gordon was faring. She hummed as she walked.

Here ends Book 1 of the Miracles and Millions Saga

Dear Consumer

Congratulations! You have taken your first sip from the giant mug of coffee that is the Miracles and Millions Saga. The one that requires two handles to hold, and resembles a white ceramic bucket.

If you are feeling frustrated, let down, and a tad bored right now, I apologise. This novel was never meant to be a standalone, and is not marketed as such. The reason it sometimes feels slow, clunky and kinda chewy is because it's designed to reflect Dorothy's state of mind. As is each of the books that follows.

Here lies Ella. The only folks who loved her series were those who actually read it.

Miracles and Millions is essentially a story of self-discovery and redemption.

How does a woman who has been hiding in plain sight for decades become a household name?

How does a man who makes his living by violence become the guy they all depend upon, and the most recognised face on the planet?

The Miracles and Millions Saga is a rollercoaster, rip roaring ride of adventure, lust, desire, blood-letting, vengeance, hatred, obsession, joy, hope and spite.

There is also a rather interesting love story (or two) thrown in.

I know that must be difficult for you to believe all of the above based on Book 1, but I promise you it's true. I have readers contacting me to say they got no chores done for a fortnight as they ploughed (plowed: Hello America!) their way through all ten. Others burst out laughing on the way to work on the bus…awkward.

Book Two (Colour) finds Dorothy growing into her wealth and becoming almost complaisant about her riches. It reads at a slightly faster pace, especially when she realises all is not well in her new world.

Book Three (Help) has a sense of helplessness about it, as the threats against Dorothy increase and she is forced to hire protection.

Book Four is called Hunted…yep. It's a fast-paced and occasionally scary step in Dorothy's journey of self-discovery. Wherever your reading takes you, I hope it brings you joy and entertainment.

Ella Carmichael

The Miracles and Millions Saga
Two minds, two bodies, two hearts, one soul

Book 1 - Avarice

Book 2 - Colour

Book 3 - Help

Book 4 - Hunted

Book 5 - Clarity

Book 6 - Sucks

Book 7 - Treachery

Book 8 - Nemesis

Book 9 - Deception

Book 10 - Death

Made in the USA
Columbia, SC
27 December 2021